Maureen Dean is the wife of John Dean, the White House counsel to Richard Nixon who exposed the facts about Watergate. She works as a financial consultant for a major Wall Street firm and lives with her husband in Beverly Hills.

D1138820

By the same author

MO: A Woman's View of Watergate

MAUREEN DEAN

Washington Wives

This edition published 1995 by
Diamond Books
77–85 Fulham Palace Road
Hammersmith, London W6 8JB

Published by Grafton Books 1988
First published in Great Britain by
Grafton Books 1988

The Author asserts the moral right
to be identified as the author of this work

ISBN 0 261 66716 5

Set in Sabon
Printed in Great Britain

To the memory of my loving parents

Author's Note and Acknowledgments

This is a story about women in Washington DC, where I spent some intense years of my life and where I still have many close and dear friends.

The story is fictional, as are the characters. But if fiction might be considered fact woven into fantasy, and founded in truth, then it is a story that is not outside the realm of the possible. Occasionally real people are used as part of the backdrop and setting of the novel. In exercising this literary license, I hope none are offended, because no offense was intended.

I remember as a schoolgirl being assigned to read a series of novels because they were 'didactic' – that is, instructive. This novel was not written with that goal in mind; rather, I hoped to give the reader a good and interesting story by focusing on and dramatizing the lives of three different women in one of America's most fascinating cities. I've tried to provide a few glimpses into the inner workings of the government, and describe how the processes are affected by the sexual attractions, tensions, and proclivities of the men and women who are involved in that process. In short, pure entertainment, a few insights, an occasional revelation, a dramatic but honest picture, and a sprinkle of history here and there were my goals.

If I have succeeded, there are many others to

thank for their contribution to the work. They include the motion picture producer who conceived the project, the past and present Washington wives who shared their insights and tales with me, the editors who helped develop and refine the manuscript, and the readers who took time to give their reactions to various drafts of the story. But mostly I must thank my silent partner lurking behind every page of this book, the ghost who also lives in my bedroom. Without his intimate knowledge of Washington and his fluent writing and editing skills, the book would never have come together.

Maureen Dean
May 1987

Prologue

Sunday, June 4, 1989 – 6.30 P.M.
The Hay-Adams Hotel, Suite 910

Washington is a city of dreams, great and small, of hopes both foolish and daringly grand. For some hours now, she'd been thinking about how simple her own particular desires were compared to the schemes and visions of so many in the capital. All she really wanted was more of him.

But there was never enough time – never enough time in his arms, never enough of the languid ecstasy of lying next to him after they had made love. But they both knew that a fleeting hour here and there was the best they could hope for. Now, even that had become too dangerous.

She stood at the wide south window of the perfectly appointed Hay-Adams suite. From the window she could see the White House across Lafayette Park. What excuse would he use to explain his absence from the briefing session in the West Wing? Even on this soft summer Sunday evening work went on in the White House. She understood that, but it seemed horrible to her that everyone needed to know where he was at all times.

The air-conditioning made the tiny hairs on her arm stand up. She shivered. A sense of physical

11

pleasure suffused her as she touched her arm. Soon it would be his hand stroking her skin. She shivered again.

Studying her reflection in the window, she saw that her hair was as he liked it, soft and loose. Her makeup was minimal but perfect.

She scanned the room. A tasteful combination of Early American reproductions mixed and matched with some authentic English antiques. The creams and blues of the Chinese rug accented the floral chintz draperies. She particularly liked the two camel-back pale pink love seats flanking the fireplace.

She noted with a smile the convex Federal mirror over the marble mantel. It reflected the butler's tray coffee table holding a silver bowl of the tiniest pink roses studded with baby's breath. Every detail seemed perfect; there was not even a hotel logo to cheapen the cut crystal ashtrays. It could have been the sitting room of any mansion on Embassy Row.

In this beautifully decorated room they would end their relationship. Neither could risk going on because they both had too much to lose. And they had become too well known, too recognizable. They would have to accept the pain and get on with their lives.

In her anxiety to set the stage, she had sprayed the room with her purse atomizer of Giorgio. Now she was sorry. Perhaps the air-conditioning would somehow recirculate and dilute the overpowering aroma.

Overkill, she thought. That touch was too much, but she so desperately wanted to control the situation down to the last detail. She would behave, she swore. She refused to have him remember her as a sobbing, clinging neurotic. He didn't deserve that.

She paced the room. Using an assumed name she had paid in cash, and felt certain no one had recognized her. When she arrived she had checked the lamp sockets, the back of the television set, under the telephone in the sitting area, bedroom and bath, behind the Federal mirror. She had even unscrewed the mouthpiece on each phone and checked for the telltale little red O-ring he had described. Nothing.

He had insisted in the gravest tones that such precautions were necessary, a vital condition of their meetings. She felt uncomfortable; yet, even today she was still excited by all they had to do to meet, as if she were living in a spy novel.

The elevator hummed from the hall and she tensed. One, two, three, four beats and then the soft tap. Hiding her face from any passerby in the hall, she cautiously opened the door.

With a backward sweep of his foot he closed the door and grasped her hips in one swift motion. She clung to him, laughing. 'Can't you wait a minute?' She knew how to build his excitement, and her own. She took a half step back and looked at him.

He looked wonderful. To her he had always been heart-stoppingly handsome. The silver temples, the crinkles around the gray-blue eyes with black lashes so thick they clumped — everything about him made her want to call off the whole idea of giving him up. How could she live without having him ever again?

'I need a shower,' he said, pulling at his knotted tie. 'The President's doctor told me to start getting some exercise, start walking more, so that's what I told the President I was going to do. Christ, I must be in bad shape to have worked up this lather.'

She held his jacket as he unbuckled his belt. 'Will you join me?' he asked with a leer.

He stepped into the tub first and stood under the pulsating water.

Her bra, garter belt, stockings, shoes, blouse, and skirt, so carefully chosen, soon followed from the door to the edge of the tub.

The water jet turned his hair into a shiny black hood, plastering it to his forehead and into his eyes. He reached for her as she stepped into the tub and pulled her against the matted hair of his chest. Their mouths met instantly, devouring each other in a deep kiss as the water streamed over their naked bodies. Then she could feel his hardness rising against her body.

'Darling,' she gasped, the water pouring into her mouth, 'we'll fall.'

'Can't wait,' he said. 'Waited all day in this condition. Thought I might embarrass myself in the staff meeting this afternoon.'

He reached for a bar of soap and tore at the wrapping paper with his teeth. 'Damn! I hate these things.'

Gently, he placed the soap between her legs and teasingly rubbed it back and forth until she thought she would scream. He stopped just before she was sure she'd lose control, and placed his hands on her hips and eased her around so that her back was against the cold tile. He entered her before she could catch her breath. For a long moment they moved in unison to the pulsing beat of the jet sequence of the shower head.

Suddenly, he was withdrawing. In one sliding motion he began moving down her body. He moaned. It was an odd sound connected more with pain than passion.

'You'll get your mouth full of soap,' she laughed.

His head did not stop where she thought it would. Half blinded by the rushing water, she saw one leg slide under his body at an awkward angle. His knees hit the floor of the tub with the full force of his weight and his upper body pitched forward against her legs. To avoid falling she grasped for the shower curtain, nearly ripping it from the overhead rod.

Steadying herself, she tried to grab him under the arms. The warm water cascading over them increased her panic. His eyes were open but blank. His mouth drooped obscenely and saliva flowed from one corner.

'Brad!' she screamed. 'Brad?'

His face was a mask of pain. His body contorted awkwardly in a heap on the floor of the tub.

Trembling, she turned off the water and stumbled out of the tub. Falling to her knees, she reached in and felt the large vein in the side of his neck. Nothing. He felt cold and clammy. He was propped at such an angle that she could press her ear to his chest. Nothing, save the terrifying stillness of death.

'Oh God, Brad,' she moaned. *I've got to find help.* 'Why don't I know how to help you?'

She began to weep aloud. She felt sick to her stomach and dizzy. Clinging to the bathroom sink, she pulled herself up and turned on the cold water. *Is this really happening?*

Again she checked his pulse. He was gone, no one could help him, she felt sure.

Stumbling from the bathroom she collected her clothes. She stuffed her underthings into her handbag and stepped into her outer clothes as fast as the trembling would let her move. Frantically, she checked the room for any belongings. Biting her lip she returned to the bathroom just in case, she thought, just in case this is some horrible nightmare. He lay as she had left him, his skin paler than before, almost blue.

Once again she checked the room for any telltale sign of her presence, using a hand towel to wipe away any possible fingerprints, but suddenly she stopped. *This is horrible.*

I can't just leave him here, she thought. *I've got to let someone know. I can't notify the hotel, I'll never get out of here in time.*

She lifted the phone and dialed nine for an outside line. When she heard the dial tone she pressed 911. Immediately a woman answered.

'What is the emergency?' the nasal voice asked.

Silence.

'Hello, what is the emergency, plee-uz?'

'Ah . . . ahh.' No words would form.

'Are you the injured party, ma'am?'

16

A shot of adrenaline seized her. 'Heart attack!' she blurted. 'Someone has had a heart attack!'

'Where is the injured party located, please, ma'am?'

'The Hay-Adams Hotel,' she shouted. 'Sixteenth Street and . . .' Her mind went blank.

'We know the hotel, ma'am. Where in the hotel?'

'In a suite, ah.' She looked around frantically, then squinted at the phone. 'Suite nine ten.'

'And who is making the report, please?'

'No one . . . a friend. It doesn't matter.'

'We need to know who is making the report,' the voice insisted.

'Just get here, damn it!' she screamed. 'Just get here, a man is dying . . . dead.' She pressed the receiver button down, wiped her fingerprints from the receiver, and slipped it into the cradle. She wanted to break down and cry again, as she forced herself to leave the room. *Could this really be happening?*

Monday

Monday, June 5, 1989 – 7.30 A.M.
Foggy Bottom

'I don't believe it, Barbara,' Jan Kirkland exclaimed into the phone.

'Well you'd better,' her administrative assistant continued, 'because his embassy has already called twice this morning.'

'The prince wants a beautiful blonde transvestite sent over to Blair House for tea this afternoon,' Jan repeated, trying to throw some humor into her tone. It was important to Jan Kirkland to act like an old pro, even though after just six months in her post of deputy chief of protocol she was still trying to figure out what her job was really all about. 'Why the Protocol office?' Jan probed. She stood naked and wet in the upstairs hall of her small townhouse in Foggy Bottom as she held the phone against her ear with one shoulder and tried to dry her feet without falling.

'Well, the Midcast desk got the first call last night from his embassy,' her assistant continued. 'I guess they didn't want the CIA to handle it, so it's ours.'

'I hope you know what you're doing because I sure don't,' Jan confessed to her closest professional confidante.

21

'What's the problem?' Mark Kirkland asked from the bedroom doorway. He was tying his favorite Brooks Brothers tie around his upturned collar.

'Thanks, Barbara, I'll be there as soon as I can.' She rushed past her husband into the bedroom.

'You're cute when you're naked,' Mark deadpanned. He had moved to the edge of the big antique four-poster bed that consumed the small bedroom. Two wooden pineapples on each post had been removed to keep them from scraping the ceiling. 'Have you seen my wing tips?' he asked, lifting the chintz dust ruffle and peering under the bed.

'Yes, hon, I did. Yesterday, on your feet.' Jan had her own problems to solve. She had to find something to wear herself.

Mark had found a long brass shoehorn on the Chippendale highboy that partially blocked the two small windows. He jabbed it into the darkness under the bed. 'Jan, we've got to find either smaller furniture or a bigger house.'

'I know,' she sighed, 'but isn't it better than the shoe box you were living in?'

The townhouse had been her father's wedding present. The furniture had been Connie's and was more appropriate to a stately mansion.

Mark had spent the fifteen years before their marriage in hotel rooms and barren studio apartments as a correspondent for *Newsweek* magazine and then as the Washington correspondent for the *Boston Globe*. His worldly goods had consisted of his clothes, a typewriter, a beat-up espresso pot, a dozen cartons of books, and a lot of journalistic talent. When they met he was camping out in a one-room apartment off Columbia Road. On their wedding day he abandoned a pull-out couch and beat-up deck chair to the next tenant and carried the rest of his material possessions in one small suitcase to the National Cathedral.

While they were on their honeymoon, Jan's father, true to form, handled everything, right down to seeing that Mark's books were moved out of storage, dusted, and placed on the newly painted bookshelves in their Foggy Bottom townhouse.

The tiny house was too small, but now wasn't the time to move out. With the pressure of Mark's job as the new President's press secretary and Jan's job at the State Department, they did not have a lot of free time – plus they had become something of a celebrity couple in the media and were invited out all the time.

The appearance of a feature story in the Style section of the *Washington Post* started it. The *Post*'s Style writer called them the perfect example of the 'bright minds' in the new administration. That was followed by an article written by Deena Simon, of the *Washington Observer*, who called them the 'most boring couple in Washington.' Jan had been hurt by the comment. Mark had been unfazed. He was accustomed to writing about people, and quickly adjusted to being written about, seeming to enjoy the visibility.

Jan dressed hurriedly. She plugged in the hair dryer over the bathroom sink and blew enough hot air on her wheat-colored hair to give it some loft.

She whisked blusher across her high cheekbones and underlined her wide-set gray-green eyes with slate-colored pencil. Her eyebrows were naturally dark arches and required nothing more than a quick brush. She looked around for the appropriate instrument, gave up, and used the toothbrush lying in a puddle by the sink. With the tip of her little finger, she ran lip gloss around her full mouth, then hurried down the narrow staircase.

Mark was already in the sun-filled kitchen gulping cranberry juice. 'Aren't you going to eat?' he asked.

'Can't,' she said, grabbing a banana from the top of the refrigerator. 'Got to get to the office and rustle up a transvestite.'

'Is that what Barbara wanted? You sure get the fun assignments.' Nothing about Washington surprised him. He had been on the national political scene too long.

She peeled down one side of the banana. 'Seems that our official visitor is lonely. Why don't you suggest to the President that he put on a blond wig when the prince pays his official visit?' Jan said with a straight face, then immediately broke into laughter.

'That would make a fine photo opportunity,' Mark replied.

As Jan hugged her husband from behind she thought, Chinese laundries must have secret bottles of man-smell that they spray on shirts. 'You'll try to be home early, right? It's important.'

'I'll try. Today should be light. The President is speaking in Pittsburgh this afternoon and has a

24

private dinner tonight. We'll be back to Andrews at five. I should be able to get away by six.'

'Great. The caterer said they'd come at four. Am I nervous?' she asked herself, making a silly face. 'Nooo.'

Mark laughed and reassured her as he headed out of the kitchen to answer his hot-line telephone that had suddenly started ringing. 'You'll do fine, darling. When you see how well it goes you'll do this once a week.'

The telephone had been installed by the Army Signal Corps so that the President could call Mark at home on a clean line, when he needed to speak to his press secretary outside office hours. The first month the telephone had been in the vestibule hall, Mark had bolted from wherever he found himself in the small house to answer its ring. But now, after six months in his post, he responded in stride, for he had come to appreciate that almost everything at the White House was important or a crisis, otherwise the White House would not be involved. And you had to deal with such matters in stride.

Jan pulled her party checklist from under the Snoopy magnet on the fridge. Whatever she knew about entertaining she had learned from her Aunt Constance, who was one of Washington's premier hostesses. Jan's little buffet paled in comparison to the fetes that Constance had arranged over the years. The sit-down dinner for several hundred her aunt was having later in the week for the President should prove to be one of the finest.

She studied the list. In truth, all the preparations

were done. As usual, Jan's father had taken care of everything.

William Buchanan Sumner, better known as Buck, was a semiretired career diplomat who had carried the title of ambassador-at-large for three presidents. He was determined that his daughter become as much a Washington social fixture as both he and his sister Constance were. For weeks he had not too subtly hinted that a dinner party was in order. Jan, overwhelmed by her new job in the Protocol office and underwhelmed by the size of her little house, kept resisting. They never had more than two couples at a time. But when the ambassador picked a date, hired a caterer, and phoned his daughter to ask whether she wanted to have a tent in the garden in case of rain, she gave in.

Buck had been pleased with her guest list. It reflected the young couple's delicately tuned insight into the Washington social and political scene. As much business could be conducted at a good dinner party, and often more, than ever could be done in the corridors and conference rooms of government. A private party was the perfect place to introduce people who would otherwise not be likely to meet and the introductions could give the hostess a double boost. Jan and Mark had intuitively recognized that you should not ignore those who were out of power today, for they could return – stronger than ever.

The size of the house and garden meant the party would be intimate. Bradford Barry, the President's chief of staff, would be escorting the First

Lady's social secretary, a delightful seventy-nine-year-old widow with the energy of a woman half her age. The President's national security advisor, General Dalton Riggs, and his wife Caroline were actually her father's suggestion, but Mark had assured Jan they were delightful.

Senator George Lowry and his wife Judy, both longtime friends of the President, were on everyone's A-list since George had become chairman of the Senate Commerce Committee. When the Lowrys accepted, Mark had suggested former Press Secretary Larry Speakes and his wife. Mark was anxious to meet his predecessor. Besides, Speakes and Lowry would have a lot to talk about since Speakes had joined a major Wall Street firm and George was planning an investigation of Wall Street's newest inroads into commercial banking.

The other outside additions included former Senator and presidential candidate George McGovern and his wife, and a couple that Jan felt were always good company — David Eisenhower, a childhood companion of Jan's from Cotillion Club, and his wife Julie Nixon. It had all of the makings for an interesting evening.

Jan glanced at the kitchen clock, grabbed her pack, and rushed out the back door. Mark was still on the phone with the President and would not appreciate an interrupting goodbye kiss. She crossed her fingers. Please don't let some crisis ruin my day — or my party.

As Jan walked through the open door of her office she saw Barbara Wilcott with a determined look on her face flipping through the giant Rolodex on her desk. Barbara wore a perpetual look of resignation that matched her drab wardrobe. She had served every administration since Eisenhower and was now, in her early sixties, surprised by nothing.

'Morning, Barbara, any luck?' Jan smiled. 'You look like you spent the night here.'

'Should have. Hookers are a snap. Blond boys in drag seem to be in short supply this week.' She went back to the Rolodex cards.

Jan was sure that her father had something to do with having Barbara assigned to her office, and she blessed him daily. Barbara not only knew where all the skeletons were buried, but which ones still had meat on them.

'Have you ever done this before?' Jan asked, still not sure this was an activity that the Office of Protocol should be involved with.

Barbara did a slow Jack Benny turn, rested her chin in her hand, and said, 'Now, what do you think?' Sensing Jan's discomfort, Barbara signaled for her to come closer.

'There are some things that they don't put in your briefing book when you come in here,' she began in a low but direct tone. 'I guess that's why old goats like me are kept on from administration to administration.' She paused and pushed a strand of gun-metal gray hair behind her ear. 'Listen, sweetie, it's not different here. Sex is as much a part of big government as show business, or any other big business. We are going to be called on this way more than we like. Sometimes we'll refer it to the CIA, but that will come from upstairs.'

She jabbed her thumb toward the ceiling and the Secretary of State's office.

'There are a few line items in our budget that the Congress never really questions, so we more or less have their blessing.' Shaking her head she quickly added, 'But God forbid we ever get caught. Those SOBs on the Hill will pretend they are outraged and start some kind of investigation. Of course, they'll never finish it.'

'What do you mean, never finish?' Jan asked, fascinated.

'I mean they couldn't risk it. During the Nixon years one of the flunkies used to take care of a few selected congressmen along with his buddies on the White House staff. He specialized in supplying some absolutely gorgeous Scandinavian ladies. They were allegedly here on a two-year trade exchange program. Actually they were really high-class call girls.'

'You're kidding.'

'Do I look like it?' Barbara quickly rejoined and continued. 'Then there was the young Reaganite who thought he'd landed in clover the first year of the administration. He was a pretty wild bachelor, and when he got ahold of our list of the finest professional ladies in the world he almost screwed himself blind. The bigwigs upstairs got word that he was sharing the wealth — hoping to endear himself with some congressmen and . . .'

Barbara stopped abruptly as a mail clerk swept through the door and deposited a bundle on her desk. Slumping down in her chair after the mail boy left, signaling she had said all she had to say,

Barbara returned to the task at hand. Jan had grown used to Barbara's habit of telling her just enough of a racy anecdote for her to get the point that she should always be on her toes. Jan valued her wisdom if not her unfinished stories.

'There's a gal I've been trying to reach. She's been an on-and-off-again consultant to us on these kinds of matters for years. I've left a message with her service. We have to start over with each new administration because these people are sometimes as skittish as we are at first. But she's good, so I think we should work with her,' Barbara said.

Jan was relieved. She was quickly realizing that the life she had led as the privileged daughter of a wealthy diplomat was light-years away from the real world of Washington power plays.

If only she could stop worrying about her party — if she could just relax about it, show up, and be herself as her father had scolded. She took three deep breaths. To work, she ordered herself.

Later that morning, when Barbara stepped through the door of Jan's office, she had a finger pressed to her lips. 'Don't say anything,' she whispered. 'The woman I was trying to reach, the "consultant", is here.' Barbara mimed quote marks with her fingers.

Jan gasped. 'She's here in the office? My word, what are we going to do?'

'*We?* . . . *You* are going to see her and make arrangements for the prince's date.'

'But Barbara, you know the woman. You can do this sort of thing. Can't you speak to her?'

'I don't know her. I've only talked to her on the phone. Besides, she insists on talking to you. Might as well get your feet wet. Just be cautious,' Barbara said as she started toward the door.

Jan wished she hadn't left her blazer in the outer closet. She glanced at her rolled-up sleeves. Quickly she buttoned them and stood up, straightened her shoulders, and lifted her chin.

Barbara opened the door and said, 'Miss Bourne, Mrs Kirkland will see you now.'

Echo Bourne was of medium height, shorter than Jan and probably in her late thirties. Her dark print dress was understated, her gold jewelry tasteful. Over her right shoulder was draped a silk shawl in a print contrasting to the dress.

'How do you do, Mrs Kirkland,' she said with somewhat exaggerated elegance. 'Thank you for seeing me without an appointment. I had other business here at State this morning and thought I'd take advantage of this opportunity to meet you. I've met your dad at several functions over the years and admire him a great deal.'

Jan shook her hand. 'Please sit down, Miss Bourne.' She realized she was staring at her too hard and caught herself. This woman looked too civilized, too businesslike.

Echo Bourne lowered herself into the chair and adjusted the hem of her dress. 'I so enjoyed the story about you and your husband in *Washingtonian* magazine this month.' She smiled.

'Thank you,' Jan said, not knowing what else to say. She tried. 'What can we do for you, Miss

Bourne?' The instant she said it she was sorry. 'Oh dear, we called you, didn't we?'

'Quite right,' Echo said, waiting.

Here's trouble, Jan thought. What am I going to say? 'Ah, well, Ms Bourne, ah, we've had a foreign embassy request on a matter of some delicacy, you see . . .'

The woman sensed her discomfort. 'You've been here only a few months, I understand, Mrs Kirkland.'

'Uh, why, uh, yes . . . I came right after President Kane took office in January.'

'Is this the first time you've had to deal with matters of this nature?' Echo opened her navy snakeskin bag and extracted a matching cigarette case bordered in gold. She snapped the latch with a long red thumbnail.

'Do you mind?' she asked, holding a cigarette between her thumb and forefinger.

Jan did mind but didn't say so. 'Oh, of course not.' She swiveled her chair around to look for the ashtray. She found it under a pile of papers and handed it to Echo.

'Perhaps I can make things a little easier,' Echo said as she exhaled. 'I've done business with the Protocol office before, as your assistant may have mentioned. The code phrase she left with my service was that she was inquiring about a ball gown. That tells me you have a VIP who requires the services of a transvestite.'

Jan cleared her throat nervously. The woman was speaking as though she were instructing her

32

dressmaker regarding a particularly intricate fitting.

'Am I correct?'

'Yes . . . yes,' Jan said, nodding. She was beginning to feel that somehow this was being recorded only to surface at Senate hearings in the distant future and destroy her career and Mark's.

'Now, there's no problem,' Echo said briskly. 'I'll need to know such details as time, place, length of stay. Our fees remain the same as during Reagan.' She paused, caught in a thought, then noted, 'During the Carter years we did very little business.'

'I see,' Jan said.

'We look forward to assisting the new administration.' Echo smiled, put out her cigarette, and rose from the chair. 'I'll work out the details with your assistant.' Echo extended her hand. 'Do give your father my regards.'

Jan shook her hand, relieved that the meeting was over. 'Yes, I will,' she said.

'Grand,' Echo beamed. 'I hope discussing matters like this doesn't make you too uncomfortable.'

'To tell you the truth, it does . . . a bit.'

'If it makes you feel any better, this sort of thing has been going on for a long time. Believe it or not, I recently had a very unofficial meeting with a group of political scientists who are studying sex in government and politics. And I think they may conclude that sex is almost as important as money. Maybe more.'

'Yes, well, thank you again,' Jan said. She wished the woman would go.

'Perhaps we can visit again. I know you have other sources you can call on, but I'd like to discuss some of our capabilities,' Echo said, adjusting her shawl.

'Yes, well . . . that would be very nice . . . uh . . .' Jan felt very much like an amateur, and was sure she sounded like one, too. But the last thing she wanted was a sales pitch on servicing the under-belly of diplomacy. Echo Bourne's departure was a relief.

Jan looked up from the pile of papers on her desk and realized that it was forty minutes since Barbara had waved that she was off to do some errands at lunch. It was nearly noon and Jan was starved, having had only a banana for breakfast. She had too much work to have time to go to the cafeteria; so the can of tuna in the office fridge would have to be enough. She settled down with the open can and a plastic fork, grateful for the brief break.

'Shoot,' she muttered in disgust as a glob of oily tuna dropped into the circle indicating where the secretary of labor and his wife would be sitting at a forthcoming state dinner for the President of Ireland. Stretching for a box of tissues, she saw Barbara walking through the outer office door. Her face was flushed, her hair coming loose from its always tight arrangement. 'Barb,' she called, 'you okay?'

Barbara stood leaning against the side of the door as if for support. 'Jan . . . I . . .'

'What's the matter?' Jan asked anxiously.

34

'Bradford Barry, the chief of staff . . . he's had a heart attack. He's dead!' she gasped.

'What?'

Barbara breathed deeply. 'It isn't even on the wire yet. I stopped by the East Wing to pick up a package from the First Lady's office and found her staff in tears.'

'Did he die in the White House?' Jan asked.

Barbara shook her head and lowered her voice. 'No, he was at some kind of meeting last night at the Hay-Adams. But listen to this. People are already talking about who is going to be the next chief of staff. Apparently the President feels he has to name someone immediately because of his Moscow trip. And one of the people they're talking about is your Mark.'

Jan stared at her. 'Mark?' Bradford Barry had just died and already the talk was of his replacement. How revolting. 'Oh, Barbara, Brad Barry was such a terrific man.' She stood silently for a long moment. 'How sad,' she continued, shaking her head. Suddenly she had an unpleasant taste of tuna in her mouth. 'I think I'm going to sit down for a sec.'

Barbara guided Jan back to her desk, tossed the tuna can in the wastebasket, and softly but firmly began to give Jan instructions. 'First, call your husband and find out why he didn't call us. We're supposed to have an inside source over there with him. Then tell him to have someone in his office try to reach the people you invited to your bash. You've simply got to cancel your party.'

'I can't call him. He's in Pittsburgh with the

President. Oh, Barbara, everything is set. What should I do?'

'Get with it, Jan. Call his secretary. She'll let everyone know. You've got clout. Start using it.'

Jan looked up at her in gratitude. 'How would I survive without you?' She smiled.

'You probably wouldn't. Now let's go see the chief. The First Lady wants Protocol to handle the Barry funeral.'

Monday, June 5, 1989 – 5.30 P.M.
The Watergate Apartments

'Shit,' she hissed.

She reached for more surgical adhesive, streaked a long white worm along the back of her index finger, and tried it one more time. She picked up a clump of lashes with a pair of tweezers and dipped the ends into the sticky mixture. She lifted them to her silver-gray eyelid and pressed them carefully among the other lashes already in place. She blinked twice. This time they all stuck.

She raised her chin, shook her mane of thick jet-black hair, and lowered her eyes to look at herself in the mirror to check the final product. Not too shabby, she thought.

At twenty-nine, Sinclare Ives knew she would never look any better. She possessed a dancer's body and carried herself with the assurance of a favored courtesan. Her showstopping asset was a remarkable face.

Her poreless skin was made paler by the frame of black hair that fell in a tangle of curls to her shoulders and shone almost indigo under direct light. Her full mouth and even white teeth made men pay attention to her every word. Staring into the wide-set green eyes circled with star-point black lashes made them deaf.

Sinclare had always been beautiful and took her looks for granted. She had learned early in life that good things come to girls who are pretty and pretty things come from men. Her mother had had a tremendous influence on her life. When Sinclare was thirteen she discovered she had something men wanted and as her mother had indelibly impressed on her, that gave her power. How much simpler could it get? And when she thought about it, which she didn't much, introspection not being an important part of her interior life, the trade was a bit uneven. Men had to work for their power and money. She only had to have a friendly smile and listen to them talk. In listening there was an implied promise of future favors to be granted. But that part of the game she controlled. She liked that.

She had married former Senator Eliot Ives because he was rich and not bad-looking, but most compellingly because she was tired of always being someone's date. The faces of the powerful men she dated, traveled, and slept with were beginning to run together in one blurred montage. Being Mrs Eliot Ives gave her the identity she hungered for and the prestige she craved. And of course, there was the money, and lots of it.

She had little comprehension of what it was that Eliot actually did. The press called him a power broker. She knew that as an attorney and former United States senator he was asked to represent companies and people who wanted something from someone in Washington and were willing to pay him a great deal to get it for them. Sometimes he made money with a simple phone call. Other times earning a fat retainer meant they had to spend endless evenings in expensive restaurants. She would smile until her jaw ached and listen to conversations she neither understood nor cared about. But she loved Eliot because he was good to her, so she just kept smiling. Tonight was going to be one of those evenings.

Now she rejected half a dozen outfits before selecting one that made her feel the way she wanted to tonight. She wanted to freeze them in their seats.

She would glide into the Jockey Club at the Ritz-Carlton with a slow sable-dragging walk and hear nothing but ice melting and deep breathing. She knew both men and women couldn't keep their eyes off her. Too bad she couldn't put this show on at the best party in town tonight: the Kirklands' dinner party. They had not been invited, even though Eliot was a good friend of Don Kane and his pals. Not being invited was really a slap in the face, she decided.

Sinclare needed a little fix. She pulled a white satin dressing gown around her shoulders and padded across the two-inch-thick, white wall-to-wall carpeting of the bedroom, through the massive double-size living area, and into the unused kitchen. The recessed lighting glowed eerily off the shiny surfaces, giving the area the look of a battle station on a spaceship. She opened several empty cabinets before locating a giant jar of Skippy. She plunged one long-taloned finger into the gooey mass and extracted a two-ounce lump. Licking her finger, being careful not to smudge her perfectly outlined and glossed lips, she walked back to the bedroom.

She found a joint in her private stash under the bed, where she hid them from the maid and Eliot. He would never approve. Sometimes she needed a little buzz when she went out with Eliot's friends. She didn't drink anymore because it made her so crazy – out of control. She always did the wrong thing after a few drinks of anything alcoholic. Besides, she'd read somewhere that it was bad for her complexion. A few hits would make the evening more pleasant. Tonight their guests were Wall Street insiders, and she had little to add to discussions about Brazilian bank defaults and tax loopholes.

She felt her body relax, as she pushed the button on the tape deck and let the sound of Bruce Springsteen wash over her.

She liked her life. She liked the sleek, expensively decorated Watergate apartment, her little red Ferrari, the jewelry, and the clothes. But something was missing. What made her unhappy was not being asked to parties like Jan Kirkland's. When Don Kane, for whom Eliot had raised so much money, was elected, all that was supposed to change. They would be part of the new administration's inner circle; the world would be at their feet. But what was taking so long?

Oh, sure, there had been rumors. Eliot was going to be named secretary of labor. It didn't happen. Then he was going to be White House counsel. But that chinless wonder who was the Vice President's former law partner got the job instead. Sinclare had all the 'things' she needed, the goodies that Eliot's money provided. In Washington you could even buy some people, but the people she wanted to be with – the people she wanted to mean something to – couldn't be bought. You had to have power to make them want you at their parties. Clearly she didn't have enough.

She looked at Eliot's photo in the silver art nouveau frame next to the bed. His Morty Sills suit and Turnbull and Asser shirt and tie made him look like an investment banker, which was the idea in the first place.

She did not regret her choice of Eliot.

Everyone saw his smoothness and hustle, and assumed he was one more in the long rank of those who had come to Washington to 'serve' in government but ended up serving himself much better as soon as he became a private citizen. But they didn't know him. Sinclare did. He'd never lied to her; sometimes Eliot's crass truths made her wince, but after every screaming fight, she'd glare at him furiously, while inside she was smiling. She knew she'd married the right man.

He had been married and divorced twice and on their second date told her, 'Never again.'

40

That was all Sinclare needed. The challenge was an aphrodisiac. She was deliberately late, forgot dates, and left the phone machine on to listen to him beg. The crazier he got about her the more she dated other men. But when she was with him she treated him like a god.

Finally, it took running off for weekends at the Waldorf in New York with George Lowry, a rich middle-aged senator, to drive him around the bend. Eliot took the shuttle and threatened to punch his former colleague in the face at the Waldorf's Bull and Bear Restaurant.

The night Don Kane formally announced he was going to run for the party nomination, Eliot gave her a seven-karat white diamond solitaire, emerald cut, bordered on each side by immense diamond baguettes. She began to relent.

When he asked her to marry him that weekend and promised they would have the world at their feet, she coyly hesitated.

When he said he was buying a penthouse at the Watergate and she could decorate it any way she liked and throw parties in it, she lowered her eyes and made a pretty pout.

When he told her that the Kanes wanted them to fly to California on the campaign plane with them, and it wouldn't be 'proper', a word he had been using more and more, for them not to be married, Sinclare said 'Yes.'

She took the ring out of her wall safe and put it on. She had learned quickly that there were times to wear it and times to leave it in her jewelry case. As glamorous as Washington wives had become since Nancy Reagan, they still weren't ready for anyone wearing a ring the size of an ice cube. If she had been invited to the Kirklands she would have left it at home, but tonight called for the big white solitaire. Tonight she was on her turf and to hell with that snooty White House crowd, no matter how high Eliot jumped for them.

She finished dressing and was sitting on the end of the bed slipping her feet into silver strap sandals when she heard the apartment door slam.

'Sinclare!' Eliot's voice boomed from the living room. 'Where are you?'

'I'm dressing, love.'

She looked up to see him at the bedroom door, his face tight with anger. 'Where the hell did you lunch today?'

'How about, "Hello, darling, it's been a terrible day without you,"' she said, scowling at him.

'It's been a crappy day. Did you hear that Brad Barry died? Hell, he and I were the same age. And he just croaked. And then the Tariff Commission hearing room had no air-conditioning. I was trapped in there like a roasting pig. Turn on the TV.' He pulled at the knot in his tie. 'Answer me, Sinclare. Where did you have lunch?'

'At Duke's. What's the big deal?'

'And who did you have lunch with?' He wasn't going to let up.

'Well, let's see. I ran into the Marshalls and Sheila Reynolds from *Dossier* magazine. She looks great since the baby. Then . . . let me think.' She looked up at the ceiling and pressed her lips together.

'Don't get cute, Sinclare, you were with Echo Bourne, weren't you?' He threw his suit jacket over the back of the chair and started twisting the big gold links out of his French cuffs.

'You know so much, why do you ask?' she sniffed. 'Sure I saw Echo, she's in Duke's all the time. She likes that jock crowd.'

'Correction. She likes that jock crowd to see her having lunch with my wife. I rode up the elevator with Judge Markey. He saw you both at the first table. Turn on the damn TV!' he barked again.

'Duke always puts Echo at the first table,' Sinclare said, knowing it was a weak defense and ignoring his order to turn on the television. Eliot had always hated her friendship with Echo and had repeatedly complained about her being seen in public with her friend. Now he would be pissed all evening. She hoped the awful news about Brad would diffuse him. She hoped to distract him further. Pawing through the makeup on her dressing table for a sharp-enough eyeliner, she said, trying to keep her voice light, 'Oh, by the way, Echo had just been to the State Department for a meeting with Jan Kirkland.' She knew that would intrigue him.

'What?' His expression changed to interest.

'Uh-huh,' she said smugly. Boy, did she know Eliot or what?

'What the hell was Echo Bourne doing in the Protocol office?'

'Apparently she has an assignment to get that Arab prince a date with a guy in a dress.'

Eliot sat down in the slipper chair and started

43

taking off his custom-made shoes. 'Now, that I find very interesting.'

'Thought you would.'

'I still don't want you to be seen with her, Sinclare,' he said, but his tone had lost its threatening edge.

'She's my best friend, Eliot,' she said in a little-girl hurt voice. 'Besides, look at all the neat information she's got.'

He pulled his shirt loose from his trousers and started walking toward the dressing room. 'I don't care. She's using you. Talk to her on the phone if you need information. Just don't go out with her. Sinclare, please turn on the television.'

He disappeared into the bathroom. Seconds later he was back with a towel wrapped around his hips, and she reached for the remote control, aimed it at the six-foot screen in the black lacquered cabinet against the wall, but kept walking toward him. An inane quiz show flipped onto the screen. She ran her fingers lightly through the mass of black hair on his chest. 'Don't be mad at me, El,' she said, her fingers moving toward the twist in the towel around his waist. 'I hate it when you yell at me.' The towel dropped to the floor. Deftly she slipped one hand between his legs.

He backed against the doorjamb. 'Sinclare, not now,' he groaned. 'I want to hear this. It's important, baby.'

'We interrupt this program to bring you an update from our ABC Newsroom in Washington . . .' The disembodied voice of the network announcer floated toward them. 'Good evening.'

The familiar voice of Jim Henderson, the ABC White House correspondent, had a sense of urgency to it. 'The White House this morning announced the sudden death of presidential chief of staff Bradford Barry. We can now report that Barry died of cardiac arrest shortly after seven P.M. last night.'

'Holy shit!' Eliot pushed Sinclare away roughly. He moved toward the television and turned up the volume. 'Something's up,' he said as he opened the armoire for a shirt. 'Barry died last night at seven. The White House didn't announce it until the end of Kirkland's morning briefing. Only now are the details coming out. I smell something cooking.'

Monday, June 5, 1989 – 5:45 P.M.
The Fort, Foxhall Road

Caroline Riggs always drove too fast. Now, with the dashboard clock heading toward six, she was doing sixty. Between the five-shop search for the shoes she wanted for the Kirklands' party tonight and the mechanic who couldn't find what was wrong with the transmission, she had less than an hour to shower and dress.

The top was down on her little tan 380SL Mercedes, and the wind lashed her dark red hair into her mouth. Caroline glanced at the speedometer and slowly pressed the brake. Dalton would be furious if she got another ticket. He'd accuse her of drinking too much wine at lunch.

She shifted down to take the grade of the steep gravel driveway that led up to the house, a mansion on Foxhall Road next to the one that had once belonged to Nelson Rockefeller. It was the dream her mother always had for her. Although her mother never saw it, her money had paid for it.

Caroline pulled the car next to the front steps and grabbed her packages out of the back seat. Where was Manuel? Usually he was waiting at the door, signaled by the photoelectric eye at the main gate.

Suddenly the front door sprang open and a sheepish Manuel reached for her shopping bags. 'Beg pardon, Mrs Riggs, the phone rang.'

'That's all right, Manuel,' she said. God she was exhausted. It was hot, too hot for June. Even the hottest day in the Texas of her girlhood hadn't the thick moist heat of Washington. She peeled off her jacket and handed it to Manuel. 'Where's Rosa?'

'She take Miss Polly's Jeep up to dry cleaner's on Wisconsin for your party dress.'

'Wonderful,' she said in a tone of relief. She stepped into the large oval entrance hall, which she never entered without a feeling of deep satisfaction. The mansion had been important to Dalton's career and it let her entertain on a social level that at first was somewhat beyond her abilities. But over the years she had learned by painstakingly observing other hostesses. Now she was among the best in the tradition of Perle Mesta, Gwen Cafritz, and Esther Coopersmith. With her outgoing manner, the elegant food, and the gracious setting, she knew she gave great fun parties – the kind she had seen her mother give, the kind people talked about for weeks.

She flipped through the mail Manuel had placed on a footed silver tray beneath the mirror. 'Who was on the phone, Manuel?'

The aging little man jumped, remembering the phone was still on hold. 'Oh! Sorry, Mrs Riggs. It's Miss Polly, long distance . . .'

'Polly!' Caroline hurried toward the library. 'Why didn't you say so?' She reached for the phone on Dalton's partner's desk. 'Hi, honeybunch,' she said excitedly in her long-distance voice, slightly louder than necessary. 'I just walked in. Manuel forgot to tell me you were on hold. How's life at West Point?'

'Mom!' Her daughter cut her off, almost shouting. 'Turn on the TV! Quick! Don't talk!'

'What channel?' Caroline asked. She reached for the remote-control gadget and aimed it at the television in the built-in bookcases.

'It doesn't matter, it's on every channel!'

Instantly Mark Kirkland's familiar voice could be heard, then his image flipped into view. He was answering a reporter's question with '. . . the President will announce a replacement no later than the end of the week. We have no further details at the moment.'

Her heart was pounding. 'What's going on, Polly?'

'Turn on NBC,' Polly snapped. 'Brokaw is talking about it. It's Uncle Brad! He's had a heart attack. He's dead!'

47

'Oh, Lord.' She sat down in Dalton's high leather chair, staring at the screen. She clicked to NBC. Mother and daughter listened to the same broadcast. The full impact washed over her. 'Oh, Polly, how terrible. I wish you were here.'

'I'm coming right down, Mother. I'll catch a ride into New York and take the late shuttle. I can make it if I leave right now.'

'Can you get away?' Caroline asked, her voice unsteady.

'Sure, it's an emergency. I'm calling from Colonel Edwards's office right now. He says it's okay.'

'All right, darling. I'll have Manuel meet your plane.'

'I'll just hop a cab at National. It's easier.' Polly paused. 'Mommy, are you all right?'

Caroline took a deep breath to steady her voice. 'Of course, hon. It's just such a shock. I must reach your dad.'

'Where is he?'

'Locked in meetings on the Moscow trip. I'll leave a message that you're on your way.'

'See you around midnight, then.'

She replaced the receiver. A soft early-evening breeze inched the heavy damask drapes forward, then released them.

Of all the people around Don Kane, they had truly come to know Brad Barry. The tall handsome chief of staff had all but become a member of the Riggs family. Before the election, as Senator Kane's administrative aide, he had been instrumental in Polly's getting into West Point. During the campaign Brad had included Polly in a swirl of activities, getting her a special job in the campaign and including her on trips on the candidate's plane. When his marriage finally fell apart because of the presidential campaign, 'Uncle' Brad spent his rare free time at the Riggs's house. Caroline knew Brad's death would be a terrible blow to her daughter.

After three tries Caroline managed to get through to her husband in his office at the White House. 'Dalton, I wouldn't have disturbed you, but Polly called. She's on her way down.'

'Quite all right, dear, you just caught me. We're all in a state of shock.'

'Do you have any more details?' she asked, knowing he must and couldn't tell her.

'Dear, I can't talk. The President has asked to see me. I'm on my way to the Oval Office and I'm late. The timing couldn't be worse with this damn Moscow trip. I'll call when I can. Don't expect me anytime soon. Oh, and Jan Kirkland said the party tonight has been canceled.'

Good soldier Dalton, she thought. No matter how involved he became in the civilian world, his instincts remained those of a lifelong military man. Now he served the commander in chief as national security advisor.

General Dalton Riggs's rise through the military ranks had been remarkable. After twenty years in the army, including two combat tours in Vietnam, he had been assigned as a military intelligence advisor to President Reagan, replacing an old West Point classmate. By the end of Reagan's troubled last two years he had made brigadier general.

When President Kane asked him to take the job as head of the National Security Council he accepted without even consulting Caroline.

He didn't have to. She knew he could never turn down the President. No matter how much she needed him, the President needed him more. There was no contest.

Was he at this very moment being asked to replace Bradford as chief of staff? Dalton was at his best in a crisis. He was trained for war, and God knows the chief of staff job would put him right in the middle of a combat zone.

'Mrs Riggs?' A tentative voice spoke from the open door behind her. Rosa stood in the door holding Caroline's magenta Norell covered with a plastic bag.

'Yes, Rosa,' she answered, her voice preoccupied and weary. She turned. 'Thank you for picking up my dress. I won't be needing it now. The party has been canceled.'

Rosa turned to go. 'We saw it on the kitchen TV. He was a nice man, Mr Barry,' Rosa said, looking down at the marble floor of the foyer. 'Always laughing.'

'Yes. We'll all miss him terribly.'

'Miss Polly will be very upset,' Rosa said.

'She's on her way down this evening. Would you see to her room and bath, Rosa? And turn on her air conditioner. It must be sweltering up there.'

'Yes, ma'am.' Rosa turned and walked back to the kitchen.

Caroline walked to the drinks tray, poured scotch on some ice, and took a long sip. She idly stepped to the campaign table beside Dalton's desk, where one of his perpetual war games was frozen in progress. He had re-created the tank-to-tank engagement at Villers-Bretonneux in 1918. He had been moving the pieces around for well over a year and had explained the battle to her too many times. She reached for one of the miniature pieces on the board, a British Mark IV. It was beautifully crafted and correct in every detail. She felt the weight of it in her hand and remembered when they had found it in a cluttered Georgetown shop.

She liked tanks. They were sturdy shells in which one could hide, impenetrable, safe yet fierce in combat – like Dalton, the way she had hoped their marriage would be.

The phone on the desk rang once and stopped. Rosa had picked up the kitchen extension.

'Mrs Riggs, there's a Mr O'Brien from the *Washington Post* on line one. He wants to speak to the general,' Rosa said. 'Do you want to talk to him?'

Caroline liked Tim O'Brien. He'd covered the White House beat for fifteen years and always whispered gossipy delicious asides to Caroline at cocktail parties. She was dying to talk to someone who could tell her what was going on. What was happening at the White House? Was Dalton being considered? Had he already been named? Most people in Washington got the news of enormous change in their life in Washington through the media. Again, her role was that of waiting wife, as it had been since her marriage to Dalton.

51

She looked at the little tank in her hand. Be a good soldier, she heard from the guiding voice that spoke from a hidden and permanent place in her head. Be a good soldier, Caroline. Good soldiers follow orders.

'Thank you, Rosa,' she answered. 'Tell Mr O'Brien the general can be reached at his White House office.'

What she really wanted to do was pick up the phone and say, 'Hi, Tim. What's happening?' And when he started talking about Dalton becoming chief of staff, to gibe back and ask him why the hell the press didn't just throw on the brakes for a minute. Wasn't it the time to talk about Brad Barry and not Dalton Riggs? And to say that the country had lost a great servant, a man who devoted his life to others? But she knew she couldn't.

Bradford Barry had been a great man, but no one was interested in him anymore. Washington reporters focused on the living, not the dead. Brad was history, and the press corps were not historians.

This is a tough town, Caroline thought, as she sipped her drink. And she would have a new role in it if her husband were to be made chief of staff.

Tuesday

Tuesday, June 6, 1989 – 8:00 A.M.
The Watergate Apartments

Sinclare heard the elevator door open and the soft plop of Tuesday morning's *Washington Post* hit the hall carpeting. She waited until she heard the elevator door slide closed, and ran naked to the front door and grabbed the paper.

She glanced at the front page, gasped, and then screamed, 'I don't believe it, Eliot!'

Squealing with excitement, she ran to the dressing room. Eliot was standing in front of the mirrored closet door smoothing his silver temples with matched brushes. She turned him around and covered his face with kisses.

He laughed, trying to keep his balance, and gently pushed her away. He was already dressed and didn't want to play again. 'What the hell has gotten into you?' he chuckled.

'Look, look, look,' she said, holding the paper at arm's length. 'It's you!'

Eliot grabbed the paper and walked over to where the light was better. 'Interesting . . .'

Sinclare stood by his side as he studied a feature story below the fold speculating on who the President might pick as the new chief of staff. Three pictures appeared under the headline 'PRESIDENT

55

TO PICK TOP AIDE BY END OF WEEK' — those of General Dalton Riggs, national security advisor, Mark Kirkland, presidential press secretary, and former Senator Eliot Ives.

Sinclare's heart was pounding.

Eliot sat down on the edge of the bed and studied it. 'Good picture,' he said, pleased.

He didn't sound nearly as surprised as she thought he would. 'Is that all you can say?'

'I see my phone calls last night did some good,' he observed as he turned to the inside of the paper. A Tim O'Brien article claimed that the FBI and the Secret Service were investigating the circumstances of Barry's death. 'One source reported' that the DC Police had been removed after they failed to seal off the room, and then gave permission to clean it and rent it the same night.

'Oh, El,' Sinclare said breathlessly, 'do you think you'll get the job?'

Folding the paper under his arm, he jammed his hands into the pockets of his pants and paced the room. 'Hard to say. I've got strong support on the Hill. What I really need is a heavy hitter to carry my case. I may call Lowry.'

'I could speak to George for you,' she said, smiling coyly.

'I'll handle it, Sinclare,' Eliot said, giving her one of his killer looks. Eliot and George had patched up their differences after George had married his present wife, Judy. But Eliot was still very sensitive about George and Sinclare.

Sinclare was sorry. Teasing him about old boyfriends wasn't fair. This was too important to them both.

He scooped a handful of change from the shelf of the wooden valet. 'I'm late. I have a breakfast meeting with Jim Morgan, that ass they made undersecretary of interior. Where are you going to be?' he asked, shrugging into the jacket of his finely tailored deep blue suit.

'I have my massage at nine or noon, I'm not sure.' No need to mention that she was meeting Echo at the salon. 'Maybe we could have a late lunch.'

'Don't know, this is going to be one hell of a day.' He leaned over and gave her a kiss on the cheek. 'I'll leave a message on the machine. And Sin, please don't talk to anyone about this chief of staff business. It's going to be rough enough as it is.'

She made a playful grab for his inner thigh, but he danced clear and was gone.

She listened for the descending hum of the elevator and pounced across the bed for the phone.

'Why are you calling?' Echo asked. 'I thought we were getting together.'

'I couldn't wait,' she said, excited. 'Did you see it?'

'See what?'

'The story about Eliot maybe being the next chief of staff.' Sinclare was irritated.

'I saw it. But did you see Deena Simon's column in the *Observer*? It's really juicy. It should help narrow your competition.'

'How can you read that rag?'

57

'Are you kidding? I'm delighted Washington finally has a tabloid. They print all the good stuff. Hold on, let me get it.'

Sinclare heard the rustle of pages.

'Ready? You're going to love this.'

Echo began to read in her throaty voice: 'Listen up, night-lifers. There are hopeful signs that the Kane administration isn't as dull as we thought. One of Don's tip-top men is a regular in the back booth of a favorite White House staff hangout where he plays kissy face with a Justice Department cutey-kins definitely not his too-too social wife. Not since Gary Hart's lady friend forgot her library book at 3 A.M. have we seen such careless courting. Word has it that the West Wing honcho has been told to cool it by the biggies or his stately wife's daddy will seriously scold.' Echo paused, then added, 'Need a translation?'

'Are you kidding?' Sinclare hooted. 'That's got to be Mark Kirkland. Oh, my God, Echo. They're going to have a fit! Do you think it's true?'

'Between you and me?'

'Of course, what do you know?'

'I'll bet it's a plant. Pure political skullduggery to hurt Mark's chances for advancement. Why, I'll bet the President has him on the Oval Office carpet as we speak.'

'Echo, what's the word on Caroline Riggs? Friends of Joan Kennedy planted stories on her drinking, trying to help her and hurt Teddy because he was playing around on his wife. Well, everyone knows Caroline has a drinking problem.

Maybe we could help her, hurt General Riggs a tiny bit, and help Eliot a lot.'

'Don't be naïve, Sinclare.'

'So you don't think we should try something like that?'

'Wouldn't do much. I'm sure the White House knows about Caroline, and the President made the general his head man at the National Security Council,' Echo said flatly. Then with a bit of mystery in her voice, she noted, 'I think I know someone who has something that would be very embarrassing to the good general.'

'The general? Give me a break. That man has to be as clean as the pope.'

'Wrong.'

'Echo, what do you know?'

'It's what I've got. A videotape.'

'Who has it?'

'Someone I know. I'll see if I can get ahold of it. It might be of help to you.'

'I really want to help Eliot to get that job. He deserves it. Besides, I'm fed up with the snotty treatment we've been getting from everybody.'

'All right, I'll try. But you owe me one, Sinclare Ives.'

'Listen, when we get to the White House you can have anything you want. I swear!'

Sinclare remembered how the town had buzzed over the alleged, but never seen videotapes of Vickie Morgan and the 'highups' of Ronald Reagan's gang. Was everybody taping everybody?

Sinclare's experience with men in high places told her that the more lofty the public image, the potentially stranger their sexual proclivities. For all of his elegant ways, Dalton Riggs might be into something really strange. Sex in Washington seldom surfaced publicly. Some of her friends were mistresses, others were among the classiest call girls in the world. They succeeded because they were beautiful and discreet. Donna Rice and the *Miami Herald* had changed the world of presidential politics by putting sex on the front page. At the time Sinclare had wondered if Gary Hart was set up. She thought she had met Donna on Adnan Khashoggi's yacht.

Suddenly it dawned on Sinclare that she and her girl friends had a tremendous role in this 'man's town'.

Maybe it was time for a sex scandal involving Dalton Riggs. God, it was exciting. Nothing exhilarated Sinclare more than being part of the action. Echo always seemed to know a lot about the action all over town. Maybe this time she was going to let Sinclare be a part of it, and help sweet Eliot.

Sinclare

1960–1977
Bide-a-Wee Motor Home and Trailer Park
Alexandria, Virginia

Sinclare Danner got the idea of being rich from her mother, Ruby, who had never been anything but poor.

At fifteen, a faulty gas heater left Ruby an orphan. Fortunately she had Big Joey, a high school dropout with a drug habit and the leader of a motorcycle gang that hung out at a seedy all-night bar on the road into Grindstone, Pennsylvania. With no one to tell her not to, Ruby had joined the group when it took off, looking for adventure. After a few months of wandering, riding on the back of a Harley hog had become too uncomfortable for the pregnant teenager. Ruby had slept with all ten of the guys in her gang, so she had no idea who was responsible for her condition.

Ruby awoke one morning in a run-down motel in Alexandria, Virginia. Big Joey and the group had moved on, leaving enough money for her to find a job and a place to live, and survive for a few weeks.

The sympathetic motel manager knew of a trailer in a mobile home park out near the airport –

the Bide-a-Wee. It provided a roof and four walls. And Ruby soon found a job on an assembly line at a small dehumidifier factory nearby that provided the means to live.

The older women on the line liked Ruby. She was sweet, cheerful, and relentlessly optimistic. Forever giving, Ruby would work two shifts back-to-back so a girl on the line could have a honeymoon. Ruby didn't mind. There was nothing to go home to in the trailer. She couldn't afford a television, and at least the factory was heated at night. Besides, she was waiting for the arrival of the first thing in her life that would be truly her own.

The men out on the work floor liked her because she was sexy and girlishly tough. Hanging around a motorcycle gang had taught her that a good scout always offered to buy a round of beers. The men at the factory never let her, but she earned their admiration for always offering. When the Machinist's Union rules meant her hospital maternity bills weren't covered, the shop steward did some clever fudging and backdated Ruby's file.

The day Ruby went into labor the entire factory chipped in. Jack, the shop steward, and two of the girls from the assembly line were at her bedside when she came to at Alexandria Hospital.

Sinclare Danner was born on a bright October afternoon in 1960. Even the hard-faced nurse who filled out the line on the admission form that read 'father unknown' had to admit that Baby Sinclare was the most beautiful she had ever seen.

With an infant to support and a baby-sitter to

pay, Ruby knew she had a problem. She needed a night job she could take the baby to if she had to.

Duke Zeibert's hatcheck room provided the answer. The restaurant had been a favorite Washington watering hole since the Eisenhower years. The story was that Duke had gotten his start as the doorman and car parker at a restaurant on Connecticut Avenue. He ingratiated himself with the movers and shakers, who gave him the backing to open his own place.

Duke, a bluff, no-nonsense man with an irreverent sense of humor, gradually made his restaurant the gathering place for lobbyists, lawyers, journalists, professional athletes and their hangers-on. Senators and jocks, reporters and judges sat side by side at Duke's bar and at his comfortably spaced tables.

The town was filling up with Irishmen who all seemed to look like the Kennedys. They all came to Duke's to drink and laugh, and have others listen to their blarney – the very things Ruby was good at.

A five-minute conversation with Ruby told Duke she could handle the late-night drinkers, and if she occasionally had to bring her baby it was okay.

Baby Sinclare soon became a pet of the regulars. She was cooed over and handed around in her plastic E-Z baby carrier. And while the customers gave Sinclare squeezes and soft toys, Ruby gave her tiny daughter a joyful, easy love that masked a ferocious desire. She wanted her daughter to have the best of life.

* * *

It was a night that would begin to define the direction of Sinclare's life. In a few months she would be graduating from high school. Tonight she and her mother were talking. Ruby popped a can of beer and sat down on the couch that served as her bed.

'I don't suppose you could work for me tomorrow?' she asked hopefully. 'You could take the car so you won't have to come home on the late bus.'

Sinclare replaced the top on a bottle of bright red polish and blew on her nails. 'I thought tomorrow was your night off.'

'It is, but Duke booked a big retirement party for some sportscaster at CBS. He asked me to work it, but I promised Benny I'd go to the basketball game with him. You know what a nut he is about Maryland winning the playoffs this year.'

Benny was one of the waiters at Duke's. Sinclare liked him and secretly hoped he and her mother would get married.

Sinclare worried about her mother. She worked too hard and was losing her looks because of it. Ruby had done so much for her, Sinclare would do anything for her mom. If she was married to Benny, Sinclare wouldn't worry about her so much.

'Can I borrow your black sweater, the one with the beads?' Sinclare asked. It was a bit too tight for Sinclare and when she wore it men said, 'I like your sweater.' She knew what they really meant.

'Sure, honey,' Ruby said. 'You look good in that sweater.'

Johnny Carson was starting his monologue. Ruby swung her feet up onto the couch and lay back against a fringed Atlantic City pillow. She extended her hand and stroked the back of Sinclare's arm. 'You get some sleep now.' Ruby smiled up at her. 'And thanks, baby.'

Sinclare walked to her area in the back of the trailer. Her 'room' could only be called that by virtue of an old floral bedspread and magazine pictures of Robert Redford tacked up on the thin, synthetic wood paneling. It was a sweatbox in the summer and freezing in the winter. Tonight it was cold, and she crawled into bed in her flannel nightie and left her socks on. She drifted off to sleep to the familiar sounds of trains clanking into the power plant freight yard a mile away and the not very distant hiss of late-night traffic on Route 1.

Washington was only twenty minutes away in Ruby's old Dodge. But it was like a distant planet to Sinclare. Filling in for her mother at Duke's was at least a chance to visit that other world. She had seen the women who came to Duke's. She'd overheard their murmured secrets in the ladies' room. One of her favorite fantasies was of walking out of the hatcheck room and sitting down to dinner with them. One day that life would be hers. Looking good at Duke's was a start.

When Sinclare pranced into Duke's his eyes lit up. 'Hey, kid, you look terrific,' he said in the avuncular way he had with her.

She knew she did. She had the top three buttons

of the black-beaded sweater undone, and wore a tight black wool skirt with it. Her dark hose and black patent leather heels teased. Her thick black hair was pinned up in a loose twist; Ruby had done her eye makeup.

'Dy-no-mite,' Duke breathed as she slipped out of her black wool coat. She stood on her toes and gave him a peck on the cheek. She loved Duke. He was the closest thing to a father figure she'd had in her life.

Everything went perfectly. She didn't mischeck a coat, briefcase, or package. By the end of the evening, there were only a few stragglers around the bar. She was exhausted but triumphant. Tonight had been special. The regulars said they barely recognized her, as their voices traveled with their eyes from her hair to her toes and back up.

One man was staring at her through the half-door with a twenty-dollar bill in his hand.

'Just a sec,' she said, 'I'll get your change.' She was looking into the bluest eyes she had ever seen. She had recognized Danny Rankin, the quarter-back for the Washington Redskins, immediately. The team's million-dollar baby, always in the paper and on television, was a god to the jocks at Duke's. He was also gorgeous.

'That's okay,' he said, his eyes on her cleavage, 'that's for you.'

'But this is a twenty,' she said, holding the bill in two fingers.

'Right, doll-face.' He leaned closer. She could smell aftershave and bourbon. 'I haven't seen you before. You new?'

'Just helping out, Mr Rankin.' She leaned on the little shelf of the half-door. Customers seemed to like it when she did that.

'Hey, baby, don't Mr Rankin me,' he slurred just a little. 'Call me Danny.' He handed her his coat check.

She was excited. He was a celebrity and he was flirting with her. He had also given her a twenty-dollar tip. She couldn't wait to tell Ruby. 'Thank you ... Danny.' She smiled and walked slowly back to get his coat. She could feel his eyes on her and so walked with a deliberate sway, pushing her hips forward as she moved.

As she handed him his raincoat he placed his hand over hers and held it. 'What time do you get off, sugar?'

'As soon as your pals in the bar call it a night.'

'Look, we're having a little party up at the Hilton. It won't start till around eleven. Why don't you consider that twenty cab fare and come on up and meet some new Redskins? You'll be my date.'

'You're kidding,' she said, not moving her hand.

'I kid you not. Suite six ten.' He slowly folded his coat under his arm, holding her eyes and delivering a steamy message.

'You may see me,' she said, dropping her eyes.

No way you won't, Danny Rankin, she thought.

She couldn't wait to get out of there. As soon as Duke started closing up she ran to the ladies' room. The makeup job had held. She fluffed her hair and covered herself with a cloud of Charlie. She tucked her sweater inside her skirt, pulling it down tight, and stood sideways to get a better view of her figure. Not quite satisfied, she undid one more button.

She could hear party sounds before the elevator doors opened. As she stepped out some very drunk, enormous Redskins lurched past her. They made kissing sounds behind her back. She stood for a moment at the open door of the suite and surveyed the room. She had never seen so many great-looking women in one place.

The couch held more people than could fit comfortably. Two girls were sprawled across several Redskin laps. The Rolling Stones screeched from two huge stereo speakers, and people were laughing and shouting over the music. Everybody seemed very drunk.

She moved hesitantly toward a makeshift bar on top of a long, low dresser. Someone had put several cigarettes out in the remains of small pizza snacks congealing on a greasy plate next to a row of liquor bottles. Empty plastic glasses and balled-up napkins were scattered in little puddles of water.

She found a clean plastic glass, dropped in two ice cubes, and had to decide what to put in her glass. She usually drank beer, but tonight she felt sophisticated so she filled her glass with Jack Daniels.

She took a sip. It tasted awful. She scanned the room for Danny and was beginning to feel awkward. If he didn't turn up in a minute or two she would just have to walk around and start talking to people by herself.

'Hey, gorgeous, you made it!'

Danny Rankin's blue eyes stared down at her. He had a firm grip on her waist and pressed his body into her side. He felt good. His shirt was open, showing a patch of black chest hair almost covering a thick gold chain. He pressed his lips to her ear and whispered, 'You better tell me your name, sugar, so I can introduce you around.'

She stretched to reach his ear and said, 'Sinclare, Sinclare Danner.'

He did not leave her side, propelling her through the noisy crowd, pulling guys by the shoulder and introducing her. She was sure they all knew she was the great Danny Rankin's date – maybe even his girl. Every time she met someone new she took another sip of her drink. She didn't know which made her higher, the flattering treatment she was getting or the Jack Daniels.

A fresh drink was pressed into her hand. Had she finished the last one already? Someone turned up the music as they were jostled into the bedroom of the suite. The king-size bed was piled with bodies. A girl in an airline stewardess uniform was necking with two guys at once. Couples were trying to dance on the wall-to-wall carpeting, which by now was soggy with spilled drinks.

Suddenly from the doorway a guy who must have weighed three hundred pounds decided to join the two guys with the stewardess. With a deafening roar he took a run at the bed and threw himself onto the pile of bodies. A horrifying crunching sounded as the bed, headboard, and bedside lamps crashed to the floor, followed by screams, laughter, and general confusion. The three-hundred-pounder had started a trend and others tumbled into the room for the fun.

Sinclare pressed herself tightly against the wall.

'Let's get out of this zoo!' Danny yelled, grabbing her by the arm. 'There's going to be a fistfight in about two minutes.'

The cold air pounding her face began to sober her up. They were driving very fast in a small, low car. Mick Jagger was screaming on the tape deck and Danny Rankin was driving. His famous square jaw was raised to the wind as he sang along with the music. His broad, Sunday afternoon hands gripped the wheel.

'Where are we going?' she shouted over the wind and music.

'Up to my place for a nightcap, beautiful lady. You game?' he shouted.

'You bet,' she replied. She held tightly to the edge of the bucket seat.

He screeched to a halt at a red light. With his free hand he reached over and pulled Sinclare's skirt above her knee. He started stroking the inside of her thigh. It felt good. 'Come here, baby,' he said, moving his hand and pulling her toward him. His breath felt hot inside her mouth and she pressed closer to him, meeting the frenzy of his mouth with her own. She was kissing a real man, not those wimps at school with the slobbering kisses and nervous weak hands. She was so turned on she would have done it right there in the car if it had been possible. It made her crazy to think of actually being in bed with him.

When the light changed he floored it. He leaned

over and opened the glove compartment and took out a small bottle of vodka. 'Come on, honey, let's party!' He unscrewed the top and handed it to her. She took a long, deep pull of the warm fiery liquid and felt it go down, then explode in her stomach.

This was as close to heaven as she had ever been. She couldn't wait to walk into Duke's on Danny Rankin's arm. Would their eyes pop! As Danny's girl she would be going to RFK Stadium for home games, having dinner at the Touchdown Club, maybe even traveling with him. There was no doubt that they would be a couple.

They were somewhere in southwest Washington. To her left she could see the Capitol dome all lit up against the black sky. Now he took a right turn into a vast parking lot in an apartment complex of what looked like small townhouses with tiny gardens.

By the time they reached the door of his ground-level apartment they were ready to start tearing each other's clothes off.

He held his arm tightly around her while he pushed the key in the lock and opened the door. All the lights were on in the living room. Sitting on the couch in front of the television were two more huge men drinking beer.

'Guys, this is Sinclare,' Danny announced. 'Ain't she somethin' else?'

The two men hooted appreciatively and nodded hello.

Sinclare was confused. 'I thought we were coming up here to be, you know, alone,' she said, pulling back as he tried to pull her farther into the room.

'Don't sweat it, honey. Frank and Doug here are just staying with me. I'm taking them through the playbook. We'll go in the bedroom.' He grabbed a bottle as they passed through the living room.

He closed the door of the bedroom with his elbow, then placed the bottle on the dresser. 'Come here, you sweet thing,' he drawled, pulling her to him. He ran his lips from her ear to her throat. She could feel his erection through her clothes. She kicked off her shoes as he eased her backward onto the bed, his hands pushing her skirt to her waist and tearing off her pantyhose. He yanked them to her ankles, unzipped his pants and belt, and his pants dropped to the floor. He was not wearing underwear and he was enormous.

He stood there admiring her, then said, 'Speaking as a professional athlete, let me say that you get greater performance out of your body when it's warmed up. Let me show you.'

And with that his head was between her legs and his tongue was soon caressing parts of her that only her fingers had touched. He was filling her with such passion she wanted to cry, or explode. Just as she was sure she would faint, he was entering her and the two bodies became one in the thrusting unity of raw body magnetism.

This was nothing like making out with the boys at school, all grabby and furtive. This was a real man on top of her, inside of her. In one sure movement he reached down and pulled her legs up over his shoulders. Instantly she started to move in a new counterrhythm with each deeper stroke. She was losing all control. She would scream if hc stopped. 'More! Danny, more!' she shouted. She had never felt anything like this.

'Danny! Don't stop,' she gasped, barely able to catch her breath.

Then, in a move that would take her to higher pleasure, he pulled out of her, flipped her over, and entered her again. His hand held her hips, as he lowered her from her knees to her stomach. She could not move. She could feel the warm sweat on his chest as he drove into her again and again. He was growling like an animal as he moved faster and faster. Suddenly she realized that they were both screaming at the same time.

For a split second it was as though she was suspended in air, awash in an ecstasy she had never felt before.

A moment later Danny shuddered and rolled off her with a deep, long groan. He lay for a long moment with his arm over his closed eyes.

'Wow . . . damn, baby, you are some kinda hot.'

'Touchdown,' she giggled under the weight of his extended arm.

She loved it. She loved being with him. As mellow as she was feeling, she instantly wanted more. Her whole body vibrated with the excitement of what she had just experienced. But she knew enough about men to know she'd have to work for the next go-around. She rolled over on top of him and began to slowly move her hips in a rolling, thrusting motion against his thigh. 'How'd you like to back the truck up and try that again?'

Then she reached over and started to unbutton his shirt. 'Now that we know each other let's try it with our clothes off,' she said laughing. She ran her hand across the deep mat of hair and down the huge muscles of his shoulders as she started flicking her tongue around one nipple and then the other.

'Oh, baby, you're going to get me started again.'

'That's the idea.'

'It may take a while.'

'I've got the time,' she said.

'You really want some more?'

'Umm,' she hummed and reached toward his crotch.

Roughly, he kicked away his slacks and cupped her left buttock in his massive hand. 'How did you like my friends?'

She stopped her efforts long enough to answer, 'Great! Wild party. I had a wonderful time.'

'No. I mean the guys outside.'

'You mean here? In the apartment?'

'Yeah.' His voice was getting husky. She could feel him getting hard against her thigh as he spoke. 'I told them we'd all have a little party.'

Sinclare pulled her head back to get a better view of his face. She was confused. 'What are you talking about?'

'You know. I mean I can see you need more than just one guy to keep you happy. Why don't I ask them in.'

Sinclare froze.

The son of a bitch! He expected her to make it with his friends.

She lay on top of him for a minute thinking.

76

Between them these three guys could lift a ten-ton truck. What would they do to her if they got angry? Angry and drunk . . . and horny.

'Look, Danny,' she said in her most sultry voice. 'I'm a mess. Why don't you go in the other room, have a drink, and let me clean up a bit. Then we'll party.'

She rolled off him, pausing to give his semi-erection a butterfly flick with her tongue. He moaned again and tried to grab the back of her head. She slipped from his grasp and stepped toward the bathroom.

'Go on, Danny. I'll be with you in a minute.' She faced him standing in the bathroom door. 'We'll have a good time. And I'll bet yours is bigger than your friends',' she said with a wink and slowly closed the door.

She could hear the raucous laughter from the living room. The bastard was telling them she was going to do it with all of them. She relaxed when she heard him making another drink; she'd have time. No way was she going to let three horny bastards near her. She pulled herself together and opened the bathroom door. She looked around the bedroom. Behind the drapes she found a sliding glass door that let out onto a small balcony. It was only six feet or so to the parking lot below.

Danny's car keys and wallet stared up at her from the floor. She removed all the cash, shredded the bills into small bits, and tossed them over the bed in a gesture of pure spite. He had hurt her feelings. Clearly, he considered her just another

77

lay. After picking up the keys, she carefully, softly opened the sliding door and stepped over the balcony wall.

The Corvette started with a powerful roar. Thank God for the stick shift on her mother's old Dodge. She could drive it — if she could find the lights. Frantically, she twisted and pulled at every knob she could find on the dashboard. Suddenly the headlights and tape deck blasted to life. She was searching for first gear when three gigantic screaming figures appeared on the balcony. The souped-up car sprang to life and shot out of the parking lot as they all leapt over the low wall and started running toward her.

The last thing Danny Rankin heard was the little dark-haired girl he'd picked up in Duke's hatcheck room laughing wildly — invitingly. It was the kind of laugh that carried over the roar of a powerful engine.

She parked the car in the garage across the street from Duke's and opened the door to her mother's old Dodge. She had to admit that she wouldn't trade a moment of tonight — her first *real* sex, her first time behind the wheel of a Corvette — and as the dying old car rattled down Shirley Highway toward Alexandria, Sinclare promised herself that before the year was out she would again feel the thrill of driving a car like Danny Rankin's. Only it would be her own.

The day after Sinclare graduated from George Washington High School Ruby married Benny. The three of them moved into a two-bedroom apartment in Hunting Towers and Ruby quit her night job. Duke suggested maybe Sinclare would like to take over full-time for the summer. She was delighted.

Congress was so clogged with legislation that they stayed in session well into August. That meant people had to hang around town, and Duke's was full every day and into the night.

Duke began to let her work as a hostess from time to time, greeting people, walking them to their tables. Everyone who met her once remembered her. And Sinclare remembered them.

One night, late, just before closing, she was seated at the bar with some of the regulars. She wasn't with anyone in particular, although she kept her eye out for Danny Rankin. She wasn't real anxious to see him again.

'Hey, Sinclare, there's a party in Georgetown,' someone yelled. 'Why don't you join us?'

'Let's go,' several people repeated, sliding off their barstools to settle up with Mac, the bartender.

The late-night crowd at Duke's never turned

down an opportunity to freeload. The hard core were mostly alimony-poor reporters. The successful lawyers and 'consultants' who courted clients and ran up sizable tabs left early.

Sinclare thought it might be fun. They drove toward the center of Georgetown. Sinclare rarely walked down its tree-lined streets or past its elegant old houses. Some were townhouses in miniature, less than fifteen feet wide; others were mansions. But what made them really interesting and important were the people who lived in them. The idea of going to a party there was thrilling. Tomorrow she and Ruby would talk all about it, what people wore, what was said. Maybe she would even meet someone famous.

By the glow of the streetlight she could see the house was large, with black shutters and a flickering gaslight beside the door.

She could hear the muted laughter and music as she pulled herself out of the crowded back seat of the cab. She knew that something wonderful was about to happen to her.

The crowd in the open doorway were smoking and laughing intimately and slightly hysterically. Sinclare wished she could join them, but she followed her friends into the roar of Billy Joel music, and through the large living room. She grabbed a Coke, lost her friends, and found her way into the tiny back garden where a sliver of a lap pool shimmered.

Let the party roar on without her for a while. She just wanted to soak in the surroundings first.

She was about to take a sip of her cola when she

felt two arms roughly pull her toward the dark side of the pool. She dropped her drink and whirled around to see Danny Rankin staring down at her in the semidarkness.

'Well, now, who is this pretty thing all by her lonesome?' he slurred. He grabbed her face and plunged his mouth over hers. She could feel the heat of his breath and smell the booze. She tried to shove him away, but he was too strong. He plunged his hand down the front of her low-cut tank top and pressed his knee between her legs. Her back hit something hard, a tree or some part of the fence, it was too dark to tell.

She tried to scream, but his mouth was over hers and she could barely breathe. Then she sensed someone else behind her.

'Take your hands off the lady, Rankin, or you'll leave here minus your balls.' It was a woman's voice, soft and low but with the hard edge of authority to it.

Danny Rankin released her instantly. He stepped back a few paces and looked like a scolded puppy as he wiped his mouth. 'Hey, jeez, like I'm sorry. I . . . I . . .' He gave Sinclare a spooked look and bolted for the door into the house. 'Sorry,' he repeated and was gone.

Sinclare leaned against the side of the house as she tried to catch her breath.

'Are you okay?' the woman asked.

Sinclare pushed her hair out of her face. The woman standing beside her stepped into the light coming through the living room picture window. She had shoulder-length ice-blonde hair and heavily made-up eyes. She was Sinclare's height and very slender from what Sinclare could see under a silky, voluminous black caftan. Across one shoulder she wore a curved diamond salamander pin with a ruby eye. Sinclare was mesmerized.

'I think so,' she said. 'Hey, listen, thanks. You sure scared him. Did you see the way he took off?'

'He better.'

'Do you know who he is?'

'Of course. He's got some nerve putting moves on one of my guests. I didn't even invite him.'

'This is your house?' Sinclare asked, impressed.

'It is,' she smiled, extending her hand in greeting. Her forefinger carried the weight of a very large purple stone surrounded by diamonds that snapped as they caught the light. 'I'm Echo Bourne, your hostess.'

Sinclare took her hand for a split second. She wasn't accustomed to shaking hands with a woman. 'I'm afraid I don't belong here either. I just came along with a group from Duke's.'

Echo Bourne laughed. 'Pretty girls are always welcome. Men with no manners can go someplace else. I could be wrong, but he seemed to know you.'

'I went out with him once, but it was a disaster.'

'Why?' Echo took a long pull on her cigarette.

'He wanted me to make it with him and two other guys at the same time,' Sinclare said, making a face. 'And I was sure they would rape me if I said no.'

'Sounds like Rankin,' Echo observed.

'I told him I'd do it. Went to the bathroom, and

82

while he was in the other room I tore up all his money, probably a couple of hundred bucks, and threw it all over the room, and then split with his car.'

Echo threw back her head and laughed so loudly people inside the house turned to see what was going on. 'I love it!' she said through her laughter. 'What's your name, by the way?'

'Sorry. I'm Sinclare Danner.' She felt uncomfortable. She should have mentioned her name. She owed the woman some kind of explanation for herself. 'I . . . I'm working at Duke's. Just for the summer.'

'Really? What are you going to do then?'

'Well, I guess I'll get a full-time job. I don't have the money to go to college.'

'I didn't either,' Echo said sympathetically. 'It's not so bad. You'll get a four-year head start on everyone who does.'

'A head start on what?'

'Living, dear. That's what it's all about. Meeting people and living, and from the way you look I think you'll do a lot of both.'

Sinclare liked the way this woman was talking to her, as if she understood her like a friend. 'Thank you, I think.' What did a woman not that much older than herself do to own a big house with a pool in the middle of Georgetown? 'What do you do?' she blurted out.

'It's called public relations. I put people together with other people. I get their names in the paper, their pictures in magazines, their ideas in the columns. And they pay me for it.' She smiled slightly but only with her mouth; her eyes remained straight and still. 'Come on, Sinclare. Let me show you around. My own party is beginning to bore me. It's been going on since late this afternoon.'

Sinclare was dazzled. She'd never met anyone remotely like this woman. A lot of the women she saw at Duke's were lawyers, stockbrokers, or important government officials. To them she was invisible — hands that took their briefcases, fur coats, and tips. She had nothing, controlled nothing and no one. Attention need not be paid, not by women. Men, well, she understood their attention. This woman, who had just taken her arm and was guiding her toward the softly lit room with white wall-to-wall carpeting and a fireplace hung with a pastel watercolor picture of herself, was like someone she had seen in *People* magazine. 'Are you married?' she asked impulsively. There had to be some explanation.

'No, thank God, and never have been!' she said huskily.

'I guess that's a stupid question, huh?'

'No. It isn't. It's one of the brighter questions I've been asked.'

The ten minutes she spent touring Echo Bourne's beautiful house determined what she must have for herself. The house was pure class, she thought.

'I would do anything to live like this,' she said as she followed Echo back down the carpeted stairs. 'You're so lucky.'

Echo stopped at the foot of the stairs, letting her pass in front of her. 'You've got it, darling. Luck had a great deal to do with it. Luck, greed, good friends, and good looks.' She surveyed the room. 'Hold on. Let me get rid of some of these people. We should talk.'

The last of the guests were leaving and the front hall was jammed with people. Echo began throwing her arms around them, kissing each goodbye, calling to them as they made their way down the front steps into the night.

Sinclare stood against the wall and watched how people treated Echo like a queen. Everyone who left invited her to do something — lunch, dinner, parties, weekends.

Echo was now saying goodbye to a short, pink-faced little man who kept holding onto her hand. She looked up and caught Sinclare's eye and signaled her to join them.

'Kelso,' Echo said, placing the man's hand into Sinclare's and holding it there. 'I want you to meet my friend Sinclare Danner. Sinclare, this is Congressman Kelso Hunt.'

'Hello, hello, hello,' the man said, running his eyes down her body and back to her face. 'I noticed you earlier. I was hoping Echo would introduce us.'

He looked important. He was wearing a white linen suit and a thick gold watch. Still holding Sinclare's hand, he said to Echo, 'Will we be seeing Miss Danner at the beach this weekend?'

'I don't see why not.' Echo turned to Sinclare, who didn't know what either of them was talking about. 'Sinclare, if you're free Saturday and

Sunday, how about coming out to my beach house at Bethany? We're having a little house party.'

'Well, uh . . . uh,' Sinclare stammered, 'I don't know.'

'Please say yes,' the congressman said, finally letting go of her hand. 'Echo, I insist. Sinclare's the prettiest thing I've seen around town in years.'

'I'll see if I can talk her into it,' Echo said sweetly, kissing the man on the cheek and easing him toward the door.

Echo closed the screen door after him and turned to Sinclare. 'So how about it? It should be fun. I'd love to have you and we can talk some more. Frankly, I'm short of women this weekend. Do you drive?'

'Uh . . .yeah, but my . . . my car probably wouldn't make it.'

'Let me send a car for you, then,' Echo said in a happens-all-the-time voice.

Sinclare was confused. What happens when someone 'sends a car for you?' She was panicking a little, but this was an opportunity and she wasn't going to blow it. 'Uh, why, sure, uh, that would be great.'

'Wonderful, done is done.' Echo reached for a piece of paper in a small desk in the foyer. 'Here, hon, I see the Cushings are leaving. Write down your address and the time you want to be picked up. Excuse me for a minute, won't you?' She floated off to say goodbye to the couple heading out the door.

Sinclare stood looking at the piece of paper she was holding. It was heavy and silky, more like stiff

86

cloth. It had a big swirly EB in raised blue and gold letters on the top. She started to write the address of Benny and Ruby's apartment but changed her mind.

She wrote, 'Duke Zeibert's, 1 o'clock, Saturday, Sinclare Danner.'

Let the guys at Duke's see her riding off in a chauffeur-driven car. That was a thousand times better than walking in on Danny Rankin's arm.

Echo said it would be fun.

Fun.

It was the weekend that changed Sinclare Danner's life forever.

The Last Sunday in August, 1977
Windswept Cottage, Bethany Beach,
Delaware

Echo Bourne lay on her stomach wearing only the bottom half of an iridescent green bikini. Her soft skin was lathered with Bain de Soleil and was honey-copper. Her small waist was encircled by a thin gold chain.

Her houseguest was Sinclare Danner, who lay next to her on an identical redwood chaise. The deck of the big gray shingled beach house hung out over a sand dune facing the ocean.

Sinclare stretched and took another sip of Tab. 'God,' she moaned, putting the cold can against her forehead, 'how much did I drink last night?'

Echo raised the brim of the big straw hat that

covered her head and shoulders and looked over the top of her sunglasses. 'I wasn't counting, but you had a champagne bottle in your hand when you led the conga line out of the restaurant. It was empty when we got back here.'

Sinclare groaned and inched farther down on the chaise. 'Who drove?'

'You insisted.'

'Oh, no.'

'It was great, right up to the edge of the porch.'

Sinclare turned her head and looked back at the house. 'You mean I drove over the dune?'

'Amazing. I wouldn't have thought that car would make it with all that weight. Kelso was riding on the fender.'

Echo Bourne had seen a lot of wild women in the five years she had been in Washington, but this kid was something else. Her personality changed with a few drinks, and nothing or no one could check her free spirit. Most kids her age were hanging out in malls, smoking pot, and damaging their eardrums with rock music. On the surface, Sinclare was like a fifties throwback, and Echo could see her becoming a man-hungry party girl with a driven 'where's-the-action' attitude toward life.

Underneath the sometimes flashy exterior there was a different person altogether. After all of Echo's houseguests had gone to bed the night before, the two of them had sat up smoking and drinking brandy. Sinclare had told her about her life growing up in a trailer park with her mother over in Alexandria. From the sound of it she had her mother to thank for the way she turned out.

The girl was a knockout. Somewhere she had gotten some terrific genes. What amazed Echo was that in a town where people have no trouble inventing themselves, Sinclare didn't bother. She would tell people flat out that she was illegitimate. If she didn't know the meaning of a word or what people were talking about, she'd speak right up and ask. And what Echo liked best of all about her was that she was a walking bullshit detector. That was something of great value, particularly to someone in Echo's business.

'Echo, we never talked last night about how you got to Washington, and in the PR business,' Sinclare commented as she rolled the Tab can across her forehead again. 'I guess I did all the talking.'

Echo laughed softly, then rolled herself onto her side, covering her breast with a towel. 'Believe it or not, I answered an ad in our local newspaper.' Then shaking her head with disbelief, she continued. 'That was over five years ago, April of 1972, and it seems like yesterday, and it also seems like a century ago.'

Echo Bourne had answered an ad in the White Fish (Montana) *Tattler-Times* for an *au pair* girl's job in Washington, DC, her senior year in high school, just before graduation. The family she came to live with had four children and a huge house on Kalorama Road. The mother, she explained, was a real society type and the father was a Nixon cabinet member. Echo spent her days caring for the kids and trying to figure a way out.

89

After a month or so she discovered it was wise to keep her door locked at night because the cabinet member took to paying her unwanted visits after she had gone to bed. One night she forgot to lock it and his wife caught him up there on the fourth floor in his pajamas. She wouldn't believe that nothing had happened, and within a week she told Echo she had a job in the mail room of the Republican National Committee headquarters.

Her ice-princess good looks and cheerful readiness to do even the most menial task soon brought her to the attention of the men planning Nixon's fall election — or coronation, as some called it once George McGovern was nominated by the Democrats.

The day she stepped into the outer lobby of the committee chairman's office she was wearing an angora sweater. It was light blue and a size too small. Her pale blonde hair was piled on top of her head and anchored with one bobby pin. Long tendrils escaped around her cheeks and down the back of her neck. The chairman first noticed the long, strong legs as she pranced toward the mail tray on his secretary's desk. He moved his eyes up to her nicely shaped thighs and tiny waist. He lingered on the sweater longingly. Pale blue was his favorite color. When she smiled at his secretary he caught his breath and slowly moved his gaze back down to the sweater.

The following day she was ensconced behind the reception desk in the main lobby of Republican national headquarters. Her duties were simple — answer the constantly ringing phone, take messages, and greet anyone entering the reception area with the smile that made the chairman hold his breath.

Echo Bourne, the 'beautiful blonde' at the National Committee, began to make a lot of friends — congressmen, Senators, journalists, and heads of special interest groups and big businesses that were courting and contributing to a winning cause. It was at that desk that she learned her first lesson in politics: to be a winner, pick a winner.

Richard Nixon won, and for a while anyone connected with him, no matter how remotely, was on a roll — none more so than Echo. In the course of her months in the lobby she had accumulated a great many admirers, the most ardent of whom was Teddy Mongrief, the owner of a chain of newspapers dedicated to conservative causes and a major contributor to candidates with whom he agreed.

Echo's ability to make and keep friends was not lost on Mongrief. After the election he offered to set her up in a one-room office in the National Press Building. She would 'represent' Mongrief's interests when he was elsewhere in the world, run errands on Capitol Hill, and be his 'man', so to speak, in Washington. She was also expected to go to dinner with Mongrief and people he wanted to impress. After dinner she was expected to sit on his face.

It was not hard work, and for a time Echo imagined herself in love with the aging publisher. But she soon realized that others would pay her for the same chores and in most cases not expect sex.

By the time Nixon walked across the White House lawn in resignation and shame to climb aboard Air Force One for the last time, she had rented a larger office and had a roster of informants – women who were part model, part call girl, part mistress, part PR executive. But they always brought Echo information. Sometimes Echo had a buyer all lined up so they had a particular assignment. Otherwise, it was panning for gold: Echo would decide what to do with the nuggets later.

Now, at twenty-three she had a house in Georgetown, a high six-figure income, and solid connections with some of the most high-powered people in the city. In a quiet way Echo was becoming a powerful woman in Washington. But she had bigger plans for herself: becoming a true force in the city became her driving ambition. She needed to expand, and had been looking for someone to entertain her 'B' list of contacts for some time. Now, miraculously, this extraordinary girl had appeared – someone who had savvy, looks, and spirit, someone she could train to run the office and who could assist her with the countless lunches, drink dates, and nights on the town with clients.

More than looks and personality, Sinclare knew who the players were around town. Her job at Duke's reminded Echo of her first job at the Republican National Committee desk.

Most of all they both lived in a world of such overpowering male ego that an attractive woman was never asked for her credentials, only her phone number. And if a woman acted truly impressed she could have anything short of an appointment as secretary of state.

Sinclare was nothing short of shocked when her new friend sat up on her chaise, looked right at her, and asked, 'Sinclare, how would you like to come and work for me?'

'Are you kidding?' Sinclare said, wide-eyed. 'What in the world could I do for you?'

'Answer the phone, hold down the fort. Keep track of people.' She laughed. 'Keep track of me for that matter.'

'Wow! You really think I could do it?'

'Yup. I'll show you how.'

Echo smiled brightly at her. Sinclare's heart began to race. A series of images flashed through her mind, each having the quality of a *People* magazine photo – Sinclare in London, Paris, Hong Kong; Sinclare at movie premieres, White House dinners, and the banquets of the most fabulous restaurants in the world. The pictures were indistinct and wavy, but they grew sharper as she burbled, 'Oh, Echo . . . thank you.'

A shout from the kitchen door interrupted them. 'Who wants a Texas breakfast?' Congressman Kelso Hunt, who smiled every time he looked at Sinclare, was standing in the door wearing bathing trunks and a ratty-looking McGovern T-shirt.

Sinclare looked at Echo quizzically and asked, 'What in the world is a Texas breakfast?'

'I think it's a six-pack and a cigarette but don't

laugh when he tells you. Like voting, it only encourages them.'

Echo's five male houseguests, all much older than either woman, tumbled onto the blazing deck kidding and horsing around. There was Tim O'Brien, who had written several big investigative stories in the early seventies and had been dining out on them ever since. Soon Tim would have to get back to work. There was a lobbyist who hung around the bar at Duke's. And there were two other members of Congress – a good-looking young one from out west and a skinny one from Illinois who told incessant knock-knock jokes.

They marched single file across the deck in a weird assortment of beach dress, hats, and sunglasses. One carried a volleyball, another a canvas beach chair, two carried either end of a Styrofoam beer cooler. They headed toward the walkway that cut through the dune to the beach.

When they disappeared over the dune Echo rolled over and stood up. She picked her bikini top off the foot of the chaise and put it on. 'Come on, pal, let's go for a swim before they discover there's water down there and join us. I'll tell you about this racket I'm in. I think you'll have some fun.'

Down on the beach in front of the house the men lolled in the sand.

Tim O'Brien was in the middle of a Washington war story. 'So we're all on Air Force One headed for San Clemente. The big Enchilada is hiding in his front cabin as usual. No real news was moving, so my editor arranged for me to substitute for the White House guy because I was on the trail of a hell of a story. I'd learned from a damn good source that some of the Nixon heavy players had forced Justice Aaron Friedkin to resign from the Supreme Court, not because of his past financial dealings, as was being reported at the time, but because he was a homosexual.'

'Come on,' injected Kelso Hunt. 'Are you talking rumor or fact or what?'

'It was a rumor, but here's what I'd been given. Apparently some young boy had been booked by the DC Police on a morals charge. Allegedly, he told them he also had a relationship with Friedkin, and the DC Police passed this on to the Nixon people. I was hoping . . .' Suddenly Tim O'Brien's voice trailed off. He noticed Sinclare emerging from the surf, and his mind was no longer able to focus on the old story. 'Will you look at that!' he said slowly, savoring the words of appreciation.

Kelso Hunt was doing just that. 'That might be the most beautiful body I've ever seen.' He removed his cap and wiped his forehead.

'One night. Just one night, dear Lord, and I'll throw the next election and go back to selling cemetery plots,' the skinny congressman said with a sigh. 'What's her name? I was too drunk last night to remember my own.'

'Sinclare something,' said the lobbyist.

'Danner, Sinclare Danner,' volunteered Kelso Hunt. 'And I'd say she can have anything she wants. That gal is definitely going to be somebody in Washington.'

Early on Tuesday, June 6, 1989
Foggy Bottom

The newsboy wedged the morning paper between the wrought-iron railing of the small stoop and the little hedge beside the door. As Jan, in her Lanz nightgown, knelt to pick it up she saw Congressman D'Anjou's driver parked across the street and waved. He waited every morning for the majority leader to emerge.

Once inside the old townhouse, she paused to sit on the third step of the vestibule stairs, and quickly scanned the predictable lead story. She also noticed Tim O'Brien had a story on Brad Barry's death, but didn't stop to read it, for as she turned the paper over she saw Mark's face, along with Dalton Riggs's picture and one of former Senator Eliot Ives.

She turned and stumbled up the narrow stairs, tripping on her long nightgown. 'Honnneeee!' she called. There were moans coming from under his pillow. She jumped onto the high bed and pulled it off his head. 'Mark, honey, wake up.'

'Huh? What?' he grumbled, reaching blindly for the pillow.

'The *Post* says you're a contender for the chief of staff job!' She placed the paper in front of his closed eyes.

He opened them into slits, squinting in confusion. 'What are you talking about?'

'Look!' She rattled the paper furiously. 'Right here.'

Mark pulled himself semi-upright and reached for his glasses on the shelf over the bed, put them on, and scanned the paper. Instantly, he was wide awake. He grabbed the paper and sat bolt upright, swinging his long pajama-clad legs over the side of the bed. 'Damn it,' he seethed, 'who wrote this crap?' He looked for the byline. 'Um, Jack Miller. I'll have his tail this morning for this.'

'Why, Mark? I think it's neat. He just says you're being considered. Why are you so angry? It's just media speculation. You get the job, you don't get the job.' She shrugged. 'I don't understand.'

'Jan,' he said with an instructive tone, 'some people will think I leaked my own name.'

'Well, you didn't. Or did you?' she teased.

'You know better than that.'

'Maybe you should have.'

'Not my style,' he said. 'Besides, all presidents hate to be second-guessed when it comes to their appointments.'

'Well, you'd make a great chief of staff. Better than Dalton, and better than Eliot Ives. Can you imagine Sinclare Ives at a state dinner. She'd probably be under the table giving the guest of honor a blow job.'

Mark burst out with laughter. When he'd contained himself he was sitting upright, and placed his chin on his own shoulder and said, 'My, my, aren't we a bit catty this morning.' He took the *Post* in hand, and as he stared at it he continued.

'Don't sell Ives short. He's an able operator. He's one of the reasons Kane is in the White House today.'

She rolled to his side of the bed and placed her hand under his pajama top. 'What this country needs is Mark Kirkland as chief of staff.'

'I'm grateful for your support, my love, but I'm afraid it will take more than an adoring wife's recommendation.'

Jan was warming to the thought. 'Just think what you could do as chief of staff! Aren't you always complaining that you can't get your advice through to the President? This would be your chance to really make things happen.' She moved closer and put her arms around his waist. 'Oh, Mark. It would be so exciting.'

'Babe, we both know the only reason I'm in the White House at all is because of your father. This stuff is just the press. The President wants me to state the policy, not make it, coordinate it, or execute it. That job will go to someone he's very close to.'

'Mark . . . ,' she said, not wanting to leave the subject, as he headed toward the shower.

'Look, Jan. I covered the story for the *Globe* during the Don Regan crunch when they brought in Howard Baker. What goes into getting and keeping the job of staff chief is some of the highest drama in this city. I think the President likes, and even respects me. But the only way I'd get the job today is by default.'

'Is the President really going to decide this week, before he goes to Moscow?'

'He sure is. Which should make this an interesting week. And this isn't an appointment your father will have diddly to say about.'

'Well, I think you should really consider taking the job if it's offered,' she said petulantly, 'I really do.'

'Forget it. It's not something I'd fight for.'

'You know what I think you need, Mark Kirkland. It's a good swift kick in the ass,' she said, grabbing a jar of moisturizer from the night table and storming out of the room.

She turned left at the end of the narrow hall and stumbled down the stairs to the tiny bathroom off the kitchen. In the small downstairs shower she let the hot water pound on her head, knowing the inadequate water heater wouldn't leave enough for his shower. She was angry enough not to care. Let him suffer.

Mark knew how mentioning her father's influence enraged her. It had been the one off-limits part of their marriage. They had told each other everything – their most humiliating moments, their saddest times, their dreams – nothing was too sacred or too awful to share. And yet sometimes she felt Mark was taking her for granted. How would he react if he thought there was another man in her life? Would he fight for her or would he let her go because he couldn't stand unpleasantness? That was why he couldn't discuss her father. Mark simply didn't have the stomach for the argument he knew could come. It was a forbidden topic.

Her father had been pulling strings for her all of

her life and things weren't likely to change. She wondered if her father had seen the morning paper yet. She knew it was only a matter of minutes before he would be calling about it. She was lucky to have such a wonderful father. One day Mark would appreciate him too, she hoped.

Jan

Early 1960s
Winterberry Farm
Fauquier County, Virginia

Her daddy always smelled so good, like lemons and burning wood shavings. Little Jan climbed into his big, comfortable lap by first grabbing hold of the fabric of his trousers and pulling herself as far as his knee. He lifted her then. She adjusted herself, curled like a kitten, her tiny feet hidden by her long flannel gown resting on the arm of his great chair.

She snuggled her head into his massive chest. When he spoke a great vibrating tremor resonated against her cheek and down the side of her neck.

'So, my mouse.' Rumble rumble. 'Tell me about the party.'

The party had been weeks ago, but he had been in . . . Paris? London? Oz?

'Caroline Kennedy and I wore the same dress.' She nestled closer, remembering how embarrassed she had been to be dressed just like the birthday girl.

'Was that okay?'

'No.'

'Did it make you feel bad?'

'Yes.'

103

'But you were prettier.'

'Do you think?' she asked, raising her eyes to look up at his great head.

'I know,' he said, his lips pressed against her forehead.

Years later she would know the words for what she felt there in her father's lap, wrapped in his arms, warm before the fire on a chilly evening of spring at Winterberry Farm. Safe. Loved. Protected.

He carried her, half asleep, up the grand circular stairway to her room. She held on tight as they moved down the long, dark corridor, past her mother's bedroom. It was dark as usual. Her mother was in the city at a ball or a party or staying the weekend with friends. It didn't matter. Her daddy was home now and tomorrow they would ride far, far out into the forest. They would have a picnic by their favorite stream on a flat rock under the fresh new leaves of the big weeping willow tree and he would tell her of all the wonderful places he had been and how he would take her there someday.

He laid her gently in her bed and pulled the puffy eiderdown up under her chin.

'Which will it be tonight? Mr Bear or Mrs Rabbit?'

'Mr Bear,' she said, kicking her feet with excitement.

He reached for her soft toy, pulled the covers back, and wedged it tightly under her arm. 'There's Mr Bear,' he said, replacing the covers. He leaned over her and kissed first one closed eyelid and then the other. It was their good-night routine. 'Who do I love?'

'Jan. Net.' She said her name as two words.

'And who is Janet?'

'The prettiest, smartest, luckiest girl in the world.'

'And how much does her daddy love her?'

'More than life,' she answered, lying on her side to watch him turn off the bedside lamp.

When he was gone she burrowed even deeper, hugging Mr Bear and silently mouthing the words 'more than life.'

When she was seven she fell while she was playing down by the grape arbor and opened a five-inch gash in her forehead.

Her mother was 'resting' and Richard, their driver, took her to Leesburg Hospital. She had to wait a long time to get stitches because the hospital wouldn't take Richard's signature for permission. Finally, her mother arrived and signed the papers so they could sew up her head. She had to stay overnight and when she woke up her mother was in her room crying. Her mother gave her a bottle of Estée Lauder Youth Dew, which smelled up the whole room. Jan later gave it to one of the nurses.

Her mother told her that her daddy had phoned from Geneva and was very, very angry when he heard that Jan had cut her head and was in the hospital. Jan knew he wasn't mad at her. He had told her he could never be mad at her.

'Can I come home now, Mummy?' she asked hopefully.

'Yes, darling, if you are very careful and don't play outside.'

'Will you take me home?'

'Sweetheart, Mummy has to go into Washington for a fitting. Richard will take you home and Odille will make you a nice lunch.'

Jan was disappointed. 'Can't you take me home, please, Mummy?'

'I'm sorry, darling, I just can't. Not today.'

Not today, she thought. Not today.

Jan's mother, Janine Sumner, was beautiful. When she was all dressed up and had her makeup on, which was all of the time except when she was 'resting', she looked like Grace Kelly.

Jan's mother and daddy were very good friends of the Kennedys and went to parties with them all the time. Her mother wore Jackie Kennedy kind of clothes, pillbox hats and sleeveless dresses that had matching coats. She even sometimes wore her hair, which was the color of vanilla ice cream, like Jackie Kennedy's.

By Christmas the gash on Jan's head was just a thin silver scar. Christmas was a special time at Winterberry Farm. The rolling Virginia hills were dusted with snow. There were evergreen swags and big red velvet ribbons hung throughout the vast house. They always had two trees that went to the ceiling – one in the main hall and the other in the library by the fire. Winterberry filled with people the week before and there was someone in every bedroom.

Jan's favorite was Aunt Constance. She was beautiful, laughed all the time, and wore knotted ropes of pearls. This time she brought her new husband. Jan hardly remembered the other two. This one was very tall with white hair and a red face. He spoke with an English accent and had very proper manners, and talked to her father too much about war and politics and President Kennedy and President Kennedy's father, whom he seemed to know and not like. Aunt Constance's new husband was named Lord Maubry, but everyone called him Tookie.

On Christmas Day her mother wore a long, dark red velvet gown with a train that had some kind of sparklers around the neck and hem. She wore her hair piled high on her head and had more sparkly things in her hair. Jan thought she looked like Grace Kelly playing Scarlett O'Hara. There was a lot of eating and drinking champagne and all the fireplaces were burning in the rooms, even in Jan's bedroom and in the kitchen.

The next day Richard, the driver, had the day off and asked if Jan would like to go to Leesburg to a double feature. Her daddy had left on an urgent trip to South America. Excitedly she ran up the big circular staircase and down the hall to her mother's room for permission.

As she approached the door of her mother's room she heard voices. Jan tried the door, but to her surprise it wouldn't open. She could hear her mother moaning and crying as though she hurt but wasn't in pain, and shouting 'More. More.'

Suddenly she felt scared, frightened of something she didn't understand – something that told her to run away as fast as she could before her mother knew she was there, listening.

Jan ran, her heart pounding and the sound of her mother's strange sounds throbbing in her ears.

Late that night when the temperature dropped below freezing Richard shone a big hanging light in her eyes. She had wrapped herself in a horse blanket and hid in the corner of an empty stall.

Her mother came to see her in Leesburg Hospital. As Jan tried to shrink down under the covers, her mother lifted the big plastic tent; her breath smelled funny and her face was puffy. She said she was crying because Jan was so sick and that she must get well quickly because Daddy had changed his mind about staying in South America for another week and was coming home.

'Your mother and I think you should go away to school,' her father said as they rode their horses side by side through the apple orchard.

'Then I'll never see you,' she said sadly.

'Of course you will. I'll come and see you every time I come home.'

The idea of leaving Winterberry made her terribly sad. She did not speak again until they reached their big flat picnic rock. She dismounted and dropped the reins over her horse's head. Her horse pulled at the patches of dead grass on the near-frozen ground.

Her father dismounted. They stood in silence watching the black water swirl downstream between the shards of ice that jutted from each bank.

'I have to go, don't I?' Jan asked, not looking at her father.

'I'm afraid so, love.' His voice was heavy and sad.

'Are you and Mummy getting a divorce? Is that why I have to go away?'

When he didn't answer she looked over at him. He was staring at the water, his hands in the pockets of his great sheepskin coat. Finally he spoke: 'I've never lied to you, Jan. I can't start now.'

'So you are getting a divorce?'

'Jan, it doesn't work. I've tried, but I can't give her the kind of life she wants.'

'Is it the drinking?'

He turned and looked at her. 'You know about that?'

'I hear and see things, Daddy.'

'Like what?'

'It doesn't matter.' There was no way she could tell about the day after Christmas. She didn't have the vocabulary to describe it without dying of mortification right there on the icy ground.

'No,' he said, slowly, 'in the end I suppose it doesn't matter. What's done is done.'

'Do I truly have to go away, Daddy?' She felt as though she was a part of the dark water, swirling, twisting, dizzyingly out of control, going down, down, down.

He reached for her shoulders and drew her in front of him. He enfolded her in his arms and she rested the back of her head against his chest. 'Oh, mouse, I can't bear it. Let me try to work some-

109

thing out. Maybe there is some way you could live with me somehow, somewhere.'

'Daddy, that would be wonderful!' she said, squeezing his arm and leaning her cheek against the soft skin of his sleeve. 'Do you really want to do that?'

'More than life,' he said and laughed. She felt the rumble of his laughter vibrating against the back of her head.

That spring Jan and Odille packed Mr Bear and Mrs Rabbit and her books and clothes into the huge trunk that Richard brought up from the cellar at Winterberry. She said goodbye to Odille and the stable hand and her horse. Her mother was in Arizona at a spa, they said. She was never mentioned again, and somehow Jan knew her mother had died.

Richard packed everything into the Chrysler Town and Country wagon and drove Jan to the Georgetown section of Washington, DC. It had all been decided. She had the entire top floor of Aunt Constance's house. All its rooms were closed except for her own large bedroom and a sitting room with a skylight that looked toward the river. It was full of large, comfortable furniture dispatched to the top of the house during the frequent redecoratings of the floors below. There were a huge television, a stereo, and a Pullman kitchen with a tiny stove and 'icebox', as Aunt Connie called it.

But the very best part was when Richard showed her the big bedroom on the second floor. That was

110

where he said her father would stay when he came home from his trips.

He came home a week at Christmas time and a few days in the summer when Jan was in music camp. There were letters, typed and signed by her father, and boxes with sweaters that were too small and books she had already read. When he phoned she would run down the hall, breathlessly, tears of joy welling in her eyes. At night she would lie awake thinking of him. They would be driving near a sea or walking in a rainstorm to a wonderful restaurant where he would order her favorite things to eat. In their elaborate fantasy conversations she said such clever things that he would laugh and throw his arms around her.

By her fourteenth birthday the braces were finally gone. To celebrate, Aunt Constance had her fitted with contact lenses. Overnight she had a face she could see without squinting and a figure that caused men on the streets to make remarks. The honey-colored hair that fell to her shoulders softened the high cheekbones and wide-set gray-green eyes.

That Christmas her father treated her like a different person, flattering her, taking her to dinner at the F Street Club, introducing her to people who clearly didn't know he even had a daughter.

Miraculously, she was blooming.

Spring 1973
St Margaret's Episcopal School for Girls
Ladysmith, Virginia

The headmistress was not amused. 'Jan, you have put us in an awkward situation.'

'I don't understand why,' Jan said politely. She was sitting straight in a Windsor chair with her anklebones touching. The pleated hem of her school uniform covered the top of her gray, cable-knit knee socks. She was seventeen years old, it was her junior year of high school and life had never seemed so exciting.

'You know the rule here is four days a trimester. You have been away for six. Your father has called and asked us to make another exception.'

'I'm sorry, Miss Daniels.' Jan dropped her head to hide a smile. Every girl in school knew that Miss Daniels was a lapsed hippie living with a George-town law professor who had dodged the draft. She hadn't shaved her legs until she took the job at St Margaret's, and if one picked through her bag, as Jan's best pal had, one could find a Ziploc stash of Maui-Wowie. Yet here she was playing Queen Elizabeth over Jan's life with her father!

'You are making it difficult for the other girls.'

'I'm sorry, Miss Daniels.'

'Well,' she said, 'I suppose, considering your father's position . . .' She scribbled her name on a piece of paper and handed it to Jan. 'He tells me you have been invited to Governor Rockefeller's for a dinner party tomorrow night.'

'Yes, ma'am.'

'You know, Jan, we've had several members of the Rockefeller family here at St Margaret's, I can't say I'm displeased at having our school represented at the Governor's table.'

'Yes, ma'am. Thank you for understanding.' Jan rose and took the piece of paper.

'Your father will send a car at noon tomorrow.' The headmistress rose. 'I'll expect you back for vespers, correct?'

'Yes, Miss Daniels.' Jan gathered the books and sweatshirt that lay at her feet. 'Thank you very much.'

Jan rushed out of the office, her heart pounding. She had beat the system one more time. Nelson Rockefeller's dinner might be important to Miss Daniels. To Jan, being with her father was all that mattered.

The next day, at the dot of twelve Ambassador Sumner's black Mercedes limousine rolled to a stop in front of the fountain outside the administration building. Trying not to run, Jan walked briskly through the door and down the wide flagstone steps. She was wearing a proper gray flannel suit, white blouse, and two-inch plain black pumps.

Her father's driver stood beside the open door of the gleaming car. She could see the legs of her father's trousers inside the car. He was seated on the far side, next to him a shiny square box tied with a white satin bow.

113

It was all she could manage not to race headlong into the car, but five years as a day boarder at a proper Episcopal school for girls and weekends with her very social Aunt Constance had taught her how to be a lady.

'Hello, Miss Sumner,' the driver said.

'Hello, Renaldo.' She grinned at him as she stepped into the car. She slid across the seat and fell into her father's arms.

'Hello, mouse,' he boomed. 'Don't scrunch your present.'

'Oh, what is it?' she said excitedly. She pulled the box onto her lap.

'You'll see,' he said. He lowered the window in back of the driver. 'National Airport, please, Renaldo.'

'Airport?' she said as the big car moved soundlessly around the circular drive. 'Aren't we expected at Aunt Connie's for lunch?'

'Not anymore.'

'Daddy,' she said with a laugh, 'why are we going to the airport?'

'That's where the planes to New York are.'

'You're kidding! I don't believe this. Why?'

'Because that's where my friend parked his plane that is taking us to Paris.'

At teatime on Sunday the ambassador called Miss Daniels from their suite at the American embassy. Jan had a 'terrible cold,' he said, 'coughed all night. Really suffering,' he moaned, 'probably caught it on the terrace at Pocantico Hills, lot of that stuff going around. Yessiree. Yessiree.' He

114

pulled silly faces at Jan as he lied. 'Yes, yes, I gave Governor Rockefeller your regards.'

Jan covered her mouth to muffle her giggles and reached for another white chocolate truffle on the tea tray.

The ambassador hung up and exploded with laughter. 'She probably won't be back for a week or more!' He mimicked himself and slapped his knee. 'We're free, mousey mine!' he shouted. 'Free in gay Paree!'

'Oh, Daddy,' she laughed, 'you're going to get me thrown out of that school.'

'Who cares!' he bellowed, beside himself with glee. 'Come on, my girl, get your new fur jacket and let's paint the town. I've booked Tour d'Argent for dinner and then it's on to La Coupole and who knows where we'll end up.'

They ended up walking arm in arm along the Seine at dawn. Jan burrowed into the luxuriant softness of her new silver fox jacket and tried to match her father's stride. She loved her new jacket. She loved Paris. She loved her daddy so much that it made her throat ache to look at him.

The Paris trip was the beginning of a conspiratorial pact between them. They were the adventurers who had to gain their freedom by stealth and caprice. The villains who had to be outsmarted were the headmistress and occasionally Aunt Constance.

By her senior year at St Margaret's Jan had missed so much school they realized she was in real danger of not graduating with her class.

'Ridiculous!' Ambassador Sumner roared.

'It is not ridiculous. The girl failed her math final and got D's in chemistry and logic,' the headmistress said, holding her ground. 'I don't know where we can find a college that will take her.'

'What about art history, Kathryn?' he pleaded, waving Jan's final report card. 'What about, look . . . look here, a B-plus in French, should be an A, my daughter speaks French better than the headwaiter at the Plaza Athenée.' He studied the card. 'And look here, a B in English!' That should count for something.'

'Buck, I've been headmistress here for many years. Long enough to have had senators, cabinet members, millionaire industrialists, and deposed kings petition me for special treatment for their darling daughters. However, my first loyalty is to your daughter's education. I can't let her graduate until she completes the requirements she simply has to meet.'

Buck Sumner sat down, seemingly defeated. 'All right, Kathryn, what should we do? Keep in mind I want her out of here. I have plans.'

'She needs a tutor. And I know just the man.'

'Man? Why does it have to be a man?'

'Because Jan desperately needs help in math and science and he happens to be the best there is.'

'I don't want some young Turk who is going to get any ideas.'

'I don't think that will be a problem,' she said, reaching for a small leather notebook. 'His name is Ian Vreen. A lovely man. A Yale graduate. He's tutored for some of Washington's finest families. I think he'll be perfect for Jan. Indeed, I believe he's

116

a somctime companion of your sister, Lady Maubry.'

'Uh,' the ambassador grunted.

'Trust me, Buck.' Kathryn Daniels smiled.

Ian Vreen wore wonderful F. Scott Fitzgerald clothes, pleated linen trousers in ice cream colors and big-shouldered double-breasted jackets before anyone else was wearing them. He reminded Jan of a picture she had seen of the Duke of Windsor when he was king. He had thin, sandy-colored hair and wore a pince-nez, tiny gold glasses that pinched the bridge of his nose and wiggled when he talked.

It was suggested that Jan live with Aunt Constance full-time for the rest of the year and attend school as a day student. Ian's tutoring schedule called for him to come to the Georgetown mansion every weekday at four o'clock and all day on Saturday. Soon Ian, who had been a friend, confidant, and escort for Aunt Constance, was living with them at the mansion as well.

From the moment she met him, Jan was enchanted. At last she had a true friend, someone in whom she could confide. It was a friendship that would be one of the most important in her life.

For all her father's influence and connections, it was Ian who got her into the University of Maryland because he had a 'close friend' on the board of trustees. Ian Vreen had a veritable network of 'close friends' in the city in every walk of life from a Supreme Court justice to interior designers, even world-famous journalists. It wasn't until she was older that Jan realized how these men knew each other.

When Jan graduated it was Ian who had a close friend working as a buyer at Garfinckel's. There was an opening in the Special Projects Department for someone to plan fashion shows and charity lunches for social Washington women. The ambassador approved. It was a proper job for a girl of Jan's breeding and background, and permitted her generous amounts of time to travel and serve as his hostess in the big old house on Kalorama Road.

It was a fundraising luncheon for Children's Hospital that brought Mark Kirkland into Jan's life. Her job was to find a speaker. The dashing *Newsweek* correspondent had just returned from Afghanistan and was greatly in demand to talk about his adventures among the rebels. She fell in love with him before he even opened his mouth.

As their love affair progressed it was Ian she told her secrets to, Ian's advice in matters of the heart that she needed, and Ian who first approached her father with the prospect that his daughter might conceivably have given her heart to another man.

The government-issue venetian blinds in Jan's secretary's office filtered out the morning sun, already high and hot. 'You don't suppose they were right, do you, Barbara?'

'Who and about what?' Barbara asked. She was typing names into the computer beside her desk.

'The people who said I shouldn't marry a man so much older.'

'Nonsense.'

'The people who said a forty-year-old bachelor was too set in his ways.'

'I take it you and Mark have had another little disagreement. You two should have been on top of the world with the *Post*'s story this morning. What happened?'

Jan dropped to the couch and quickly rescued a pile of newspapers that started to slide to the floor. 'Oh, Barb,' she sighed, 'it never ends.'

'What was it about this time?'

'Same as usual. It's either matchbook house with the megafurniture or my dad. Today it was Daddy. Usually it's him.'

'Oops, you've got a real problem,' Barbara said. She stopped typing and looked up at Jan. 'Mark's job can't help. It's a killer. I honestly think being chief of staff would be more relaxing than facing

119

those bloodhounds every morning. Maybe you both need a vacation.' She smiled. 'In the meantime, madam, we have a funeral to handle here.' She pointed to the printout of the funeral service and reception guest list. 'This list is a mess. If only someone in this administration had died earlier. I just know I'm going to leave someone out.'

The mention of the reception snapped Jan out of her funk over Mark. 'Barbara, isn't it curious that Bradford Barry was in the Hay-Adams on Sunday night? Nobody has said who he was meeting with either.'

Barbara pressed her lips together and nodded her head.

'You know, I completely forgot to ask Mark about it,' Jan said, shaking her head.

'Sounds like you'd better not mention it at the moment.'

'I'd really like to know more about what's going on. Do you think there's a cover-up in the works?'

Barbara gave a customary noncommittal shrug. 'Maybe, maybe not. Things over there work in mysterious ways.' Barbara turned away from the computer and drummed her fingers on the desktop. 'Uh . . . Jan,' she began hesitantly.

'Uh-oh, whenever you start like that it's bad news.'

'You didn't happen to see Deena Simon's column this morning, did you?'

'I try to save the *Observer* until my breakfast settles. Why? Whose life is she destroying now?'

'I think you'd better read it.'

Jan felt a chill go through her body as Barbara

folded the paper to the page where Deena's column always ran. 'Do I really want to see this?'

Barbara tapped the page. 'No, but you'd better.'

Jan's mouth fell open as she read. She lifted the paper slowly from the desk and walked with it back to the couch, reading the column a second time. 'Barbara, what is this garbage?'

'Garbage,' she said casually.

'But this sounds like Mark. One of Don's tip-top men . . . stately wife.' She tried to control her voice. 'Why would she write something like this? If this is supposed to be Mark it's an absolute lie!'

'You know that and I know that. Others might not.'

'But what an awful thing to do. There are laws against this. I'm absolutely stunned.' Jan felt as though she was going to cry.

'Don't be shocked. It's not worth the energy. In this town the press likes to build people up so they have someone to shoot down. Deena Simon likes to shoot you down first prematurely. Why let facts get in the way of a good story. She'll take a lying plant from anybody.'

'Barbara, I feel sick. I suppose Mark has seen this. What are they going to say over at the White House?'

'By now he's had his nine o'clock briefing. Someone's already asked him about it, I'm sure.'

Jan could no longer contain herself. 'Goddammit! I'm going to call my father.' Her hands shaking, she started toward her office.

'And say what?'

'Well . . . he knows Deena Simon very well.

Forget that, he knows the publisher just as well, he can make them . . .'

Barbara held up her hand like a traffic cop. 'Wait . . . wait . . . wait. Think before you go calling in the heavy artillery. You may be making more trouble for yourself. I think you should leave it alone for a day or two. See what's going on.'

'Going on?'

'Maybe someone wants you to overreact. Planting nasty items is an old trick in this town. This item is aimed at starting a whispering campaign to discredit your husband and take him out of the running for Brad Barry's old job.'

Jan sighed, returning to the couch. 'Barbara, I know this is dumb, but I really don't understand what the big deal is about being chief of staff.'

Barbara looked at Jan with a half-smile of exaggerated impatience. 'You're not dumb, because you're smart enough to ask when you don't know. Let me see how I can explain it. Look at the executive branch as a corporation, if it will give you a frame of reference. The President is the chairman of the board, but he doesn't really use his cabinet like a board of directors. Cabinet members are more like heads of divisions or heads of their departments.'

'Okay,' Jan nodded.

'Anyway, the President, like a chairman of the board, is the long-range planner. He's the man who sets the policy and decides what issues are important. He doesn't make the little everyday decisions. There's no way he has the time to make them all. That's why the chief of staff is important.

He's the day-to-day manager who interprets the President's policy and makes countless decisions in the President's name. Or he decides who on the staff, or in the cabinet, should make a decision.'

'Sounds like he's more important than the Vice President or even cabinet members.'

'Absolutely. Now, knowing that much, do you think Mark wants the job?'

'I honestly don't know. I think he does. He started muttering this morning about other chiefs like Haldeman who was an advertising man and Dick Cheney who came down from someone's staff on the Hill. The one he drew the most comfort from was Ham Jordan. He called him a "good ol' country boy."'

'And look what each of those guys did for their presidents. Nixon quit and the other two got beat for reelection. That should tell you something about the job. So you see, it is a big deal.'

Jan, who had been idly trying to make a cat's cradle out of an outsized rubber band, looked up at her friend. 'Oh, Barb. It all seems so scary. What in the world can I do to help Mark through all this – win or lose?'

'Just do what a good Washington wife is supposed to do, sweetheart. Stand by to pick up the pieces.'

Tuesday, June 6, 1989 – 9:20 A.M.
Kalorama Road

When did he start hating Echo? Buck Sumner looked down at her, at the cleanly washed platinum hair. The straps of her black teddy fell off her shoulders giving her a seductive, slutty look. As she reached up to his zipper her gold Piaget watch glinted in the early-morning sun. She unzipped the fly, resting her head against the trouser fabric of his Savile Row suit. He ordered five every year from his London tailor. Gently she reached inside his forty-dollar Egyptian cotton broadcloth boxer shorts. Money, old and earned, had its privileges. He was beholden to no one. It had bought him this grand old house in a prestigious neighborhood; it had given his daughter an expensive education at the best of private schools and had kept his secretary, Belle, in a large luxury apartment on Connecticut. For Buck Sumner the best that money could buy was his entitlement. Materially he wanted for nothing, but he knew it wasn't his money that brought Echo to his house at least once a week to service him with his only sexual pleasure. No. Echo was on her knees before him because of his power.

God, she was good. He drew in his breath, making a sharp hissing sound, and momentarily grasped the leather arms of his chair. His gaze blurred as he watched the light playing in her platinum hair.

Their morning meetings had become ritualized and formal. In the early years they had made real love, spending endless hours of the nights and days in exploration and discovery of each other's bodies. Even now, as she approached forty, Echo was still a knockout, but he didn't like to get too close to her. The tiny lines around her eyes disturbed him, reminding him that he was getting old.

She had the most exciting mind of any woman he had ever known. She was devious and clever about getting what she wanted out of life. He knew she didn't want money. Echo lusted after power and friends in the right places. People who owed you not only their livelihood but their own hold on power made, if not the most loving, certainly the most loyal of friends.

Yes, he hated her, but he needed her and she knew it. He loathed this dependency, this need for another human being to do something for him that was better than anything he could do for himself. He could always change his tailor, his vintner, his masseuse, but Echo controlled the last vestige of his youth with her mouth and hands.

He gasped as she twirled her tongue to tease him, staring up at him with smiling, taunting eyes that mocked his need and confirmed her power over him.

She moved very slowly, taking him in all the way, almost swallowing him whole. It was a shame she left this sort of work to her girls these days.

The world would be a richer place if Echo would share her special talents.

During these sessions with Echo, Buck loved to fight his body with his mind, anything to prolong the pleasure, to make her work harder, be more creative.

She tilted her head to one side. He could see her long black lashes pressed in determination against her cheeks as she went about her work. Seeing her eyes close brought back the memories of that morning five years ago when he began to hate her. They had fallen into the linen sheets of the Danieli in Venice, at dawn, and made rapid, almost violent love in a huge canopied bed.

The night of drinking and music had ended with a screaming fight in the Piazza San Marco. Echo had spent hours dancing in some pitch-black club with some stranger she had taunted into a visible erection on the dance floor while Buck sat getting drunk and outraged at a corner table.

After the lovemaking he had sat on the edge of the bed watching her sleep. Long black lashes fanned out against the almost transparent white skin. At that moment, as now, he knew he was looking at a woman who served only herself. She loved sex with him not so much for any pleasure it brought her but for the control over him, the man who had made her, taught her, and had total control over her – once.

Fighting the urge for violent release he pushed his mind further back, back to the men he had served – Roosevelt and Truman as a young man. With Eisenhower he had learned to lose at golf. It was not until the Kennedy election that he became deeply involved. Indeed, he had left government service to help a man he'd thought his friend. He'd discovered too late that Kennedy was never really serious about being President. Actually, Bobby was the serious one, and Buck had helped Bobby in a number of special projects ranging from his vendetta against the Teamsters Union to the Bay of Pigs. But after what Jack Kennedy had done to him, he never regretted turning Bobby down on some behind-the-scenes assistance to the Warren Commission, or Bobby's own effort to sort out the fateful events in Dallas.

Several presidents had come to know that Buck Sumner obtained results. But the upright Mr Clean, Donald W. Kane, had been reluctant to use Buck at first, but now appeared ready to explore his services.

Echo was moving faster now. He found it impossible to continue his game of disinterest in her artistry. Her mouth was as soft as cashmere, but her lips were firm. She was breathing faster, and sweat was beading on her forehead. He stretched his arm now and pressed his hand hard against the back of her neck, forcing himself toward that velvety moist spot at the back of her throat. He threw his head back and closed his eyes, vaguely aware of the flashes of light behind his eyes as he felt himself explode.

He handed her one of his Irish linen handkerchiefs, as she rose with a smile he'd seen so many times before.

Echo turned and walked toward the bathroom

and closed the door. He knew she would linger there to pleasure herself. He had caught her at it once and commented. It was never mentioned again.

He poured himself half a crystal tumbler of scotch and returned to the leather chair. Relaxed and satisfied he pulled together the threads of his thoughts before Echo had worked her weekly magic.

Less than a month after Kane's election, the President had dispatched Dalton Riggs to the house on Kalorama Road on a very private mission. Riggs had been uninterested in Buck's electronic toys, the teletype, mainframe computers, the fax machine, and the state-of-the-art recording devices . . . the tools of a modern-day information and intelligence-gathering operation. Briskly dismissing Buck's offer of twelve-year-old scotch, General Riggs informed the ambassador that his very special talents would not be needed by this administration. The straight-arrow new President would be handling everything 'through government channels.' Buck could see Riggs mentally running a white glove over along the dusty shelf of Buck's decades-old service to his government. Inwardly Buck had smiled. He had heard it all before, only to have presidents find they needed him as much as he enjoyed serving them.

However, Riggs continued, the President did not want to appear ungrateful for Buck's many years of service, so Riggs had been authorized to offer him an appointment to a high government commission, a subcabinet post, or whatever he might be interested in.

At the time, Buck had been worried about the reporter that Jan had married. It was a chance to take care of his daughter, so he'd arranged for Mark Kirkland to become press secretary.

He'd not talked with the President until six months later, when President Kane found he indeed needed Buck Sumner – urgently. The call came very early Monday morning. President Kane sounded shaken. 'Mr Ambassador: Don Kane here. I apologize for calling so early.' Buck was well aware that presidents pretended informality, as if the personal touch would accomplish more.

'Mr President,' Buck had answered with an implied salute in his voice.

'Have you heard that Brad Barry died in the Hay-Adams last night? The circumstances are odd by far, perhaps compromising, and I am concerned.'

Buck had heard that Barry died within a half hour of the DC Police's arrival at the hotel. But there was no need to mention this; besides, it wasn't a superior intelligence feat. Anyone in the metropolitan area with a police band radio knew about it. 'Why, no sir, what a shock!' he answered the President innocently.

'I've lost a good friend and an able chief of staff. But let me get to the point of my call, Buck,' Kane said brusquely. Then he had another thought. 'Oh, Buck, by the way, Mark Kirkland's doing a fine job for me, but we can talk about that later.'

Clearly he had not called to chat. 'Either Bradford was getting laid and the woman abandoned the scene because she was terrified of the scandal. That's a very likely scenario, I might add. Or there could be a breach of national security. I've got the FBI, the Secret Service, the CIA, and those incompetents at the District police department checking it out. Someone will be getting back to us soon. We've got that under control. However . . .' The President hesitated and cleared his throat.

Here it comes, Buck thought. He wished he had put money on the timing six months ago.

'I'd be grateful if you'd do some checking for me. We're moving immediately to name a new chief.'

Hah! There it was. Buck smiled and nodded, pleased with himself. 'What can I do for you, Mr President?' he asked, keeping his voice cool.

'I've got three candidates for the job, and I've got to make a decision before I leave on Friday morning.'

Buck reached for his gold Mont Blanc pen and began scribbling notes. Ordinarily he would have activated his elaborate taping equipment, but taping the President was not just bad manners, it was downright stupid. 'I see, sir,' he said.

'We've got FBI reports on two, and nothing on the third, although I requested full reports on all, but the bureau can only do routine stuff in the next three days. I'll explain in a second, but let me tell you who I'm considering to make sure they don't cause you a conflict.'

'Go ahead, sir.'

'There's General Dalton Riggs, Eliot Ives, and
. . . Mark Kirkland.'

'That's very interesting, sir.'

'Interesting? That's all you have to say, Buck?
Thought you would have liked Kirkland. As I said,
he's good, and he's honest, and he's got the energy
and humor you need for the job.'

Buck kept his voice flat. 'He's all of that, sir.'

'You know, sooner or later it may come out that
Brad Barry was playing around. You know my
campaign position against adultery; I can't have it.
But I don't want the moralists in the media dis-
qualifying every able man in this town from a top
job. I'd like you to assist me. Find out what you
can about each of them, even your son-in-law, and
get back to me. Let me know if any of them has
anything that might be a serious problem . . . I'm
not looking for saints, but I've got to protect
myself here.' The President's voice was getting
irritable.

'I'll have everything you need by Thursday, Mr
President,' Buck said quickly.

He didn't bother to replace the receiver. He had
pushed '1' on the phone to activate a direct dial
call to Echo. He did not tell her of the President's
call, only who was under consideration. He was
becoming increasingly careful about what he told
her, and now he was worried that even asking her
for information about any secrets these men might
be hiding was a serious mistake. She was moving
beyond his control, and for the first time in their
life together he actually worried that she was
abusing *his* information. She didn't understand

131

that while his methods might be suspect his motives never were. He had to give the President an honest answer because that was why presidents called him. He suspected that Echo was inventing the answers. She had denied it, but he'd been at the game too long not to be suspicious. They had discussed little else but the candidates in the thirty-eight hours. This sort of power game was nectar of the gods to Echo. Buck figured this was her true sexual pleasure.

Buck straightened his clothes and stepped to the bar. By the time she returned from the bathroom he was back in his favorite chair with another half a tumbler of scotch.

She had fluffed her hair and freshened her makeup, and walked with the familiar strut she affected after one of their sessions. Her power walk, he observed, amused.

'So what's the program, Buck? What's the latest?' she asked impatiently, reaching for his glass and taking a gulp. 'My money says they're all turkeys. None of them deserves the job. Riggs has the American flag up his ass. And his wife is shit-faced before the soup at too many dinner parties.'

God, she could be crude sometimes, Buck thought, taking another sip of his drink – crude but on target, he had to admit. 'That wouldn't bother Kane. She's not the first White House wife who drank too much. See what else you can find on him.'

'Why bother? Your son-in-law is perfect,' she said with only a hint of sarcasm.

Buck stared at her. She knew how much he had grown to dislike Kirkland. Not only had he stolen Jan, but he was a reporter to the core; Mark looked through him as though he were a tower of Jell-O.

'He's history,' Echo observed. 'I told you last night that Sinclare got that sex story in the paper, and she'll start spreading the word 'divorce' around town to polish him off.'

'How do you know Sinclare planted it?'

'Because she read it to me before it was in the paper, that's how.'

'Look, Echo, I don't want anyone hurt, you understand.'

'Hey, I can't tell Sinclare what to do,' she said, holding her arms up. 'Now, about Eliot,' she said, ignoring him as she began to pace the frayed oriental rug. 'He must have a résumé that reads like a rap sheet. I can't believe the President would consider him.'

Buck was well aware that Echo had never liked the ex-senator. Sure, she had been delighted when Sinclare started dating him and encouraged her. Echo was thinking jewelry, furs, a hot car, and a cool apartment. She was disgusted when she realized Sinclare was thinking marriage and actually did it.

'There I think you're wrong, Echo,' Buck corrected. 'If I were President I'd want a man like Ives. He's good, even if I don't like him. He's smart, and straight from what everyone tells me.'

'I may puke!' Echo stopped pacing and stared at him.

133

'You have a problem with Ives. Okay. What else?'

'It's not Ives so much as the idea of Sinclare as the wife of the chief of staff!'

'Now is not the time to let personal feelings get in the way. One of these men is going to be sitting in the best staff job in the White House by this time next week unless we have something to report to the President, or if the FBI finds something.'

'They're all clean, according to my sources at the FBI.' Echo mashed her cigarette into the Senate ashtray on Buck's desk. She had a disgusted look on her face. 'And whoever gets it isn't going to owe us a damn thing.'

'On the contrary. Haven't I taught you better than that?'

Echo stared at him.

'A man owes you when he knows you've got something on him and don't pass it on,' Buck said with a sly grin. 'And it would be very nice if the next chief of staff was indebted to us, wouldn't it, my dear?'

Tuesday, June 6, 1989 – 9:45 A.M.
The Fort, Foxhall Road

'It's all right, Rosa,' Caroline said softly. 'General Riggs is still in the solarium. He didn't get home from the White House until five A.M. this morning because of the Moscow trip plans and the time difference between here and there.' Why try to explain? She wasn't sure she understood herself. As the sound of her own voice vibrated in back of her eyes, she hoped Rosa understood her, for if she spoke any louder or longer she would die.

Her housekeeper crossed the carpeted bedroom and placed the breakfast tray across Caroline's knees. Caroline was lying back against three Porthault-covered pillows and manipulating the remote control around the early-morning talk shows. She turned the volume up on Jane Pauley's interview with a professional sperm donor and helped Rosa adjust the tray.

'I thought you'd want the papers right away,' Rosa whispered. After years of waking her mistress she knew what her mornings were like. Rosa pulled the *Post* and the *Observer* from the carrying space at the side of the tray and unfolded them. She pointed to Dalton Riggs's picture at the bottom of the front page of the *Post*.

Caroline reached for her scarlet-framed half-glasses. 'Rosa, what is this?'

'It says General Riggs might be the next chief of staff,' Rosa said, pulling her shoulders back proudly.

'Oh, Lordy me. I can't deal with this right now.' Caroline leaned forward and looked through the archway to the solarium, where Dalton kept his exercise equipment. She could see he was still upside down suspended from his gravity machine.

She'd wait for Dalton to finish his morning routine. After such a late night on the job, she knew this would make him feel better.

Her head was still pounding, her throat hurt,

and her legs ached as though someone had whacked them with a baseball bat. Not that she would have felt it the night before, but lately she was discovering odd bruises and marks in various places where she had bumped into things around the house. If they didn't show she ignored them. When they did, a little touch of foundation made them disappear.

Dalton entered the bedroom with a monogrammed bath sheet twisted around his trim waist. 'Morning, Caroline,' he said briskly. 'You were dead to the world when I got in. Wish I could sleep like that.'

'You could, if you took two yellows and a blue. Works like a charm,' she told him.

He leaned down and kissed the top of her head. 'How's Polly?'

'Like she's been rode hard and put to bed wet,' she quipped in her best Texas twang. Then she added with less exaggeration, 'I hope a night's sleep picks her up a bit.'

She did not mention that Polly seemed distraught as well as exhausted when she arrived after one A.M. 'The *Post* here's got you runnin' for chief of staff,' she said, trying to be light about it.

'Let me see what they're saying,' he said, taking the paper from the bed. 'This broke earlier than I thought it would.'

'You knew they were doing a story?' She pulled off her glasses and looked up at him.

He tossed the paper back on to the bed, trying to be nonchalant. 'Ah . . . yes, that fellow Miller was in my office yesterday.'

136

'His idea or yours?'

'His, of course,' he said brusquely. 'You know I don't leak.'

Why was it that no one ever admitted to leaks? Yet they flowed constantly. That's why they could hold a top-secret meeting in the subbasement of the White House and it would make the evening news; why every word said at secret closed-door congressional hearings got printed on the front page.

'But you're not upset that he wrote the story?'

He picked a slice of melon from Caroline's plate and popped it into his mouth. 'Let's put it this way. I'm not going to call Kay Graham and demand a retraction.'

'The job's a mighty tough go,' she said, punching her pillow and rearranging herself higher in the bed.

'So were two tours in Vietnam,' he said around the melon.

Of course he wanted it. Wanted it as much as he'd wanted every promotion in the army, every presidential commission, every mention in the political columns. She had to admit, she wanted it for him too. She always wanted the next step up for him. Every star on his shoulder was a testament to her ambition for him. Wanting what he wanted was as much a part of her as Polly was.

But at the moment, with her tongue thick and head pounding, she was in no condition for one of their intense strategy sessions. Anything she said would be gibberish until she got herself together.

'Dalton, sugar, could we talk about this a little

137

later? I'd like to shower and get dressed. I promised Pol I'd have breakfast with her.' She glanced at the bedside clock. 'Good heavens, look at the time! And Rosa said your driver's downstairs waiting. You better get a move on.'

He stood by the side of the bed for a long moment as though he wanted to say something. He didn't. She wanted him to just go so she could get her act together. He did.

She poured herself another cup of coffee from the thermos Rosa brought on the tray. In the bottom drawer of her night table under a copy of *Vogue* were two of those little splits of brandy they sell on a plane. Caroline liked them so much she asked the nice man at Embassy Liquor to get her a case of them. They were easy to carry.

She opened one and poured it into her cup. Within minutes she felt better. The clenching feeling in her head released its grip and the knots in her legs relaxed.

She wondered, Does the wife of the chief of staff see her husband any more often than the wife of the head of the National Security Council? Probably not, she concluded.

She poured a second split of brandy into her coffee and carried it into the shower.

On warm spring mornings Constance Maubry took a light breakfast of tea and fruit on the huge screen porch of her Georgetown mansion. She and her secretary-companion, Ian Vreen, discussed the morning papers and checked over her schedule for the day.

The stately old house sat high above the Potomac. Its possession had required a considerable amount of negotiation at her late husband's deathbed. Somewhere in Europe were two middle-aged daughters from Lord Maubry's previous marriage who angrily believed that Constance had no right to the landmark Georgian mansion.

From her wicker peacock chair Constance could see hummingbirds fluttering at the hedge that encircled the swimming pool one terrace below the tennis courts. She and Ian sat opposite each other, separated by a small table holding a breakfast tray.

'I had a lovely phone visit with Beth Kane this morning. She gets up earlier than even I do,' Lady Maubry said as she freshened her cup. She gestured toward Ian with the porcelain pot.

'No thanks,' he said, shaking his head.

'She's absolutely amazing. I think she's going to be the most popular First Lady since Eleanor.'

'Prettier, too.' Ian smiled, lowering the morning

paper. 'I voted for her as much as I voted for her husband.'

'I think a lot of people did.' Lady Maubry dusted her strawberries with powdered sugar. 'Now Lady Bird had a lot of Beth's gumption but then again . . .'

Ian folded the paper and half-listened as Constance droned on about her intimate knowledge of first ladies. Of the last seven presidents, Constance was on a first-name basis with all except Pat Nixon and Rosalynn Carter.

'She's awfully upset about it,' Ian heard her say and snapped to attention.

'I'm sorry, dear,' he said, now alert. 'Who's upset about what?'

'Beth,' she said sharply, 'Beth Kane. She's taking Brad Barry's death very hard. Both she and Don were very close to him. Of all the people on the campaign Beth said Brad was her favorite. She's very disturbed about the rumors that Brad was having a secret affair and not the least bit pleased with Tim O'Brien's mention this morning that the FBI and Secret Service are investigating it.'

It served him right for not paying attention. Ian smiled to himself. Constance always had the best information, but over the years he had learned that there were times when she would share inside gossip and times when she would not. He knew if she had spoken to the First Lady she knew more about the Barry situation than even the FBI.

'Why would they be investigating his private life now? The poor man is dead,' he said, hoping to keep her in a generous mood.

'Between us?' Constance asked, leaning forward in her enormous chair. The wicker whispered as she moved.

'Always darling, you know that.'

'Ha! I know no such thing, Ian Vreen. But I would like to get your thinking.'

Ian ignored her. Clearly she was going to tell him. All he had to do was to be still and let her go on.

'Well,' she began, 'Don Kane very nearly didn't name Barry chief of staff. It seems Brad had a, shall we say, compromising affair during the Kane campaign with a left-wing French journalist sent over to cover the campaign. She was sharing an apartment at 2500 Q Street with another lefty, some Spanish woman the FBI had under surveillance. Anyway, along with pictures and phone taps they gathered information on Barry's nightlife. Seems he was interested in romance, not revolution, so it all worked out. The President named him chief of staff.' Constance sat back, patting her mouth with her napkin.

'Fascinating, my dear. Absolutely riveting. Your, ah, sources didn't tell you more?' he said, trying not to name the First Lady directly. It was a game he and Constance played – I'll-tell-you-something-but-I-won't-name-my-source.

'Nope,' she said blithely, a tiny smile playing at the corners of her mouth. She pushed herself out of her chair more to change the subject, he was sure, than to give attention to her parakeet. She walked to the brass cage suspended from a ceiling

141

chain and made chirping sounds to the excited bird.

Ian unfolded the *Observer* and turned to Deena Simon's column. 'Did you read Deena's item on Mark Kirkland?' he said to her back. 'Pretty nasty stuff.'

'I did,' she said, poking her finger into the cage, 'but only after Buck called this morning to point it out. I try not to read her. She upsets my day. Buck says Sinclare Ives planted that story.'

'Sinclare?' Ian said, surprised. 'How would your brother know something like that?'

Constance turned and moved back to her chair. 'Buck knows everything, Ian. You know that.'

Ian stood, his body tense. Sinclare was his friend, and for all her madcap behavior he doubted she was capable of deliberately planting an item to hurt someone.

'You look upset,' Constance said kindly. 'Did I say something that offended you?'

'No, not you, Connie dear. It's just upsetting to hear Sinclare's name thrown around so irresponsibly. It's not her style to be hurtful. I wish I knew where Buck got such a story.'

'Well, if it makes you feel any better, Echo Bourne told him.'

Ian ran his fingers through his thinning hair. 'Echo? I'd hardly call her a reliable source.'

'Be that as it may,' Constance said, dismissing the subject. 'The only person I care about in any of this unpleasantness is my niece. What hurts her hurts me. I'd really like to know more about this but my contacts aren't at that level.'

142

Ian smiled. 'You mean a level that low, like mine.'

'Ian, I would never even imply such a thing,' she said, seemingly shocked. 'But you do know a lot of people that I don't . . . socialize with.' She looked up at him bright-eyed.

'Let me see what I can find out around town. If, and it's a big if, Sinclare had anything to do with it I'm sure she is just trying to help Eliot. I know she was angry at not being invited to Jan's dinner party, but she wouldn't be so petty as to plant that story.'

'Well, you know her much better than I do,' Constance said, ringing the tiny silver bell on the breakfast tray to summon Celia.

After the housekeeper left with the dishes Constance asked, 'How far do you think Sinclare would go to get Eliot that job?'

'I don't know,' he said slowly, 'but pretty far.'

Tuesday, June 6, 1989 – 10:00 A.M.
The Fort, Foxhall Road

Polly overslept for the first time she could remember. It felt wonderful not to be jolted awake by reveille.

The pitch and whine of the yardman's electric mower came from far out on the grounds, down by the boxwood maze. She could hear the sound of her mother's shower running downstairs. It

143

would be at least an hour before Mom had assembled herself for the day.

She stared up at the underside of the Laura Ashley canopy, which matched the draperies and wallpaper. The middle shelves of the bookcases between the windows held soft toys battered by years of being packed, loved, and repacked. The top shelf held her dog-eared copies of Dickens and Jackie Susann and a manual on the M-16 rifle. On the dresser was a silver-framed collection of family photographs – her father in the dress blues of a brigadier general, her mother as a young woman seated at a grand piano, a satin ribbon across her strapless evening gown on which glittering letters spelled out Miss Teenage Texas.

She needed to talk to her mother, but having breakfast with her meant actually eating something . . .

That did it. Suddenly she was sick again. She threw back the light cover and bolted toward her bathroom. At least at home she didn't have to flush the toilet repeatedly to cover the sound of retching.

When she finished she sat on the fluffy white bath mat and leaned against the cool tile of the bowl. Great, three years at the United States Military Academy down the drain.

Polly Lawton Riggs, daughter of a general and West Point second classperson with a straight A average, had been betrayed by the thing she could always count on – her own body. It was a wondrous machine – strong, lean, and beautiful to boot. It could outrun, outjump, and outdo most

144

boys in almost any competition, but the competition ended when it came to sex. She had lost.

Her dark red curly hair needed nothing more than a finger comb. A light dusting of a few pale freckles danced from one high cheekbone to the other. Two of the biggest freckles had gone astray and landed directly under the lower lashes of each big blue eye, giving her a look her father called perky.

Now she felt trapped and weak, and very sad. She pushed the intercom button on the bedside phone. The thought of breakfast was more than she could bear.

'Good morning, Miss Polly,' Rosa's cheerful voice answered from the kitchen far below. 'Welcome home.'

'Morning, Rosa. Thank you.'

'Your mother said you and she would have a late breakfast.'

'Well, I . . .'

'I've got blueberry waffles,' Rosa said eagerly.

Polly felt her stomach lurch again. 'No . . . no thanks, Rosa, I'm going up to Rock Creek Park to see Eagle for a quick ride. Is the Jeep around?'

'Yes, Miss Polly, in the back drive. Manuel washed it for you.'

Quickly she looked through her closet for her jodhpurs and boots. The riding pants had a crease pressed into them. 'Dry cleaners,' she sniffed. She found her riding boots standing at the back of the closet. They had been reheeled and spit-shined. Manuel knew from years of service to a military man how boots should be cared for. She pulled on an old brown turtleneck sweater and found her black velvet hacking cap on a hook in the back of the closet.

She looked at herself in the full-length mirror. Nothing showed, not yet. Maybe a bumpy Jeep ride and a morning on horseback would do the trick. She might not have to tell Bob or her mother after all. It would all go away like a bad dream. No, she thought, not a dream, a nightmare.

Perfect Polly, that Riggs girl who did everything right. 'Sweet as a peach, but tough at the core,' her dad liked to say. Sweet, perfect Polly had screwed up. Probably the first illegitimacy in the long Riggs/ Hardaway family tradition, she thought, as she rushed from the house.

Caroline

June 1960
The Double H Ranch
Bexar County, Texas

The sprawling Hardaway ranch hadn't seen such a commotion for almost a decade – since that movie company used the house as background in *Giant*.

Caroline June Hardaway had been nine then and away at boarding school in Dallas. She had only her mother's letters to describe the trucks and vans that tore up the front lawn, the grips and electricians who ran miles of wire around the porches, and the barbecue Martha Hardaway and the help laid on for a 'wrap party'. Martha Hardaway had been proud to write that one thousand pounds of side meat had been sliced, grilled, and served to 'perfect strangers', except for Elizabeth Taylor, Rock Hudson, and James Dean, who were now, of course, her best friends.

Martha was thrilled that for once her daughter would be home to see how grandly the Hardaways could entertain. Caroline June, who had just graduated from Beauchamp Rise as valedictorian of the Class of 1960, had come home to do one of two things: prepare for the debut her mother insisted on next Christmas or go stark-raving mad. Martha Hardaway always got her way, mainly because everything was hers – her ranch, her cattle, her money. Actually it was Martha's Daddy's money, but it had been left to Martha years before, and though she didn't bring it up, the population of Bexar County was too small for everyone not to know.

Caroline had been sitting in her favorite hiding place for over an hour. For as long as she could remember she had brought her inner thoughts to the window seat under the bay window on the staircase landing. If she brought her knees up almost to her chin and leaned against the wall, the high damask drapes concealed her from view completely.

Out on the airstrip just past the pond, planes had been landing since early in the morning – Pipers and Comanches and executive jets owned by big oil companies and construction firms and banks from all over Texas. By late afternoon there was barely anyplace left for them to park. The latecomers had to taxi out onto the bumpy grass of the north pasture.

The passengers had one thing in common: they had all contributed money to Lyndon B. Johnson's presidential campaign and were coming to the Double H Ranch to contribute still more. With the Democratic convention only two weeks away, the smell of victory was loosening purse strings.

The ranch hands had been stoking the barbecue pits for days, and the pungent smoke now permeated the upper floors of the house. A Houston TV reporter named Dan Rather and his crew were set up on the part of the porch that looked toward the airfield. They were awaiting the arrival of the star of the fundraiser, Senator Lyndon Baines Johnson and his wife Lady Bird.

Caroline desperately wanted to be a part of it all, but her mother had other plans. Politics was Tom Hardaway's preoccupation. Her daughter Caroline was hers.

Tom Hardaway had been a close associate of Lyndon Johnson's since their days at a small state teacher's college and had put aside his small-town law practice to direct the senator's campaign for the Democratic party nomination. Martha had served as his hostess and social organizer, but her overriding goal in life was to see that her only daughter became a Southern lady in every sense of the word. A proper introduction into Texas society was mandatory.

Caroline thought of the daylong fittings at Neiman-Marcus, the endless girlish luncheons, the obligatory parties and balls where she would be forced to smile and make small talk with a succession of pasty-faced young men.

She pulled her knees higher and rested her cheek against the rough fabric of her jeans. She wanted to be down in the library with the cigar smoke and the liquor and the men who talked about real life — money, power, politics, and winning.

From her hiding place she could see her mother out on the flagstone terrace in front of the house. Her mother was wearing silver cowboy boots and a denim blouse and skirt studded with rhinestones. Resting on top of her dark red beehive hairdo was a straw boater with a red, white, and blue satin band that read 'Ladies for Lyndon.' As each of the guests made their way up the long stone walk from the road she greeted them effusively and pinned them with a huge beribboned button. Even from where she was sitting Caroline could read the button slogan – ALL THE WAY WITH LBJ.

'Damn!' she said out loud. In a few days some of these people would be leaving as delegates to the convention in Los Angeles. They would be part of something really meaningful. And what would she be doing? Practicing the piano and going to lunch and listening to her mother tell her to keep her shoulders back and her legs together.

Caroline had been raised to put a good face on everything. No pouting, temper tantrums, or arguments were permitted. For seventeen years her mother had been running her life. She never particularly liked the show-off things her mother pushed her into, such as baton twirling and ballet and piano lessons, even the Miss Teenage Texas contest. But she had to admit they had taught her how to handle herself, and how to keep smiling in the face of any humiliation.

She had gone along with it to please her mother. Now she was bored with it all and the thought of a debut made her cringe. More and more she had been drawn to politics. At home on vacations from school she had listened to the wheeling and dealing going on in her father's library and ached to do more than simply curtsy sweetly to the powerful men who came to the house. They treated her like a pretty little girl, a budding flower of Texas womanhood. But Caroline knew what they were really thinking. She was a pretty girl with a well-connected father and an oil-rich mother. And she was sole heir to some forty thousand acres of prime Texas land — breeding stock.

'Caroline! Where are you, girl?' Caroline heard the unmistakable sound of her best friend Natalie Bowen's voice at the foot of the stairs. She pushed back the drapes and saw her standing in the foyer wearing a gingham square dance skirt and one of Caroline's mother's Ladies for Lyndon boaters.

'Nate! I didn't know you were coming,' Caroline shrieked and ran to the stair landing. The two girls met halfway and threw their arms around each other. 'God, it's good to see you,' Caroline cried. 'I thought you were in Europe.'

'I'm not going,' Natalie said breathlessly. 'I'm going to the convention!'

Caroline stood in the middle of the stairs and stared at her friend. 'Are you serious? How did that happen? I'd kill to go.'

'Let's go somewhere and talk, okay?'

Caroline glanced toward the front door. 'We'd better. If Mom catches me in jeans, I've had it. I was supposed to be dressed an hour ago.'

They lay on their stomachs on Caroline's high canopied bed on the third floor.

'A Pom-Pom Girl for Lyndon!' Caroline whooped, rolling from side to side. 'Natalie Bowen, I don't believe it. You of all people!'

'So what's so funny?' Natalie said, sounding hurt. 'We all don't have to look like Ann-Margaret, you know.'

'I didn't mean that, Nate. I just pictured you

153

doing stone rubbings in French graveyards, not jumping around waving crepe paper and yelling "Happy days are here again."'

'Beats a bike tour,' Natalie said, reaching for the last Mallomar in the box. 'You wanna go?'

'You're joking, of course.'

'No. Mrs Thornberry is in charge of the group. There are twelve of us. I'm sure she'd love to have the campaign manager's daughter, particularly Miss Teeny-Tiny Texas.' Natalie licked the chocolate off her fingers.

'Back off, you know that was Mom's idea.'

'I'm serious, Caroline, come with us. It will be a ball.'

'I don't know,' Caroline said, shaking her head. 'It seems kind of mindless.'

'Oh, and what would you rather do? Write position papers for Senator Johnson? Maybe he needs some clear thinking on Cuban sugar quotas.'

'Now you're talking,' Caroline said.

'Look, I'll speak to Mrs Thornberry. Let her ask your mother. It will be a kick. All you have to remember is to keep your mouth shut.'

Caroline swung her legs over the side of the bed and walked toward the closet. 'What are you talking about?' she asked sharply.

'Well, you have to admit you have a way of saying what's on your mind. We are supposed to be smiley little girls whose sole function is to make the delegates think Lyndon is the greatest thing since FDR.'

'You mean we're supposed to be fakes,' Caroline

said, examining the freshly pressed white linen dress her mother had sent the maid up with.

'Caroline June, you bite your tongue.'

Martha Hardaway was hesitant. Was this something ladies did? But after much consultation she gave her approval. The Pom-Poms for Lyndon were the daughters of some of the finest families in Texas. They would undoubtedly be invited to some smart parties and Louella Thornberry would see that Caroline was properly looked after. The fittings and functions attendant to Caroline's debut could wait a couple of weeks. Within a week Martha Hardaway was dying to tell her friends about her daughter's good fortune.

Caroline was of two minds as she packed to leave for Los Angeles. The idea of wearing a cute little uniform and parading around at rallies and airports was less than exciting. Being around history in the making made up for it. She would meet a lot of people who shared her interest in politics. And Johnson might just win.

July 1960
The Biltmore Hotel
Los Angeles, California

Caroline's life had been saturated with the mystique of the great Lyndon Johnson. When she reached Los Angeles she was in for a shock. The Democratic convention of 1960 was fixated on one thing – the hatred between Lyndon Johnson and the gorgeous young senator from Massachusetts.

The Johnson campaign people had booked six rooms at the Biltmore Hotel in downtown LA for the Pom-Poms. Since both the Johnson and Kennedy staffs were headquartered there, the lobby, elevators, and halls were filled with staffers, delegates, and press who talked openly about the vicious tensions between the two camps.

The Johnson people hated the Kennedy people. The Kennedy people treated the Johnson people like a bad joke. One LBJ lieutenant had started a whispering campaign about Kennedy having incurable Addison's disease. Johnson himself was meeting with state delegations and telling them that Kennedy's father was the man 'who held Chamberlain's umbrella.' And everywhere Caroline turned she heard Kennedy people openly referring to Johnson as 'that shit kicker.'

Caroline loved it. She thought the conversations she had eavesdropped on in her father's library were fascinating, but what she was witnessing here only moments after her arrival was raw, gut-level politics that made her blood race.

While the other Pom-Poms worried about getting to the hotel hairdresser in time for their first appearance, Caroline wandered through the crowded halls in awe. Purely by accident she found herself standing across from the Johnson press office, which served as the nerve center for rumor and strategy.

The Pom-Poms' first assignment was a welcoming rally for the Texas delegation in the main ballroom of the hotel. Mrs Thornberry told the girls to be in their white blazers, boaters, and red pleated skirts in the lobby to pick up their Pom-Poms no later than five-thirty.

At five a man rushed out of the Johnson press room and shouted at Caroline, 'Can you collate?'

Caroline didn't make it to the Texas rally. She didn't make it to the party afterward either. By the time she got back to her hotel room, wearing the same blouse and skirt she had worn on the plane, Natalie was furious.

'Where the hell have you been?' Natalie asked angrily as she turned on the bedside lamp.

Caroline collapsed on her bed without even taking off her shoes. 'In the press office,' she said, exhaling with exhaustion.

'All night?'

'Since five o'clock.'

'Doing what, for God's sake? Mrs Thornberry is really pissed.' Natalie frowned, propping herself up on her elbows.

'First I collated a three-page press release. Then I started answering the phone. I tried to leave, but the guys in there begged me to stay. They were swamped. It was a madhouse. They say Kennedy is going to take it on the first ballot and we'll be up shit creek.' Caroline lay flat on her back and spoke to the ceiling.

'Such language, Caroline June!' Natalie said, feigning shock.

Caroline rolled over and faced Natalie's bed.

157

'Nate, what would happen if I decided not to be a Pom-Pom?'

'Mrs Thornberry would be on the phone to your mama fast as a scalded dog,' Natalie said, rubbing the sleep out of her eyes. 'Your mama would have you on the next plane home. Why?'

'They want me to come back in the morning. They're really shorthanded down there. It's not like I wouldn't be working for Lyndon.'

'Gee, I don't know, Caroline. You kinda made a deal to be a Pom-Pom.'

Caroline rolled over on her back again. 'I made a deal to help Lyndon Johnson get the presidential nomination. I think I've found a better way to help than shaking my butt to a brass band.'

By the time Wyoming put John F. Kennedy over the top Caroline had had four hours' sleep in three days. Natalie had been to five rallies, eight cocktail parties, and Disneyland. She was also temporarily in love with a Johnson advance man from Waco.

Caroline was having a love affair of her own. She was besotted, engulfed, and overwhelmed by a passion for politics. While Natalie fussed with her eye makeup Caroline paced the hotel room in a frenzy. 'They say Johnson is going on the ticket with Kennedy,' she said, wringing her hands.

'Is blue me?' Natalie asked, looking at her eye shadow sideways in the mirror.

'Kennedy is telling people he's too young to die in office so the vice presidency doesn't mean anything.'

'Up or down?' Natalie held her straight dark hair up with the back of her wrists.

'Huh?'

'Should I wear it up or down?'

Caroline exploded. 'For chrissake, Natalie! Don't you have any appreciation of what we're living through here? This is important! If Johnson goes on the ticket it's a sellout. It will tear the Democratic party right down the middle.'

'I think down,' Natalie said, dropping her hair and picking up a bunch.

'I give up,' Caroline sighed. She popped up when the phone began to ring. It was probably the press office wondering where she was. 'Yes,' she said abruptly. 'Oh, Mrs Thornberry, I'm so sorry. I thought ... uh ... well, I don't know. I'm supposed to work tonight.'

Natalie turned and stared at her. 'Did she call your mother?' she whispered.

'Oh, well, in that case. Yes, ma'am, yes. I'll be at the suite at eight sharp.'

'What was all that?' Natalie asked excitedly after Caroline hung up.

'Mrs Thornberry wants me to keep Luci Bird company while the Senator and Mrs Johnson are on the convention floor,' Caroline said smugly. 'Lynda's going with them and she'll be all alone in the suite.'

'In the Johnson's suite?'

Caroline rose slowly from the bed and smoothed her skirt. 'I may even get to meet the Senator.' She smiled, enormously pleased with herself.

* * *

159

The younger Johnson daughter was already asleep when Caroline arrived at the candidate's suite. There was little for her to do but meet Mrs Johnson, listen to brief instructions about calling room service if she was hungry, and settle down to watch Johnson's name be put in nomination on TV.

The Johnsons returned well after midnight. Lady Bird Johnson thanked Caroline and said good night. To Caroline's astonishment, Lyndon Johnson, possibly the next Vice President of the United States, poured himself a glass of scotch, sat down on the end of the couch, pulled off his shoes, and asked Caroline if she thought he did the right thing.

She said yes and it seemed to be what he wanted to hear. She told him that from what she had heard in the press room and halls of the hotel, Kennedy couldn't carry the South without him. He seemed to like that, too.

'Tom Hardaway's got a right smart daughter, I see,' he drawled, patting her on the arm. 'How long have you been working for us?'

'Five days, plus the last five hours, if watching your television and signing for room service can be called work.'

'Your daddy get you the job in the press room?'

'No, sir. I came out as one of Mrs Thornberry's Pom-Pom girls and was hanging around when they needed an extra hand.'

'And you've been there ever since?'

'Yes, sir.'

Johnson rose wearily from the couch. He didn't

look nearly as imposing as he had when she first saw him at the fundraiser back at the ranch. At that moment he looked like a tired, slightly crumbled giant with a lot on his mind. 'I tell you what, little lady. We've got a lot of work ahead of us. We could use someone like you in Washington. How would you like to come work for us?'

Caroline was dumbstruck. Her first impulse was to say something smart-alecky, as she usually did when she wanted to hide her emotions. Now was not the time. What was she going to say? I have to go home and make my debut so my mother can marry me off? You don't want to hire me, I don't have any experience? This was all a dream, she thought. I'll just play it straight.

She stood and picked up her handbag. 'Senator Johnson,' she said, looking directly at him, 'if you really mean that, I'll be on the next plane to Washington.'

'Well, I mean it, little lady.' He hiked up his belt. 'I'll have young Bill Moyers call your family in the morning.'

He held out his arm and gently guided her to the door of the suite. 'You're a mighty pretty thing, Caroline Hardaway,' he said as he closed the door.

That night Caroline lay in the dark watching the pattern of light on the hotel room ceiling. Natalie flopped about in her sleep muttering the Waco advance man's name.

Let her moan over some jerk, Caroline thought, let Senator Lyndon Johnson think she was a mighty pretty thing. He wasn't the first and wouldn't be the last to think that was what she wanted to hear about herself.

Caroline knew there was more to her than the way she looked. Now, at last, she had a chance to prove it.

Winter 1961
Maubry House, Georgetown

Caroline was nervous about going to dinner at Lady Maubry's. Her mother, who was still having a hard time adjusting to Caroline's refusal to make a debut and going to work in Washington, had written several curt notes asking her to give Lady Maubry a call. Long experience had taught Caroline that some of the people her mother considered her best friends were merely passing acquaintances who barely remembered her.

But Lady Maubry had been very sweet on the phone and without hesitation had asked her to dinner. All week when Caroline thought about going to dinner she pictured a stuffy, middle-aged society lady who would treat her with the bored tolerance one shows the daughter of someone they owe some vague social favor. Her co-workers had been impressed when she told them about the invitation. Lady Maubry was Washington's *grande dame* and she had promised a full report.

The house, just a few blocks' walk from her apartment, was as large and imposing as Caroline had been told. Lady Maubry, on the other hand, was quite a surprise.

As Caroline mounted the steps leading up to the massive oak front door it sprang open. Standing there was a tall thin woman wearing a silver satin floor-length gown with a Grecian drape. Her hair was the same tone and shine as the dress. It curved under in a pageboy that just reached her jawline and was held in place on one side by a diamond clip. Her flawless skin was reflected in a triple rope of burnished pearls. 'You must be Caroline,' she said. 'Welcome to my den of intrigue.' Her accent was that of an American who had lived among the English. It rang bell-like and made Caroline self-conscious about her Texas twang. Constance Maubry was extraordinary. Why had she expected someone like her mother?

'I'm Constance Sumner Maubry. Thank God you've come!'

Caroline, a little flustered, said, 'Hello, Lady Maubry. Do you need some help or something?'

'Absolutely,' she said, shutting the door. 'Oh, mums! My favorite.'

Caroline stood holding the flowers she had picked up at a shop on the corner of Wisconsin Avenue. Behind Lady Maubry's head on round tables covered with velvet drops were the largest flower arrangements she had ever seen, even in Texas.

Lady Maubry reached for Caroline's sorry little offering and held them as though they were some rare and precious species. 'You know, Caroline dear, I have spent the entire day trying to figure out how I know your mother.'

Somehow Caroline was not surprised.

'Well, never mind, we'll figure it out. Come, let's go into the library and have a martini. I always like to have a bit of a buzz on before dinner.'

Constance Maubry led the way into a room Caroline hadn't seen the likes of since she toured the furniture exhibit at the Metropolitan Museum on her senior class trip. Tufted and fringed velvet couches and armchairs in deep tones of red or gold sat at angles through the high-ceilinged room. High on the walls above the dark paneling were crossed swords and mounted antique guns. A massive carved fireplace mantel was flanked by eight-foot-high tapestries depicting knights with lances spearing small animals with terrified eyes. The entire room was paneled in dark smooth wood that gleamed with the light of porcelain sconces. The floor was covered by a brilliant, elegantly worn Tabriz. There were round tables covered with jewel-toned watered silk drops to the floor, their glass tops cluttered with photographs framed in silver, awards framed in tortoiseshell, engraved boxes, and 'things' she would not be able to describe to Natalie.

Lady Maubry positioned herself in front of the burning fire and reached for a needlepoint bell pull. Over the mantel hung a larger-than-life portrait done in the manner of Boldini, very romantic, of a beautiful woman mounted sidesaddle on a rearing stallion. The hooves attacked the stormy sky. The woman sat regally, a full black split skirt to her ankles. She wore a tall silk hat. A tiny black veil played across her high forehead and wide-set eyes.

Caroline stood staring at her surroundings.

'What do you think of this room?' Lady Maubry asked, gesturing at the walls.

'Mussolini would have loved it,' Caroline said matter-of-factly. She quickly pressed her lips together, realizing she must sound rude.

'Wouldn't he just!' Lady Maubry laughed. 'Come,' she said, indicating that Caroline should sit in one of the wing-backed chairs that flanked the fireplace. She gave the bell pull another yank and sat down opposite Caroline. In the firelight she was even more beautiful than Caroline had realized. 'How are you finding the men here in Washington, my dear? You know everyone always complains that there are too many women. I have found it quite the contrary,' she continued without missing a beat. 'I find that if you move in the right circles there are more than enough men to go around. They may be flawed somewhat, if you know what I mean. Ah! There you are. Ian, this is my new friend, I hope, Caroline June Hardaway. Caroline works for Lyndon.'

Constance leaned forward in a girlish, confidential way. 'Darling, has he pinched you yet? You must tell all.' She turned back to the man who had just entered the room. 'This is my friend and companion, Ian Vreen. That's what you are, darling, right? Yes. We haven't figured out anything better to say. Ian, be a dear and fix us a thundering jug of martinis. You probably don't take martinis,

165

do you, Caroline? Well, time to start. The Kennedys have brought such élan to our town. During Eisenhower everyone was drinking prune juice. Now tell me what you think of Lyndon.'

Caroline stared in disbelief. The woman had not taken a perceptible breath. 'Some people say he's all hat and no cattle, but I like him.'

Ian Vreen stepped toward her and offered his hand. He looked like a character out of a twenties play – tall and very thin, with a long aristocratic face and an expression of bored amusement. He was wearing a pink cashmere sweater over a pink-and-gray tattersall shirt. In the open neck was a carefully pouffed gray silk ascot. He wore black silk trousers with inverted pleats. On his feet were black velvet slippers with some sort of crest on the toes. On his long nose he wore tiny gold pince-nez. He was smiling at her. 'All hat and no cattle. I like that.' He extended his hand. 'I met John Connally at dinner the other evening. What's he like?'

'Slick as a two-dollar suit, but I like him too. My mother and Mrs Connally are on the Dallas Symphony Ball Committee.'

'That's it!' Lady Maubry said, clapping her hands. 'Your mother is Martha Hardaway. The Dallas Symphony Ball. But of course.' She turned to Ian. 'Tom Hardaway, Ian, is a great friend of Sam Rayburn. And what a dancer.' She turned back to Caroline. 'Did you know your father was the most superb dancer in the world?'

Caroline could only nod. She had no idea anyone considered her father a superb dancer, but it was fun to hear.

'Why, I remember, it was the Symphony Ball in, oh, my, last year. Right after the unpleasantness with Lord Tookie. I accepted an invitation to the Kelberg ranch. Your father and I danced a paso doble that cleared the floor.'

'Connie, my dear . . .' Ian tried to interrupt.

'Tom Hardaway,' she said dreamily, gazing into space.

'If you ladies will excuse me for a moment I'll go get us something to drink.'

Lady Maubry snapped out of her reverie. 'Yes, do that, Ian. There's a love,' she said brightly.

'Can I get you some fruit juice or a Coke, Caroline?'

'Aren't you making martinis?' Caroline asked.

'Why, yes, but I thought – '

'That's what I'll have then, thank you.'

Ian cut his eyes at Lady Maubry, who ignored him. She was studying Caroline with a look of surprised interest. 'You're quite sure?' he asked cautiously. 'Have you ever had one?'

'No, but if Lady Maubry needs a buzz before dinner perhaps I've been missing something.'

Ian's hand went up to his mouth to suppress a smile. He cleared his throat. 'I think we're going to like you, Miss Hardaway. Martinis for all coming up.'

He returned a few minutes later with a silver tray. He served Caroline her drink and stepped to Lady Maubry's chair. 'You know, Connie, you really should have hired a waiter for the evening. I don't think Celia is up to serving such a crowd.' He disappeared through the foyer.

167

Crowd? What was he talking about. Caroline assumed she was the only guest. 'Are you expecting guests?' Caroline asked, surprised.

'Just a few of my young friends, nothing overwhelming. I thought you might enjoy meeting them.'

Lady Maubry had invited eight others – all men.

Summer 1961
Georgetown

The eight men Lady Maubry asked to dinner that night became the nucleus of Caroline's social life. As the months passed she got slimmer and dressed more in the style of Jackie Kennedy than a Texas teenager. She wore simple sheaths in good fabrics, tailored suits, and her first fur, an eighteenth-birthday present from her parents. They were finally accustomed to her living in Washington and adjusted to the fact that she would not be coming home to go to college. Her picture was appearing more and more in the society pages of the *Washington Post* and the *Dallas Times Herald*, more for whom she was dating than because she was a member of the Vice President's staff.

She was seen about town with Senator Scoop Jackson, the last remaining bachelor in the Senate, with the correspondent for the *Manchester Guardian*, and with various young Kennedy aides at parties at Hickory Hill, Georgetown mansions, and dancing the night away at Washington's Whiskey-A-Go-Go, a trendy new disco.

None of them meant anything to Caroline. She thought constantly about the one man at Constance Maubry's dinner she couldn't have.

Lady Maubry had invited Dalton Riggs only because his wife was out of town. He was a major in the United States Army. His father had served in Europe with Constance Maubry's first husband. When Constance learned that Dalton and his wife Eleanor were posted to the War College at Washington's Fort McNair she began inviting them to dinner. Eleanor was considered plain and vague, but everyone was impressed with Dalton. The tall, rugged young officer, with his movie-star good looks, quick mind, and grasp of world affairs, was a fascinating dinner partner.

Caroline made Sunday afternoon tea with Constance a habit. It gave her a place to collect her thoughts and someone to tell her problems to. She had grown increasingly fond of the older woman. No one knew Constance's age. Ian always said when pressed, 'Sixty and lying.'

The Sunday before her parents expected her home Caroline sat in the quiet screened porch staring into her teacup.

'Caroline, dear, I feel so guilty,' Lady Maubry said, adjusting her skirt as she slid back in her large wicker chair.

'Guilty? For heaven's sake, whatever for?' Caroline said, putting her teacup aside.

'If I hadn't needed an eighth to round out my table none of this would have happened.'

'Something tells me I would have met him anyway,' Caroline said wistfully.

'Are you quite sure he is divorcing? You know how married men can, well, bend the truth.'

'Of course I'm sure. You sound disapproving.'

'Not I, my dear. But people can be so unkind.'

'You mean people are talking about us?'

'I'm afraid so, dear. This town runs on gossip.'

'And you disapprove?' Caroline said, an urgency creeping into her voice.

'Caroline, darling. I have had many husbands. Three were mine, the others were someone else's. It's just that Dalton Riggs is something I suppose all young women have to experience.'

'You talk about him like he's some sort of rite of passage. Like your first botched body wave or a car crash.'

Connie laughed. 'Well, in a way he is. There are many women in this town who have had a passing crush on Dalton. They get over it, but it's terribly painful when it's going on.'

'Is it because he's so much older?'

'Oh, my dear. I see you aren't going to listen to me. Nobody in love ever has. I don't know why I try.'

'I'd like to think you try because you care for me.'

'I do, Caroline dear. I care terribly about you, and because I do, I want you to be happy.'

'I'm happy, Connie. I've never been so happy in my life.'

* * *

It hadn't really started at Connie's dinner. But a week or so later Caroline had bumped into Major Riggs at the bar of the Carroll Arms Hotel on Capitol Hill. They recognized each other immediately. They stood talking among the noisy after-work crowd at the end of the bar. The Armed Services Committee staffer Riggs had been with said good night and before they realized it the group Caroline had been with had also left.

'Do you have dinner plans?' he asked, checking his watch. 'I'm starved. My wife is still in Atlanta with her mother and the pantry is bare. Why don't we grab a burger?'

Clyde's was jammed with the young crowd that hung out there after work. They found a table in the back and he ordered hamburgers and a salad. After the waiter left he leaned across the table and said, 'If you're free one night next week, Caroline, I'd like to take you for something more elegant than a hamburger.'

She looked into Dalton Riggs's handsome face and then down at his hands. They were broad, hard hands, the nails short and immaculate. She imagined what they would feel like on her body. She thought about what her mother would say.

Caroline said, 'Dalton, I know this is kind of unpleasant of me to say, maybe even square, but I know you are married and – '

'Do you know I am also getting unmarried?'

She paused for a long moment. 'No, I didn't know that.'

'That's why my wife is in Atlanta. Her family is down there. She's already filed for divorce, but let's forget that for now. I want to hear about your work. How in the world did you wind up working for the Vice President?'

Hold on, Caroline told herself, just because you're attracted to him doesn't mean he feels the same way. She began to talk about Texas politics and how different the people around Johnson were from everybody else she met in Washington.

By the time the check arrived they each had had two cups of coffee and a snifter of brandy. She watched the candlelight on his thick black lashes as he bent to sign the check.

She reached over and started peeling wax from the guttering candle on the table. 'I'm free any night next week, Dalton,' she said, not looking at him. 'In spite of my sheltered Southern upbringing, I don't mind letting a man know when I like his company.'

'Great!' he said, leaning back and rearranging his napkin. 'I tell you what. How about this Saturday? Lunch in the country. We'll go to the Olney Inn. Ever been there?'

Caroline shook her head. Saturday. She mentally counted the days. She guessed she could wait that long.

'You're in love,' Constance said, pulling one of her fluffy Lhasa apsos into her lap. 'It's written all over your face.'

Caroline had been talking so long her mouth was dry. She reached for the teapot and freshened her cup. 'I didn't know it could be so painful,' she said sadly, as she poured more tea for Constance.

172

'You didn't?' Constance laughed. 'There is a world of music and art and literature dedicated to the pain you are feeling, Caroline.'

'I know, but for me it's something new.'

'I forget that you are eighteen,' Constance said sympathetically. 'Forgive me.'

'And he is thirty-two.'

'And married.'

'For the time being,' Caroline said.

Constance shook her head slowly as she stroked the tiny dog in her lap. 'You're a strong girl, Caroline Hardaway. Something tells me you can take what's in store for you.'

Their date for lunch in the country had lasted until midnight the next day. By the time he left her tiny apartment near George Washington University she felt as though she had known him all of her life.

They had talked throughout a three-hour lunch at the beautiful old inn deep in the Maryland woods. They talked all the way back to her apartment – about his life as an army brat, living all over the world, his love of the military and politics; about Caroline and all her dreams.

By the time he walked into her living room they both knew why they were there. No words were needed, only arms and hands and mouths and his great strong body, protective, insistent, and engulfing.

Not until afterwards as they lay entwined in each other's arms did he tell her he would be going to Southeast Asia on a special assignment. He couldn't tell her any more, and he held her tightly when she began to sob.

Tuesday Evening, June 6, 1989
Foggy Bottom

Jan spent the entire day trying to figure out a way to squeeze two hundred more people than there were seats into St John's Church for the Bradford Barry memorial service. Brad Barry's friends in government were legion. The fear of making a mistake or leaving someone out made Jan tense and agitated, and especially eager for her usual evening jog.

She rounded the corner of her block at full sprint, her breath coming in deep, lung-bulging bursts. Her T-shirt was drenched. It was still hot, though the sun had set and dusk was fast turning to darkness.

As she moved up the familiar block she slowed her pace to a lope. She turned the corner of the small alleyway that divided her house from that of the neighbors, a nice couple who worked on Capitol Hill. Suddenly her running shoes skidded on a slick of coffee grounds. Startled, she noticed the alleyway was strewn with garbage.

'Damn,' she muttered, 'what is this mess?' She assumed the garbagemen had been careless or Congressman D'Anjou's monstrous hound had been snacking again. As she bent to pick up a slimy

174

freezer bag and the skin from her morning banana, she froze.

Fifty feet or less down the dark alley she saw a tall figure wearing dark glasses and workman's coveralls yanking open the gate of her small back-yard. It was the entrance to the service road that ran in back of the houses facing the street. A flash of sneakers disappeared and a surge of adrenaline coursed through her limbs. Without thinking she shouted, 'Hey!' No sooner had the sound left her throat than she felt a rush of fear that the fleeing figure might stop and come back after her.

Trembling, she jogged back up the alley to the well-lit street. A black Ford screeched away as the figure in the workman's coveralls ducked into the passenger's seat. With the sound of her heart pounding in her ears she watched as the car disappeared down Twenty-first Street.

She was still shaking when she dialed the kitchen phone, safe now inside the house. 'Belle,' she said breathlessly, 'let me speak to Daddy right away!'

'Sure, honey,' her father's secretary chirped. 'He's on long distance. I'll get him off.'

Jan stretched the phone cord as far as it would go as she paced the kitchen.

'What's up, love?' her father's voice boomed.

'Daddy, I just got back to the house and there was this creature in the alley, you know the alley that runs along the side of the house? There was garbage strewn all over.' The words spilled out as fast as her mouth would move.

'Hey . . . hey . . . hey, slow down, sweetheart. Just slow down.'

'I can't, Daddy, I'm scared to death.'

'Are you all right? You're not hurt or anything, are you?'

'No . . . nothing like that. Whoever he was just made a mess, and when he saw me he ran out through the gate and jumped in the car that was obviously waiting to pick him up. I don't think he was trying to get in the house or anything. He just seemed to be going through the garbage.'

She could hear her father breathing heavily. 'This is very upsetting,' he said finally.

'I'll say. You don't suppose this has something to do with Mark? You know, with that filthy stuff you said Sinclare put in the paper. It just seems weird. Two creepy things in one day.'

'Now don't go getting paranoid, Jan, honey,' he said. 'Have you told Mark about this business just now?'

'He's not home yet.'

'Who's not home?' Mark asked from the kitchen door.

Jan jumped in surprise. 'Oh, hi honey. I'm talking to Daddy.' She turned back to the phone. 'Listen, Mark just walked in. I'll call you later. Bye. I love you.'

'What's going on?' Mark said, dropping his corduroy jacket over the back of a chair. 'You look like you've seen a ghost.'

'I was just telling Daddy, Mark, someone was going through our garbage can when I got home just now. Do you think we should call the police?'

'Why bother when you can call your father,' he said sarcastically.

The words stung. *Please don't start again on that, Mark, not after the day I've had.* Jan said nothing, hoping silence would change the subject. It didn't.

'You call your father for everything, don't you?'

She couldn't stand it anymore. 'Some creep is going through our garbage and you have a problem with me talking to my father about it!' Jan picked up a crumbled dish towel and aimed it toward the sink.

'You could have called me.'

'For heaven's sake, Mark, you've been out of pocket all day. Besides, it just so happens that Daddy is my only family. I don't see anything wrong with going to him when I'm upset.' She wished she could recall the words. Instantly, she knew they were wrong.

'Goddammit.' Mark slammed his hand down so hard on the kitchen counter that the top of the automatic coffee maker popped loose and rolled to the floor. 'Family? Your only family? What am I? Your prom date? For Christ sake, Jan, I'm your family, too.'

'Of course you are, Mark,' she said softly. 'Please try to understand.'

'No, I don't think I will ever understand, and one of these days you are going to have to choose. Probably sooner than later. Frankly, I'm very close to saying "I've had it."'

Jan reached for his sleeve. 'Honey, don't. Mark . . . please . . .'

He yanked his arm away from her and strode

toward the kitchen door. He slammed it hard enough to make the hollow wood shudder.

She stared at the door. Her throat felt as if it were glued shut. She gasped for breath and when she exhaled a sobbing escaped. 'Why do I have to choose? Can't I have you both?' she whispered.

Wednesday

Wednesday, June 7, 1989 — 6:00 A.M.
The Hay-Adams Hotel

The FBI sweep team marched through the lobby of the Hay-Adams Hotel four abreast. The investigative work had been made virtually impossible thanks to the DC Police, which had given the hotel the okay to clean the room on Sunday night after Barry's body was removed. They even gave the suite out that night to a late-arriving family from Canada. So the room had been cleaned a second time on Monday morning before they were called in by the White House to investigate.

This was their third visit since Brad Barry's death, and none of the men were particularly pleased to be back. The order to go over the suite one more time meant someone in the White House would be on the director's case if they didn't come up with something soon.

Agent Vinnie DeSanto had the word from the DC Police that the woman who called 911 emergency for an ambulance had been taped, and they would have a copy soon. One hotel employee, a janitor, had seen a woman leaving the hotel about the time of Barry's death, but the description was hopelessly vague. The man, an undocumented Filipino, was terrified he would be sent to jail or deported. The bureau cracked a deal with Immigration giving him six months' amnesty. They hoped today he would be calm enough to review a stack of pictures, for he was almost trying too hard to cooperate now.

Vinnie was pissed. They had nothing. They had gone over the suite inch by inch the day before with everything but a Q-tip. All of them was sure there was nothing to find.

When they reached the suite they began again, starting with the outside door, now black with fingerprinting dust. The once beautifully decorated rooms were in a shambles from their earlier efforts.

Vinnie took the foyer leading to the bedroom and the bathroom. Nothing, completely clean. He'd checked the toilet drain with a plumber's snake the day before. He checked the razor slot in the medicine cabinet, all the crevices, and even tapped the grouting between tiles. He probed the shower drain.

The shower drain. Shit! How could he have been such a jerk?

He leapt into the bathtub, removed a collapsible probe from his inside coat pocket, and extended it to its farthest length. He inserted it into the drain.

Two minutes later he was back in the living room of the suite holding a gold chain bracelet set with diamonds. It hung from the end of the probe, glittering in the lamplight.

'Bingo!' he said to his partner, who was lying on his back, his head inside the fireplace.

Tomorrow Bradford Barry would be buried. For
one last day the ghost of the tough, respected, and
feared chief of staff would linger and then he'd be
gone – a simple footnote in the history books. In
another six months few people outside politics and
Washington would remember just why the name
seemed familiar. But for now, the media treated
him like a sweeping figure. Editorials pondered
'Quo Vadis, Kane Administration?' and conjec-
tured on 'Dismantling the Barry Machine.' Contenders Riggs, Ives, and Kirkland were profiled and
analyzed. Herblock, the political cartoonist for the
Washington Post, drew a witty composite of
Riggs's military background, Ives's business
acumen, and Kirkland's charm, to signify the ideal
chief of staff – Bradford Barry.

Dalton Riggs knew that when he left the house at
7:30 A.M. Caroline would still be sleeping. Once
she would have hopped out of bed, shooed Rosa
out of the kitchen, and served him breakfast,
chatting merrily over the morning papers.

At dawn he'd tried to stroke her awake, hoping
they would make love. Mornings used to be their
favorite time. But she was in such a stupor that he
rested his hand on her back to check her breathing.

183

Some part of her had died or at least was in deep hiding. The world outside their bedroom saw a bright, charming, successful wife and mother. At home she wore only a mask of serenity.

He had to do something for her soon. Talk to the damn doctors who were giving her the pills. There were probably a half dozen of them, for all he knew. Jerry Ford had faced the same situation. Perhaps he could have a private word with his old friend and get Caroline into Betty's clinic. It wasn't the sort of thing someone in his position made casual inquiries about. He didn't want to humiliate her, and yet something had to be done. He knew the answer lay in her deep disappointment in their marriage, and he alone was to blame. He knew she was bored and lonely, but accepting guilt took time and concentration. Somehow, he must find both to save her.

In an hour he would brief the President on the upcoming Moscow trip. Only last week President Kane had praised him in a speech for having restored 'intelligent détente' to US-Soviet relations and for advancing the cause of arms control. The speech had editorialists pounding their word processors elevating Dalton as the President's ideological twin. It was heady wine. *The New York Times* profiled him as the quintessential Kane man. He only hoped the President agreed when he chose his next chief of staff. As much as he enjoyed his present job, and felt secure in his broad knowledge and experience in foreign affairs, he would welcome the expanded responsibility of a new challenge. The only job he would like more would be secretary of state.

He looked down at Caroline again. She hadn't moved at all while he was dressing, opening drawers, and flopping on the bed to lace his shiny black shoes, or blinked when he'd opened the shades to let in the bright June sunlight.

As soon as the President made his decision he'd do something about Caroline. He touched her limp hand and ran his thumb lovingly over the miniature of his West Point class ring that he had set with a yellow diamond. Where was the girl he had given it to? Somewhere inside this unhappy sleeping figure was the vibrant Caroline he once knew. I promise, he vowed, together we can find her again.

Wednesday, June 7, 1989 – 9:15 A.M.
The Watergate Apartments

Eliot Ives pulled the chaise closer to the balcony railing so the rays of the early-morning sun were full on his face and bare chest. He liked to keep a perpetual tan to enhance the look he cultivated – that of a rich, successful, vigorous man of action.

He scanned the morning papers for mention of his name, an indication that his relentless telephone campaign might be paying off. Evans and Novak had one line about him – nothing he could take to the bank. He found himself buried on the

185

Op-Ed page of the *Wall Street Journal* in a long piece on Bradford Barry's impact on the White House, way back on page forty, where people would miss it.

Damn! He glanced at his watch. It was too early to start calling anyone. The only person not in transit to his office at this hour would be President Kane himself. The thought of going directly to his old friend the President crossed his mind. He dismissed the idea immediately. One thing no one ever accused him of was being a fool.

There had been a time when Don Kane shared everything with Eliot, his master political strategist, savvy advisor, and finder of lost dollars. Eliot had found millions of them deep in the pockets of people who wanted to see Don Kane in the Oval Office. Now he was there and Eliot was losing patience with the slowness of his gratitude.

Eliot picked up the spiral notebook he'd pored over the day before. On one page he'd made an elaborate box chart of the possible contenders for the chief of staff job. Appended to each boxed name were smaller boxes designating their contacts and his relationship to each.

He studied it carefully. It was an accurate road map of who owed whom. A lot of people owed Eliot Ives, none more so than Senator George Lowry, his old crony from his days in the Senate. The time had come to call in that due bill. But that would be hard, because Eliot didn't want to owe Lowry *anything*. The two of them had vied for Sinclare, and George had recently intimated that he'd *given* Sinclare up so that Eliot could have her. Talk about rewriting history! George was so full of bullshit sometimes.

Eliot took one more swig of lukewarm coffee and eased himself out of the chaise. He looked over the railing at the stream of rush-hour traffic on Rock Creek Drive below. George was probably in his office by now. What the hell, why not take a shot at him. He'd get him early – make an appointment to see him before the day got away.

He patted his bare stomach, hitched up his pajama pants, and pushed open the sliding glass door. In the semidarkness of the bedroom, Sinclare lay sprawled across the king-size bed, her skin almost translucent against the black satin sheets. God, she was a piece of work.

He felt himself growing rigid under the flimsy fabric of his pajamas. He could call George Lowry later. First things first.

Wednesday, June 7, 1989 – 10:00 A.M.
The White House

For Mark Kirkland it promised to be a brutal day. He started it off with a hangover, avoided his wife, moved on to his normal 9:00 A.M. briefing, and ducked questions and follow-ups there about his own chances of being the next chief of staff. 'I serve at the President's pleasure.' He smiled at what he had begun to consider his tormentors.

'Thank you for asking.' That was on the record. Off the record, his tongue firmly planted in his cheek, he said, 'Sam, I was hoping for a post in Paraguay. I love rain and mosquitoes.'

He gathered his papers and made a break for the door. A *Chicago Tribune* reporter blocked his path. 'Mark, what can you tell me about the FBI investigation of Barry's death?'

Mark blinked. Other than what he'd read in Tim O'Brien's article he didn't know anything, but he couldn't say that. 'Can't comment, Bill. Check me later.'

He made a dash for his office and slammed the door.

'Goddammit!' he blurted out, throwing himself into his desk chair. 'Why doesn't anyone tell me anything around here?' It was a problem almost every press secretary had, and the reason was simple: if the press secretary didn't know anything he couldn't lose his credibility with his peers by lying to them.

He took a deep breath and tried to calm down. Mark had a love-hate relationship with the press secretary job. He took the job, heady with the flattery of having been asked by the President of the United States. He received a lot of good-natured joshing from his journalist pals, but he knew very well that deep down they envied him the limelight, the power, the control over what they knew and didn't know about the most powerful man alive. In the frantic rush of the first days of the Kane administration he had not had time to analyze what the job would do to his relationship with Jan. More subtle but just as damaging was the position it put him in with his father-in-law — one of gratitude combined with an implied loyalty to a man he neither liked nor particularly admired.

When was Jan going to wise up about that old spy anyway? She thought he walked on water. The week he met Jan he was preparing a profile on him for *Newsweek*. Mark had tried to get the ambassador's file when he first came to the White House. In his reporting days he would have killed for that file. Now as White House press secretary he had been able to finagle around the old man's pals at Langley somewhat. The bits and pieces he got suggested Buck led a more thrilling life than James Bond. No wonder Jan never saw her father when she was growing up. He had been up to his ass in espionage at least since Eisenhower, possibly earlier. And Jan believed he was a roving diplomat! This was a man who shipped arms, tapped phones, and negotiated with every flimflam artist from Bangkok to Beirut, yet he was the yardstick by which she measured her husband.

'I told you to hold my calls, Betsy,' he said irritably when his secretary poked her head through the door.

'I am, Mr Kirkland, but your wife — '

'That goes for my wife as well.'

'But she's here.'

'Here? Where?'

'Right outside.'

'Why didn't the gate call?'

189

'They did. I told them it was okay. Wasn't that all right?' Betsy said, cringing.

'It's okay,' Mark sighed. 'Tell her to come in.'

He had not talked to her since their spat in the kitchen last evening. After he had stormed out of the house he had gone out drinking with several White House staffers he'd found in a favorite Georgetown watering hole. He had stayed out very late and left the house early to avoid her. In his way he was trying to make the point that he would no longer tolerate her always bringing her father into their lives. Something had to give or he would stay angry until it did.

He looked up from the pile of papers he was pretending to study. 'Hello, Jan. What are you doing here? Shouldn't you be putting together tomorrow's funeral arrangements?' He was sure she could not miss the coolness in his voice.

'Barbara's taking care of that,' she said. 'Everything is on the computer anyway. My biggest worry is that our transvestite shows up across the street.'

'How's that going?'

'It's been taken care of.'

It felt awkward having her in his office. She looked wonderful, slightly flushed, her hair shining from its morning shampoo. He could smell her cologne clear across the desk.

She carefully crossed her legs as she sat down on the couch. Great legs, he thought.

'Mark, I'm sorry,' she said softly. 'I came to

190

apologize. I hate it when you get mad at me — when you get cold and refuse to fight.'

'Why do you do this to me, Jan?' His voice broke. He nervously cleared his throat. She was intentionally turning him on, damn her. The top three buttons of her rose silk blouse were open, her eyes wide and innocent.

Quickly, Mark moved toward the door and locked it, then flipped a switch that had been installed back during the Nixon presidency by Ron Ziegler, which lit a red light outside his door indicating that he was not to be disturbed by anyone, even the President of the United States!

She knew exactly what he was doing. He had once told her of the 'Ziegler Switch'. She also knew he couldn't resist her.

Jan thought sex solved everything. That was something women never understood. Mark could be angry enough to strangle her and still want to make love to her.

He closed the shutters of the long windows of his office, which faced the West Portico. He moved directly in front of her. Without a word he pulled her off the sofa. He could smell her hair and felt her tight, hard body underneath her clothes.

Suddenly he lifted her skirt. She was wearing her little Miss Muffett pink garter belt with white stockings and black patent leather pumps — just the way they had taught her at St Margaret's, he bet. Those frozen old deaconesses thought it was virginal and proper. It made him hotter than any porno flick ever could.

191

He unzipped his pants and leaned her back onto the desk. Papers, magazines, a mugful of pencils cascaded on to the floor. He wondered if the rumors he'd heard about his predecessors having similar moments in this office were true, but passion interrupted such outside thought. She was pushing herself against him, insistent and yielding, almost begging him to enter her.

He could wait no longer. With a single thrust he drove his erection deep and immediately withdrew. He knew what drove her crazy.

'No, Mark, please,' she moaned. 'Don't go away.' She reached out and tried to force him back inside her.

'Do you really want it?' he taunted softly. Of course this is what she wanted. Getting laid in the White House was like joining the mile-high club, except the membership was far more exclusive. And Jan was excited by being in a special class of anything.

She gasped when he went inside her again. Breathing hard, she was trying to be quiet, conscious of Mark's secretary sitting on the other side of his door.

He pinned her to the desk so that all she could move was her behind. She was grinding into him. He heard her gasp a pleasure sound, and then he came, biting his lip so he wouldn't cry out.

Gently, he pulled her skirt down and slid her off his desk to her feet. Her makeup was smudged, her hair hung in damp strings and stuck against her face. Together, as if someone had pushed a button, they both burst out laughing. They had passed the initiation ritual for a very exclusive little club.

Mark felt like asking her if her father could do that for her. Instead, he said, 'I hope we can keep your father out of our lives for a while.'

Jan's smile disappeared. She stepped back from him and her words came out in a slow hiss. 'You are a total son of a bitch, Mark Kirkland.' She looked away and proceeded to smooth her rumpled skirt, pick up her bag from the couch, and storm toward the door. 'Open the goddamn door!' she ordered.

Stunned at the implied violence in her voice he did as she asked. She shot past him before he had a chance to apologize. He had been crude and heavy-handed, he had to admit. Their lovemaking had simply been a temporary cease-fire.

Wednesday, June 7, 1989 – Noon
La Reine Salon de Beauté, Connecticut
Avenue

La Reine was packed.

Sinclare took one look at the crammed reception area and swept up to the receptionist. The four women ahead of her were Washington matrons who moved away like startled pigeons, cocking their heads in disapproval at Sinclare's bright yellow linen duster, yellow linen boots, and leopard skin print scarf that hung nearly to the floor.

'My appointment was at twelve,' Sinclare said grandly, extending her chin and watching herself in the mirror behind the reception desk. Through the archway she could see Caroline Riggs with a towel on her shoulder being ushered to a heat lamp at the far end of the salon.

Sinclare looked back at the frazzled receptionist hurriedly pawing through her calendar.

'It's going to be at least an hour . . .'

'Excuse me,' Sinclare said coldly, the baby girl dimples dissolving into a mask of outrage. 'Either you honor my appointment right this minute or I'll have to speak to the owner about your work.'

'Excuse me.' The timid voice of one of the manicurists interrupted Sinclare's escalating tirade. 'Miss Bourne is in booth seven and would like to see Mrs Ives.'

'What?' Sinclare turned. 'She's here? Why didn't someone tell me?' She turned and marched down the hall, her boots digging little divots in the thick pink carpeting. She enjoyed putting on her bad girl act. Actually, when driving over to La Reine, she remembered she had forgotten to make an appointment. She slammed through the swinging doors into the booth on the left and flounced into the room to complete her show of rage.

Sinclare had learned her bad girl act from watching other women at Duke's – ladies who arrived without reservations, or wanted better tables, and threatened to make a scene, and got away with what they wanted. She had tried it later and it worked. The next time they treated you with respect, particularly if you had made a scene, for fear it would be a repeat performance. She was pleased that all around town she could find seats at the best restaurants and be rushed to be taken care of at the best shops. Ah, the art of intimidation. Oh well, if it worked, why not?

Actually, she was in a wonderful mood. Eliot had stayed home to make delicious love to her this morning. He was good in bed, and knew how to satisfy her insatiable need for sex.

Echo was lying on her back on a narrow sheet-covered cot. She was wrapped from head to toe in towels that smelled of eucalyptus. 'Sinclare, for heaven's sake, they can hear you yelling in Chevy Chase. What in the world is going on?'

Sinclare plopped down in a plastic chair next to Echo's head. 'Just having some fun.' She smiled.

'Well, how about having some more?' Echo lifted her towel-wrapped head and nodded toward her handbag on the small table near the wall. 'Hand me my bag.'

Sinclare scurried around the foot of the massage table and retrieved Echo's bag. 'Oh my God! You got it?'

'Here,' Echo said, handing Sinclare a rectangular package the size of a book. 'You might just want to cancel everything, run right home, and throw this on the old VCR.'

Sinclare stared at the package and then at Echo. 'It's the Dalton Riggs tape, right?' she whispered.

'Uh-huh.' Echo pressed her index finger to her lips and with the other hand gestured toward the open space between the wall and ceiling over which, they both knew, even whispered conversations could be heard.

'Look, Sin, if the person who gave me this finds out you have it, I'm in trouble. What I want you to do is take it back to the apartment and watch it a couple of times — enough so you can describe it to anyone you talk to. Okay?'

'This is fabulous. Eliot would die if he knew I had this.'

'I wouldn't say anything to Eliot, hon. It would be better for him not to be connected to it in any way. You know Eliot's never approved of dirty tricks.'

Sinclare had wanted to get her legs waxed. To hell with it, seeing the tape was more important. She might really be able to help her husband become the next chief of staff by eliminating his strongest competition, Dalton Riggs. She was about to leave when Echo signaled with her forefinger to come closer.

Echo pulled her toward her and whispered, 'Told you to talk softly in here. These walls are paper. Before you go I want to tell you something else. They put Caroline Riggs over there.' She pointed to the booth beside hers. 'I heard her talking to her hair stylist about her husband being up for the chief of staff job, and you know what she said?'

'How would I, Echo?' Sinclare said sharply, annoyed with the obvious.

'Caroline said something about Eliot Ives being no competition because the President could never appoint him since his wife was such a tramp!'

Sinclare exploded. 'I'll tramp her!'

'Shut up, Sin,' Echo insisted as she reached up to put her hand over Sinclare's mouth. 'Be smart on this one. Go watch the tape.'

'You're right, E.B.' Looking very depressed, Sinclare quickly left La Reine.

In all the years Echo had known Sinclare, she'd never seen her take anything harder than the information she'd just imparted. Maybe she had overplayed it, and Sinclare would figure it all out. The girl was shrewd. No, Echo thought, she had always been shrewder, and able to stay one step ahead of Sinclare. She had given Sinclare a life and shown her a world she could never have dreamed of, and Sinclare had betrayed her. She had married Eliot, and, rightly or wrongly, she felt Sinclare had joined the enemy camp. Sinclare knew too much, and by switching loyalties now became suspect, dangerous, someone with something 'on' Echo and not to be trusted. She had not the slightest qualm about what she had just done. After all, she was a master at survival. Buck always told her that and she believed it as much as she believed in her own acquired power. Sinclare was a threat pure and simple and had to be dealt with.

The eucalyptus fumes from the hot towels she was wrapped in were beginning to make her gag.

'Mildred, take this crap off me now, will you?' she shouted. 'I've got to get out of here.'

Her masseuse hurried into the booth and started unwinding the towels. 'Feeling a bit peckish today, are we, Miss Bourne?' she said with exaggerated servility.

'A little, Mildred, just a little. Dealing with problems always does that to me.'

Driving home Sinclare felt awful. Could she be the reason the President would not appoint Eliot chief of staff? She thought about what Eliot had said as they were lying there in bed this morning just talking – how much alike they were, how they both had to fight for everything. But Sinclare felt more like crying than fighting. She'd always liked that feisty little Texas bitch who was clearly spreading rumors for her husband. Thinking about the tape in her pocketbook made her feel better. Thoughts of revenge were delicious under these circumstances.

Wednesday, June 7, 1989 – 6:00 P.M.
Secret Service, White House Detail,
Command Center
Basement, Executive Office Building

Agent Robert Kadanoff punched the code to unlock the outer door into the Command Center. At last they had some major breaks in the investigation of the events surrounding the death of Bradford Barry. FBI Agent Vincent DeSanto, the FBI's White House liaison officer was enroute to the command post at this moment to give him and his boss at the Secret Service, Dick Riley, a full report.

The Command Center was filled with television screens from the cameras perched around the White House and grounds. It was also the nerve center for the network of sensor pods placed throughout every area of the grounds, and the ultrasonic movement detectors in the White House.

From the blinking lights on the floor plan diagram, Kadanoff could see that both Don and Beth Kane were in the Oval Office. Riley would be giving them an update tonight. The pressure for the President had been relentless, and Kadanoff was sympathetic. Even though Barry and Kane had been close friends there was a danger that Barry had been in some way involved in espionage and compromised. God, wouldn't it be an ugly mess if a political scandal erupted so early in the administration?

DeSanto slipped into the room behind Kadanoff and Riley, and soon the three men were seated at a small conference table off to the side of the command post. They spoke in hushed tones that would not be overheard by the other Secret Service agents who were keeping tabs on the President's safety.

'Thanks for coming over, Vinnie,' Dick Riley

began, pulling a notepad in front of him. 'The boss wants to know what you've come up with.'

'Sorry I don't have a written report, but we haven't had time to pull all the field reports together,' Vinnie apologized as he opened his briefcase and retrieved an assortment of notes and reports.

'Let's see, where should I start?' He paused. 'We've had over a hundred agents out today, across the East Coast, and in Western Europe.' He looked over at Riley, who was taking no notes. Might as well forget the politicking for the bureau, Riley wasn't going to put in any good words for the FBI unless they had gotten results, which they had.

'Let me start first with the voice tape of the woman who called 911. DC Police gave us the original yesterday afternoon. It's standard procedure to tape those calls. We ran a voice print analysis, and then checked it against similar analysis of those we'd done on all the female voices we picked up on the tap we had on Barry. Remember? He was under surveillance during the campaign.'

DeSanto was reading now from his copy of the FBI lab findings. 'It was definitely not Monique Delvay, his French lady friend, nor her former roommate, Nina Estevez, who was killed in a drug deal in Miami. Barry seemed to prefer rather colorful women.' He smiled and returned to his notes. 'The lab also ran some matches through their computers for other counterintelligence potentials. Zip. No evidence of anybody of that

200

nature, so the President has no concerns in this area, as we see it. Looks like it was a romance. Barry had recently gotten divorced, and we're pretty sure he was having an affair with a married woman.'

'No evidence at all of a security breach?' Riley asked as he began to take notes.

'I'll say that's ninety-nine percent anyway. We've discovered no national security problems, but that doesn't mean the President doesn't have some problems. This whole thing came out a little strangely.'

Riley looked up from his pad. 'What are you saying?'

'Well let me tell you what developed with the bracelet.' DeSanto sifted through his notes and reports. 'Here it is. That thing had a total of eight karats, in twenty-three small stones, fourteen-karat gold, estimated value eighteen grand. No, that's not what I want, hang on.' He flipped through a few more documents. 'We found that the bracelet was manufactured locally by a jeweler on Connecticut Avenue named Charles Ernest. Class place.'

'How do you know it was worn by the woman with Barry?' Kadanoff asked.

'That was the first thing we established before we put agents all over the East Coast on the pavement. The hotel desk clerk has never been able to give us much. He was trying to get a plumber to make emergency repairs at the same time as the check-in. The woman paid cash, and we now know she used an assumed name. She was wearing a turban around her hair and large sunglasses. She had attractive features, but he really wasn't paying much attention. He has no recollection of what she was wearing. Today he was shown the bracelet, and he remembered seeing it when she held the top of the registry. It was on her left wrist. He was positive on this and says she was wearing no other jewelry. He remembers thinking at the time that maybe he should give her one of the little cards the hotel has to tell people about the safety deposit box. Then he got distracted by his plumber problem and never did.'

'Interesting.'

'You may find this even more interesting. Charles Ernest made that bracelet for William Buchanan Sumner over a year ago. Ambassador Sumner designed it himself. So we had an agent call the ambassador to see if he'd lost it. He said he'd given it to his daughter for an engagement present.'

'You shitting me?!' Riley said it, while Kadanoff mouthed it. The two men looked at each other as if they'd just been told their mothers were whores. 'Do you know who Jan Sumner is?' Riley asked Agent DeSanto.

'Sure, Mark Kirkland's wife.'

'Are you saying she was having an affair with Brad Barry?'

'We're not saying anything. We don't know yet. We do know it was her bracelet we found in the drain.'

Kadanoff just kept shaking his head in disbelief.

'Let me tell you guys why we haven't reached any conclusions. I said we ran checks on voice prints of all the females who called Barry against the 911 print. Well, he had several calls, while under surveillance, from a female at a number up in Northwest Washington, 973-2021. The voice prints from the lady at that number are close to a perfect match to the lady who called 911, and that number belongs to Dalton Riggs and the caller was his wife Caroline.'

Kadanoff was perfectly still for only a second, then both his hands landed on the table flat. 'No way,' he said.

Both other men were surprised at his reaction, which he explained.

'I know Mrs Riggs. She's just not the type to go around having affairs. She's from a fine old Texas family, and there's about as much chance of her having been in that shower with Barry as me. Besides, it was Jan Kirkland's bracelet.'

'Hey Bob, ease off,' Riley said. 'Obviously, the bureau's not reached any conclusions about any-body. I don't think you need to defend the general's wife.'

'Sorry,' he said, and rested his back against his chair.

'You didn't let me finish on the Riggs matchup,' Vinnie said. 'The lab says while there could be a match, because the 911 caller sample is brief, and because the voice is under stress, they can't be sure. So this is iffy, maybe coincidence.'

'Is that it?' Riley asked, since Vinnie was starting to put his papers back into his briefcase.

'Not quite. Investigations at this early stage can be very confusing, and this one is certainly that. You know that illegal Filipino we've been working with?'

'Right.' Riley nodded, back to taking notes.

'We ran pictures by him. Nothing on either Jan Kirkland or Mrs Riggs. But today he thought he saw a woman walking down Connecticut Avenue who looked exactly like the woman who left the hotel about the time of Barry's death. As you know, that hotel's got a small lobby, and not a lot of traffic on Sunday nights.'

Vincent DeSanto had one sheet of paper in his hand. 'Let me take you through the field office report in summary form: This little fellow was walking to work today. He goes in at one P.M. until nine P.M. every day except Monday and Friday. At approximately twelve-thirty P.M. he's walking down Connecticut Avenue south, toward the Hay-Adams Hotel, and he sees the woman he thinks is the same one. He's scared shitless. This thing's been like a bad dream for him.' Vinnie laughed. 'That last part is not in the report, it's what the interviewing agent told me.

'He doesn't know what to do. The woman had come out of a beauty salon – La Reine, we believe. So he follows her into the parking lot, where she gets into a little red Ferrari. He takes down the license plate number, goes to the public phone booth, and calls the number we gave him.'

'Who's the lady?' Kadanoff asked.

'We traced the car to a Mrs Sinclare Ives.'

'Hey, Vinnie, are you pulling our leg with this whole report?' Riley asked, but without a smile.

Vinnie held up his hands. 'I know, I know. The director asked me the same damn thing.'

'Anyway, we brought Emmanuel into the office and showed him the pictures of Sinclare Danner Ives in our files. Nice-looking gal. And Emmanuel smiles and says that's the woman he saw in the lobby. How could he ever forget such a beautiful woman?'

'You're serious, aren't you?' Riley asked as he scribbled intently.

'Pure coincidence that these three happen to be the wives of men under consideration by the President for the chief of staff job. Obviously, it can't be all three. In fact, it might be that none of them was with Barry last Sunday. We can shoot holes in everything we've got.'

'We understand, but the President is not going to be real pleased to hear all this,' Riley observed.

The three men sat in silence for quite a while. Kadanoff finally broke in, and again he was shaking his head. 'Jan Kirkland and Caroline Riggs, I think, are non-starters. From what little I've heard around town, Sinclare Ives might be a possibility.'

'I sure hope so,' Vinnie DeSanto added, 'because then I can rest easy that Brad Barry died a happy man.'

All three men laughed a good tension-breaking laugh. The meeting ended, and Dick Riley gathered his notes and headed to the Oval Office.

Thursday Morning

Thursday, June 8, 1989 — 8:00 A.M.
The Fort, Foxhall Road

Today, at high noon, was Bradford Barry's funeral service. At least that was one event on the crowded agenda. In the early afternoon, following the service, there would be a reception. Bradford Barry had lived and would die in a very public way. By nightfall, Washington's social life would sparkle anew. There was a cocktail party on the *Sequoia* for some of Washington's money people. And Lady Maubry's 'Party of the Year', as *People* magazine would subsequently dub it, would begin at seven-thirty at the sweeping Sumner estate in Virginia's bucolic hunt country. Nothing short of the death of President Don Kane, the guest of honor, could cancel such a momentous event.

Why was it that big days so often started for Caroline with extraordinarily painful headaches? Her heart pulsed rhythmically and loudly. The only reason she could rise unsteadily and move shakily to the small refrigerator tucked beneath the skirt of her vanity table was the thought that by tomorrow, one way or another, the decision would be made. The President would be over the Atlantic on his way to Moscow, and he would have chosen his chief of staff.

Caroline opened the freezer and removed the iced face mask Polly had given her as a gag gift last Christmas. The card attached had read, 'For all the headaches I cause you.' Some gag. Polly didn't give her headaches. Too much drinking did.

Caroline tied the face mask around her throbbing head, covering her eyes and forehead. She gingerly lay back on the goosedown pillows and let her thoughts roam.

To this day Dalton could not understand her driving need to know things, a need that sprang from her deep insecurity at never having gone to college, of living for two decades in a man's town in a time when women were becoming more important and powerful each year. Every day Caroline opened the paper and saw that women were being appointed to the Supreme Court and to the cabinet and as ambassadors to the United Nations. Once she'd had so many wonderful dreams, but she was no closer today to being part of it all than she had been as a young girl on the other side of her father's closed library doors. Caroline was smart enough to step outside herself and see herself as others saw her. Every morning she awoke and saw a frozen image of what she'd become: one of those Washington wives who was 'just a wife', with the added label of 'a marvelous hostess'.

Beneath that charming, chatty Southern exterior was her driving need to understand, to know what made people do the things they did, and the best way to get straight information was with a direct question or answer. And that's what always got her into trouble, although she never meant to be blunt or rude. Now that she had a beautiful antique-filled mansion, politically significant people were more generous. Some thought her remarks were intentionally funny. The only thing Caroline meant by them was to locate the shortest conversational distance between 'How do you do?' and real gut-level, fundamental, down and dirty details of what made different people tick.

Like most well-born Southern women she had been instructed in the fine art of nano-talk, conversation so airy and weightless that it would propel one of Malcolm Forbes's hot air balloons halfway to Patagonia. But she just couldn't do it. If the earnest gentleman on her right droned on through the bisque to the filet mignon about the restructuring of the national debt, she would finally interrupt and ask him what he thought about the new shrink in town, the one everyone on the Hill was seeing. What would he have said was Henry Kissinger's reason for marrying a woman two heads taller? Sometimes being a bit outrageous was the catalyst for creating a lively, unforgettable party. The man could fall silent, but then again she might get truly interesting conversation going. The sparks could fly; they'd connect and she would learn far more than she had from his whole tedious show-off monologue on world economics. She tried, God knew she tried.

She knew the small white and brown plastic bottles in her medicine cabinet and handbag were testament to her losing battle to be herself, but she considered them temporary 'friends'. Every time she swallowed a gulp of 'pick-me-up' she told herself she didn't really need it. Each pill was just to ease the worry of the moment. She considered stopping in the same inconsequential way she thought about someday getting around to putting China silk drapes in the library or body-waving her hair. She'd get to it, but today's schedule was far too crowded. Besides, you shouldn't make such a serious decision when you're feeling down.

Caroline was not unaware that if she had looked like Bella Abzug or Barbara Mikulski she might be considered profound rather than witty. But Caroline was a pretty little redhead with wide-set emerald eyes and a figure that defied the ravages of the grape and remained only two pounds heavier than in her days as a Pom-Pom girl.

She was sure she had offended people at last night's dinner party, but she couldn't help herself. Deep under the comforting and womblike eiderdown quilt Caroline started to laugh, sending ripples of thunderous pain that moved through her left eyeball, broke into a Y, and shot up into her frontal lobes. A bitchy female lobbyist had asked her if she thought Eliot Ives could become chief of staff. The woman just wanted to see how Caroline would handle such a question. The dozen guests grew silent. Then Caroline carelessly tossed off the remark, 'How could the President risk it, when his

212

wife has AIDS?' Kelso Hunt actually fainted and fell on the floor. How was she to know he'd had an affair with her?

She moved her arm across the broad expanse on the other side of the king-size bed. She wouldn't be torturing herself like this if Dalton were here. She sighed and rolled over. The sheets felt like cool, smooth sand – the sand they had been making love on that night so many years ago when they made Polly. Would all this pressure ever end? Would they ever make love like that again?

Polly. She pulled herself up in bed and pulled off the eye mask. Polly had left a brief note by the phone saying she wanted to talk at breakfast. It wasn't like Polly to leave notes.

She reached for the phone and buzzed the kitchen intercom. 'Rosa, is Polly downstairs yet?'

'Oh yes, ma'am. She took the Jeep up to Rock Creek Park to ride Eagle. She said she'd be back to have breakfast with you.'

Two mornings in a row on that horse, Caroline thought. I wish I had that kind of energy. She slipped out of bed and reached for her pink silk dressing gown. She would dress after breakfast. Right now Polly was more important.

Rosa was pouring her a second cup of espresso when Caroline heard the kitchen door slam. 'I'm in here,' she called.

Polly pushed open the swinging door to the dining room. Her face was flushed, her curly hair damp and matted from her cap. She was wearing her old riding clothes and carried the hard cap under her arm. 'Hi, Mom,' she said breathlessly. 'What a glorious day! I've got to have Eagle's right front fetlock looked at. I think he has a spur.' She threw her cap on an empty chair and surveyed the sideboard.

'You oughta eat, honey,' Caroline cautioned after Polly ignored the plate of croissants and poured coffee.

'I'm a bit off food at the moment,' she said, sitting across from her mother.

'Oh?' Caroline pushed away the *Washington Post*. 'Something wrong?'

Polly stared into her coffee.

'Polly?'

'I'm pregnant, Mom,' Polly said with no inflection.

For a moment Caroline could not speak. Oh, Lord, please don't let this be happening. Not to my Polly.

'I'm sorry, Mom,' Polly said, her voice heavy.

'Oh, honey, it's not like you have to apologize to me. All I care about is that you're all right. Have you seen a doctor?'

Polly nodded. 'Yeah, I went to a civilian doctor in Highland Falls after I took one of those drugstore tests.'

'How far – '

'Four months.'

'Four months! Why so long, sweetie?' Caroline fought the panic she felt spreading through her chest.

Polly stared into her cup. 'I don't know, Mother.

At first I didn't believe it. Then after I missed the third period it was exam week and . . . I don't know, it just got away from me.'

'An abortion at four months is still safe, you know.'

Polly scratched her arm under her fisherman's sweater. 'I know. The thought of it gives me the creeps.'

'But, Polly!' Caroline rose and closed the swinging door to the kitchen. 'What other answer is there? You have your education to consider. You've worked so hard. It breaks my heart to think of you throwing it all away.'

'I don't know, Mom. I'm so confused.' Caroline sat back down and took her daughter's hand. 'Darling, it's not such a terrible mess. We can work something out. I'll call Dr Williams.'

'Mom, don't. I don't need to see Dr Williams. I've seen a doctor. I don't need a second opinion. There are only two alternatives. I either can have an abortion or I can have the baby.'

'Have the baby?' That had never occurred to Caroline. 'Darling, how can your father possibly . . . I mean . . . an illegitimate grandchild. I realize we're almost into the nineties here, but the Riggs family . . .' She was stunned into sputtering. Caroline didn't think she'd ever been at a loss for words.

'Don't forget to include yourself in that, Mom,' Polly said sarcastically. 'Besides, who's talking illegitimate?'

'What?'

'If I have the baby I'll be married.'

'Married? To whom. If you don't mind my prying.' She was caught up in Polly's sarcasm. This was turning out badly. She had to back off. She loved Polly too much to play the outraged mother. 'I'm sorry, Polly. It's just that I'm so upset for you. For us. Now, who is the man? Is it someone at the Point?'

'No,' Polly said.

God, it was like pulling hen's teeth to get this girl to open up. 'Polly?' Caroline said sharply.

'Okay. For what it's worth, he's someone very special.'

'I'd say that's worth a lot,' Caroline said. 'Can I take it that you're in love?'

'Yes.'

'And what about him?'

'He doesn't know about this yet. I don't know how he will react.'

Caroline was disappointed. 'I can't imagine you would love a man who would change the way he feels because of something like this.'

'One never knows, does one?' Polly said doubtfully.

'Do you want to tell me who he is?' Caroline persisted.

'Does it matter?'

'Polly, I love you. Everything matters. And if he's the kind of man you could love, he's a part of this, too.'

'I suppose,' she sighed. 'He's someone I met on the Kane campaign last summer.'

Caroline felt a ping behind her eyes. Please, please don't let it be some married man, some husband of a friend. 'And . . .?' she asked.

Polly took a deep breath. 'He was . . . is . . . a Secret Service man. He sat next to me on the press plane that time Uncle Brad fixed it for me to go on the Midwest swing. We got to talking and one thing led to another. You know.' Polly looked at her mother for the first time.

'I never mentioned him. You and Daddy were so busy. That was when you had the Symphony Ball fundraiser to put together and Daddy was tearing around the country with the Kane people. Anyway, before I knew what I was feeling I realized I couldn't live without him. He came up to the Point last February. That's when he asked me to marry him.'

'I see,' Caroline said, letting it all sink in. 'And do you want to marry him?'

'Yes,' she said. Caroline could hardly hear her. 'I'm in love with him.'

'But, Polly,' she said, trying to keep the despair out of her voice and not succeeding very well, 'what do you know about this . . . uh, this Secret Service man?'

'Mom,' Polly suddenly flushed with anger. 'You should hear yourself, you sound like you're saying this serial killer! I know what you're thinking. A glorified cop, not good enough for your astronaut. Well, he's single and good-looking and graduated from the University of Michigan with honors. His father is the chief of detectives in Cleveland and he has great teeth and clean fingernails. Okay?'

'Just asking, dear,' Caroline said in her most casual voice.

'Come on, Mom, it's me, Polly. I know what a snob you can be.'

Caroline could feel the heat rising in her cheeks. She studied the corners of the thick linen napkin and traced her raised monogram with one finger, first the little C, then the big R, and on to the little H. She was remembering the dancing lessons Polly wouldn't take because she hated the short squirming little boys, and the Laura Ashley dresses with bows she despised and refused to wear. The full scholarship to Smith she turned down over an appointment to West Point.

Her mind suddenly flashed back to a night years ago when Dalton was working late. It was the evening of Polly's fifth birthday. They had waited for him to get home until well past nine. Their birthday supper of Polly's special, and dreadful, 'white food' – creamed chicken, mashed potatoes, corn-off-the-cob, and coconut cake with marsh-mallow sauce – was ice cold. Polly was cranky from a long day, her birthday party, and other children playing with her toys.

Finally Caroline had carried the painfully disappointed child up to her room. She bathed her and dressed her in her favorite fuzzy nightgown, then pulled her onto her lap in the big white rocking chair Constance Maubry had sent before Polly was born.

Caroline sat, quietly rocking, holding her most precious creation in her lap. She pressed her lips into the fat red curls on top of her head and sang 'Itsy, Bitsy Spider.' Before she got to the part about the waterspout Polly said something into Caroline's chest.

'What, Buttons?'

'Only Mommy loves me,' the tiny voice squeaked.

'Honey, don't say that. Daddy loves you more than anything in the world.' Poor baby, Caroline had thought. How could she know how much her father adored her? Like any child, she could only see the immediate moment.

'Does not. Only my Mommy.' She balled her tiny hands into fat fists and ground them into her closed eyes.

Caroline would never forget the feeling that engulfed her at that moment. Dalton had been asked to kill in his life by his government, Presidents Kennedy, Johnson, and Nixon and General Westmoreland, and he did it. Caroline couldn't have done it for them or her country or the flag or God. But for this warm, soft little person she would have killed without a moment's hesitation, with no remorse, fear, or guilt. If anyone ever harmed, threatened, or hurt this creature she would do it with her bare hands.

And this was the way she felt now, even though Polly was grown. Some stranger had come out of nowhere and touched her child, damaging her. Whoever this man was she wanted to kill him.

'Justifiable homicide,' a jury of mothers would say. 'Next case,' the lady judge would command. Her baby would be safe again.

'So what are we going to do, Pol?' she asked with a sigh.

'I don't know yet, Mom. Not till I talk to him. All I ask is that you don't say anything to Dad yet.'

'That I can promise. This is not a week to distract your father.' Caroline tried to push their other problems out of her mind.

'I guess my timing sucks.'

'If you must put it that way.' Caroline grimaced. You couldn't send your daughter to West Point and expect her to speak like a debutante.

'Do you think he'll be named chief of staff?' Polly asked. She seemed eager to change the subject.

'Anything could happen. Mercifully, we'll know by the end of the week.'

Polly pushed her chair back and rose from the table. 'We'd better get dressed.'

'Polly?'

'Umm?'

'When are you going to talk to . . .' She stopped, realizing that she didn't even know the man's name.

'Bob, his name is Bob, Robert Kadanoff.'

'. . . Bob.'

Polly picked up her cup and saucer and headed for the kitchen. 'Today,' she said. 'He'll be at the Hay-Adams reception after the memorial service. That is, if the President comes.'

'What does he have to do with it?'

'Bob's on the White House detail,' she said, pushing through the swinging door. 'We better move it or we'll be late.'

She disappeared down the back hall toward the kitchen. Caroline sat for a long time staring at a middle distance in the lovely room.

Polly was nineteen and in love. Caroline knew. When she was nineteen she was in love. At least the man her daughter loved wasn't already married.

She picked up the *Post* to carry it back to her bedroom. Her eye locked on the first line of an article by Tim O'Brien. '. . . The FBI believes that Bradford Barry was with a female friend at the time of his death.'

Thursday, June 8, 1989 – 9:40 A.M.
US State Department
Office of the Chief of Protocol

'Office of Protocol.' Barbara squeezed her eyes at Jan as she listened to the caller. 'I'll see if she's in. One moment please.' She put the caller on hold. 'Are you in for the *Christian Science Monitor*?'

'I don't think so. What do they want?'

'The same as everybody else. Seats in the sanctuary.'

'Tell them absolutely not. No press inside the church. The reception only and only if they have

221

White House press credentials!' Jan was getting exasperated.

Barbara punched the last blinking button in the line. 'I'm sorry. No press is permitted inside the church. There will be one print reporter and one pool camera crew. I'm sorry. Have a nice day.' She hung up and hesitated before moving on to the next blinking button. 'It takes a true ghoul to be a reporter.'

Jan smiled wearily. It had been a dreadful morning. She had spent a sleepless, restless night. Mark didn't get home until almost midnight again and smelled of beer when he came to bed. She was sure he had been with the White House staffers who hung out at the Class Reunion. She knew he was nostalgic for the old days, the camaraderie of his fellow journalists, standing around in some grungy bar, jacket off, tie pulled down, trading war stories. With them he could relive the happy times of his life before he married Ambassador Sumner's demanding, spoiled daughter. This was the first time Jan wondered if she hadn't forced him against his true will into the press secretary's job. But he'd seemed to want it so much and they had been so crazy in love, and Mark so dazzled by the life Jan had introduced him to. Being a member of the A-list was a big leap for someone who had spent his life nosing around after information that could destroy an A-list career. She swore she'd never have forced him into something he didn't want.

When they started dating there had been rumors that Mark had been keeping a file on Buck Sumner and was preparing a major profile for his magazine. People whispered that he'd killed it when he fell in love with Jan. Jan had dismissed it as typical malicious gossip that was the inevitable result of two prominent Washingtonians dating. They never spoke it. But that wasn't the only thing bothering her. She was still quietly seething over the item her father told her Sinclare Ives had planted in the paper. She might be angry at Mark for preferring to go out drinking with the boys rather than be with her, but she was sure he wasn't playing around. She couldn't forgive Sinclare for planting the item and she couldn't let it go. Somehow, some way she would retaliate.

Jan walked to her desk and picked up the computer printout. The guests were listed alphabetically, each first initial on a separate page. Her eyes landed on the sheet for 'I' and read:

Itoh, Ambassador and Mrs Toshido K.
Itzkovitz, Chancellor and Mrs Solomon G.
Iulo, Reverend and Mrs Davidson L.
Ives, the Honorable and Mrs Eliot

She carried the sheet back into Barbara's office as Barbara was hanging up the phone. 'How long would it take to punch up this sheet again?' Jan asked, showing her the printout.

Barbara looked surprised for a second. 'Oh, I thought you had left for your ten o'clock meeting.' Then reaching for the sheet, she said, 'Gimme, I better do it right now; this has to be over to the White House in half an hour.'

223

'I have one change,' Jan said. She picked up a thick black felt marker. 'Weren't we told that people had to let us know before nine this morning if they would be attending? Secret Service crowd count, all that stuff?'

'That's right,' Barbara singsonged. She missed nothing.

'What time is it?' Jan asked.

Barbara glanced at her Seiko. 'Quarter to ten.'

'Have you heard from the Iveses?'

'Nope.'

Jan reached over and ran a heavy mark through the line that read Ives, The Honorable and Mrs Eliot.

'Something troubling you?' Barbara asked with a smile.

Jan said nothing.

'Oh, that was your father who called. I'm sorry but I told him you'd gone to a meeting. Anyway, he wanted to know if you realized that you'd lost your diamond bracelet. The one he gave you.'

Jan momentarily looked puzzled. Could that be? she asked herself. 'Barbara, I think I feel awful,' she said slowly, then rushed from the room.

Thursday, June 8, 1989 – 10:30 A.M.
Maubry House, Georgetown

Ian Vreen examined his image carefully. He stood
in front of the oval dressing glass in his room in
Lady Maubry's Georgetown mansion debating the
sartorial overkill of a tiny pink rose in his button-
hole. In dress, as in life, God was in the details. He
decided against the rose.

There were only a few things he would not do
for Constance Maubry. Attending funerals was
one of them. Besides, he hadn't cared much for
Bradford Barry. In all his dealings as chief of staff
Barry had endeavored to leave the impression that
his finger was closer to the nuclear button than
was that of his overworked employer, the President
of the United States.

When he thought about it, Ian didn't care for
most of the new White House crowd, with the
exception of Connie's nephew-in-law, Mark Kirkland, and his darling Caroline's husband, Dalton
Riggs.

Though he felt Eliot and Sinclare Ives pushed
the borderlines of vulgarity, he had to admire their
energy. Without their type Washington would be
as dreary as Toledo. What he loved about Sinclare
was her relentless capacity for naughtiness.

The first time he saw Sinclare was at a dreary
State Department reception for the new Russian

press attaché. It was a snowy night, and no one in the room was under fifty except Ian and the bartender.

Suddenly he saw this creature working her way down the receiving line in sheer black stockings and a dress so tight you could read the label on her pantyhose. An odd-looking man wearing bowler's trousers and an ill-fitting jacket accompanied her. He turned out to be her cabdriver, whom she had breezed through security. She was afraid of being stranded on a snowy night and simply invited him to the party as her captive date. When the whispering about it reached Ian's corner of the room he was transported. He introduced himself and asked her to lunch the following day. They had been co-conspirators ever since.

His dressing completed, he dropped into his favorite pose, his left foot turned out, head high, arms folded. Adolphe Menjou, twirl in your grave.

Ah! He knew he was forgetting something. He stepped to the armoire between the windows.

The *coup de foudre!* Lord Tookie Maubry's homburg, good as new. He balanced the hat at a jaunty angle, reached for his walking stick, and admired himself one more time. Perfect!

As he made his way down the curved staircase he heard Connie's voice in the library. It couldn't be Celia with her, she was out doing the marketing.

As he reached the bottom landing he recognized Caroline's Southern lilt. Quickly, he stepped to one side of the double doors and slipped behind the coromandel screen.

At the foot of the stone steps he could see Polly Riggs at the wheel of Caroline's Mercedes. This must be a short visit then.

Damn. It enraged him to be left out. After all these years Caroline still came to Constance with problems, and the problem was usually Dalton.

He fidgeted in the hall trying to overhear. Their voices were too soft to carry. He removed Tookie's homburg and dabbed at the sudden perspiration on his brow. He decided not to interrupt the two women. He would find out soon enough what was going on. Connie could never hide anything from him for long.

Thursday, June 8, 1989 – 10:30 A.M.
The Watergate Apartments

Sinclare held the apartment door open with her hip as she shifted the weight of the shopping bags hanging from both hands and each shoulder. Thank God for the Yves St Laurent boutique downstairs. It had taken her less than an hour to find a complete outfit for the *Sequoia* party tonight, but maybe she'd wear that little dress she'd found in New York. Oh, well, she'd see what her mood was later. But she had found, in addition to an adorable satin jumpsuit, a lime-green linen dress, shoes, a new bag, two ribbon-knit sweaters, and a divine lavender marabou throw.

Her eyes swept the huge living room. Empty. She was safe.

She had been waiting for an opportunity to look at the tape Echo had given her. Eliot and two clients had spent all yesterday afternoon out on the balcony.

She hurried to the bedroom and tossed her purchases far back in her closet. The little red light on the phone machine was winking. She rewound the messages.

Beep. 'Mrs Ives. This is Tilden Morse at UPI, Washington Bureau. We'd like to set up an interview if you and your husband are available later today. Please ring me back at 555-1700.'

Beep. 'Sinclare, are you there, goddammit? Something extremely important has come up. I have to go up to the Hill to meet with George Lowry. Looks like I won't make it to Barry's service. You go on. Watch yourself, for chrissake. Everybody will be there. Don't forget the *Sequoia* party tonight. I'll need my tux pressed. Call the desk, will ya.'

'What am I, the maid?' Sinclare muttered as she took the videotape from the drawer in the bedside table where she had hidden it and slipped it into the VCR. She pushed the start button, and the machine whined and spun. She waited impatiently for the squiggly lines to pass.

Now she could recognize the back of a woman's torso wearing a garter belt and high boots. Other figures were in the picture, but the camera was stationary so the things kept moving in and out of

228

focus. There was no sound and the black-and-white film was grainy and underexposed. Suddenly a male form appeared, naked except for a half mask and black leather gloves. The figure was carrying a whip and seemed to be hitting a shadowy square that looked like a bed. Amateur night at the movies.

No doubt that what she was watching was an S and M party, but the faces were really blurred. The man in the half mask turned toward the camera. Sinclare recognized the broad, straight neck and the beginning of the jawline as the whip came up again. Snap. The squiggly lines began again.

'Was that it?' she asked Echo a moment later on the telephone. In the background Sinclare could hear people talking; she had interrupted Echo in a meeting in her office where she tracked her down. Echo's voice sounded hollow under her cupped hand.

'Yeah, well it only runs a minute or two. What do you think?' Echo whispered.

'Jeez, I don't know, Echo, it looks like him. Where did you get it, anyway?'

'Remember Deirdre?'

'That black girl from Congressman Niediger's office.'

'Yeah. It's her tape. She swears it's General Riggs. I played it a couple of times and I think she's right. As right as she needs to be for our purposes, you know what I mean.'

'All right, so I have the tape,' Sinclare said. 'What do I do now?'

'Perhaps you might have a reporter friend who'd find it useful.'

'Yeah. Then what?'

'Then leave it up to them. Look, Sinclare, I can't talk. There's too many people around. Do what you can. It might just help. You know what I mean.'

'Okay, okay,' Sinclare said irritably.

She was beginning to wish she didn't have the tape, even if it could help Eliot. Right now she had more important things on her mind – the message that had been waiting for her at her desk: 'Mrs Ives, please call FBI Agent Vincent DeSanto, Washington Field Office, 470-3600.'

Thursday, June 8, 1989 – Late Morning
Pennsylvania Avenue and K Street

Ian drove the Rolls, nervously drumming his fingers on the wheel. They had less than ten minutes to get to the funeral service. Lady Maubry sat beside him wearing a gray silk dress, the hem just brushing her ankles, and a gray organza cartwheel hat with a huge gray balloon rose with a pink satin center. Instead of her ubiquitous triple rope of pearls she wore a high pearl choker with an opal-and-diamond clasp centered on her Adam's apple.

He waited until they turned onto Pennsylvania

Avenue before he asked. He had to know why Caroline had been at the house. Now, with Connie rattling on about the party tonight, the weather, and the condition of the Rolls, it was clear that she was not going to share this information. Nonetheless, he pressed on.

'So?' he said brightly as they waited for the light before the traffic circle. He glanced at George Washington Hospital on their right, as he waited.

'Sorry?' Connie said, just fluttering her lashes at him.

'What did Caroline want?'

'Caroline?'

So that's the way it was going to be. 'Yes, this morning?'

'Oh, yes, Caroline. Well . . .' She paused.

'Well, what?'

'Ian, darling, I rather promised it would be a private conversation. Besides, I have something more important to discuss with you.'

They had stopped at the light at Pennsylvania and Seventeenth Street. Ian was all ears, hoping it was truly 'more important' than Caroline's conversation.

'I had a little chat last night with Beth Kane. She called just as I was getting ready for bed,' she began as the big car resumed its journey down Pennsylvania Avenue. 'Beth said that the FBI investigation has been concluded, and while she didn't elaborate, she did say it had revealed more than they'd really wanted to learn.'

'About what?' Ian asked petulantly.

'About I don't know,' Lady Maubry said as she lowered the front sun visor to check her makeup in the mirror behind it. They were approaching the church.

Ian and Constance had spent too many years together for him not to know what she was up to. She'd been mildly annoyed at his pushiness about Caroline, so she was reminding him in her nice way that she was very much in charge of her life. If there was more for him to know, she would decide.

Just as they found themselves confronting a small traffic jam, Constance turned to him and said, 'Ian, darling, would you find out for me where your friend Sinclare was on Sunday evening?'

He sighed inwardly and stared out the windshield as though deafened by his concentration on his driving. Fine, he sulked, she won't let me in on what's going on in her life, but she wants me to spy on my friends. He glanced at her with a thin noncommittal smile but said nothing.

Ian hated anything that had to do with dying. Receptions, on the other hand, meant living people. As soon as he dropped Constance off at St John's, they had agreed, he would wait for her across the street at the Hay-Adams, where she would join him at the reception that was to follow the memorial service.

Sixteenth Street was cordoned off by security people for the President's arrival. A battalion of District Police milled about, waving limousines,

232

cars, and taxis off from making the turn from K Street. He nodded to the familiar faces passing him on the way to the church, grateful that he didn't have to sit there for an hour.

He let her out at the corner of Sixteenth and K Street. By the time he found a parking lot that presumably carried enough insurance to take a six-figure car and made his way back to the hotel he was ready for a drink. He knew that Constance didn't have anything more to tell him. Once again the great lady had been called to action. He willed himself to relax. He knew from past experience that whatever Caroline was up to, sooner or later, he would become a part of it.

Thursday, June 8, 1989 – 12:10 P.M.
The Hay-Adams Hotel Bar

'Ian!' a female voice shouted as he stepped through the bar door. He squinted in the semidarkness, mildly offended. It was so rude to call out in public. He removed his hat as his eyes swept the room. At the far end of the room, at the bar, he saw Sinclare Ives waving both arms. Fortunately there were no other customers. Everyone was outside peering at official Washington arrive at the memorial service.

He couldn't have been more pleased at the chance encounter until he got to within a few feet of where she was standing. Sinclare was clearly drunk, and a drinking Sinclare was dangerous.

'Thank God you're here,' she gasped, throwing herself against his chest. 'The most terrible thing has happened!'

He removed her firmly from the front of his suit. He always felt women shed on him like cats. 'Sinclare, darling, aren't you supposed to be across the street? What in the world are you doing here?'

She was dressed head to toe in black. Her hair was encased in a black velvet turban, emphasizing her high, poreless forehead and prominent widow's peak. Her superb figure was encased in a wide-shouldered, smartly cut black silk suit. She wore no blouse under the jacket and the deep cut of the lapels revealed a distracting expanse of milky white skin.

'I'm so pissed! I was barred from the church,' she hissed, adjusting the single black summer shawl over her left shoulder. 'In front of everybody. I could just die!' He let go of her and she momentarily lost her balance and bumped a passing waiter.

'Let's sit down,' he said, intrigued. He put one hand under her elbow and propelled her back to where she had been sitting. 'You can tell me all about it.'

She must have bathed in Obsession. He had an image of plants wilting as she passed.

There was a half-finished orange-colored drink on the bar by her stool. As they arranged themselves the bartender placed a fresh drink next to it. 'And for you, sir?' he asked, smiling at Ian.

His nerves cried out for far more than the Bloody Mary he'd been thinking about walking back to the hotel. 'A double Tanqueray, bone dry, up, no veggies,' he said. Then Ian swiveled to face her. 'Now, what's going on, my precious?'

'You better tie me down, Ian. I think I'm going to kill somebody.'

'Sinclare, just calm down and start at the beginning.'

'When I got to the church this little prick of a Secret Service man looks for my name. Then he says, "You are not on the list." I mean, I knew there had to have been some dumb mistake, so I tell him who I am again and he says no. Then I tell him who my husband is. He acts like he's never heard of Eliot! I mean, where has this twinkie been? He goes and checks some kind of master list with another guy and comes back and says, "Sorry, no."'

She threw back two gulps of her drink, coughed, and continued, talking as fast as her lips would move. 'All this time I'm standing there. People are trying to get past me. They're hearing all this. I couldn't believe my ears. Someone behind me says, like, step aside, you're holding things up. Do you believe it? They say that to me!' She pointed a long red fingernail toward her cleavage.

'Then I see a network film crew moving in on me while I'm arguing with this turkey. Getting it all down for the six o-fucking-clock news. Ian, I wanted to die!' She pushed the knuckle of her index finger under her right eyelid to protect her mascara from the tears that were reaching the spill level.

Oh, Christ, Ian thought, looking away, if she cries with all that makeup she's going to look like a raccoon.

Sinclare searched in her snakeskin clutch for a tissue. Ian offered his handkerchief, and she blew her nose loudly into it, then made a ball and popped the hand-rolled, monogrammed, pure linen square custom-made in Madeira by blind nuns into her bag.

'Honeybunch, don't cry. I'm sure it was just a clerical error. After all, they put the thing together in two days.'

She shook her head violently. 'It was no mistake, Ian.'

'Where was Eliot while all this was going on.'

'Up on the Hill waiting to see George Lowry. I mean, where are men when you need them?'

Quite. Ian took another sip of his gin and felt himself relax under the slow liquid burn. Sinclare had a problem, but it was of passing note. Poor Sinclare, all she wanted was a little respect. But wasn't that what we all wanted.

His thoughts were interrupted by Sinclare shouting to the bartender: 'Another New York shower.' She giggled and corrected herself: 'Sour.'

Ian studied her. She was swaying a bit on the stool and holding on to the side of the bar with both hands. 'Are you planning to go to the reception?' he asked sweetly.

'You bet I'm gonna go. Ya wanna know why?'

'Why, sunshine?'

'Because I got something here in my bag that I want to get to someone important.' She waved her clutch in front of Ian's face. 'It's a motion,' she hiccuped, 'picture of someone we know doing dirty things. Wanna see?'

Ian was all ears. 'What's to see?' he asked.

She unsnapped her purse and held it open. Inside, taking up most of the space, and next to his best handkerchief, he noted, was a plastic video cassette holder.

'Oooooh, fun! Whatever is it?'

'Cross your heart and hope to die?' she said, leaning very close to him.

Ian nodded enthusiastically.

She pulled herself up, pressed her cheek next to his, and purred into his ear, 'It's General Rambo Riggs doing naughty things with a whip.'

Ian pulled back in surprise. 'Sinclare, you're putting me on!'

'Am not,' she said smugly, with a childish pout, and closed her purse. 'I looked at it this morning. That's what it is, all right.'

'What are you going to do with it?' Ian asked.

'I'm gonna give it to the first important person I see in there.' She gestured toward the general area of the reception. 'Gonna fix that tight-assed wife of his. And take care of my El.'

Ian laughed, then reconsidered. Oh God, he

thought, this was bound to blow up in Sinclare's face. He had to make a move before Sinclare acted. He excused himself to go to the men's room, where he knew there was a pay phone. He would try to reach Eliot on the Hill. It was worth a shot. His first two calls did not locate Eliot and he rushed back to check on Sinclare. If she drank yet another whiskey 'shower' she'd be singing and crying and completely embarrassing herself.

Sinclare was gone. Ian tried Senator Lowry's number once again and remembered that he'd forgotten to ask Sinclare where she'd been Sunday night as Constance had asked.

Nervously, he listened to the Hill operator switching him from place to place in search of Eliot. He tried to still his panic over where Sinclare had gone and the possibility that she might have gotten herself into some kind of real trouble.

Thursday, June 8, 1989 – Noon
The Capitol Building, Senate Side

Eliot had been waiting for George Lowry's return for more than an hour. He didn't mind. At last he felt that he was effectively doing something to get himself the chief of staff job.

These were the senators' offices that constituents never saw. The folks from back home who visited the crowded quarters in the Senate Office Building went away thinking how preciously their great

238

elected officials spent their tax dollars. Indeed, to some visitors it seemed incommensurate with their position that their senator should be asked to work in such a small, cramped space.

As he jumped up to pace Lowry's beautifully decorated and spacious office, Eliot Ives thought what a testament it was to the collective wisdom of the Senate to provide these secret offices in the Capitol Building to the more senior members of the body. Once, Eliot's Capitol office had been two doors down the hall.

If walls could talk, Eliot thought, these walls of the hidden Senate quarters could tell some tales — wild tales, for sure, for there was no safer place to bring a female friend since the Capitol Police prevented tourists and others from accidentally wandering these halls, and tales of deals, trade-offs, and compromises — the things that made lawmaking possible when so many conflicting interests had to be resolved. That was why Eliot and George were meeting — to make a deal.

Eliot had been riding high all morning. The President had called just as Eliot arrived at the office. During the campaign they'd spoken almost every other day, but since the election they'd chatted only superficially. This was the longest conversation Eliot had had with the President since he'd been sworn in. After the President's call Eliot sat back in his high leather chair and smiled with delight. He couldn't have written a more satisfying script. The President had been most apologetic for not calling earlier, but as he quipped with his dry wit, 'I'm still trying to find the damn drinking fountains over here.' Eliot could appreciate that he'd been up to his neck learning the reality of the new job.

'Eliot,' the President had said, 'I know you as well as anyone in this town and owe you a lot for helping me get into this office. Also, I know that I can trust that our conversation will never be repeated.'

'Absolutely, Mr President,' Eliot assured him, conscious of how much added weight this promise carried because the man he made it to was the President.

'I almost asked you to be chief of staff six or so months ago, when we had trouble getting Brad cleared by the FBI, but I'll tell you that story some other time. The reason I've not called to offer you another position is, frankly, that I didn't want to waste you. Almost any of the cabinet jobs would be a waste of your talents, Eliot.'

'Thank you, Mr President, I think.'

'You can smell me coming, can't you, El?' the President asked.

'I'm not sure. Please continue. Flattery is addictive.'

They both laughed.

The President continued. 'Here's the situation. I need your help. George Lowry is a good friend of mine. He's given me a lot of help over the years, but he's giving me a hell of a hard time on my Eastern bloc nations trade bill. He doesn't like it, and he says he'll have to kill it in committee if I send it up. I need to turn George around before I go to Moscow, since the boys in the Kremlin want normalized trade with us. Those fellows over there never seem to understand that we write our laws a little differently than they do.'

'Agreed.'

'Here's what I need. I can accept that for political reasons George can't sponsor my bill. But I need a promise from him that he won't kill it.'

'I understand.'

'You know, El, before I got here I was naïve enough to believe that if you had a good cause nobody turned down the President, particularly an old friend. I was never very good at getting my colleagues to change their position when I was in the Senate, and I've not gotten any better. Have you still got the old touch?'

Eliot understood what the President wanted before he even finished speaking. Deliver George Lowry neatly roasted with an apple in his mouth and he would be appointed chief of staff by the end of the week. Easy to figure out; more painful to do.

The only problem with delivering George would be having to talk to his former friend. He knew his antipathy to George was illogical and purely emotional, and he hated himself for it but there it was: every time he looked at George Lowry he wondered if Sinclare had made love to him with the same passionate attentiveness that she did with him. The fact that Eliot had, in the end, won her mattered hardly at all. He felt no differently today

241

than he had the night six Waldorf waiters had to restrain him from smashing George through a plate-glass window.

Now he looked at the large clock built into the wall – 12:40. The illuminated stars along the top of the clock indicated the Senate vote would be concluding in a few minutes. The crowded calendar had caused the Senate to go into a pre-noon session at eleven, so Eliot and George only had had time for a few pleasantries before three roll call votes in a row.

When the telephone rang Eliot reached across George's desk and answered it, thinking it would be George calling from the Senate cloakroom.

'Senator Ives, is that you?'

'Yes.'

'This is Nancy Raymond in Senator Lowry's office. I'm glad I found you. We have a call for you from a Mr Vreen. He says it's urgent. Shall I transfer the call?'

Eliot was totally bewildered. 'Yes, please do, Miss Raymond.' *What the hell was this all about?* He heard clicking noises, then he barked 'Hello.'

'I'm sorry to have to track you down, Eliot. It's Sinclare.'

'Yeah, Vreen, what's up?' he said impatiently, fully expecting to be told that Sinclare had smashed up his BMW again. The crazy broad drove like a blind woman with a lead foot.

'I'm with her here at the Hay-Adams bar. She's pretty upset.'

'About what?'

242

'She'll give you the details later, but it seems she was barred from attending Bradford's funeral. She's had a bit too much to drink and insists on going to the reception. I thought it better to alert you in case you could talk her out of it.'

Eliot's confusion changed to anger. Barred from the funeral? Why the hell would she be barred? She had as much right to be there as anybody else. And drunk. That spelled trouble any day, anywhere. 'Thanks, Vreen. Can you put her on?'

'I'm afraid I've lost her.'

'Lost her? Wasn't she with you?'

'She was, but she's not here now.'

'Look, Vreen, do me a big favor, will ya? I'm really tied up. I can't get down there for at least an hour. Would you see if you can find her? Send her home in a cab. I don't care what it takes.'

'I'll do my best.'

'I'd appreciate it,' Eliot said. 'And Vreen?'

'Yes, Eliot?'

'Watch yourself. When she's mad she bites.'

'Oh, not true,' he said playfully.

'I'm dead serious. I have the scars to prove it.'

Eliot hung up and crushed out his cigar. Great, he thought, just great. Sinclare, the wild cannon on his ship of life, was loose again.

Thursday Afternoon

Thursday, June 8, 1989 – 1:15 P.M.
Hay-Adams Hotel Reception Room

Half-deaf, paper-thin Abigail Marblehenny, whose husband had been Truman's deputy press secretary, had never heard the word 'cunt' before, at least never so loudly. From her seat along the wall of the Hay-Adams ballroom she plucked at the sleeve of a passing waiter. 'What did she say?' she cackled.

The waiter, who had worked many Washington affairs and had heard everything, looked down at Abigail and said, 'You cunt,' and kept on moving with his silver tray of coffee cups and saucers.

Abigail's companion, who had missed the goings-on by seconds, jumped back clutching her lace jabot and stood slack-jawed with shock at the waiter's unpardonable behavior. What Abigail's companion had missed was a completely fried Sinclare Ives, furious and somewhere over Pluto on New York sours, soaking the pale linen suit of that sweet Caroline Riggs who gave such a lovely luncheon for the board of the Kennedy Center just last week.

Sam Donaldson, Connie Chung, and the new ambassador from Kuwait saw it. It was pretty hard to miss.

247

A stunning, dark-haired woman dragging a black scarf strode right down the middle of the ballroom and tossed a glass of champagne directly on the head of the national security advisor's wife.

They were also witness to Caroline Riggs's retaliation.

Caroline was standing by the side of the cold buffet talking to columnist Tim O'Brien, *Washingtonian* magazine editor Vera Glaser, Caroline's daughter Polly, and President Kane's new domestic advisor.

Suddenly Sinclare broke free from Ian Vreen's firm grasp and stormed through the crowd.

People's attention was first attracted by the sound of Sinclare screaming something at Caroline, something that sounded like, 'Who are you calling a tramp?!'

Several versions of the obscene phrases Sinclare used shot around the room like exploding squash balls.

Senator Konrad (D.-Wisc.) told a *Washington Post* reporter, who instantly yanked her notebook out of her bag, that Sinclare had told Caroline to go 'fuck herself.' The *Washington Post* reporter seemed disappointed that Sinclare had not said something she could print. The wife of the Bolivian chargé d'affaires demurely reported that Sinclare had called Caroline a 'tight-assed bitch' and said something about stealing a hairdresser. The wife of the Bolivian diplomat had heard of violent reactions from Washington wives who had their cooks stolen, but hairdressers?

Nonetheless, both the *London Express* correspondent and White House counsel Tad Michaels recalled hearing 'up your giggie' and speculated on the anatomical location of the 'giggie' until both their wives excused themselves and hurried off to find out more.

Everyone, however, heard the words 'you cunt.'

There was a hushed and horrified silence while Caroline blinked in astonishment, champagne dripping from her hair and face. A widening dark stain began to appear on her dress.

She reached into her handbag without a word and retrieved a linen handkerchief. She wiped her face and hair as a waiter leapt to work on her suit with napkins.

Sinclare just stood and stared at her, clearly shocked at what she had just done. As Caroline replaced her handkerchief she withdrew two dollar bills. She reached out and with one stroke folded them into Sinclare's cleavage.

Both Jack Anderson and Diana McLellan, who had years of experience getting quotes correct, verified that Caroline said, 'Here, Sinclare. I believe two dollars is your price.'

It got worse.

Everyone started talking at once. That's when Sinclare screamed 'you cunt' again, loud enough for Abigail Marblehenny to hear it and inquire.

Fortunately, the hotel manager was standing nearby and swung into action. He grabbed Sinclare by the wrists and held her arms behind her back. Her turban was askew and her black scarf had fallen to the floor and become entangled in several pairs of legs. The champagne on the marble area of the floor had turned it into an ice rink, and the people began slipping about and grabbing at the cloth on the buffet table, and each other to get their balance.

Into this improbable melee jumped two Secret Service agents. Onlookers recognized them as the men who had been checking names at the door of the church. For some reason this seemed to further enrage Sinclare Ives, who began to scream more colorful epithets, which were reported in the next day's editions of the *Post* and the *Times* as 'gestapo gangsters,' 'murdering turkeys,' and '**** heads.'

There was a heated argument as to whether the four stars stood for 'shit' or 'dick'.

Sinclare, with an agent at each shoulder and the hotel manager taking up the rear, was hustled through the astonished crowd and out the side door of the reception room.

Abigail Marblehenny told her companion she wanted to go. She said she didn't know what the town was coming to with this new Donald Kane person in the White House. Later, when she was settled in a comfortable chair back in her vast Kennedy-Warren apartment she would go for her dictionary to look up the word 'cunt'.

Living in Washington, no matter what your age, meant keeping an open, active mind.

Deena Simon had missed all of it and was fit to be
tied. When the juiciest story of the Kane administration was taking place, the city's premier gossip
columnist was seated at the best table in the Jockey
Club sipping a free glass of Moët & Chandon.

Deena had not paid for a mouthful of food or
drink that she could remember. There was no
need.

Her thrice-weekly column filled a space no larger
than the average supermarket receipt and was
loaded with enough blind items and mortifying
innuendo to make or break a marriage or a career.
It was not easy work but she loved it. Still, during
those lonely hours when she contemplated what
she had to do to make her living, she wanted more.
She was comforted by the untidy pile of yellow
typing paper next to her bed. Her manuscript, the
great Washington novel, could someday, somehow
give her a way to real money, and power born of
more than fear. For now, however, being feared
was fine. It meant Deena could have anything she
wanted in Washington and usually did.

Deena had the hair but not the face of folksinger
Mary Travers, bone straight and blonde to her
shoulders. Her long bangs caught in her false

251

eyelashes, causing her to flick her head with annoying regularity. Too many trips to the plastic surgeon in search of Tuesday Weld's nose had left her with a tiny protuberance; it made anyone sitting opposite her feel as though they were staring up the business end of a double-barreled shotgun.

The wide succulent mouth was magenta and capable of language that would make a teamster blush.

'You're shitting me!' she said to Martin, the city's most elegant and erudite maître d', when he whispered the news to her.

Martin lowered his eyes, bowed, and took several tiny steps backward. 'Can I get you anything else, Miss Simon?'

'A phone, Martin. Instantly!'

The public relations man she was lunching with exchanged glances with Martin as a busboy plugged a princess phone into the outlet behind the banquette.

For several minutes she pushed numbers, her wrist-to-elbow bangle bracelets clattering as she worked. She gave her host a running commentary of the event as she gathered bits of information.

The wife of former Senator Eliot Ives had verbally and vulgarly assaulted Caroline Riggs, wife of National Security Advisor Dalton Riggs, in front of God and everybody at the memorial service reception at the Hay-Adams Hotel. Not since Sondra Gotlieb, wife of the Canadian ambassador, smacked her social secretary across the face in front of the entire press corps while in a nervous-hostess frenzy had Deena missed a story of such moment.

'God, I've got to get ahold of Sinclare. I'll get a front-page feature out of this.'

She began to gather up her cloud-light maroon sheepskin Fendi and a handbag large enough to accommodate a complete change of clothes. With some difficulty she dragged her large body and accessories across the velvet banquette and struggled to her feet. 'Sorry, Jeremy, I've got to run. Catch you later.'

She made her way, waving and calling out 'darling, darling' and flicking her bangs out of her eyes, through the tables as her companion stared at the forty-dollar *Homard en Chaud-froid, Blanche Neige* the waiter was placing on the table in front of Deena's empty seat.

As Deena passed Martin at the entrance to the restaurant she brushed her bangs away from her eyes and said, 'Doggie bag that lobster for me, would you, doll-face? I'll send a cab around for it later.'

Martin lowered his eyes again and said, 'Of course, Miss Simon.' Under his breath he said, *'Vache.'*

By the time Deena reached the Hay-Adams she learned the reception was almost over, guests were starting to leave, and that Sinclare Ives had been ushered into the manager's office, slamming the door on several reporters and an NBC camera crew. Deena hammered on the manager's door until he was forced to open it.

She shoved a booted foot between the door and the jamb. 'I'm Deena Simon of the *Observer*. I want to see Mrs Ives,' she said in a piercing voice.

The manager stared at her with a coldness he reserved for people who had forgotten their wallets or pocketbooks. 'I know who you are, Miss Simon. I'm afraid Mrs Ives is indisposed.'

'Deena!' Sinclare shouted from somewhere inside the beautifully decorated office. 'Let her in. I want to see her.'

Reluctantly, the manager eased the door open. Sinclare was sitting on a red leather Chesterfield that faced the manager's desk, cradling a telephone receiver against her shoulder. Her hair was in disarray and her eye makeup smudged as if she had been crying.

'Sinclare, darling,' Deena cooed, oozing her way past the unhappy man, 'are you all right?'

The two women embraced, then released each

254

other and sat down on the couch. Deena looked up at the confused manager and said, 'Would you excuse us please, sir. Mrs Ives is terribly distraught. I'll stay with her until she feels better.'

The manager looked around the room for a moment, decided they'd do no damage to his office, shrugged, and stepped toward the door.

The reporters waiting in the hall pounced on him as soon as he closed the door.

'Can you tell us what caused the incident?' Helen Thomas of UPI asked, notebook poised.

'I'm sorry, I really can't say anything at the moment,' he said, waving them away.

'Is Mrs Ives ill?' asked a man from the *Baltimore Sun*.

'Look, not now. I really can't . . .' The manager fled down the hall as the reporters stood murmuring among themselves.

During the confusion Ian Vreen had again called Eliot, told him of the emergency, and agreed to wait for him in the lobby. He saw Eliot jumping from his car before it came to a complete halt in the small portico in front of the entrance to the hotel. Eliot flew through the door. The doorman stopped his car.

The manager rushed to greet him. 'Senator Ives, I'm Walter Rudolph, the manager director. I'll take you to Mrs Ives.'

'Where is she?' Eliot demanded, fighting to put his coat jacket back on. 'This is the damnedest thing I've ever heard!'

'She's a bit upset. She's in my office with Miss Simon at the moment,' the manager said calmly.

'With who?'

'Miss Simon, from the *Observer*. They seemed to be friends. Your wife said she wanted to – '

'Deena Simon? I don't believe what's going on.' He turned, red-faced, to see Ian standing a few feet away. 'Hello, Vreen, thanks for the call. We've got to get to Sinclare before she launches another one of her unworkable, dangerous schemes. Come on!' He grabbed the sleeve of Ian's coat, pulling him along as the three men walked rapidly in the direction of the manager's office. Suddenly, Ian hit his brakes.

'Eliot,' he commanded with uncharacteristic authority. 'Come over here. I must speak with you privately for a moment.'

Sinclare curled her legs up under one thigh and made herself comfortable. It wasn't often that she had the undivided attention of one of the more important women in Washington. This was an opportunity not to be missed.

'Now,' Deena said in her most confidential voice, 'tell me exactly what happened, darling. I'm sure it wasn't your fault.' Flick, flick.

Safe for the moment, Sinclare snuggled into the corner of the manager's sofa. She was delighted to see Deena. Deena was one Washington reporter who had proved she couldn't keep a confidence. She could circulate a story faster than a full-page ad in the *Washington Post*.

Sinclare patted the cushion next to her. 'Deena, where have you been?' she asked, smiling at her. To Sinclare, the woman had always looked like an enormous sheepdog. She wondered why she didn't fix herself up. Never mind, it didn't matter; she was useful. 'I was looking for you at the reception. Then I saw Caroline Riggs.'

'Darling, I heard! What in the world happened?'

'I don't know what got into me. I guess I just freaked at the sight of her.'

'But why, sweetheart.' Deena whined as she fidgeted with the clasp on her huge handbag. 'What did Caroline do?'

'Deena, I have to tell you something very important, but you've got to promise not to tell a living soul this came from me.' Sinclare laid her hand on one of Deena's linebacker shoulder pads.

'Of course, love. You don't even have to ask that. You know I'd die before I'd give out a source. What is it?' she cooed, her tiny eyes peering out from under Miss Piggy lashes.

'Eliot's going to be here in a minute, so I'm going to give you the bare bones.'

Deena frowned with concern. 'Can I take notes?'

'No, no, no,' Sinclare said, frantically waving her hand back and forth as if to erase the words before they were spoken. 'I've seen a videotape of Dalton Riggs. He's with two women, naked, and doing something with a whip.'

Deena gasped. 'Wait a minute, I want to lock this door,' she said, getting to her feet rather ungracefully.

* * *

257

Jan missed the actual scene at the reception but saw the commotion of Sinclare being rushed from the room. People were crowding around Caroline, shielding her from view.

Aunt Constance was standing off to one side right next to old Mrs Marblehenny and her companion. Constance had offered to take the ladies home, but all three women were still craning their necks to see what was going on.

'Aunt Connie,' Jan called.

'Jan, darling. Come over here,' Constance called back.

Jan reached her side and they both turned to look. 'What in the world is going on?'

'Darling, it was so bizarre,' Constance said, clearly enjoying the excitement. 'Something about Caroline's expression seemed to have incited Sinclare Ives. Sinclare called her some awful names.'

'Why would she do that?' Jan asked, puzzled.

'Well, Ian was in the bar with her earlier. He said she was quite drunk. She's been barred from the funeral and was drowning her humiliation when he showed up.'

Jan froze. 'Oh, no,' she whispered.

'Darling, what's the matter? You look terrible.'

'I think I know what happened. Oh, Lord, let me find out. Aunt Connie, I'll see you tonight at Winterberry.'

'But dear . . .'

Jan pushed her way back through the crowd and out into the lobby. She spotted a Secret Service man standing in the corner. 'Hello, I'm Jan Kirk-

258

land from Protocol. Would you happen to know who was at the door at the church? Who had the guest list?'

'Why, yeah, ma'am, I was.'

'Was there some problem with Mrs Eliot Ives?'

'You might call it that,' he said, maintaining an agent's Easter Island mask.

'What happened?' Jan asked, feeling her hands go clammy.

'Mrs Ives's name was not on the list. I couldn't let her pass.'

'What did she do?'

'She wasn't real happy, ma'am. She, uh, used some strong language.'

Jan paused. That was it. She must have figured out that she was deliberately left off the list. She came over here to the bar and got drunk. Why she took it out on poor Caroline Riggs was beyond her. 'Did anyone see? I mean, there wasn't a big scene or anything, was there?'

'Well, there was a television crew right behind her. They kept rolling. Yeah, I guess you could say people saw it. We checked with the White House. They had the Iveses on a master list. Someone must have taken her name off.'

'Thank you,' Jan said briskly, 'thank you very much.'

She turned and nearly ran to the ladies' room. Oh, God, she thought, they're going to find out it was me. How could I have been such a jerk? She felt a wave of nausea rush over her and leaned her

259

cheek against the cool wall of the booth. How am I going to explain this one?

Liars were good copy.

Beautiful, ambitious Washington wives with dubious backgrounds who lied were even better copy.

Deena Simon would bet her secret source at the closed-to-the-press Alfalfa Club dinner that Sinclare Ives had just spent the better part of the last hour lying through her opalescent teeth right into Deena's trusty hidden tape recorder. A miniature microphone was disguised in the clasp of the handbag that never left her lap. She hooked her thumb under the top of her girdle to relieve the pressure and dusted the cigarette ashes off her voluminous linen tent.

Deena glanced at herself in the mirror behind the door of the manager's office, unlocked it, and raked her long fingernails through her bangs. She flicked them once, twice, and charged through the door and down the hallway.

Ah, the Muskie syndrome, she smiled to herself. A man with political ambitions could wheel and deal throughout his entire career; his hand could be clawing at the very last rung of the slippery political ladder, and then one ill-timed incident, one fleeting act involving his wife, and he'd be on his ass by the time the morning paper hit the doorstep.

Deena liked that. It was what kept her going. A lot of female reporters in town balked at covering

260

the social side of politics, thinking it demeaning fluff, but Deena knew better. The real story at the heart of politics and male power was their wives and lady friends. Just ask Gary Hart. All the rest was tax policy, arms control, and international flimflam.

Seeking and, if need be, causing domestic disaster, professional destruction, humiliation, and personal pain was what interested Deena. She did not care that her work didn't make her popular. What was important was to be feared. It was her power base, for now.

As she lumbered through the revolving door, the immaculate doorman snapped to attention and tapped the visor of his cap. 'Good afternoon, Miss Simon,' he said. 'May I – '

'Cab,' she snapped, stepping in front of a waiting couple. Having the doorman hail a cab meant a tip, something Deena spent a lifetime letting other people do. She threw herself into the first taxi in line. 'Press Building and move it,' she barked, slamming the door on the hem of her dress.

The doorman stood smiling as the cab pulled away with a three-foot hunk of linen flapping from under the closed door.

Deena was anxious to get to the club. The taproom would be buzzing with variations of the verbal and champagne brawl between the wives of the President's men.

* * *

Jan leaned against the cold metal door of the ladies' room booth and took several deep gulps of air. She had to get a grip on herself. She could see a pair of alligator pumps under the door and hear water running in the sink. She opened the door a crack and breathed a sigh of relief. No reporters. The woman brushing her hair at the sink was a trusted friend.

Judy Lowry, the slender, stylish second wife of the senator, was a veteran of the publicity wars herself. She had met George Lowry when he came into her fashionable boutique in Old Town to buy his secretary a Christmas gift. That led to a stormy romance, and eventually George left his twenty-year marriage and teenage children in a conservative New England state to marry her. Jan had stuck by Judy when most of the wives muttered 'home-wrecker' and wouldn't invite her to parties or dinners with George.

'Hi, Judy,' Jan said, stepping out of the booth. 'Boy, am I glad to see you.'

'Hey, Jan,' Judy said cheerfully. 'How're you doing?'

'Today has not been my day,' she said, slowly shaking her head.

'I seem to have missed all the excitement. What happened at the reception between Sinclare and Caroline Riggs?'

Jan took one more deep breath and squinted at herself in the mirror. 'Please, I'm pretending it never happened.'

She didn't like what she saw. Her face was gray.

What little makeup she'd put on had worn off. Her hair hung in damp strands around the side of her face. She started splashing cold water on her face.

Judy moved closer. 'Are you okay. You don't look so hot.' Judy had heard all the hushed gossip at the reception about Brad Barry's last tryst. Looking at Jan made her ask herself, Could Jan have been the woman? She didn't think so, but anything was possible in Washington.

Jan reached for a paper towel. 'I just felt a little faint for a minute. I'll be all right.'

'Come and sit down. I haven't seen you for weeks. I've been seeing Mark all over the paper lately. I'm dying to know what's going on.'

Jan dried her face with the rough towel. 'Have you got any makeup with you?' she asked. 'I left everything in my bag at the checkroom.'

Judy rummaged around in her purse. 'Sure, here.' She handed her a lipstick, compact, and comb. 'Why don't you let me get you something. Coffee? A Coke?'

Jan shook her head. 'No, really, Judy, thanks. I'll be okay.'

Judy walked with Jan to the couch in the foyer and sat down beside her. 'What has you so upset? Certainly not those two women.' She gently probed, as a friend, to see if Jan wanted to open up to someone she knew she could trust.

Tears began to well up in Jan's eyes. All she could do was nod her head.

'Jan Kirkland, don't be a goose. That wasn't

263

your fault. Sinclare Ives is an uncontrollable lunatic, you know that. Absolutely everyone said how lovely everything looked. I think you're amazing to have put this whole thing together on such short notice.'

'I had a lot of help, Judy. The White House did the reception. We only did the guest list. But that's not it,' she said. 'You don't understand.'

'What's to understand?'

Jan blew her nose. Speaking from behind the tissue, she said, 'No. I think she was furious at something I did.'

'What in the world could you do to someone like Sinclare Ives?'

'Judy, I've got to confess to someone.'

'You know it won't go further than here.'

'This morning, at the office, I deliberately took Sinclare's name off the guest list.'

Judy shrugged. She thought back to when she started having an affair with George, a married man, and how slow she was in telling anyone – how at first she shared little unrelated things with friends, to build the bridge of trust a bit at a time, so that it was strong enough to carry the weight of her big secret. Judy would help her friend build her own bridge.

'That's your guilty secret? Big deal. There's nothing that says Sinclare had to be invited,' Judy added with reassurance.

'That's not the point. I did it out of spite. She planted a story in Deena Simon's column that had me really mad. I shouldn't have used my job that way. If the press gets onto it I'm out of a job, not to mention what the publicity would do to Mark's chances of becoming chief of staff.'

'Ah hah! So you do want him to get the job.'

Jan stared at her friend. Suddenly, she realized how much she wanted him to have the job.

'So what have you done to help Mark?'

'Used my job to one-up Sinclare Ives. Aren't I smart?' Jan said, pounding her fist against her thigh in anger.

'I think you're blowing that all out of proportion. So what if you made a clerical error in the rush to put this thing together in two days? Perfectly human. If the press gets onto it just admit it and shrug it off. And you know what else I think? I think you want Mark to get this job so badly you're losing your perspective. If I wanted George to get something I'd be looking around to see who I knew that could help him.'

Jan stared at her wide-eyed. 'You mean actively campaign for him?'

'Well, I wouldn't rent a billboard, but look, Jan, you've got a lot of powerful connections. Start using them.'

Jan thought for a minute. 'You know my dad got him appointed press secretary.'

'So? Just shows you how powerful your father is.'

'What I mean is, I don't think Mark's real happy in the job. More and more I feel I pressured him into it. I'd be doing the same thing with the chief of staff job. What if he got it, hated it, and blamed me?'

'Why don't you and Mark take a bottle of wine, crawl into bed, and talk to each other, damn it!'

'That would be tough at the moment. We're barely speaking.'

'Oh, great.' Judy threw up her hands. 'Look, kiddo, who's your best friend? Husbands don't count.'

'Hmm. Next to my Aunt Connie, I'd have to say my dad.'

'Okay, here's my advice,' Judy said, opening her purse and handing Jan her compact again. 'Get yourself together, call your father, and tell him you're coming to see him.'

'Now?'

'Right now, if he's available.'

'Oh, he's available. He never leaves that mausoleum up on Kalorama Road.'

'Then beat it. You need to sort yourself out, sweets. And fast. A shot at the second most powerful job in the world is a high-stakes game, and you're not even at the table.'

Jan sat very still and digested everything Judy was saying. She was making sense. She did need to talk to her father. He would tell her what to do. He always did.

Each time Eliot reached the edge of the oriental rug in the manager's office he gave the fringe a vicious kick with his custom-made glove-leather shoes. 'Why the hell were you even talking to that woman?' he roared.

Deeply engrossed with drawing a new lip line, Sinclare said, 'I dunno,' through the perfect O of her mouth.

'I dunno,' Eliot mimicked. 'You've got to know she'll cut my balls off with a rusty razor. She's done it before!'

Sinclare recapped her liner pencil and dropped it and her jewel-encrusted compact into her bag. They nestled into Ian's handkerchief. 'Get off the cross, Eliot,' she said calmly. 'Deena's my friend.'

'That snake is nobody's friend and don't you forget it.' He rolled his cigar from one corner of his mouth to the other when he spoke, giving his words an odd, undulating sound. 'Am I right, Vreen, or am I right?' he asked, turning to Ian for support.

Ian had been listening to the two of them go at it for the last ten minutes, waiting for the appropriate moment to leave. He elaborately cleared his throat. 'He's probably right, precious, she is not known as a truly trustworthy person.' He had hoped to stay out of this whole business, but Eliot had made him stay – for an audience, Ian was sure. 'Eliot,' he said pleasantly, 'perhaps you should give Deena a call. Chat with her about her vacation plans, if you get my drift.'

'Huh? Vacation? Why should I give a damn about her vacation?'

'Perhaps the offer of your condo in Charlotte Amalie would interest her.'

267

'No way, Vreen. I don't play those games. I like all the cards on the top of the table or I'm out of the game. I'll figure out another way to get her to kill the story.'

Eliot paced the floor a few more times. He didn't want to confront Sinclare with the information Ian had given him outside until he had more control over the situation. 'Uh, listen, Vreen, thanks for your help, hear. I appreciate it.'

Relieved to be dismissed, Ian stepped to the couch and gathered up his gloves and Lord Maubry's homburg. Eliot sounded genuinely grateful. That was a change. The husbands of his women friends almost always hated him. He supposed they had good reason to – he knew all their secrets.

Sinclare rushed to kiss Ian on the cheek. 'Thank you, darling, for the moral support. Can I call you this evening?'

Ian hesitated. He would be driving down for Connie's big do for the President at Winterberry. She had never even considered inviting the Ives. It served no purpose to bring it up now. Sinclare had had enough humiliation for one day.

'Try me, hon, but I'll probably be out.' He smiled and gratefully moved toward the door.

As Ian entered the lobby, Jan Kirkland was standing by the main entrance door with George Lowry's smashing wife.

'Good afternoon, ladies,' he said with exaggerated grandness, sweeping his homburg in an arc. 'Have we all had an exciting time?'

268

'More than we can stand for one day,' Judy said to Ian, her hand cupped under Jan's elbow.

Ian noticed a long black limousine with official government plates idling at the curb.

'Can I drop either of you someplace?' Jan asked them as they pushed through the revolving door. 'Might as well take advantage of our tax dollars.'

Ian hesitated. Connie had the Rolls. She had scooped up a shaken Mrs Marblehenny and her companion and was probably applying cold compresses to their throbbing temples. Riding in a State Department limo was acceptable transportation.

'Thank you, Jan. I'll hop a cab,' Judy answered. 'I'm late to pick up my dress for tonight.'

Jan's shoulders drooped at the mention of Connie's party. 'Oh, darn, I haven't even thought about what I'll wear. You going long or short?'

'Long, of course, darling. Your aunt would expect nothing less,' Judy said, signaling the doorman for a cab.

'Thanks, pal. Now along with everything else I have a fashion crisis.' Jan gestured to Ian to get into the limousine as the driver patiently held the door.

The three friends blew each other kisses as Jan and Ian slipped into the darkened elegance of the huge car.

When the limousine pulled out into Sixteenth Street traffic Jan spoke to Ian without looking at him. 'I need to talk to you, dear.'

'Oh?'

She turned to face him. He was startled by what he saw. Jan had always looked like a soft little girl. Now her chin had character and her voice was strong. 'I'm going to Daddy's. I have some sorting out to do.'

Jan leaned back against the plush headrest and lowered the window between them and the driver. 'Drop me at my father's, would you, David, and then take Mr Vreen where he needs to go.'

The driver raised his hand in acknowledgment as Jan pushed the button to raise the window again. She might put on a façade of calm determination for Judy and Ian, but inside she was churning. Within the past few minutes she had recognized what she was really feeling — exhilaration.

This was why Washington excited people so! When power beckons, all but the emotionally numb follow, at whatever cost to their comfort and their private lives. She wanted Mark to be chief of staff. She wanted him to have everything that mattered. She was sure that if events had not been rushing headlong at them — if they could do what Judy suggested, take a jug of wine and crawl into bed together — she would discover that Mark wanted it as badly as she did.

Her father knew the intricate ways of gaining power. She couldn't wait to talk to him. She knew her eyes were sparkling; her body felt alive, charged.

As the limo drove into the underpass below

Dupont Circle, Ian drummed his fingers on his knee. 'I'm waiting,' he singsonged.

Jan turned to him. 'Sorry, love. I guess I was working out how I would put this.'

'We'll never know unless you do,' he teased.

'Okay, how's this? I'm going to ask Daddy to get Mark the chief of staff job.'

'Wham!' Ian said, lightly smacking his forehead with an open palm. 'Just like that, history is made.'

'I'm not kidding.'

'I believe you. I haven't seen you like this since you brought Mark home to meet the family.'

Jan laughed, remembering that weekend. 'Was it that obvious?'

'It wouldn't have been if you'd let go of his hand at some point.'

'Oh, Ian, stop.'

'Long enough for the man to eat dinner at least,' he giggled.

'I was so in love,' she said softly. 'I was afraid he'd get away.'

'Well, he didn't, and clearly you are still in love or we wouldn't be taking this ride, right?'

'Right.'

'What do you think the ambassador will say?'

'I'm sure he'll have some ideas.'

'Have you discussed this with him at all?'

'Not really, with the funeral and all I haven't had a chance. I spoke to him the other morning, but I was so crazed I didn't bring it up. Anyway, I wasn't nearly so sure of what I wanted then.'

'And you are now?'

271

'Dead sure.'

'What if he has another candidate in mind?'

'Don't be such a cynic, Ian Vreen,' she scolded. 'Daddy adores me. He'll do anything he can to help.'

Thursday, June 8, 1989 – 2:30 P.M.
Kalorama Road

There was no need to call ahead. Jan knew he was always there in the afternoon, doing whatever it was he did on his five telephone lines, his computers, and his telex machine.

She seldom visited him at the gloomy four-story house. It had never been home to her. She had always preferred the gaiety and comfort of Aunt Connie's house in Georgetown or the farm. Since her marriage she had avoided coming 'up the hill', as her father referred to it, more than ever. The place was ominous. Most of the rooms were closed off, lending an air of secrecy that made her uncomfortable.

As the limo pulled up in front of the house Jan squeezed Ian's shoulder. 'Wish me luck,' she said.

'Nothing but, my peach. You can tell me all about it tonight. You are coming out, aren't you? Long or short.'

'Of course. Hopefully to celebrate. Don't say

272

anything to Aunt Constance, okay? This is our secret for now.'

She was about to push the doorbell a second time when Mrs Crackney smiled out through the crack in the door. 'Hello, Miss Jan,' she said brightly. 'I can't believe it's you.'

'Hello, Mrs Crackney. Is my father in?'

'Of course. He's upstairs on the phone. Come in! Come in! He'll be so pleased to see you,' she chirped.

Jan wondered exactly what Mrs Crackney did. Her father ate at his club. She certainly didn't clean, she thought, noticing the dust on the hall table, a plant long dead drooping underneath.

'I'll tell him you're here,' the housekeeper said, starting toward the stairs.

'Please don't bother,' Jan said. 'I'll trot on up and surprise him.'

Mrs Crackney looked relieved.

Buck Sumner made his working headquarters at the back of the second floor. The large paneled room looked out on an overgrown garden.

Jan climbed the wide staircase, her footsteps muffled by the frayed carpeting. The second-floor landing contained the only bright spot in the house. The tiny alcove outside her father's office was the battle station of Buck's loyal, longtime secretary, Belle Auslander. It was brightly lit. The windowsill behind the antique desk held a lacquered bowl of daffodils from Belle's apartment

273

balcony garden. The plastic cover on her high-tech typewriter signaled she was out running errands.

Jan paused. On the corner of the desk, next to the sophisticated tape machine on which Belle monitored all of her father's calls, stood a silver-framed picture of Jan in her cap and gown with her arm around Belle. She felt a tug of guilty gratitude to Belle for all the years of sending birthday cards, notes of encouragement, and gifts, for each contained a note from Buck in Belle's distinctive handwriting. Jan promised herself she would be a better friend.

She could hear her father's muffled voice on the telephone. Then she heard the receiver drop into place and the click of the tape recorder turning off. She rapped gently on the side of the door. 'Daddy, it's me,' she said. 'Can I come in?'

He was seated at his huge desk, his feet on a stack of papers. Buck Sumner snapped his feet off the desk. He paused for a long moment that surprised Jan, for he seemed lost in thought. Then he gingerly stepped around the desk with both arms spread wide. Engulfing his daughter, he squeezed her until she giggled and playfully begged to be released.

'My, my, what a surprise!' he boomed.

Jan settled into the Hitchcock chair with a Harvard seal decal on the back. 'Don't you look splendid!' she said, taking in his double-breasted blazer complete with its ancient Knights of Malta crest and custom-made brass buttons. His shirt was dazzling white and he wore a gray-and-blue striped tie. She was used to him working in an open shirt and drooping Henry Higgins cardigan.

At well past sixty, he was still one of the best-looking men she knew. She remembered how her heart would nearly stop when she saw him coming toward her at school, his great long legs striding across the lawn, his coattails and scarf flying behind him. His hair was as silver as it had been coal black in his youth. Not a hair of it had left the edges of the Cary Grant hairline. If anything, it was fuller and more luxuriant.

He buttoned his blazer and tugged at it, straightening his shoulders as he received the compliment. 'Why thank you, my dear. Sorry I couldn't make Barry's service. I had a luncheon appointment I couldn't cancel,' he said, walking back behind his desk and sitting down. 'Now, how did the reception go? I heard some rumblings at the club about Ives's wife getting into a dustup with Caroline Riggs. What was all that about?'

'A minor embarrassment. Hopefully, it will blow over.'

'Oh?' he said, his black eyebrows rising with interest. 'Perhaps the ladies are getting edgy about this chief of staff business.' He smiled. 'Now, to what do I attribute the honor of your visit?' he said grandly.

She arranged herself in the chair so that she was sitting absolutely straight. 'It's about this chief of staff business,' she replied, making quote marks in the air.

'Somehow I'm not surprised.'

'Daddy, I need . . . we need your help.'

'Mine?' he said, too innocently.

'Well, we've been under a lot of stress lately and I'm convinced it's because of Mark's being mentioned for the job. I've got to help him. I know he wants it. I'd like your advice on working out a strategy. Perhaps, for a start you might put in a word for him with the President.'

'I see,' Sumner said, reaching for a meerschaum pipe in a holder of several by the telephone. He began an intricate ceremony of filling it from a brass canister on the windowsill, tamping it down, and lighting it several times before it caught. Jan knew the routine and had come to recognize it over the years as a stalling device.

She waited. She could see he did not share her excitement.

'If I had to estimate your Mark's chances, I'd say they were not good,' he said finally through a cloud of blue-gray smoke. 'I'd say he's the fallback candidate, if the others falter.'

'Do you base that on anything other than instinct?'

'No, not really.'

'But would you make a call for Mark?'

The ambassador chuckled. 'You overestimate my influence, Janet.'

'I don't think so,' she said firmly. 'And I don't think the President does either.'

The ambassador took another long pull on his pipe. Jan could not tell from his expression what he was thinking. 'I admire you for coming here to plead Mark's case, Jan, but I'm afraid I have to disappoint you. I can't do what you are asking me to do.'

Jan didn't think she heard him correctly at first. Perhaps he said 'can' and the stem of his pipe slurred his speech. 'I'm sorry?' she said.

'I said I can't do that.'

'What? Call the President?'

'I can call the President day or night.'

'Then you mean you won't give your support to your own son-in-law,' she said, trying to control her anger.

'That's what I'm saying, but not for the reasons you may think.'

'Daddy,' she said, struggling to keep her voice under control, 'don't you want Mark to be the next chief of staff? I don't understand.'

Now she wished she hadn't come. Not only was he going to turn her down, but he was going to attach some unpleasant lecture to it. Whatever his reasons, she didn't want to hear them, but she knew it was too late.

'Jan, I have received some information that I had hoped I could avoid mentioning to you. I think you should know, if you don't already, that there was an investigation into Bradford Barry's death.'

'I saw something in the *Post*, but what has that got to do with Mark, for God's sake?' Her cheeks burned.

'Bradford Barry was not alone when he died.'

'That's a juicy piece of gossip, Daddy, but I

don't see what it has to do with Mark's career, or my life, for that matter.'

'You don't?' he said.

'So Bradford Barry was having an affair. Not a major Washington scandal for a divorced man.'

His look of reproach intensified. 'My dearest girl, I didn't want to talk about this so soon, but now that you are here I have to tell you that this is as uncomfortable for me as it must be for you.'

'Why don't you tell me what is making you uncomfortable? Perhaps I can help,' she said with exaggerated patience.

Her father put his pipe in the big crystal ashtray bearing the presidential seal. He had a collection of them from an array of presidents. He folded his arms and looked directly at her. 'Jan, did you get my message about the diamond bracelet I gave you when you got engaged to Mark?'

'Yes, and there must be some mistake because it's not lost. It's my best piece of jewelry and it's at home.'

'When is the last time you wore it?'

She tried to think through the confusion his line of questioning was producing. 'I don't know. I only wear it when I really dress up. I think the last time I wore it was in January, to the inaugural ball. Why do you ask?'

Buck Sumner swiveled his chair, tenting his fingers. He stared out the dusty window for a long time, then turned and faced Jan again. 'The FBI found your bracelet in the bathtub drain in the suite where Barry died.'

'My bracelet! How in the world do they know it's mine?'

'They checked the jewelry shops around town. It's routine. They discovered it came from Charles Ernest, the jeweler where I had it made. Jan, it is undoubtedly yours. You can imagine how I felt when the FBI called me with that bit of news.'

'I'm sure there's a simple explanation, Daddy. I'll check my jewelry box. Perhaps I lost it. It might even have been stolen.'

'Possible but not plausible,' he said. His eyes were level with hers. They were as cold and black as she had ever seen them. 'Jan, I have to ask you this. Were you with Bradford Barry when he died?'

She wanted to laugh, join him in the joke, but as she looked at his expression she knew he wasn't joking. 'You . . . you, don't think I was really with him?'

He waited a long time to answer. 'Everything is possible with women, Jan.'

Jan's mouth fell open. 'Then you do think it was me! Daddy, how can you be saying this to me?' Hot tears sprang to her eyes.

'I can see why you are pleading Mark's case. There must be a good bit of guilt involved here.' He leaned across the desk and poured whiskey into an empty glass. He offered none to his daughter.

In the fractured light from the leaded window he no longer looked like the elegant, influential ambassador. This man accusing her of adultery, maybe even murder for all she knew, was a dangerous stranger, an enemy she hardly knew. She

279

had always assumed that because he gave her material things he treasured her. But it was Belle who bought the presents with his charge card. It was Belle who came to her graduation. The ambassador was in Saigon and cabled congratulations. It was Belle and Aunt Constance who arranged for her wedding and cried when she and Mark drove off on their honeymoon. A mere request for help had turned him into a nightmare.

He took a long pull at his drink. 'At least you're one up on your mother. I'm sure she didn't feel any guilt at all.'

'My Mother? I don't believe this! You haven't mentioned her since I was a child.'

A small vein in the side of his head was visibly pulsating as he avoided her stare. 'It's been my experience that the apple doesn't fall far from the tree.'

Jan gripped her bag and stood up. 'I'm sorry. Somehow we aren't communicating. I'm asking you for help. Not only are you refusing it, you're accusing me of something I didn't do, and speaking about a mother I hardly remember. I barely knew Bradford Barry. I don't know what my bracelet was doing in his hotel bathroom. And the only things I know about my mother I read in old society clips at the school library when I was twelve.'

She turned toward the door, fighting back an explosion of tears. 'Our conversation is finished.'

'I don't believe you any more than I believed

your mother.' His words were level and threatening.

She was trembling with rage as she plunged down the stairs and out the door and on toward the street. The bastard. As each heel of her pumps hit the cement of the sidewalk words pounded into her head.

Bracelet.

Your mother.

I don't believe you.

She was barely aware of the taxi screeching to a halt at the corner of Connecticut Avenue.

'Where to, miss?' the driver asked as she threw herself into the back seat and slammed the door.

'Where to?' she said as if awakening from a dream. She was hurt and confused. Thoughts were rushing through her mind as she tried to sort it all out.

'Yes, ma'am, you wave down a cab, you must wanna go someplace.'

'Yes . . . yes . . . take me to my aunt's house.' Her chest felt as though it would burst.

The driver spoke slowly and calmly and in the modulated voice used to deal with the mentally disturbed. 'You'll have to give me your aunt's address, lady. I forgot it.'

281

Caroline kept one eye on the road, the other on the speedometer. The patrol cars along upper Massachusetts Avenue were particularly vigilant at this time of day.

'Loony bitch,' she muttered, looking down at the dried stain on her skirt. Of all the social insults she had been party to on her climb to the top in Washington, this was the worst.

Now she was glad Dalton had had an out-of-town speech scheduled that he couldn't cancel to attend the memorial service and reception. He wouldn't have been one bit amused. In a different time Dalton would have confronted that parlor rat's husband and 'called him out'. She could picture the two of them, sabers at the ready, on some misty bluff over the Potomac.

She wondered how long it would take for the story to reach him. It was bound to rival the chief of staff gossip as topic A at Connie's party this evening.

He had promised to meet her at the club by four-thirty so they could drive out to Winterberry together. But how many times had she heard that promise?

She depressed the gas pedal and downshifted as

she turned the little Mercedes into the steep drive up to the house.

It was not yet three. That left time to shampoo out the sticky mess Sinclare's drink had left in her hair and take a nap.

The phone was ringing as she opened the screen door. 'I'm here only for Dalton, Rosa,' she called. She paused at the bottom of the stairs. Rosa stood holding the hall phone with her hand cupped over the mouthpiece. 'If anyone from the press calls tell them Mrs Ives is a frustrated hair stylist,' she cracked and continued up the stairs without waiting to hear who was calling. She stripped off her clothes and left them on the bed for Manuel to take to the dry cleaners.

The last three days had given her a chance to consider her feelings about Dalton's future. If anything was needed to convince her that she wanted him to get the chief of staff job it was the scene at lunch. If Sinclare had pulled that stunt on the wife of the President's closest aide she would have been brought up on charges.

She didn't feel the slightest remorse at having implied that Sinclare was a whore. She was worse than that. She was a crazy whore. No one in town who was sane would disagree.

Caroline stepped into the shower and let the cold water pound against the back of her neck, loosening the tension that had accumulated. She needed a drink.

She stepped out of the shower and pulled on a huge terrycloth robe. It smelled of Dalton's aftershave. She missed him. The house was silent except for the dim babble of Rosa's soap opera in the kitchen.

As she entered the darkened library a soft breeze from the open French windows cooled her damp face and hair. She stepped to the drinks tray against the wall and poured three inches of vodka into a brandy snifter. No need to alert Manuel by asking for ice. He might say something to Dalton, not that Dalton mentioned her drinking often. But she recognized the sideways look, the thin-lipped smile of disapproval toward her glass at dinner parties or when she walked too many times to the drinks tray.

She congratulated herself on her stealth. She knew to have a couple of quick ones before Dalton got home. She refused to drink in front of him until he was well into his second. Whoever invented vodka was a genius. A quick swirl of toothpaste was all that was needed.

Thursday, June 8, 1989 – 3:00 P.M.
Maubry House, Georgetown

Jan desperately needed to talk to Aunt Connie. As the cab she had found near her father's house inched its way down Wisconsin Avenue she tucked her hands under her hips to control the shaking.

She could feel the dull pain of a migraine starting just above her eyes. She hadn't had one since the day she'd introduced Mark to her father.

Had the whole world gone crazy? How could her father believe she was having an affair with Bradford Barry? What was most disturbing were his ominous words about her mother, a subject so repressed and forbidden that she had never even seen a picture of her. She had only a mental image of an exquisite young woman in a red velvet ball gown slowly descending a wide staircase. She had always assumed she was dead and the subject was too painful for anyone to mention.

She realized that she had been lied to by omission all her life — that information about her mother had not been rewritten, twisted, or embroidered, but deliberately withheld. She tried to remember how old she had been when she gave up asking questions. Somewhere along the way she had learned that it was better not to ask, not to risk the censure, the icy looks of disapproval.

She had blocked so much.

Dear Aunt Connie. All these years she had kept the faith, never mentioning her mother or what clearly were the bad times. But out of loyalty to whom? Jan's father? Certainly not out of any love for Janine Sumner.

And what was this insane business about her diamond bracelet?

A sharp pain shot through the dull throbbing of her migraine. She had been thrilled with the bracelet when her father presented it, partly because it

285

was a unique piece that he had designed himself, but more importantly, because it officially signaled his acceptance of her marriage to Mark. The bracelet was something precious from her father to her. She seldom wore it because she was so afraid of losing it. She had worn it the night of the inaugural ball to please him. Aunt Constance had given a spectacular buffet before the ball attended by the new President and First Lady. It was the most glittering evening she could remember and she had consumed far too much champagne. She and Mark had not gotten home until dawn and fell into bed in their evening clothes. Had she lost it? Was that possible? The nerve endings began to knit together into a fist and her mind went blank.

As the cab turned into Constance's street she saw Ian leaning into the trunk of the Rolls. He was trying to make four big wicker hampers fit into a space already taken up by two wooden boxes marked Meursault 1983 and Chassagne-Montrachet 1985 that Connie had especially ordered for the President's table. He was dressed in the full banana republic gear he affected for trips to the country.

Jan looked at the meter, threw a five-dollar bill over the front seat, slammed the door, and, hoping Ian wouldn't see her, ran up the front steps. She didn't want to explain herself.

The front door was open, and she stood in the hall and listened for a moment. Liza and Libby, Constance's little doggies, sensed a strange presence. She could hear the yapping starting from the second floor. As she made her way up the stairs the two animals hurled themselves at her, excited to see a familiar face.

'Who is it?' Constance's voice trilled from the upper floor.

'It's me, Aunt Connie, can I come up?' Jan called as she ran up the stairs. The yapping of the dogs prevented her from hearing any answer.

She rapped softly on the doorjamb of Constance's bedroom. 'Come,' said Constance's muffled voice from somewhere in the room.

Jan stepped into the room to see Constance bending over deep inside her walk-in closet. Clothes were strewn around the vast room and more were flying over her shoulder, landing on the Aubusson rug and missing the dogs, who were now circling in a frenzy.

'Was anybody hurt?' Jan asked, picking a lavender egret boa off the floor and draping it on the bedpost. 'This room looks like it exploded!'

Constance straightened up and turned around. 'Jan, darling, what in the world are you doing here? Are you coming out with us? Ian didn't tell me. How delightful.'

Jan sat down on the foot of Constance's draped and festooned bed. 'Aunt Connie, I know my timing is terrible, what with your big party tonight, but I need to talk to you.'

A look of concern creased Constance's flawless brow. 'Of course, darling. I didn't realize it was going to be so warm. I haven't a thing to wear. What do you think of this?' She held up a peach linen Lily Pulitzer that had seen better days. 'I suppose not, it's too sporty.' She cast it aside. 'I don't know what possessed me making this thing black tie.'

'Connie?'

'Oh, how about this?' She yanked a hanger holding a long beaded Galanos and held it out toward Jan. 'Bought this to wear to one of Nancy's White House galas. You know, darling, I was very fond of her, but she's the reason everyone over-dresses.' She held it against her chest and stepped to the full-length mirror. 'Ugh, too much. You know, in a way I'm glad they're gone. We all tried to outdress her and we're still doing it. I should have bought something new.'

'Constance, please!' Jan's eyes began to fill with tears. 'I need to know something.'

The minute Constance noticed the state Jan was in she dropped the dress and rushed to the bed. She sat down next to her niece and put her arm around her. 'My sweet, forgive me. Here I am jabbering away. I had no idea you were upset. What is it, lamb?'

Jan fumbled in her skirt pocket for a tissue. 'Aunt Constance, I want you to tell me about my mother.'

There was a silence so total Jan raised her head and looked at her aunt. 'Connie?'

Constance Maubry slowly removed her arm and walked to the bedroom window. She stood with her back to Jan and said, 'I've always known this day would come. I'm a little surprised it's taken this long.'

Jan had never heard her voice so low, her words so slow and considered. Gone was the bubbling, sometimes daffy but always grand lady Jan had known. As Constance turned, Jan saw her beautiful face transformed with pain and remembering.

Suddenly Jan was awash with guilt. 'I have a right to know, don't I?' She knew she sounded as though she was pleading. She was.

Constance sighed deeply. 'You have every right, Janet. You have always had the right to know. In a foolish moment many years ago I promised your father I would never speak.'

'He spoke of her to me just now in his office,' Jan said. 'In a white rage. I've never seen him like that.'

'Your father talked to you about your mother?'

'That's right.'

'I don't believe it. What happened?'

Jan told her aunt about the bracelet in Bradford Barry's suite and her father's accusation. 'He said, "The apple doesn't fall far from the tree,"' Jan related, blowing her nose again. 'Then he started comparing me to my mother, saying that he knew how rotten women were because of her. Connie, how could he think I would do something like that? He knows I adore Mark. Then to imply something obscene about my mother!'

'Jan, I am appalled. What did he actually tell you about her?'

'Nothing direct. I was so shocked that I couldn't

289

ask him to elaborate. Connie, what is going on? You've got to tell me about my mother. How bad could it be?'

Constance dropped slowly to the foot of the chintz chaise longue and said, 'It was pretty bad, honey.'

Old Southern families like the Sumners were no strangers to madness. It was as common as the love of horses and good bourbon. If one shook most family trees hard enough, a brother, a cousin, or someone's in-law who was slightly 'off' was likely to drop out.

'But what happened to your mother,' Constance told Jan, 'was more than any of us could understand.'

For twenty-five years Constance Sumner Maubry had been the keeper of the family's dark secret, and not a day passed that it did not trouble her conscience. Buck was two years younger than his sister, and as the last male of a grand old Southern family, their hope for the future. As had generations of blue-blooded first families of Virginia, he had graduated from the University of Virginia. After spending two secretive years in army intelligence, he entered Harvard Law School, which provided the final polish and style. His good looks and courtly manner made him terribly popular with women, and there were many in his life, momentarily desired and soon discarded. By the time he was thirty-five, his family began to despair of his ever marrying.

Since graduation from law school, he had worked for what was then referred to as 'the Special Services'. In actuality he worked for the tight little group that started something that would one day become the CIA, but in those days one didn't speak of such things. His cover as a diplomat lent legitimacy to his unexplained travels.

One spring he phoned the family from London to say he was coming home with a bride whom he had met and married abroad. Her name was Janine Stanfield. He gave no further details and the Sumners braced themselves for someone of whom they would most assuredly disapprove. How could Buck Sumner, reared in the gracious manner of the old South, bring home 'a foreigner'?

Any resistance to Buck's new bride was soon dispelled. Janine Stanfield was the most ravishing thing ever to set foot in Fauquier County. She was tall, blonde, and possessed a fashion model's figure. She spoke with a lilting British accent so admired and badly imitated by elite southerners. She never spoke about herself, but disarmingly asked others to tell her about their lives. By the end of the first week the men in Buck Sumner's household and circle of friends were falling about in a swoon. The women took a few days longer, but when they learned that she could dance, ride, crochet, and properly instruct servants they too talked of nothing else. That Janine Sumner only had eyes for her handsome husband won them over completely.

Buck Sumner was bewitched.

* * *

Hearing the front door slam, Constance broke off her story and walked to the top of the stairs. 'Celia!' she called. 'Would you tell Mr Vreen I've been delayed. Tokido can drive me down when he finishes the hedge around the pool.'

'No, Aunt Connie,' Jan protested. 'It's such an important party. I mustn't keep you.' She prayed she would continue, but knew she was being inconsiderate. In just a few hours Connie was hostessing what would undoubtedly be the social event of the year. And yet Jan had to know.

Constance waved her suggestion away and stepped back into the room. 'If I'm there by seven it will be fine. The staff always does better if I'm not there bothering them. The White House said the President wouldn't be there until after eight. The caterers are wonderful. Don't worry.'

'You're sure?'

Constance nodded and went back to the end of the chaise. 'You have to hear this, Jan. It's the only way you will understand. But before I go on I have to ask you something.'

'Yes?'

'You must know that your mother . . .'

Constance hesitated. She pinched the bridge of her nose, her eyes tightly closed as though she were in pain. 'What I'm trying to say is that we've never been sure if she is dead or alive.'

'It never occurred to me that she hadn't died,' Jan whispered. 'If she's still alive where would she be?'

'Only your father knows for sure.'

292

'Please go on. Maybe if I know the whole story I'll be able to make sense of all this.'

Constance leaned back on the pillows of the chaise and picked up where she'd left off.

She had never seen her brother behave the way he did around Janine. He was like a tomcat, prowling, pacing, never completely comfortable unless she was in the same room with him. If she was in the garden long enough to cut three roses he would start wandering around the house calling for her. If she slept late he would come in from riding and run up to their room to check and see if she was still breathing.

Parties were a nightmare. Once she saw she was accepted Janine became a bit of a flirt and it killed Buck. He just couldn't stand it. He spent most of his time keeping an eye on her. When it got more than he could bear he would interrupt and whisk her away. Later, there would be terrible rows.

'Poor Buck.' Constance smiled sadly. 'He had never been in love before so he had never been jealous. He didn't know how to handle it.

'Every time they had a fight he would feel guilty. He was forever giving her things — cars, furs, stock, an apartment at the Kennedy-Warren so she would have someplace to rest between parties in town.

'And the jewelry! My dear, you have never seen such jewelry. Emerald earrings because it was Tuesday. Diamond and ruby cuffs because the sun came up. Drawers and chests of it!

'On their first anniversary he bought her a tiara to wear to the Christmas ball at Beaulieu, the

293

Montgomery estate near Middleburg. Here I was married to honest-to-God English nobility and I didn't have a tiara! All those beautiful things . . .' She paused, shaking her head. 'Later, after you were born, he gave her the Sumner pearls. At the time I was livid. I thought that as the only daughter I would get them. It doesn't matter anymore; besides, all of those beautiful things should have been yours.'

'What ever happened to them?'

'Gone.' She shrugged. 'When he found out he went up to her dressing room that night and took it all. One of the grooms saw him take a pillowcase down to the abandoned well near the potting shed and throw it in. They were gone forever. There's an underground river feeding that well.'

'Connie, back up. When he found out what?'

'Patience, dear. I'm an old lady and I've never told this to anyone before. I have to get the pieces in the right place so you'll understand and not blame your father too much.'

'Okay,' Jan said, leaning against the tufted head-board, both horrified and fascinated.

'In the mid fifties Buck was approached by some people he had known at Harvard. John Kennedy was going to run for the Democratic nomination and they wanted Buck to take a leave and help them. The family had been lifelong Democrats, but they hated the Kennedys. Not Buck. Like so many he was absolutely sold on Jack Kennedy. Thought he was the hope of the free world. He wouldn't listen to any of us. He up and quit his government work and announced that he was going to join the Kennedy campaign staff. Well, my dear, a Catholic! With a father who had been a bootlegger! And worst of all a Yankee! For a while there I thought Buck was going to be disowned.

'You were in the terrible twos. Buck got terribly busy with the campaign and was traveling a lot. Your mother was stuck at Winterberry, and not happy about her life. She didn't take to domesticity. She wanted to wear beautiful clothes, go to parties and fine restaurants in town, and have her man at her side.

'You turned five the night Kennedy was nominated, but Buck wasn't there. He was in Los Angeles at the convention. I think that was the turning point for Janine. She felt there was nothing she could do that would interest Buck as much as working for the Kennedys. As soon as she got her figure back she started going into Washington to parties when Buck wasn't around. She had made a lot of friends, and if someone was having a dinner party she would just up and go. It would drive Buck crazy when he found out, but he couldn't stop her.

'She and I saw a lot of each other. I was not getting along with Lord Maubry at the time and welcomed her company. We had the villa at Cap d'Antibes then. Buck was traveling back and forth to Latin America. We didn't know it then, but he was involved with the Bay of Pigs business. He had no time for her, or you for that matter. She would leave you with the Munsons at the farm and flit off to stay with me in the south of France. There she would really let go, doing her Lady Brett Ashley act, dancing on cafe tables, drinking Calvados right out of the bottle. Not wearing a bra in those days when it was unthinkable. After a week in the sun she was so beautiful she literally stopped traffic.

'It didn't take long for people to start talking. I learned that before she married Buck she had quite a reputation among the wealthy layabouts in London society who ended up involved in the Profumo scandal. She had somewhat misrepresented herself to the family simply by not talking about herself. In Buck she had found herself a rich Southern boy and bowled him over. I kept my mouth shut and prayed he wouldn't find out and blame me for not telling him.

'That summer she got in with a really fast Hollywood crowd. Ava Gardner had a place there, the Pecks, Gable, real Hollywood royalty and the types that hang on to famous people like that. Friends of Peter and Pat Lawford invited her to Palm Springs, and she was on the next plane. That's where she met him and the real trouble started.'

'Met who, Aunt Connie?' Jan was riveted by what she was hearing.

'President Kennedy. I was told the romance began within minutes.'

'Oh my God,' Jan breathed. 'Poor Daddy.'

'Exactly.' Constance nodded. 'In those days no one would believe the President of the United

States was having affairs. Particularly not this handsome Catholic boy with a stunning wife and babies. It was unthinkable. Oh, some well-connected people in the press knew, but they protected him. I think their protection only made him bolder. I was told that his staff spent most of their waking hours in cardiac arrest trying to cover up his womanizing. Harold Macmillan once said John Kennedy spent half his time talking about committing adultery and the other half talking about secondhand ideas. Too bad they didn't print it when he said it, but in those days anyone who was a Kennedy was royalty.

'Well, Janine was caught up in all this and had no one to talk to about it but me. I kept mum about the whole thing, it scared me half to death. The next thing I knew they announced that the President was buying the dreary place down the road from Winterberry so Jackie could ride her horses – and, I discovered, so that Jack could slip away and see Janine.

'Your father found out. It was the most terrible thing that could happen to a man. He worshiped Kennedy and, of course, he was mad for your mother. Finally the betrayal became too much for him. He drove out to Winterberry in the middle of the night to have it out with Janine. He simply couldn't stand it anymore. Janine called me here at the house hysterical. Tookie and I must not have been fighting that week because I remember we drove down to the farm at three o'clock in the morning. The thing I was most afraid of was that

Buck would go nuts and call the press. Not that they would have printed it, mind you.

'By the time we got to the farm, Janine had locked herself in the wine cellar. That was the night he threw the jewelry away.

'It was a kind of double betrayal for your father. Politically he had gone over to the enemy camp to help elect a man who then stole his wife.'

'Where was I when all this was going on?'

'Sleeping peacefully in your nursery on the third floor.'

'I see,' Jan said.

'Buck stormed and raved until well into the next morning. All we could do was sit in the library and let him get it out of his system. I must say Tookie was terribly ungracious. He said something about "lying down with dogs and getting up with fleas," referring to Buck's throwing in with the Kennedys. Your father realized that he was helpless. If he had confronted the President, Kennedy would have denied it. Buck knew that no one would believe such a story. His wife and the President? They would have thought he was some kind of black-mailing smear-monger.

'Things eventually smoothed over, sort of an armed truce because of you and Buck's work. Your mother stopped seeing Kennedy and pretty much stayed at home for the next few weeks. Then there was the big party we have every Christmas. Do you remember any of this, darling? What happened was so dreadful.'

Jan stared at her aunt. 'Me? Connie, I don't

remember any of this. It's like you're talking about two strangers. I think my earliest memories were of Mother going off to parties in her wonderful clothes. Then Daddy said they were getting a divorce and I went to live with you. After that she wasn't there anymore. Somehow I knew better than to ever speak about my mother. I knew it would upset him and all I wanted was for him to love me. But please go on. What happened that Christmas?'

'If you truly don't remember I don't think I should. Sleeping dogs and all that.' Constance's voice trailed off and she studied the pattern in the rug.

'Connie, I have to know. Please.'

'It was the Christmas party weekend. You went to your mother's room and saw her in bed with my husband. You ran away and the servants didn't find you until morning.'

'Connie! Did I end up in the hospital with pneumonia?'

'I think it was pneumonia. You were terribly sick. We were all so worried about you.'

'God, it's coming back to me. I can remember standing outside her door. I heard voices. Oh, Lord. Was that why I ran? How awful for everyone,' Jan said sadly.

'It was about as awful as anything that had happened in the family, worse, in its way, than the Kennedy business. Tookie was family, and yet I couldn't really blame your mother. She was ill, far more than I realized at the time. I can't say I was amused, but I wasn't in nearly as bad shape as Buck was when he found out.

'I was in a frenzy trying to keep everyone from doing something foolish. The only answer seemed to be to get Janine out of there before Buck returned from South America and did something horrible. The following day we took a plane out of National to New York and then on to Nice. The villa at Cap d'Antibes was closed for the winter, but we made do. At least it was a safe haven until we could figure out what to do. It wasn't high season, but some of the old Hollywood crowd were there for the Christmas holidays. Janine started right in drinking and dancing all night, sleeping with everything in pants.

'After a couple of weeks I noticed how thin and pale she was. She seemed tired all the time and slept most of the day. One night, at dinner, she reached for something on the table and I saw long red scratches on her arm. They weren't marks from drug needles. I knew what those looked like. These were like knife cuts. I asked her about them and she just smiled and said something about the cat. Well, there weren't any cats at the villa and I didn't believe her. I thought perhaps she got them when she fell; she did that a lot when she was drunk.

'One day I walked into her dressing room and found her cutting herself.' Constance rubbed her arms and shuddered.

'Cutting herself?' Jan said, horrified. 'With what?'

'Razor blades, pieces of glass. She wanted to see

300

her own blood. Apparently this had been going on for some time. She was naked and I could see long silver scars on her thighs. That's when I knew it was deliberate. A few days after that Buck's lawyer called and said he was going to get custody of you and that she would never see you again. If she tried he would file for divorce and name the President as corespondent. She started cutting herself again and hit an artery in her arm. We raced her to the hospital. When I asked her later why she tried to kill herself she said she wasn't doing it to die. She did it because it felt good. She was in love with the pain; it made her feel alive. When she saw her own blood it made her feel in control. That's when I knew she was seriously disturbed and probably had been for a long time. I didn't have a clue as to what I could do about it.

'Then one night my maid woke me and told me Janine had called her into her room and asked her to twist her feet around.'

'What!' Jan uncurled and sat straight up on the bed.

Constance nodded. 'She wanted her to twist her feet around in such a way that, if the poor woman could have done it, it would have broken every bone in her ankles.'

'Oh, Connie, I think I'm going to be sick.'

'I'm sorry, Jan, I shouldn't be telling you this.'

'Don't apologize, Connie. You're right. I do have to know,' Jan said softly. Her arms and legs felt strangely cold in the late-afternoon heat. 'What you're telling me is that she was truly mad.'

'I'm afraid so, my love.'

'What happened to her?'

'I didn't know what else to do. I called your father and he flew to France with a doctor and took her away,' Constance said without elaboration.

'Where did he take her?' Jan asked.

Constance glanced out the window. The buzz of the gardener's electric hedge clippers had stopped. The only sound came from a slight breeze rustling the trees outside the bedroom window. 'We don't know. We've never known. We've always been too afraid of Buck's pain to ask.'

Jan sat perfectly still, her hands folded in her lap. Her first reaction was an overwhelming pity for her father. 'Aunt Connie?' she said, her voice barely above a whisper.

'Yes, dear.'

'Do I look a lot like her?'

'Yes, you do, Jan. Your hair is a darker blonde and you have your father's eyebrows. Other than that you are the image of your mother.'

'Aunt Connie, how do you suppose he would respond if I asked him where she is?'

'Are you afraid of his anger?'

'No,' she said, her mind absorbing everything she had just heard. 'Not anymore.'

'Then ask him. That's the only way you're ever going to know. He may not tell you, but you have to ask.'

'I think he'll tell me.'

'How can you be so sure?'

'He'll tell me when he finds out he's going to be a grandfather.'

Constance's hands fluttered to her cheeks. 'Jan! You didn't tell me.'

'I haven't even told Mark. I just got the test back last Friday. I sort of knew anyway. I've been throwing up for a month.'

'I'm going to be a great-aunt. How splendid!'

Jan walked to the end of the chaise and put her arms around Connie. 'Thank you, Aunt Connie. I know this wasn't easy for you, but it was terribly important to me.'

'Well . . . yes, dear,' she said, slightly flustered. 'It makes me feel better just being able to talk about it. Now, let's get moving. It's getting late and I still have nothing to wear.' She walked toward the huge closet. 'Perhaps the beige chiffon. I wore it to the Laxalts'. There were no photographers there. Or perhaps the celery silk. No, I was in *Dossier* magazine in that . . .'

Jan only half-heard her chirping away deep inside the closet. Her mind traveled back, searching for what she remembered as an idyllic life at Winterberry so long ago.

'Smile and keep right on walking, goddammit,' Eliot growled through his clenched teeth. He alternately pushed and pulled Sinclare through the hotel lobby. 'If anyone says anything, stiff 'em. You've done enough talking for one day.'

Sinclare wobbled along beside him, unsteady in her high sling-back pumps. The effect of the drinks she'd had with Ian had long worn off and left her with a dull headache.

'Don't push me,' she whimpered, 'my head hurts.'

'You're lucky your ass doesn't hurt from my foot.'

They moved down Sixteenth Street, where the doorman had parked Eliot's car. Sinclare wrenched her arm out of his grip. 'You're such a hot shit aren't you, Eliot? Did it ever occur to you that I might be trying to help you get that job?'

Eliot refused to argue with her. He had too much on his mind. Five minutes after Vreen called him in the Senate office, George and Eliot had a crisp, businesslike meeting. Eliot tried to throw some charm into his voice, but he refused to sound like a beggar. George coolly informed him that he would not change his vote, and Eliot was forced to scurry out quickly. He knew how stubborn George

304

could be; he would have to end-run him later that night.

Now Eliot was in the blackest of moods. Had the man forgotten the all-night poker games and the hookers they had shared? And what about all those campaign funds Eliot had arranged for him? Didn't that count for something?

Eliot and Sinclare didn't speak to each other until they were inside his BMW with the windows safely closed, the air-conditioning turned on full blast. 'Now,' he said in a slightly calmer voice, 'you want to tell me what your little talk with Deena was all about?'

'No,' she said, fluffing her hair in the rearview mirror she'd turned in her direction. Whenever she looked at herself in a mirror she sucked in her cheeks and lowered her eyelids. It irritated him every time.

He ground the floor shift into low, then second and shot up the garage ramp and out onto K Street with an aggressive roar. 'So what am I supposed to do, catch it on the news?'

'Oh, shut up, Eliot,' she said languidly.

'I won't shut up. Do you know Vreen got me out of an extremely important meeting with George Lowry? If I hadn't been forced to leave I might have been able to convince him to change his mind. You may have blown the whole deal right there . . .' He cut himself off from saying more.

'I should have blown George Lowry. Then you'd get his support.'

'Watch your mouth!'

'It's always been your organ of choice,' she said, smirking at him.

He ignored her remark. She was trying to pick a fight to avoid discussing the afternoon's disaster. Eliot's thoughts returned to the conversation he had with Ian Vreen upon arriving at the hotel.

Eliot had to hand it to Vreen. He was made of stronger stuff than he had believed and had proved it by telling him that Sinclare possessed some goddamn porn tape starring Riggs. Vreen obviously was afraid for Sinclare and of what she might be up to. Now that was real friendship, when you cared enough about someone to try and save them from themselves. He'd make it up to Vreen somehow, but for now he had to get to the bottom of this video business.

'Sinclare, did someone give you a tape of Dalton Riggs?'

'I don't know what you're talking about,' she answered in an almost sweet tone.

'You know exactly what I'm talking about. And if you're planning to help me out by sharing that tape with Deena or anyone else, just toss that idea in the toilet along with the tape. Now, let's start at the beginning. Where is that tape, dammit?'

Sinclare moved as far to her side of the car as she could. She wished he would stop grinding away. She couldn't tune him out. But he continued.

'I was a city prosecutor, a county prosecutor, a state prosecutor, and a United States attorney. I can tell you this, little lady, you could go to jail for a long time if you extort, blackmail, or fraudulently intimidate a high federal official. And God knows what kind of civil lawsuits, libel, slander, and defamation you'd be open to.'

'Drop me at the salon,' she insisted suddenly.

'Are you crazy?'

'Everything I had done this morning is messed up,' she shouted. 'How am I going to go to the yacht party with my hair like this?'

'Your hair is fine. Just comb it, for Christ's sake.'

'What do you know?' She was trying to think fast. She studied her hands. 'Look! My nail!' She held up her right hand, showing four magenta talons and one pale stub on the index finger. 'I just had this one wrapped. Now look at it.'

He stopped short at a red light, pitching her forward. 'Buy some of those drugstore things and stick another one on. I'm taking you back to the apartment.' He was going to get that tape and find out what she was up to if he had to beat it out of her possession.

'El, I'm not going home. Let me out or I'll jump out.'

She yanked open the door and had one leg out of the car before he could reach across and pull her back into her seat. 'Are you crazy! Get in here!' he shouted. Her door was still half open as he slowed and then had to brake hard to avoid rear-ending a city bus. Sinclare immediately leapt from the car.

'I'll see you at the apartment in a couple of

hours,' she shouted back at him as she strode off in the direction of La Reine.

'Tell him to soak your head while you're at it,' he yelled after her. Maybe she really is crazy, he thought. Not just wild, but over the edge. He looked down at the floor. Her small black patent leather bag lay against the gray carpet. It bulged oddly. When he felt the hard tape inside the bag, he thought, no she isn't. She knew she'd left it with him.

He laid the bag on the seat, and as he maneuvered back into traffic with one hand he punched Deena's number into the car phone.

He'd change for the *Sequoia* party first, and try to get to the yacht before George; then he'd up the pressure. If Eliot could deliver George before the President arrived on board that would make an impression!

Thursday, June 8, 1989 — 3:15 P.M.
Kalorama Road

Buck Sumner made no attempt to keep Jan from leaving his office. What good would it do? Having spoken to her about her mother for the first time in more than two decades there was nothing more to discuss.

Speaking of her now brought back the dull ache of betrayal. What Janine Stanfield Sumner had done to him had irreversibly colored his attitude toward women.

Now, sitting alone in his darkened office, the memory of her came flooding back. The information he had received about the bracelet had ripped the self-protecting scar tissue away. He had to look into the gaping wound of humiliation that was her only legacy. Again, he faced the self-inflicted guilt.

When the doctors finally declared that Janine was mentally ill his pain was overlaid with the feeling that he somehow might have been the cause. He had watched his daughter grow, looking for signs that she might have inherited her mother's dreadful malady. Mercifully, while she had grown as tall and beautiful as her mother, it was always clear that her mind was intact. And yet today, when Jan had walked into his office, it was as though he had looked up to see the young Janine smiling at him, her arms outstretched.

He shivered. Jan would have learned a lesson if he'd told her about her mother, but there never seemed to have been the right time or place. He couldn't tell her when she was small, it was too painful. And by the time she was old enough to understand too much time had passed to relive the whole sordid mess through her eyes. It was best she not know.

His ruminations were interrupted by Belle on the intercom. 'Mr Ambassador, the White House is on line one. It's the President's personal secretary just to say he's running behind schedule. Do you want to take the call?'

'No, Belle, not if that's the only message,' he said.

'She said the President will return your call sometime early tomorrow.'

'Thank you, Belle,' he said briskly, concealing his disappointment.

Damn, he figured as much. The President was avoiding him again. But why?

Buck's pulse began to throb with tension. Here he had hard, solid information on each of the contenders, information the President needed to have before he made his decision. But the winds had turned again, and clearly the President was now depending on other sources. He swore softly: it had seemed likely he was going to play an important role in this administration. The next four years would be dreary indeed if he were forced to sit them out. Could the President have heard rumors about him and Echo? Or about Echo? What was that woman up to?

When he maneuvered his son-in-law into the press secretary's job, ignoring his own personal feelings about Kirkland, he'd thought that an inside contact at that level was a virtual guarantee of continued White House influence, but having Mark on the inside had proved worthless. He was getting the fast shuffle and he didn't like it, not one bit.

For nearly forty years his special skills had been at the service of the man in the White House. His information network had ranged the world, though in recent years it had shrunk considerably.

His operatives had died, retired, or simply folded their hands and left the table on which his special game was played.

Buck knew his own value and always had. Well born to a wealthy and prestigious old Virginia family, the University of Virginia and Harvard Law School were only starters to a lifelong career in intelligence.

He had left government service during the Ford administration and set himself up on his own, advising, counseling, and generally making himself useful on special assignment to both the private sector and the government. And although he did not have the network of agents at his disposal that he once had, he still had inside access to the Washington scene through old chums, intelligence colleagues, his social contacts, and, most importantly, his last remaining operative – Echo Bourne.

Over the years Buck had spent a fortune of the government's money on her upkeep, training, and cover. She had been worth it. Echo's office, the house in Georgetown, the house at the beach, and the cars were handled through a maze of corporate fronts and offshore sources. Between the two of them they had once had the town wired. They knew things before the press did. They mastered the fine art of leaking information when it would serve their purpose.

No one except Belle knew of his complicated relationship with Echo, and that served both their purposes. Neither admitted to anything more than a knowledge of the other's existence. There were parties, dinners, and receptions that would develop an entirely different atmosphere if Buck Sumner were present. Not so with Echo. She could go to the ladies' rooms and girlie lunches and even to bed with valuable sources. In time, she started 'assisting' other women, introducing them to the right man, and her network began expanding. That's where the real information was in Washington. Now it was Echo's vast network that reached into all the important places in town.

More than once Echo had called him from some guy's bathroom phone, still damp from an encounter, to tell him what he needed to know. She made friends with the important wives and could overhear a conversation at twenty paces. More amazing was her ability to repeat whole conversations near verbatim.

The situation that was developing between them had been his own fault. He had been lazy, permitting her more and more independence to do what she wanted, and he had begun to distrust her. There was nothing specific, just a general feeling of discomfort. She seemed to be off on a lot of little projects of her own — 'unavailable', 'tied up on another call' — all the cover stories a good assistant could dream up. The days when Echo took his calls before any others seemed over.

The last vestige of what they had together was now his sexual dependency on her. He knew it — and dangerously she knew it, too.

Belle buzzed. 'Miss Bourne is on your private line, sir.'

'Tell her I'm tied up,' he barked. Let her have a taste of her own medicine.

'Excuse me?' Belle asked, incredulous.

'You heard me.'

A minute later Belle was back on the intercom. 'Sir, I'm sorry to bother you, but Miss Bourne said she would see you at the farm this evening. She had something important to tell you.'

'Winterberry? I didn't know my sister invited her.'

'She didn't, sir. Miss Bourne is accompanying the new Saudi ambassador.'

'Jesus Christ, she never gives up, does she?'

'No, sir. And neither should you.'

'Belle, you know too much for your own good.' He chuckled, but it did little to relieve his anger at the situation with Echo.

'She doesn't know you aren't going tonight.'

'She's not supposed to, Belle. You know that.'

'Yes, sir. I know that.'

He leaned back in his chair. He felt no qualms about what he would have to do. He had made Echo Bourne, and he could break her with a lot less effort. It was time.

Thursday, June 8, 1989 – 3:20 P.M.
Echo Bourne's Townhouse
P Street, Georgetown

Echo Bourne leaned her head around to the kitchen door on her way up the stairs of her townhouse. 'You can go, dear,' she said to her maid, who was wiping crystal wineglasses with a fresh linen cloth.

'It's only three, Miss Bourne.'

'That's all right. I'm having company.'

'Company?' Conchita said with a lascivious grin.

'Go, Conchita.' Echo smiled and headed up the stairs to her bedroom.

Hidden within the white lacquered bookshelves next to the French windows was a hidden video camera. She engaged the automatic switch. The camera would activate as soon as any weight was on the bed.

She had represented the Saudi ambassador for only a week, and this would be her first opportunity to show him how clever he had been to retain her. Deirdre and Ony were on their way, and soon the young Oxford-educated diplomat would discover how unique entertainment could be in the nation's capital.

She pulled off her linen dress and stepped out of her heels. There was time enough for a shower and a change into something more diaphanous before the girls arrived.

The girls worked for nothing when the client owned his own 747 and had a habit of tossing around gold Rolex watches like confetti. As for Echo an OPEC contact was a must. Her latest had been reassigned and after this afternoon the new ambassador would most certainly be cooperative. If not, there would always be the tape.

Echo's were her Swiss bank account. They lined the shelves of a specially built closet in the hall, pitch dark and temperature controlled, each labeled by Echo's own secret code. A well-endowed senator from Texas was marked 'Giant', a black cabinet officer who liked to be fully made up and dress in French couture ball gowns was labeled 'The African Queen'. One of her favorites, a highly decorated Pentagon general who liked to be verbally abused, was labeled 'Star Wars'.

The Arab, like all the men, would be work; the only fun part would come afterwards when Echo and the girls would break open a bottle of champagne and dream up a code name for the burnoose-wearing Arab who was at this moment telling his secretary he would be 'over at State and unreachable for the entire afternoon.'

The bedroom phone rang while she was still in the shower. After the fourth ring she remembered she had given Conchita the afternoon off and not turned on the machine.

Soaking wet and covered with bath gel bubbles she stumbled to the bedside phone. If this was one of the girls canceling she'd have a fit. 'Yes!' she snapped.

'You called,' Buck said matter-of-factly.

'Oh, it's you. I'm sorry. I was in the shower. Yeah, I called. What's the business about you being busy when I needed to speak to you?'

'Well, I was,' he said petulantly. 'Jan was here.'

'I really needed to talk to you, Buck.'

'So talk. I'm here.'

'Only for a sec. I'm expecting the new Saudi ambassador for tea.'

'Tea! At this time of day?'

'Old Arab custom. What's this about Jan?'

'She wanted me to speak to the President on Mark's behalf.'

'You're kidding. What did you say?'

'I told her I knew about her affair with Bradford.'

'Damn, I wish you hadn't done that, Buck.'

'Why not?'

'That's what I called you about. I got a tip from a friend at the FBI today. The President's calling off the investigation. Seems Justice says whatever Barry was up to was personal. No security problems. You ought to sharpen up your sources, love. You just know about the bracelet. Seems that Sinclare Ives was seen leaving the hotel right after Barry died. Well, Sinclare was at the Hay-Adams, all right, but she wasn't with Barry, for sure. I know who she was with. And it wasn't your baby daughter Jan because she and Mark were having dinner at Lion d'Or. The maître dates one of my

316

girls and saw them together at the restaurant Sunday night. So Bucko, I think you should give your daughter a call and apologize because I think I know who was playing in the shower with Barry and so does the FBI.'

'Jesus, will you slow down? I'm going into information overload here.'

'I can't,' Echo said. From her bedroom window she could see Deirdre and Ony sliding out of a cab in front of the house. She'd have to answer the door any second. 'I see the ambassador's limo pulling up.'

'To hell with the ambassador! Who was with Barry?'

'Caroline Riggs. Goodbye, Buck.'

Thursday, June 8, 1989 – 3:30 P.M.
The Fort, Foxhall Road

Caroline glanced at the eighteenth-century English grandfather clock in the hall. It was almost three-thirty. She didn't want to be late meeting Dalton at the club. The drive to Winterberry would take over an hour. She'd better get moving.

Upstairs, she dressed carefully. She decided on her favorite Adolfo. The raspberry raw silk with pink satin lapels was perfect for Constance's garden dinner party.

She opened the felt-lined drawer of her jewelry chest. Everyone would be wearing their showiest trinkets tonight. As she lifted out a double chain of pearls and garnets, she automatically checked the other pieces – her huge cameo, the diamond and emerald earrings Dalton had given her when he made brigadier, her good pearls . . . the bracelet . . . maybe she should take a chance and wear it?

But where was it? She made a well in the satin comforter on the bed and upended the drawer into it. A tangle of chains, rings, earclips, and pins glittered in the afternoon sun. Frantically, she pawed through them, telling herself not to panic. She loved the delicate gold and diamond bracelet, mostly because she and Brad had found it together the night they had declared their love for each other. They had danced all night while Dalton stood in with a small group of advisors. Everyone thought it kind of the new chief of staff to spend so much time with her. Brad noticed the bracelet first, and swooped down and picked it up, then wrapped it around her wrist and said, 'With this bracelet I do pledge my love for thee.'

There were so many diamonds that they'd thought the bracelet was just costume jewelry. She'd turned it in to the Secret Service, but no one had ever claimed it so it was returned to her. Even though it was now legally hers she didn't tell her husband about it. It was the only thing that was hers and Brad's, theirs alone, and she didn't want to share their secret. She had worn it only when they were together.

Caroline sat down on the edge of the bed. Her forehead beaded with perspiration, although the bedroom air conditioner was on full blast. She separated each piece, lining them up alongside one another on the comforter. The bracelet wasn't there.

Oh . . . my . . . God. Sunday night! *What was I wearing? Did it have pockets? What handbag was I carrying?* The questions darted through her consciousness, escalating her panic.

A twenty-minute search of every drawer in the room, all the pockets of bathrobes, jackets, and handbags in the walk-in closet produced nothing. She even looked inside her shoes.

The car! Maybe I dropped it in the car. The clasp was probably bent or open or . . . She sat back down on the bed. She knew it wouldn't be in the car. Polly had used it twice. Manuel, even Dalton, had taken it the night before to run to the drugstore.

Her worst fear was realized. She started to laugh, a painful, near-sobbing sound. She lay back on the pillows. Any psychologist would tell her that wearing the bracelet and losing it revealed a self-destructive desire to be caught.

She was sure that by now the FBI and the Secret Service would have found it in the suite and would be tracing it. Somehow, she knew, they would find their way to her . . . or Dalton!

Suddenly she stopped laughing and sat up. It had been four days now. What if they were already speaking to Dalton? What if he confronted her at the club? Dalton wouldn't want a scene at the White House. The club was his sanctuary, his turf.

Where better to accuse a lying, cheating wife? He'd said he was going there to change for the party. But why couldn't he change at the White House?

Her heart began to race. She knew what she had to do. If Dalton didn't know, he didn't deserve to learn of her treachery in such a humiliating way. She would tell him herself.

She held the car in the far right lane at twenty miles an hour all the way down MacArthur Boulevard. She didn't care if the drivers behind her blasted their horns at her for driving so slowly. She needed time to think — to find the vocabulary for telling her husband that she had made love to another man. She wondered if she would have to give the details, explain to a husband who always got undressed in the bathroom that it had not happened on a tipsy spur of the moment, but languidly, rapturously, almost obscenely for hours on end for the past six months. Would she tell him that they had made love in hotel rooms, motels in Virginia, and just last week on a thick blanket spread on the rocks above Great Falls? Do you tell your husband that you and your lover had done things to each other she had only read about in deliciously tasteless novels one takes to the beach? Things that would have shocked Dalton had she ever suggested they do them?

That had been Bradford Barry's charm. He didn't expect her to be perfect. He didn't idolize her or treat her like a sacred being. With Bradford she could be abandoned and not feel obscene. She

320

could be a woman who wanted, needed to have sex a million different ways.

With Bradford she was someone else, a different Caroline, not the charming hostess, the gracious Southern wife. He had made her feel alive, wanted and needed. He'd filled her loneliness and ended her boredom.

She started to shake. The little Mercedes swung into the left lane. A blue Fiero narrowly missed her left fender.

Would she be able to make him understand why she did it, how she was feeling the summer Dalton announced that he was going to assist the Kane campaign? A whole new life was opening up for both of them, he said.

For Dalton perhaps, life was going to change, but not her life. She would go on sipping her evening drinks, waiting for him to come home. She would go on arranging dinner parties and lunches for the ladies and wishing something . . . anything . . . would happen to make her feel alive.

Dalton began a travel schedule that kept him on the road for days at a time. Bradford Barry ran the candidate's Washington office. One weekend Dalton brought him to the house 'for a home-cooked meal.'

As the campaign heated up, Dalton was working eighteen-hour days. When he was home he was dog-tired.

One night Bradford gave Polly a lift home from campaign headquarters where she was working during her month off from the Point. Caroline was on her second drink and insisted he stay for one. As the weeks wore on, Bradford found more excuses to stop in — important papers for Dalton, 'just passing' on his way home.

They were both aware of the sexual tension between them. One night after Polly had gone to bed, they sat in the kitchen trying tipsily to make French toast. Suddenly his mouth was covering hers. It was as though every nerve in her body was exposed.

Alone in her bed the next morning she ran her hands down her body, touching her skin, feeling it respond with the remembered sensation of his kiss. What she was feeling was what she had wanted, craved, for so long. She was alive again.

Up until their last horrifying moments together she had been in ecstasy.

Thursday, June 8, 1989 – 3:30 P.M.
The Watergate Apartments

Eliot Ives was frustrated and angry. Sinclare was driving him crazy, and not the kind of 'crazy' he had bargained for. He couldn't trust her enough to tell her what was really going on with the President, and he couldn't stop her from her bizarre campaigns to help him. This business with the tape was sheer lunacy. He knew Dalton Riggs well, and Dalton's ramrod personality didn't have a kinky bone in it. He didn't have to search hard when he wondered who in hell had given Sinclare the tape. There was one prime suspect, but how to get to her? First: damage control.

After several tries on the car phone he reached Deena, whose meeting with Sinclare still worried him. His conversation with Deena confirmed his worst suspicions. She was planning to write an item about the tape in her column. He had to get to her fast.

When he suggested they meet at four at the Willard Hotel, she countered with five. Already, she was in control and it would cost him something – how much, he would simply have to deal with. The story could destroy him and Sinclare. Something had to be done – today.

Meeting Deena would press him for his meeting with George Lowry. Goddamn you, Sinclare.

The Watergate apartment was empty. Eliot cursed Sinclare again as he rewound the answering machine tape. The complex provided live phone answering service at the concierge's desk in the lobby, but Sinclare had insisted that she didn't want other people on her phone line.

Beep. 'Eliot? Sam Donaldson, ABC News here. Would you call me at the White House press room as soon as possible? We'd like your comments on today's events.'

Eliot snorted and shook his head.

Beep. 'El, I'm leaving the hairdresser's now. I'm running to Garfinckel's. I don't have anything to wear. I'll meet you at the Sequoia by six. Hope you're not still mad. Kiss. Kiss.'

Eliot snorted again, this time with less amusement. He glanced toward the mirrored wall of the bedroom. Behind the twenty-foot expanse hung enough clothes to dress a Las Vegas chorus line for a lifetime, along with every feather Frank Perdue ever threw away.

Beep. 'Sin, it's E.B. Urgent I speak to you about that TV opportunity. I'll be back to my house by four. Need to talk to you about last Sunday. Call me.'

'That bitch,' he chortled. 'The line about the 'TV opportunity' left little doubt in Eliot's mind that Echo Bourne was connected to the tape he was carrying in his hand.

He flipped on the wide-screen television and the power button on the VCR. The early local news flickered on to the huge screen.

Anchor Tiffany Dunsmore was reporting:

'Services for the White House chief of staff, Bradford Barry, were held at noon today at St John's Episcopal Church. Barry died suddenly on Sunday evening while attending a private meeting at the Hay-Adams Hotel. Government officials from cabinet members to White House staffers were in attendance. Shortly before the ceremony there was a brief confrontation between Secret Service agents controlling the door and the wife of ex-Senator Eliot Ives.'

The hair stood up on the back of Eliot's neck. He leaned forward in his chair, his mouth agape, as the picture switched from the newswoman doing a stand-up on the sidewalk in front of the church to a close-up of the church door. Between the shoulders of guests waiting in an orderly line to enter he could see Sinclare. She was hanging on to the lapels of an agent and was shouting something – the microphone was too far away to pick up the clearly hysterical tirade. Her turban was askew, and a black shawl over her shoulder was dragging on the ground.

The cameraman and electrician moved closer and to Eliot's horror caught the words 'I don't give a flying . . .' The station mercifully beeped out the next word. 'I'm Mrs Eliot Ives. You can't keep me out. I'm a personal friend of the President!'

As the camera pulled back to show Sinclare being held under both arms by two burly agents, a wave of humiliation washed over Eliot from the back of his eyes down to his sphincter. The agents half-pushed, half-lifted her down the sidewalk to the street.

Eliot sat frozen in the chair as the station returned to the studio. Tiffany Dunsmore began to explain how the scene had come about. Eliot barely heard the words.

The glass that Eliot threw at the bookcase beside the television set shattered a framed portrait of Sinclare. He stepped back over to the VCR machine and pushed the play button.

The tape was over in a few seconds. In black and white taken in dim light, and mostly out of focus, a woman was decked out in nothing but a garter belt and boots, and a bare-assed guy was cracking a whip. There was no sound or voices. Eliot rewound the tape and replayed it.

He started laughing. Sure the guy looked like Dalton Riggs, but anyone who knew Riggs would nail this as a fake in a second. At one time Eliot and Dalton had golfed together regularly. In the locker room they'd discussed the sorry state of Dalton's butt and how it was the same color as the Purple Heart that remained in Dalton's bureau drawer. A Viet Cong land mine had almost killed him, but other than his wife and the guys in the Army-Navy Country Club locker room, no one understood the ugly reality of Dalton's quip, 'I gave my ass for my country.'

The humor of the situation was fleeting. Eliot wondered if this phony tape was meant not just to get Dalton but him and Sinclare as well. He was mad, but his anger was measured – controlled.

He would use an old prosecution trick: smoke out the evidence, then confront the perpetrator – Echo Bourne.

He detested the woman and the influence she had over Sinclare. He had become aware of her years ago when she successfully blackmailed a Senate colleague into changing his negative vote on a bill that favored a client of hers by threatening him with compromising pictures. The senator was romping in the buff with two of Echo's girl friends. Obviously she hadn't changed her trade. Although she moved in the highest circles she was basically evil, always manipulative, always looking for the edge.

As Eliot searched Sinclare's big phone book for Echo's unlisted private number, he considered the best way to deal with the situation. Because Echo had no scruples, no hesitation about lying, falsifying evidence — anything to protect herself — Eliot had to be careful not to be drawn into her sticky web.

By the time he'd found her number, dialed it, and heard the phone ringing at Echo's Georgetown house, he knew exactly what he'd do. It was right, safe, and also, the only route.

She answered after several rings.

'Echo, this is Eliot Ives.' He could hear muffled voices in the background but plunged ahead. 'Sinclare needs to talk to you.'

'Oh, thanks, Eliot.' She paused. 'Ah, I have company, but I do need to speak to her.'

Eliot was relieved. He had made sure that Sinclare and Echo had not spoken, or that Sinclare was not at her house as he spoke. That would undercut what he was about to do. He listened carefully to her response. She was clever, probably a damn good little actress, but he'd had too many witnesses under cross-examination, and now he was on his turf.

'But while I have you on the phone, Echo, I need to speak to you. Got just a second?' Put her at ease. Be non-threatening. There's no formula for interrogation, it is pure feel, and Eliot knew he was one of the best.

'I really should get back to my . . . yeah, okay, Eliot, what's up?'

327

'Echo, the tape you gave Sinclare ... well, it could be very useful to me in dealing with a little problem.' She'd like thinking she was a co-conspirator. It was added protection for her.

'Eliot, I really must have that tape back immediately.'

Bingo. It *was* her tape!

'Hold on just a minute, will you, Echo. That call-waiting click is going on this line and I have the damnedest time working this newfangled phone.'

Actually, Eliot prided himself on his mechanical ingenuity. He loved gadgets and sophisticated electronic toys and had them all, including the latest BMW.

The conference call he had placed to his office just before he dialed Echo was coming in right on cue. His secretary, a woman of unquestioned probity and background, who had served as the personal secretary to the archbishop of the Washington diocese before coming to work for Eliot, was sitting poised to take notes of his conversation, after he brought her on the line. As soon as she was on Echo would overhear a conversation she would believe had been the result of a mistake on his part in switching the line.

'Miss Harmond, I'm in the middle of a very important conversation with Echo Bourne. Would you please call the President's secretary and leave word that I would like the President to consider Mark Kirkland as my deputy chief of staff. I'll give the President my reasons when we meet this evening.' This was neither a true nor a false statement, but he knew how Echo would interpret it.

'I guess I should congratulate you, Senator Ives,' Miss Harmond responded as rehearsed.

'I hope you'll be coming to the White House with me, Miss Harmond.'

'Oh, Senator. Why of course.'

'Please hold on now, Miss Harmond.' Eliot's finger hit a phone button at random, creating a click-click sound on the line. Miss Harmond had been instructed to take notes from this moment on. 'You still there, Echo?'

'Yes, Eliot,' she said somewhat breathlessly. 'Sure, I'm here.'

He knew she would be stunned at what she had overheard, exactly what he had hoped for. He knew the minute he ended the conversation she would call whoever was involved with her, if anyone, and tell them what she had just overheard. Then the telephone log of her calls would reveal her co-conspirator.

'Good. These damn phones. They should never have deregulated the phone company. Let's see, where were we?' He waited a long time for her to respond. That was one of the secrets of a good interrogator. Most people are extremely uncomfortable with a pregnant pause in a conversation, and will rush in to fill it, even more so, face to face, Eliot thought. He'd love to be doing this and see her expression when he unloaded.

'Eliot, I really need that tape of Riggs back. What do you have in mind?'

'Well, I was not really sure it was Dalton Riggs,

it's very short and out of focus. By the way, who's the woman?'

'A friend.'

Gotcha. Number two! He'd hit the jackpot!!

Click. Click. Again, his fingers tapped the phone buttons. 'Damn it. Listen, Echo, I know you want to talk to Sinclare. Let me get her, and I'll take this call, and when you and Sin finish I'll tell you what I had in mind. Hold on, I better not put you on hold or I might lose you.' Turning from her open line, he shouted to the empty room: 'Sinclare, here's Echo.' Pause. 'Sinclare.' Pause. Back into the receiver he said, 'Listen, Echo.' Click. Click. 'Echo, I don't know where she is. Let me take this call and then call you right back.'

'Promise. This is urgent, Eliot.'

'I promise. You can count on it. Give me five or ten minutes. I'll be talking to ya,' he said with a smile on his face, and with intended clumsiness put the receiver back into the cradle of the telephone.

He waited for about forty seconds, then dialed Echo's number. Just as he'd hoped, it was busy. He pressed the receiver down again, released it, and when the dial tone came on pressed automatic dialer for his office.

'The office of Eliot Ives,' Miss Harmond answered.

'Did you get all that, Sara?'

'Yes, sir. What do you want me to do with it?'

'Nothing, don't touch it, and forget about calling the White House. Right now I want you to place another conference call.' Eliot instructed her

330

to connect him with the head of the Criminal Division, Assistant Attorney General Wilbur O'Neil, and the US attorney for the District of Columbia. He knew both men well from his days on the Senate Judiciary Committee. Both knew Eliot was a straight shooter.

Soon he was explaining to the two prosecutors, while Sara Harmond first listened. Then Sara repeated the conversation she had heard during the three-way conversation with Eliot, Echo, and herself. Eliot then asked the prosecutors to hold so he could bring Echo back on the line and confront her. He called Echo back and before she could say a word, explained what he had done from the moment he had first called her, and identified those on the line with him.

'You shit-ass bastard, Ives,' she yelled, edging on hysteria.

Then the US attorney cut her off. 'Miss Bourne, please report to my office on Monday morning with your attorney. If that is unacceptable, I will have a warrant issued for your arrest immediately.'

'Fuck you all!' Echo shouted. 'I'll be there with the best goddamn lawyer in this city. I'll sue every fucking one of you before this is over. You just wait and see.'

Eliot felt neither good nor bad about what he'd just done to protect himself and Sinclare. Sooner or later that woman would get his wife on the other side of the law, he was sure, not because Sinclare was evil, for he honestly did not believe she had an evil inch in her body. Rather, it was

because Sinclare so believed that Echo was responsible for all that was good in her life.

Realizing he was pressed for time, Eliot quickly
dressed for the *Sequoia* dinner and scribbled a note
for Sinclare: 'Sin dear. Will meet you at the
Sequoia. Love, El.' He hoped the tone of his note
would keep her from stirring any more action into
his rather chaotic day.

Thursday, June 8, 1989 – 4:00 P.M.
Crystal City
Arlington, Virginia

Polly roared into the passing lane on M Street and
hung a left. She shot across Key Bridge in thirty
seconds flat, whipped around the traffic circle on
the Virginia side of the bridge, and drove down
the off-ramp onto the drive that ran along the flat,
Virginia side embankment of the placid Potomac
River.

She eased up on the gas and dropped back down
to a speed still worth a ticket and fast enough to
vent some of the emotions she had been swallowing since Sinclare Ives had attacked her mother.
That scene at the Hay-Adams had been the distil-
lation of everything she disliked about the wives of
the Washington power elite.

When she was ten Polly vowed she would never
live life vicariously in the shadow of the man she'd
marry, like so many of the women who came to

332

her mother's luncheons and cocktail parties. These women lived in the void of their own lives, clinging to what existence they could find in the lives of their husbands. They weren't comfortable as women, mothers, or whatever, without the identity of an important husband.

Avoiding their fate had a lot to do with her choosing West Point. Her father took it as a compliment to his own military career. Polly told neither of her parents, whom she loved, her real motivation because it would only have hurt them. She knew her mother had not chosen her life, which surely accounted for her drinking. It made Polly sad not to be able to help. She had vowed to fall in love with a man who was her equal – no more, no less.

Of the wives, she loathed Sinclare Ives the most. This morning she had wanted to slam-dunk her head into the salmon mold. She would have, too, if she hadn't been afraid of further embarrassing her mother. She enjoyed the thought of flipping Sinclare Ives over her head and face first into the pâté. After three years at West Point and routine twenty-mile hikes carrying forty pounds of field gear, she was at the peak of her physical strength. Her svelte, compact body had the strength and agility it required to compete with men twice her size, and that gave her a feeling of total confidence in her ability to react to any threat – anything except downright cheap shot, bitchy behavior like Sinclare Ives's. Polly had never understood why her mother, until today, had always enjoyed Sinclare's outrageous behavior. Polly had hated her since their first encounter at Judy Lowry's boutique, where Polly had taken a summer job her last year in high school. When Sinclare tried to charge over a thousand dollars' worth of clothes without a credit card Polly gave her a polite but hard time. Sinclare's final argument was to stand in the door of the dressing room in her black bra, garter belt, and no panties, shrieking at Polly, 'Don't you know who I am?'

Polly had stared at the angry woman standing bare-assed in plain sight of all the other customers. At the time, Polly had been dumbfounded and very embarrassed. She had never heard of Sinclare before, but Polly would never forget the name.

'Don't you know who I am?' That scream had stayed with Polly all these years as the motto of those Washington women who were, in fact, no one.

At the Hay-Adams this morning there hadn't been one woman, except perhaps Justice Sandra Day O'Connor and, of course, former Transportation Secretary Liddy Dole, who Polly felt didn't harbor a silent scream, 'Don't you know who I am?'

Over the years at her mother's parties and luncheons she met many such women with that same silent scream inside the designer clothes or too skinny bodies, so fragile that they looked as though they could be snapped in half between thumb and forefinger.

They would circle and size each other up for

334

some flaw, some hint that someone else was less than they were, an ounce heavier, a wrinkle older, an inch of hemline less well-turned-out. They batted their eyes like cartoon fawns and said airhead things they didn't mean. She shuddered just thinking about those women, whose lives were based not on talent or worth but on their husband's last appointment or election.

She had never thought of marriage in a positive way until she met Bob. Men thought she was dainty and vulnerable and were attracted. But cockiness and self-confidence usually turned them off, and, if that didn't, her sharp intellect or her physical superiority did.

That hadn't been the situation with the big, shambling Secret Service man who plopped down next to her on the campaign plane last fall. They were thirty thousand feet in the air somewhere between Sioux Falls and St Paul, Minnesota. His ready smile and obvious self-confidence immediately put her at ease. A few of her old sarcastic tricks only made him laugh, his soft brown eyes crinkling at the edges. Immediately, attempted one-upmanship on her part seemed childish, so she quit. By the time they touched down in St Paul she knew she had found someone special.

She pulled into the underground garage of Bob's Crystal City, Virginia, apartment complex seconds before he arrived and screeched to a halt behind her. Their timing had been near-perfect. She looked at his handsome face as he approached.

They hugged and she buried her head into his neck. 'God, I missed you so much.'

Gently he pulled her chin up and stared down at her. 'Let's go up to the apartment.' Their kiss lasted the length of the elevator ride from the garage to the floor of his apartment. Despite all they had to talk about, they said nothing. They both knew that it would be impossible until they satisfied their desire.

She led the way into the bedroom, undressing as she walked. By the time she reached the bed he was down to his shirt and shoulder holster.

Naked, they fell into the cloudlike loft of the feather comforter and wordlessly went about assuaging their hunger for each other. It had been that way their first time together. No explanations, no games, no excuses – just their overwhelming need. That need had been in their phone calls, their rushed meeting in airports and the little motels in the towns and villages within a few miles of West Point.

They had never been able to manage an entire night together. She had her life and he had his. Through careful planning and the power of their need for each other they managed to come together for a few glorious hours, promising themselves their next meeting would be calmer, longer, more peaceful, and less pressured. It lent an extra edge to their passion. Their fantasies about each other took on geographic overtones. Someday, they told each other, they would be on a beach, in a mountain cabin, trapped in a blizzard, marooned on a desert island.

Sated and reluctant to rouse himself, Bob glanced at his watch. 'Polly, it's four already. I'm on duty at five-thirty. The President is going to the *Sequoia* for a drop-by, then to a big party.'

'Desert him,' Polly mumbled from under a pile of pillows. She was just drifting off into a gauzy sleep.

'Can't be helped, my sweet,' he said, gathering her into his arms and pulling the comforter over them. 'Polly, we have to talk,' he continued, in a tone that sounded amazingly official for the circumstances, as he brushed his lips against her forehead.

Polly stiffened slightly. She was the one who had to talk. She had to tell him she was pregnant, but she couldn't bear to bring it up. She would let him go first. Her news could wait.

'You know I've been on the detail investigating Bradford Barry's death at the hotel.' She nodded, uninterested. Bob took a deep breath. 'That's what I need to discuss with you.' He sensed that Polly was not very anxious to think about the 'uncle' she had just buried. She was going to be downright miserable after she heard what their investigation had turned up about her mother.

'Hey sweetie,' Polly said, turning to him and stroking his head as he sat staring sadly at her, 'what's going on?'

'Damn, Polly, I've got to tell you some things that I've got no business telling you, but because I love you, I can't not tell you. And to make it worse, I'm afraid it's pretty unpleasant.'

'Bob, I'm a big girl. Let's have it.'

He lit a cigarette slowly, then casually told her about the matching voice print in such a manner that it sounded like pure coincidence. Polly was more surprised to hear that Uncle Brad was such a swinger than that he'd been under surveillance during the campaign for sleeping with a 'left-wing' French journalist. The fact that he'd been trysting the night of his death gave her a pleasant kind of memory that he'd been enjoying himself during his last minutes.

'Pure coincidence that the woman calling the 911 number and Mom's voice sound alike,' she stated confidently. Then she laughed. 'Bob, I can't imagine Mom and Uncle Brad making it, can you?'

'Well, I couldn't until this morning. Let me tell you what else has come up. The FBI found a piece of jewelry in the shower drain of the tub Brad Barry was found in.'

Polly pushed away her thoughts of her adopted uncle to a more comforting image.

'Wow, you mean he was doing it in the shower?' Polly said. 'That's great. It takes real strong legs to do it standing up.'

'Polly, stay with me and listen.'

He was still too serious, too concerned for her to do otherwise. She had barely moved since he'd started, so she adjusted a leg that felt cramped under her.

He continued. 'We traced the bracelet to a

338

jeweler and got the name of the person who had it made. So we knew that much.' He paused for a moment, wondering if he should tell her that Ambassador Sumner had given it to his daughter Jan. No, he was already breaking so many rules. It was necessary, anyway, now. He reached over and put out his cigarette. 'Anyway, the bracelet was returned this morning by the FBI to the Secret Service. Valuable property is always logged on to our computer so that whoever is handling it is responsible for it, even if we only have it overnight. That was done and, in doing so, the agent noticed there was a record of what appeared to be the same bracelet already in the computer from six months earlier. It had been turned in to the White House lost and found the night of the inaugural ball. It was your mother who turned it in. She said she found it on the ballroom floor.'

Bob paused because he'd been giving her a lot of details and wanted to make sure it was sinking in.

'The bracelet was locked up in our office for about a month. When no one claimed it, it was given to your mother. Polly, I hate to say this but it looks like she was the one wearing it when they were in the shower together.'

Polly listened to her heart beat three times, trying to think through what Bob had just said. 'My mother?' she said, in stunned disbelief.

He reached over, took her hand, and looked into her stricken face. 'You know I shouldn't be telling you this. I could end up pushing a desk in the counterfeit detail in Cheyenne, or worse, they'd throw my butt out of the Service. But you mean too much to me.'

Polly jumped from the bed, pulling her cover sheet angrily about her naked body. She paced between the window and the bed. 'Okay, assuming it really was her, and I'm still not positive of that, what does it have to do with anything?'

'Polly, don't overreact. I've got more to tell you.'

'I don't give a flying fuck! What are you people, the gestapo or something? The thought police? If it's some kind of crime for consenting adults to fuck, maybe you and I had better turn ourselves in, too.'

As Polly continued to pace, her anger turned to worry. She walked silent in thought, then stopped. 'The FBI! Holy shit, Bob, how big a deal is all this?'

'Well it is a pretty big deal, but I'm trying to shrink it down to manageable size. Keep the whole damn world from knowing about it. I want to protect you and your parents. This could be pretty rough for your dad.'

'Who knows so far?' she asked, fighting the feeling of total panic at the mention of her father.

'Polly, I'm the only person in the world who knows that the bracelet found in the hotel is the one your mother found. I discovered it on the property log because it was sent back to me to handle. It was sent to the White House because the President has ended the investigation. There was no reason to believe there was any security breach, so it's over. The bracelet will be returned to its owner tomorrow.'

'Poor Mom. I don't know if she can handle something like this,' Polly said, swallowing hard to clear the lump in her throat.

Bob reached across the bed and pulled her into his arms. He held her, rocking gently back and forth. 'I'm trying to make it easier on all of you, hon. But I've done all I can do.'

'I want to die,' she said, reaching over and hugging him hard.

'Polly girl, that's not like you. Where's my kick-ass cadet, huh?' He continued to rock her slowly back and forth.

Finally she said, so softly he could barely hear her, 'Your kick-ass cadet is pregnant.'

'What?' he said, in shocked surprise.

'Sorry, Agent Kadanoff. A slight goof-up.'

He stopped rocking and held her away so he could look into her eyes. 'That's no goof,' he beamed, 'that's damn wonderful!'

'It's a mess, Bob. I feel stupid.'

'Cut it out. What's to feel stupid about? I love kids. I love you, now more than ever.'

'West Point uniforms do not accommodate protruding stomachs.'

'Screw West Point!'

'If I have it, it will be the other way around.'

'If you have it . . . What are you talking about?'

'We have an alternative.'

She would never forget the look on his face. It was part startled pain, part white fury. He pointed

341

to her stomach. 'In there is a part of us,' he said, 'just you and me. It's what we made by loving each other. There is no alternative. Never.'

She gave in and let the tears come. 'Oh Bobby, I do love you so.'

'Polly, we can talk about this later. Right now I think you should get to your mother as soon as possible. She has to know we're on to this, and maybe we can help if Sumner is rumbling around.'

'By the time I can get back up to the house she'll be gone.'

'Where?'

'She's going to a big dinner party out at Lady Maubry's estate in Virginia, somewhere out in Fauquier County.'

He stood and walked toward the shower. 'That's where we're headed on our second stop with the President tonight. You'd better get out there pronto.'

'Yes, sir! Will that be all, sir?' she said with a wry smile, snapping to attention and saluting. She was standing stark naked as the sheet fell from her body.

They stared at each other for a moment and then rushed back into each other's arms.

The Cosmos Club

Caroline had Dalton paged and sat down to wait
in the ladies' lounge. The elegant old Cosmos Club
at the corner of Massachusetts and Florida avenues
was deserted. The luncheon stragglers had long
gone and it was too early for the cocktail hour.
From her seat in a high-backed leather chair near
the window she could see four blue-haired ladies
quietly playing bridge in the card room.

She smiled sadly to herself. It occurred to her
that in twenty years she would very likely be one
of those ladies, whiling away her afternoon playing
meaningless card games. Washington was littered
with widows – women who had followed their
ambitious husbands to the capital city, established
their place in its pecking order, then lost a husband
to the ravages of stress and achievement that haunt
the banks of the Potomac. Rather than return to
the small town or big city they had come from, to
friends and family who didn't understand the
dazzle and energy of Washington, they stayed and
kept each other company. They had a common
bond, and some were even active, forming the
backbone of Washington's many charities.

After what Caroline had been through in the last
six months the prospect of living like these ladies
seemed reassuring and comforting, but boring as

343

hell. She wondered what her future held now that her marriage would most assuredly be coming to an end.

She ordered a martini from the handsome old black waiter who had been at the Cosmos Club as long as she could remember. She had just taken a sip of her drink when she saw Dalton striding toward her. He wore the banker's gray suit, striped silk tie, and dazzling white shirt she remembered him selecting that very morning. He'd flown to Atlanta and back for his speech this morning, only a million years ago.

Dalton signaled the waiter before brushing Caroline's cheek with a kiss and taking the seat opposite her. She held her breath and fixed her eyes on his West Point ring, afraid to look directly at him. 'Dalton, we need to talk,' she began.

'If it's about Polly,' he said, 'it's all right. She called a few minutes ago. She's working things out with that young man. Then we'll talk. Please don't worry, darling, it will all work out.'

Caroline stared at him. Either he was a monster torturing her or he didn't know. All her resolve vanished. She wanted a reprieve, a stay of execution. She told him about the incident at the memorial reception for Brad. At least it would serve as a distraction. But he'd heard all about it and complimented her on how well she'd handled a difficult situation.

'Any new thoughts or information about the new chief of staff?' she asked, searching for another change of subject.

344

'I think the President will probably ask Eliot Ives to come on board; he could even elevate the acting chief of staff, David Klein. I doubt he'll give it to Mark Kirkland, but he thinks Mark is very able and underused at the Press Office.'

'Dalton! You're talking like you've given up all hope.'

'I have, Caroline. That's what I wanted to talk to you about.'

The waiter silently placed a ginger ale in front of Dalton and disappeared. Dalton pulled his chair closer, so their knees almost touched. 'I was going to tell you this evening on the way out to Connie's. It's rumored in the press corps that there's a videotape circulating around town. On it are people indulging in sadomasochistic sex. I am purported to be one of those people.' He spoke as though he were presenting his position on nuclear disarmament, matter-of-factly, without emotion.

Caroline flushed. 'That's the nastiest, slimiest thing I've ever heard! It's a fake, of course!'

Dalton held up his hand to silence her. 'Now, now, dear, that's why I hesitated to bring it up. I knew how upset you'd be. Of course the tape is a fake, but a lot of damage can be done before people realize that. You know how rumors spread like fire in this town. It doesn't take much to get a smear going. The wires pick it up. The television networks lead off the evening news with it, true or not, and, well, there you are. I can't do that to the President. His administration has been spotless so far.'

'But what are you going to do about it?' Caroline demanded, trying to keep her voice down. 'You can't let someone get away with this.'

'That's why I wanted to meet you over here, out of the office. I have an appointment with the President at five. With your permission, I'd like to withdraw my name from consideration.'

'Oh, Dalton, this is awful.' She was surprised that he shared this with her. Thoughtful Dalton. 'I want you to do whatever you think is best. How did you find out?'

'David Klein called me this afternoon. The Press Office had a couple of calls on it this afternoon. It's buzzing around over at the Press Club. He wanted me to know before he went to the President. It was decent of him. He didn't have to, but he wanted me to know before whoever made the tape leaks it. He's also informed the Justice Department and requested the FBI to find out who's behind it.'

'How can people be so vile?'

Dalton shrugged. 'That's the name of the game, love. The closer you get to power the more threatening you become. Your enemies can get amazingly inventive.'

He signaled the waiter. When he arrived seconds later Dalton told him to leave the tab open. 'I'm running, darling,' Dalton said, squeezing her hand. 'Why don't you relax. I'll send a White House car to pick you up in about forty minutes. Then we'll head out to Virginia. Wish me luck, I have to do this.'

'I know, darling,' she said softly, blowing him a kiss.

When he was gone she sat for a long time staring out the window. The apple tree next to the old building was losing the very last of its blossoms. A late-day breeze had sprung up, urging the pink-white blossoms to the ground. It was as though the tree were weeping.

Wordlessly she raised her hand to signal the waiter. As he approached the table she pointed to her empty martini glass and indicated that she would like another.

She was on her third when a White House aide called to tell her a White House car was en route to pick her up, but that the general had requested she go on to the dinner by herself. The President's meeting was running late, and General Riggs would meet her at Winterberry later.

Now she didn't know if she felt better or worse for not telling Dalton what she'd come to tell him, for again she felt very much alone – very much away from being a part of anything of significance. She looked at the ladies still playing bridge and said aloud to no one, 'No thank you. That's still not for me.'

Eliot, pressed for time and annoyed by his mission, scanned the Willard bar twice. The bartender had not seen her.

No Deena!

Dammit! If that bitch has stood me up I'll . . . 'Ah! There you are!' he said, throwing up his hands in relief.

She was sitting in an alcove just outside the bar, almost as though she were hiding. A low fringed lamp next to her squat club chair made her dull gray-blonde hair look like a fright wig.

At the sound of his voice she quickly shoved a hefty sheaf of papers she was reading into the oversized handbag on her lap. She flicked her bangs at him and spoke through her teeth. 'Well,' she said, affecting the Queen Mother attitude he had seen many times before, 'I see you finally arrived.'

Eliot smiled his most charming smile. If there were a way to reach down, lock his hands around the folds of her neck, and squeeze the life out of her, he would. At this moment he loathed her for the power she had over him, for making a man of his standing come here, to a damn hotel lobby, to plead his case.

348

Eliot counted to three behind his teeth and sank into the plush of the chair opposite her. 'What's that you have there? You haven't taken up reading manuscripts in your spare time, have you, Deena?'

'What spare time?' she snapped. 'Three columns a week, a magazine article a month, and a daily radio show. Who has time?'

Eliot suppressed a moan. 'Well, Deena, since you're so busy I won't take much of your time. I want to have a word with you about your conversation with Sinclare today. She wasn't herself this afternoon, and if you could just forget anything she may have said I'd be most appreciative.'

After a moment of silently staring at him, she asked, 'How appreciative, Eliot?'

Eliot was good at reading people. He had thrown out the bait, not sure what useful clues it would pick up. Deena's continual unconscious stroking of the bag in her lap did not go unnoticed.

He reached for a cigar. 'Mind if I smoke?' he asked.

He didn't have much time. He was supposed to meet George Lowry at six, but he'd have to hide his urgency and act as if he had all evening. It would take fifteen minutes to reach the navy shipyard where the *Sequoia* was docked. He had only a few minutes to bring her around.

He blew a funnel of thick blue smoke that filled the air around them. She didn't flinch. 'Tell me what you've got in mind, my dear. Then we'll know how appreciative I've got to be.'

He could see by the look in her eyes that she

was going to make him squirm, if she could. One thing he had loved about being in the Senate was that he dealt with gentlemen – men who knew when to press and when to pull back. Deena always pressed as hard as she could.

'Well, I assume you are a bit worried by the fact that your wife is running around town slandering, perhaps blackmailing a public official, which could make a must-read column for tomorrow's edition.' She reached inside her voluminous dress and yanked a bra strap into place. 'I'd have to have a really good reason for not running it.'

'All right, Deena, what's the manuscript you've got in the bag?'

She looked down at her lap and peeped at him through her long fake eyelashes. One was coming unglued and looked like an escaping centipede on her eyelid. 'You won't believe this,' she said proudly. 'It's mine.'

He believed it. He held out his hand as she hoisted the heavy bag on her lap into her arms, like a child. She held it against her chest, cradling it and lowering her voice to a confidential purr. 'Eliot, I've been working on this for over two years. It's got everything – sex, glamour, power-fucking, intrigue, real inside Washington stuff that only I could know. Sally Quinn, Allen Drury, Barbara Howar – none of 'em could capture what's in here.'

Eliot withdrew his hand. He would have to listen before she would part with her treasure.

'You know, people have been telling me for

years to do a big Washington novel. Everyone says I could make a killing if I wrote a book. Well, Eliot, I've done it.' She flicked her bangs at him, and then stared toward the ceiling. 'But I feel so unprotected, so vulnerable. What if I sent my manuscript off to someone and they stole it? You're a lawyer. They could do that, right?'

'Highly unlikely, Deena, it doesn't work that way.'

'That's it! It doesn't work that way,' she repeated as though he had summoned up a clever Eleventh Commandment. 'Eliot, I need someone to help me. You know, show me how things work. I know I'm sitting on a gold mine here, hardcover, paperback, book clubs, mini-series, maybe a movie. I just don't want to get taken. You understand.'

He understood. He also understood that she knew he represented the Washington interests of a number of New York book publishers. 'Why don't you get an agent, Deena? That's what they're for.'

'An agent! Anybody can get an agent!' she shrieked. 'I want real protection. I want a heavy hitter, someone who knows the ropes. I want a lawyer like you, Eliot.'

'I don't think you can afford me, Deena, dear.'

'Afford? Afford? You mean there would be some kind of fee?'

He took a long pull on his cigar and watched the smoke rising. What she wanted was clear. Indeed, if the book was good, he could help her. 'Deena, you need an agent to evaluate your book –

someone who knows what the market for it might be, and then cracks the best deal,' he said patiently.

'Maybe you need an agent to keep your ass out of trouble for letting your wife run all over town blackmailing a public official, Senator.'

'Easy, Deena,' he said, controlling his temper. Long ago he had learned that confrontations resolved nothing. 'You want to make a deal. Let's act like grown-ups and make a deal. I have no doubt that you can write a hell of a book and I'll be glad to be of assistance. But I want you to back off of Sinclare even faster than you moved in on her.' His voice was firm but non-threatening. As he spoke each word he looked at Deena square in the eye.

'I'm sorry, Eliot. Perhaps I was too heavy-handed, but this book is more than just important to me. It's my life.' Her lower lip began to tremble.

He had never seen Deena drop her guard. 'And Sinclare is my life, Deena — more than my life — and I don't want to see her hurt. Ever.' He reached out again for the book she was still clutching. 'Here, let me have it. Now that we understand each other, I think we can do each other a favor.'

She pulled the manuscript out of her bag and placed it on her lap, lovingly stroking the top page. 'You promise, Eliot?' she asked plaintively. 'You promise you'll take care of it? Promise you won't let anyone else see it?'

'Deena, I can hardly help you get it published if I can't let anyone see it,' he said gently. 'The publishers have to evaluate it, right?'

'Well, yes, but you know what I mean. There's a lot of hot stuff in here. You won't . . . like talk about it around town . . . tell people?'

'But, Deena, dear. Isn't that what you do for a living?'

'Sure . . . yeah . . . but this is me. My heart.'

'I assure you it is safe,' he said and extended his hand.

Reluctantly she released the pile of paper.

Together they walked across the lobby discussing how Eliot would proceed to 'place' her book. He knew exactly where to send it, and he figured he'd better do it soon – immediately. He realized that he had struck a better deal than he had expected. As long as he had Deena's manuscript in his hands, she would not dare write anything nasty about him or Sinclare. It could be months before her book was published, and then after publication she would need the continued good will of the publisher, through Eliot. That would keep Deena in line. It was a hell of a deal.

Deena was thrilled. She hugged him and kissed him goodbye, embraces he would rather have been spared.

Eliot was still smiling when he got into his car to race traffic to the *Sequoia*. He hoped he'd have as good fortune with George Lowry.

Thursday Evening

Thursday, June 8, 1989 – 6:05 P.M.
The White House, West Wing

The sound of Marine One landing on the south lawn all but drowned out the six o'clock news, even though the Press Office was on the north side of the building.

Mark Kirkland hurriedly tried to clear his desk of last-minute items as he watched the three television screens which enabled him to check the news on each of the network stations. Only recently had he learned that the three-screen viewing tradition at the White House had been started by Lyndon Johnson during the last year of his presidency, when he wanted to know everything that was being said about his handling of the Vietnam War. What Johnson got was a triple dose of bad news, as had many of his successors. But the Kane administration was still enjoying a honeymoon with the press, so getting away from the White House this early in the evening was no real problem.

All three stations were carrying the local news. A tractor-trailer jackknife on the Beltway led on Channel 9. A story on a betting scandal at some Maryland junior college was on Channel 2. On

Channel 7 Tiffany Dunsmore was standing in front of St John's Church with a microphone in her hand. He turned down the volume of the other two stations.

'Services for White House Chief of Staff Bradford Barry were held at noon today at St John's Episcopal Church,' she began.

Mark watched with increasing fascination as Dunsmore reported the embarrassing incident between Sinclare Ives and the Secret Service. Sinclare's reputation for histrionics was well known. His mild amusement at the report turned to sudden interest as she ended her report. 'We tried to learn from Jan Kirkland, the State Department Protocol officer who planned the event, just why Ms Ives was barred from the services. As of airtime Ms Kirkland's office had not returned our calls.'

His hand reflexively reached for the phone. He asked the White House operator to ring his home. He was about to hang up after the fourth ring when Jan answered.

'It's me,' Mark said.

'Honey, I'm sorry. I was in the shower. I'm frantic. Aunt Connie is downstairs in the car with the gardener. Are you coming down with us?' Her voice had a wavy quality as though she was balancing the phone and moving around.

'Have you seen the six o'clock news?'

'No, I've been running. What's up?'

'Did your office have anything to do with Sinclare Ives being kept out of the Barry service?'

'Damn,' she said under her breath, 'I was afraid of this.'

'What's it all about, anyway?'

'Honey, please come home. We need to talk.'

'But you're leaving.'

'I'll send Aunt Connie on. We'll drive down together and change at the farm. I've got your tux in a plastic bag right here.'

'And my shirt?'

'Shirt. Check.'

'Studs, links, cummerbund, shoes ... forget it, I've got on black shoes and socks.'

'How about your Dracula cloak?'

'Huh?'

'Kidding,' Jan sang.

'Don't kid. I'm running. Kiss.' He dropped the receiver into place.

He surveyed his office. There would be no more news coming from the White House Press Office, since the President would be leaving within the hour.

Jan and Mark said little as he maneuvered through the triple lanes of suburban-bound traffic. Jan squeezed her eyes against the blazing sun. In another hour it would dip below the rolling hills of northern Virginia and the earth would begin to cool.

She adjusted the air-conditioning vent and let it blow directly up the soft folds of her dinner dress. 'Pretty dumb, huh?'

'Not too smart,' he agreed.

'I didn't think this would turn into a Pulitzer Prize for an investigative journalist,' she asked sarcastically. 'Do you think the press will follow up?' she asked in a serious tone.

'I doubt it. It's a one-shot story.'

Jan stared out the window. She knew Mark didn't approve of her taking Sinclare's name off the guest list. But that nasty lying news item had hurt her so.

'I did it for you, Mark.'

'For me?'

'I'd learned Sinclare planted that item in Deena Simon's column. She was trying to hurt you and I was furious.'

'You're a good woman, Janet Kirkland,' he said. With exaggerated seriousness, he was making light of the incident, trying to say it should no longer concern her.

'Well, I've got a good man. Have they offered you the chief of staff job yet?'

The set of his jaw told her something was bothering him and he wanted to talk about it. As desperately as she wanted to tell him what Aunt Connie had told her that afternoon she wanted him to talk first. 'Honey?' she said to prod him.

'Jan, I've always figured I was a default candidate. And I don't see any defaulting yet. But I'm not really tuned in to what's going on.'

They sat silent for the next minute, as she watched the heat rising up from the melting tar on the highway, creating shimmering mirages around the tires of the cars in front of them.

Then, turning to him, Jan said quietly, 'My father isn't everything I thought he was, Mark. I found that out this afternoon.'

'What do you mean?' he asked, surprised.

She told him. At first the words stuck in her throat. When she got to the part about her mother they came tumbling out in a stream of pain and relief. When she finished they both sat staring straight ahead.

The car was climbing now. The flat pastureland on either side of the road had given way to slowly rising hills. On the other side lay the valley stretched out in all its muted early-summer glory. She knew that from the crest of the hill they would see the place she loved most. Far to the left the low white fence of Winterberry Farm ran seemingly for miles, marking the land that had belonged to the Sumner family since long before the Civil War.

At the turn at the top of the hill there was a scenic rest stop where tourists took pictures of the valley below. 'Pull over, Mark. We can stop here like we used to,' she said, pointing to the sign ahead. 'We have time.'

He guided the car into the rest stop. Without speaking they got out and walked toward the low railing. The air was fresh and sweet and smelled of honeysuckle. The sun fractured into shreds of gold that fanned out over the valley below.

Jan slid her arm around Mark's waist and leaned her head against his shoulder. 'I only wanted you to have that job because I thought you wanted it,' she said softly. That hadn't been true yesterday.

Then it had seemed like the most important goal of their lives. But today she meant it.

He put his arm around her shoulders.

'Mark, I need your help. I'm afraid to ask my father where my mother is.'

'But you must,' Mark said, his face filled with concern. 'We must.'

'You mean you'd go to him with me, feeling the way you do about him?'

'I wouldn't let you go alone.' He pulled her into his arms. She lay her head against his shoulder and felt his lips covering her forehead.

'I have to find out,' she said. 'I have to know once and for all.'

'We'll go to him. First thing tomorrow morning if you like.'

She burrowed farther into him, letting his strong straight body protect her from the rising wind, from the hurt. 'Maybe later in the day would be better. Mornings are getting pretty grim.'

'Why? What's wrong with your mornings?'

'Morning is when I get sick.'

'Huh?'

'The doctor says I'll probably stop getting sick after the third month.'

She waited. His only response was to increase the pressure of his arms around her. Finally he whispered, 'Oh, Jan, now, we'll be forced to move out of our ridiculous little house.'

Senator George Lowry leaned against the brass railing of the presidential yacht. He held his patrician face in profile against the evening breeze. In soft focus he looked somewhat like Gregory Peck – or so he enjoyed being told. Suddenly he broke into a broad smile. This was exactly his kind of Washington party, free of dull bureaucrats and the drooling sycophants who hung around the powerful. The small group invited were men of enormous influence, successful in the private sector. In the group chatting nearby he recognized California mega-developer Doug Munsinger and his stunning cover-girl wife, Michelle Fox. They were talking animatedly with the chairman of the board of the Bank of America. George was watching Michelle's long blonde hair catching the wind when he sensed someone at his shoulder.

'Excuse me, Senator.' A ramrod-straight young naval ensign interrupted his thoughts. 'We have two calls for you. The White House switchboard is patching them over to us right now. Your wife and Senator Ives.'

Lowry placed his drink down on the small deck table. 'Thank you. Where can I find a phone?'

'Follow me, sir,' the ensign said as he turned to

lead the way back into the main dining room off the aft deck. 'Senator, we don't have secure lines.'

'I understand,' he nodded, picking up the phone in the small elegant room. 'George Lowry here,' he said briskly.

The White House operator asked which call he would take first.

'I'll speak with Mrs Lowry, please.' He heard the operator sign off. 'Hello, dear. Are you ready for the Winterberry party?' He spoke sweetly. He knew Judy was not amused at the logistics of his dropping by the *Sequoia* and her having to pick him up there for the drive to Winterberry.

He also knew his meeting with Eliot would be short, and disappointing to Eliot, so the sooner Judy got there the better. He didn't want Eliot working him over – the bastard had a way of getting through – so he would tell Judy to come on ahead now. They lived just across the river in Old Town, Alexandria. She could be at dockside in twenty minutes.

'I'm ready, George,' Judy said tightly, 'but that's not why I called. That Echo Bourne woman called here for you about twenty minutes ago. I've been trying to find you, and your office told me to call the White House.'

Shit. What did Echo Bourne want? he wondered. It didn't take long for Judy to tell him.

'She was very cold, George – hostile. I've never liked that woman, and I don't understand her call.'

'What did she say?'

'She wanted to know where you were. I told her.

364

She said she was going to Winterberry tonight. I find it odd that Constance would invite someone like her.'

'Judy, skip the social commentary. I've got Eliot Ives holding.'

'Good, maybe you'd better tell him what she said, too. Let me repeat it as best I can. She said, "Tell your husband if he doesn't get Eliot Ives and his pack of dogs to back off immediately, I'm going to blow up this whole effing town, starting with our effing house."' Even with her husband, Judy couldn't bring herself to use the 'F word'.

'Is that all?' He was taken aback by the message.

'Don't you think that's enough?'

'I don't understand, but I'll find out. Listen, darling, why don't you head over. I don't need to wait to say hello to the President. We'll see him down at Winterberry.'

As he waited for the White House operator to hook him up with Eliot, George scanned the room. From the looks of the dining room, about twenty people were going to be attending the cruise dinner. The *Sequoia* crew would start with cocktails with the President, who would ride with the guests to Mount Vernon, where he would disembark and be helicoptered over to Winterberry Farm. After the President departed, the guests would have a beautiful seated dinner on the cruise back up the Potomac to Washington. George knew the routine; it would be a pleasant evening. He and Judy had attended these dinners on several occasions: Rosenthal china, the best crystal and silver, superb wines, great cigars – not your usual boating fare. The White House knew how to entertain. He reached for the phone after half a ring. 'Eliot?'

'George, sorry, I'm running late. Can you stay put? The President really wants us to talk.'

'I don't know, Eliot. Judy and I are due out at the Winterberry dinner . . .'

'I know, I know,' he said impatiently. 'Listen, is Sinclare there yet?'

'Haven't seen her. Why?' As George spoke he felt a warm presence at his shoulder, then a soft peck on the cheek. He turned. He was about to say her name when Sinclare pressed her finger to her lips. With her free hand she reached down and began stroking his crotch. Panicked, he scanned the stateroom. Empty. He could feel the perspiration building on his forehead.

'Ah . . . Eliot, could you hang on a minute? The steward is trying to ask me something.' George covered the mouthpiece of the phone so tightly his knuckles were turning white. 'What in blazes are you up to, lady?' He smiled at Sinclare. He could feel himself growing rigid as she stroked him.

'Just trying to say hello,' she said coyly.

'Hold on, Sin,' he whispered, both excited and flustered. 'I'm talking to your husband, so just hold on.'

Sinclare shrugged and smiled.

'Look, Eliot . . .,' he said, returning his attention to the phone call, 'the steward says there's another call coming through and Judy's on her way. If you can get over here pronto, we'll chat.'

'Fine, George, but I think I've got something you'd better hear right now.'

George firmly clasped Sinclare's wrist to prevent her from any further manipulation of his crotch. George listened and then in a tight and urgent voice informed Eliot of Echo's bizarre threat, and they agreed that it was a dangerous situation.

Sinclare stood beside George listening to his side of the conversation. She looked particularly beautiful, dressed to attract the kind of attention she wanted at such a party. Her dress was bold and sexy, a yellow and black print of a thin fabric with a short puffy skirt and a strapless top that showed her creamy shoulders and abundant cleavage. She was beginning to fidget. He could tell she was absorbing enough to put the pieces together and wasn't liking what she was hearing.

George hung up and turned toward her. 'Does your pal Echo know about us?' he asked in a demanding tone, glaring at her.

'Hey!' Sinclare shouted at the young Filipino waiter in a crisp white jacket passing at the end of the dining room. 'Bring me a martini.'

Sinclare plopped down on a chintz-covered dining room chair she had pulled away from the table. 'What was that all about, Georgie?'

'I want to ask you something, Sinny dear,' he said, standing over her. 'Did you tell Echo we were still a number?'

'I didn't have to tell her. She had already figured it out. That lady's plugged in everywhere in this city. One of her FBI contacts told her I was seen leaving the Hay-Adams last Sunday night. Some janitor saw me. The FBI thought I'd been with Brad Barry. Some agent actually called me, but don't worry, he never called back, and Echo said the investigation has been called off.'

'How did she know you were with me at the Hay-Adams?'

'Well, she knew Judy was in New York last weekend because one of Echo's friends sat with Judy on the shuttle. She's not dumb. She asked me if I was seeing you and I told her. So what?'

'Holy Christ, that woman is going to cause us some terrible problems. Eliot turned her over to the US attorney this afternoon because of the fake Dalton Riggs tape she was pushing. She's got to be some kind of pissed to call my house with a threat.'

Sinclare's expert makeup job did not conceal the sudden whiteness of her face. 'Shit, George, I'm dead! That's it! Eliot will throw me on the street before dawn if he finds out.' She paused as a waiter suddenly appeared with her martini on a silver tray. She lifted it with a trembling hand and took a long sip. 'Not to mention you. Christ, they won't even find the pieces!'

'Only if he gets to me before Judy does.' He snatched the martini out of her hand and swallowed the remaining mixture in one gulp. 'You know Echo, Sin. You think she'd hurt you or me?' George answered his own question with a groan. Of course she would.

Sinclare looked ill. She pounded her fists against

her knees. 'Shit on a stick. What the hell are we going to do?'

As a lawyer, and a former attorney general of his state, George had been through the process. He knew that once Eliot had placed the wheels in motion it was hard to stop them from rolling. They would have to figure out how to cut off the investigation of Echo without obstructing justice. 'Look, Sin, she doesn't care that she's blackmailing us. What are a few more counts on an indictment. She'd pull down the whole damn town before she'd go down alone. The woman's a walking time bomb.'

Sinclare pushed herself off the chair and started pacing the pattern of the presidential seal woven into the rug. 'George, when I was working with Echo she recorded everything. And I mean everything – phone calls, conversations in her office. She even had a pair of earrings made that were tiny receivers so she could pick up everything at parties and stuff. I typed up a lot of that crap for her over the years and I'll bet anything she's still doing it. She had the transcripts locked up somewhere like the goddamn crown jewels.'

'A tad more valuable I'd say,' George said. He could feel a black depression weighing in on his shoulders. Not only was his marriage in jeopardy, but so was his political career. Add to that double disaster the prospect of ending his relationship with Sinclare. She wasn't just a little piece of tail. She was damn near a drug, an addiction, so much so that he wasn't even that upset when she had married Eliot. At least that meant she would stay in town where he still had a chance. He had to have her. If he went longer than a week without arranging a meeting he couldn't think. She could walk into a restaurant where he was lunching with some boring old constituent and he would get an erection under the table. How Judy didn't find out he never knew, but she didn't. How Eliot never found out was another miracle. They had been careful, but with Echo looming in his life it was becoming clear that they had not been careful enough.

'Come on, we've got to move. Eliot's going to be here soon. If he finds us together . . . well, I don't want to think about it.'

Suddenly, George felt the whole world knew about them. He rose and brushed the trousers of his spotless tux. 'Look, I want you to come down to Winterberry. We need time to talk this out with Echo, try to get her to back off, somehow. Once Eliot gets here you're stuck.'

'I can't go to Winterberry! I wasn't invited and I'm not going to go through the kind of humiliation I went through at the memorial service ever again. What the hell is Echo doing at that party?'

'Sinclare, I have no idea why Echo was invited to the party,' he said with exasperation. 'But if you don't go down there and see what you can do with Echo, I know this: you might as well kiss your husband goodbye. And me.'

'Listen, George, I've already kissed you goodbye. Sure I enjoyed our little visits, but I plan to stay

370

married to Eliot. My marriage means a lot to me and it's more important than our physically enjoying each other.'

'Well, then I suggest – ' Before he could finish, she cut him off.

'The reason you want me to go to Winterberry is to save *your* ass, George. You don't want to ruin your marriage any more than I do mine. But more importantly, you don't want Echo to screw up your political career. The media isn't a bit shy anymore about revealing the private lives of politicians, and yours would make juicy reading.'

George felt like a whipped dog.

'Now,' she said, 'this is what we'll do. I'm going to go down to Winterberry all right, but only to keep Eliot from being hurt. He doesn't deserve it, and I want your help.'

'I'll help any way I can, Sin, you know that.'

'Good. I know Eliot has been meeting with you about something that is very important to him.'

'Oh no you don't,' George said angrily.

'Just back off, George. I want to know what Eliot wants.'

'He wants me to support the new administration's trade legislation. But politically I can't do it.'

'I think you'll find a way.' She smiled smugly.

'No I won't.'

'You will, George, if you want to stay where you'll even have a vote in the first place.'

He knew Sinclare, and her tone of voice was one he had learned never to argue with. When Sinclare made up her mind to do something there was no stopping her. She would go to Winterberry to settle her score with Echo on her own terms or not at all. 'Okay, Sin,' he sighed. 'You've got yourself a deal.'

Sinclare gave him a peck on the cheek. 'Don't forget to make arrangements for me to get in. I'll call Ian when I get there. And tell Eliot my mother had an emergency. That's where I am, as far as he's concerned.' She turned to leave, and then with her wonderful laugh added, 'At least he'll think I'm out of trouble.'

Thursday, June 8, 1989 – 6:15 P.M.
Virginia Route 7
The Road to Winterberry Farm

Sinclare was barely out of the navy shipyard gate when from her rearview mirror she saw Eliot's BMW turn into the same gate. She was more than pleased with herself. George had been easy, but then again he always was. She loved sex with him, but she loved being Mrs Eliot Ives more. She wasn't quite sure what she would do if George changed his mind about delivering whatever damned support Eliot wanted for some boring trade legislation, but she would think of something. She always did.

As she steered her car toward Virginia, through now-moderate expressway traffic along the District side of the Potomac, she thought about how she was going to handle Echo. It wouldn't be a pretty scene, but after her victory with George she was warmed up.

She kicked off her shoes and turned on the radio, finding a soft-rock station. Poor El. He had just been trying to save her from making a terrible, possibly criminal mistake. Why had she ever messed with that damn tape in the first place? She really didn't want to hurt Dalton Riggs, despite his snotty wife. It had only been to help Eliot. God, she wished Eliot had talked to her before he'd turned Echo in. She could have gone to Echo and straightened things out before things had degenerated into this sorry state. Old times had to count for something.

But something more bothered her. Why had Echo given her the tape in the first place? To help Eliot? Or to set her up? These new suspicions of Echo hovered in the back of her mind like threatening black clouds.

Thoughts of Echo, and Eliot, preoccupied her for miles until the glare from the setting sun interrupted. She took one hand off the wheel and pawed through the glove compartment for her shades. Driving west at this time of day meant squinting into a blinding setting sun.

She found a pair of dusty Ray-Bans behind a pile of maps and pushed them on. As she glanced into the rearview mirror she realized she had chewed off all her lipstick. Her mascara was smudged and her hair stood out in clumps from the wind on the yacht.

She saw the white picket fence and the bright green and white striped awning of the Fox and Hound Inn beckoning invitingly ahead. She and Eliot had had Sunday brunch there often enough that the captain would certainly allow her to freshen up in the ladies' room. She knew she was in the vicinity of Winterberry, but she also saw she would get hopelessly lost once past Leesburg. She would have to call for directions.

As she circled the parking lot looking for a space she noticed a White House senior staff car parked directly in front of the canopy. The Lincoln Town cars with gray uniformed drivers from the marine base at Quantico were one of Washington's most coveted perks. The driver stood, ramrod straight, beside the fender. She wondered who the passenger was. A friend, perhaps?

'Hi there,' Sinclare called as she approached the young marine. She slowed her pace, letting him get the full picture. She knew from experience that facilitated cooperation from men.

'Yes, ma'am,' he said, his body snapping to attention a second after his eyes.

'You must be driving someone from the White House to the big party at Winterberry.'

'Yes, ma'am.'

While driving she had pinned her hair loosely on top of her head against the heat and humidity. Now, she reached up and released it. Her thick ebony hair cascaded to her shoulders. The young marine's eyes grew noticeably wider. 'Are you driving someone real important?' she asked breathlessly.

'Why, ah, yes, I'm driving Mrs Riggs. Her husband is the national security advisor.'

Oh, God. Of all people. 'And she's in *there*?' Sinclare gestured toward the restaurant.

'Yes, ma'am. She's on the phone.'

She remembered the public phone was in the back of the dining room. Perhaps she could get in and out without running into her. The last thing she wanted today was another confrontation with Caroline. Sinclare waved goodbye to the young driver as she opened the door. 'Don't stand out in this heat too long.'

Sinclare loved tormenting cute guys when they were on duty and couldn't respond. There was something very sexy about watching them try to control themselves.

She tentatively made her way back to the ladies' room, her small silk makeup case clutched in her hand. The captain was busy seating dining patrons, and she slipped directly through the main dining room unnoticed, but before she made her way down the tiny back hall she saw Caroline. She was seated in a booth by the window, her hands over her face, sobbing.

Sinclare stood stark still. She couldn't just walk by the woman as if she were invisible. Yet if she stopped to say anything there could very easily be a nasty scene. She and Eliot were too well known at the Fox and Hound to let that happen.

Before she could move, Caroline took her hands

away from her face. They were now face-to-face. Caroline's makeup was streaked, and her cheeks and neck were mottled in big pink splotches.

Caroline's shoulders drooped as she closed her eyes and then slowly opened them. 'Oh God, it's you,' she said, her voice heavy with resignation and fatigue.

'Sorry about that,' Sinclare snapped. 'It's a free country and this is a public place.'

Caroline nodded and stared into what appeared to be an untouched cup of coffee.

Amazed at Caroline's lack of response, Sinclare asked, 'What's the matter with you anyway?'

'None of your business.'

'I didn't say it was, Caroline, but when I see someone I know crying alone in a restaurant it upsets me.'

'Oh, please,' Caroline said with exasperation. She was searching hurriedly through her bag. 'Damn, damn, damn,' she said and tossed her bag onto the table next to her coffee.

Sinclare continued to stare at her.

Caroline's eyes were filling with tears. 'I can't stand it, I just can't stand it,' she gasped and slumped against the wall with her hands over her face again.

Sinclare sat down on the banquette opposite her without being asked. What the hell was going on here? she thought. The woman is cracking up! 'Look, Caroline, I know what you think of me but how about a truce, okay? You look like you need a friend.'

376

'You are certainly no friend of mine, Sinclare Ives,' she said angrily from behind her hands.

'I don't think this is the time to be picky, lady. Look, I'll have a cup of coffee with you and you can get yourself cleaned up.'

'I can't. I didn't bring any makeup.'

Sinclare extended the makeup case she had in her hand. 'Here, Estée Lauder bought a Mercedes with what's in here. Take it. We don't have the same coloring but like they say, any paint in a pinch.'

Caroline lowered her hands and looked at Sinclare's extended hand and then back at Sinclare. 'All right,' she shrugged, 'momentary cease-fire, but I still have a bone to pick with you.'

'Okay.' Sinclare smiled. 'I can handle it.'

Caroline located a compact and a small bottle of foundation in Sinclare's bag and started applying it to her mottled skin. 'I've kept the car waiting too long. I really should go.'

'Those sweet little soldiers are paid to wait. Relax, there's plenty of time to get to the party.'

'Is *that* what you're doing here?' Caroline said, raising her eyebrows. 'I didn't think you were . . .'

'You can say it. No, we weren't invited, but I'm going anyway. I have some serious business to take care of.'

'How are you going to get in?' Caroline said, feathering her eyebrows with one of Sinclare's tiny brushes.

'I'll call Ian Vreen from the gate. He's expecting me.'

377

'Ummmm. I don't know . . . the security is going to be real tight.' Caroline gave her hair a final smoothing.

The plastic sign on the waiter's waistcoat read Bruce. 'Will you ladies be having dinner?' he inquired politely. Then he looked at Sinclare. 'Oh, *hello*, Mrs Ives. How *are* you? My goodness, what are you doing sitting way back here. Mr Marcus would want you at your regular table.'

'Hi, Bruce.' Sinclare smiled. 'We just wanted a little privacy. It looked so crowded up front. Is it okay if we just have coffee?'

'Of course, Mrs Ives. And you, ma'am . . .?' He eyed Caroline's untouched cup.

'Thank you,' she said simply. 'Do I look okay?' Caroline asked after the waiter left.

'You look fine. You should wear a darker lipstick more often. It looks good on you,' Sinclare offered. This was going better than she could have dreamed. She had been fully prepared for Caroline to step out of that booth and punch her lights out. Now here they were having coffee and being perfectly civil with each other. 'So what were you so upset about a minute ago?'

'I'd rather not talk about it,' Caroline said, staring into space. Quickly she turned back to Sinclare. 'What I would like to talk about is why you came at me like a banshee today.'

Uh oh, the party's over. 'You don't know? I can't believe that.'

'I never did *anything* to you, Sinclare. Quite the contrary. You're the one who has done something

378

terrible to me, and to my husband. Not just terrible – possibly criminal.' Caroline's voice was growing louder.

Sinclare looked around nervously, then moved her hand downward to signal Caroline to keep her voice down. 'Criminal?' she whispered. 'What are you talking about?' Caroline couldn't know anything. She couldn't.

'That tape. My husband took his name out of consideration for chief of staff because of your criminal, and I repeat it, criminal slander about some dreadful videotape.'

Sinclare's hand flew to cover her mouth as her jaw dropped. Had this tape business gone further than she thought? God, why had she tried to be such a big deal with Deena?

'Oh, don't act so surprised, Sinclare . . .' Bruce deftly placed two fresh cups of coffee on the linen tablecloth and disappeared. 'Your friend Echo Bourne told me all about it at La Reine.'

'Echo! What did she say?'

'She caught me as I was leaving my booth and apologized for you. She said she was so upset that you were going around saying Dalton was a sex pervert and you had a videotape to prove it. Now you *know* that's a lie, Sinclare. How could you do something like that?'

'Wait . . . wait . . . wait,' Sinclare said, slamming down her hand and nearly spilling both coffee cups. '*You* are the one who's been going around slandering *me*.'

'What! I've never said anything about you I wouldn't say to your face, Sinclare Ives.'

'Oh no? You said Eliot couldn't be named chief of staff because he was married to a *tramp*.' Sinclare spat the word out as though she had found a mysterious slimy object in a mouthful of her coffee.

'Now you wait a minute, Sinclare. I never said that about you. Where in the world did you hear that?'

'From Echo. She made a real point of telling me. That's why I laid into you at the reception. Granted, I'd had a ton of New York sours in the bar earlier, but when I saw you I went berserk. I may be a lot of things, Caroline, but tramp isn't one of them. I've earned my own living since I was seventeen years old. It's been an honest living and I can hold my head up. Sure I dated a lot of big shots – senators, hot shot lawyers. I almost married George Lowry. I had affairs, plenty of 'em. But I never took a dime from any man in my life until I married Eliot.' She paused and took a deep breath. It felt good. There was something wonderfully therapeutic about confronting an accuser. 'You hurt me, Caroline. You hurt me terribly.'

Caroline looked directly into Sinclare's eyes. 'Sinclare, I never said that.' She spoke softly and with such conviction that Sinclare almost believed her.

'Then why would Echo – ' Sinclare stopped speaking and stared straight ahead. Her thoughts were coming too fast for her to articulate them.

'Exactly,' Caroline said, 'Echo. Think for a minute. She lied to me about you. She lied to you about me.'

The realization of what Caroline was saying infuriated Sinclare. 'I could kill her with my bare hands!'

Caroline blanched. 'I wouldn't go *that* far, but something really should be done about her.'

Sinclare felt her cheeks flush. 'I'm sorry, Caroline. Sorry about everything. I can see now we've both been set up. But why? I've known Echo for years. I worked for her, I talk to her on the phone every day. Why would she do this to me? To us?'

'I don't know the woman, Sinclare. She's playing a dangerous game. The White House asked the Justice Department this afternoon to begin investigating the source of the tape. If we hadn't met I would have told Dalton that the word was that you were behind the tape.' She looked at Sinclare's eager, concerned face. 'I'm glad I didn't. Listen, why don't we get going? We can talk some more at the party.' Caroline signaled the waiter serving the next booth. 'This is my treat. Okay?'

Sinclare smiled and nodded as she slid out of the booth. Together, they walked to their cars. 'Caroline, Eliot has already told the US Attorney's office about Echo and the tape. She's on a rampage. That's the reason I'm going down to Winterberry.'

'Do you know how to get there.'

'Oh dear, I forgot to ask in there.'

'Corporal Samuels,' she called to the driver. 'Which way to Winterberry from here?'

'Straight down Route 7 to Middleburg. First

light after the intersection. It's exactly one mile to the gate.'

'Leave it to the marines.' Sinclare fluffed her hair at him.

'I'd offer to take you in with me, but you know they'd give us a hassle,' Caroline said apologetically.

'No problem, I like gate-crashing. It's one of my favorite sports.'

'How about Echo bashing?' Caroline smiled as she stepped into the open door of the Lincoln.

'Now there's a game we can both play.' Sinclare laughed.

The marine driver started the engine as Sinclare leaned into the open window and said to Caroline, 'You still don't want to tell me what had you so upset in there?'

Caroline lowered her eyes and pressed her lips together. 'I'll tell you some other time, Sinclare. I have a feeling I'm going to *need* a friend.'

Sinclare reached through the open window and placed her hand over Caroline's. 'You have one.'

'Thank you. And thanks for the loan of the makeup.'

As the car pulled out into the highway traffic Caroline leaned back against the seat exhausted. She adjusted the air conditioner vent so that it blew directly on her.

She ached to talk to someone. Under other circumstances she probably would have blurted out the whole story to anyone who would listen.

382

She always felt she had a legion of friends, but when Sinclare offered to listen she realized that in a personal crisis there wasn't a living soul she could truly trust with her sorrow.

She had asked the driver to pull into the inn for cigarettes and decided to check in with Polly, to see how she was feeling. She expected a three-second phone call to say she was okay; instead, a distraught Polly came on the line and told her she knew all about the affair with Brad. Caroline had stood at the pay phone with total strangers passing her by, trying to believe her ears. Her Polly, her darling baby girl, was on the other end of the line telling her it was 'all right,' she 'understood.'

'The only reason I'm even mentioning it, Mom,' she had said, 'is to tell you not to worry. I know about the bracelet and the investigation, too. Everything will be fine. Bob is taking care of everything. Don't worry. No one will ever know – ever – not from me, not from Bob. It will be like it never happened.'

That's when she knew she was going to cry. She thanked Polly and said she would see her later, hung up, and fled to the ladies' room. Her chest felt about to burst as she ran past the counter down the tiny hall blinded by tears she couldn't hold back.

She locked herself into the booth, sat down, and fell quietly to pieces. All the fear, all the sneaking around, all the planning and the memory of the joy and pain her relationship with Bradford Barry had produced poured out of her. She thought she

383

was under control when she went back out to the restaurant, but she hadn't been able to stop crying. That's when Sinclare Ives walked in.

Amazing, she thought, as she watched the rolling Virginia pastureland fly by the window. A woman she had been contemptuous of for years turned out to be a real human being. And perhaps, no, very likely, she was someone who could truly understand what she had been through.

Thursday Evening, June 8, 1989
Winterberry Farm
Fauquier County, Virginia

No one in Washington could remember anything like it. A seated dinner for six hundred people at a private residence like Winterberry Farm boggled the mind of even the most veteran partygoer. Constance Maubry was an acknowledged genius when it came to putting the right mix of people, food, and entertainment together in an exquisite ambience, but tonight she had outdone herself.

The stately antebellum house was twice the size of Monticello. Bathed in footlights hidden in the surrounding shrubbery, it stood out against the indigo night sky as though washed with moonlight. The soft glow of hundreds of candles mounted in brass candelabra glowed from every window.

A hundred-foot-long white canvas canopy ran from the massive front door, down a brick walkway to the circular drive. The underside was strung with thousands of tiny white light bulbs the size of two-karat diamonds. Spaced at ten-foot intervals under the canopy, liveried footmen stood at unblinking attention like life-size toy soldiers.

More footmen were deployed to meet each car pulling up to the canopy. They opened car doors for the guests, then moved the cars to a wide side lawn near the stables.

Judy Lowry gasped as George slowly maneuvered their car toward the entrance. 'George, look! It's like a movie set. Isn't Constance amazing!'

'It's pretty impressive.' George uttered the first consecutive three words he had spoken since Judy picked him up at dockside at the *Sequoia*. During the hour's drive down to Winterberry his responses to anything Judy said had consisted of grunts, groans, and long pregnant pauses.

He slowly braked to a full stop to permit the passengers in the white Rolls Corniche two cars in front of them to alight.

'Oh my God, George, it's Elizabeth Taylor!' Judy squealed like a crazed teenaged fan. 'I can't stand it!'

'Eh.' George shrugged.

That was it. Judy exploded. 'George Lowry, you might as well keep driving because I'm not getting out of this car until you cut it out!'

'Cut what out?' he groused, not looking at her.

'You know damn well what. You haven't said a word since I picked you up. What the hell happened on the *Sequoia*? First I see Sinclare racing

385

past me in the parking lot. Then I see Eliot Ives roaring up in that single-man's car of his. He runs up the gangplank and I sit there in the car cooling my heels for ten minutes waiting for you. Then I sit through an hour's drive trying to be pleasant and you don't have the courtesy to even speak to me. What is this?'

'I got my nuts squeezed,' he said flatly.

'What! By who, Sinclare or Eliot?'

George paused and inched the car forward as the Rolls slowly pulled up the drive. 'Eliot.'

'You didn't answer that quite as rapidly as I would have liked.'

'Huh.' He grunted again. 'Here we are, get out.'

A footman was running beside Judy's door, his white gloved hand resting lightly on the handle.

'No, not until you tell me what happened.'

'Judy,' he glowered at her, 'get out of the car.'

'George . . .'

'I don't want to talk about it. *Not now.*'

'Damn,' she muttered as the footman opened her door and extended a hand to assist her. She gathered the folds of her long skirt in one hand and smiled up at him. 'Wonderful, George, just wonderful.' She spoke through an artificial smile, and flashbulbs from carefully selected press photographers momentarily blinded her.

She waited until George made his way around the front of the car. He adjusted his cummerbund and took her arm as they started their walk up the canopied walkway.

As a former 'other woman' and now second

wife, Judy was keenly alert to any outside forces from George's former life, and Sinclare Ives certainly qualified. Any time that woman was within a country mile of George her antennae went up and started to quiver. Her antennae were sensitive as well to George's position in the Senate. Obviously Eliot Ives had asked George for something that he was reluctant to give. Now that they were out of the car she had lost her chance to find out more. She decided to forget it for the moment and enjoy what clearly promised to be the party of the year.

They moved grandly up the walkway just behind the British ambassador and his wife. As they entered the great hall a string quartet played Bach to their right. To their left a row of waiters dressed from head to toe in white with dark green satin sashes at their waists stood holding silver trays of champagne. Each guest was expected to take a fluted glass and move ahead to the French doors leading to the wide terrace that ran the length of the house.

As Judy and George stepped out on to the terrace they could see white ribbon-festooned tents spotted about a sweep of blue-green velvet grass that led down to the stream. At least four hundred guests had already arrived and stood in conversational groups. They spoke softly as though awed by their surroundings, not wanting to disturb the bucolic elegance of such a stately place.

Judy and George moved to one side of the terrace to sip their champagne. Too vain to wear her glasses and unable to endure even soft contacts,

Judy squinted as hard as she could to pick out familiar faces. Jan and Mark Kirkland stood with the secretary of commerce and his wife, chatting merrily away as though totally oblivious of the murmured speculation that Mark would be named the next chief of staff.

Judy soon lost George to a gaggle of Reagan holdovers. He wasn't talking to her anyway so she leisurely strolled on by herself. As she paused to watch a black swan gliding downstream at the foot of the rolling lawn she caught a sharp female voice behind her.

'. . . No wonder little Miss Kirkland doesn't smile much. I can tell you from firsthand knowledge that Mark can barely get it up; he's not what I'd call a wimp, actually I'd say he was a wilt.'

The raucous laugh that followed the anecdote made her turn and look. She knew it! Echo Bourne. *What a perfectly nasty story to be telling. That bitch . . . and in Jan's family's house, too.*

Judy had to admit Echo looked smashing. She was wearing a wide-shouldered white satin gown with jeweled epaulets, very high heels, and a tiny white satin pillbox hat with a veil pulled tightly over her beautifully made-up face.

Judy flattened herself against the ivy-covered side of the house, where she wouldn't be noticed. She was separated from Echo by a tall trellis covered with climbing roses. They were only three feet away from each other, but Judy was pretty sure she couldn't be seen.

Echo seemed to be with an Arab wearing a

flowing robe and a white burnoose, and most of her chatter seemed aimed at amusing him. Judy could hear Echo greet Donald Slezack, the dour syndicated columnist everyone called the Prince of Darkness for his gloomy view of the world of politics. If you blew in his ear today it would be in tomorrow's column. Echo made elaborate introductions all around and asked, 'Well, Donald, you know everything. Who's going to be our new chief of staff?'

'Of the three, you mean?' he said, puffing himself up like an overinformed adder.

'We can start with those.' Echo smiled at her Arab.

'Kirkland, I doubt. Ives . . .' He wobbled his open palm from side to side as a gesture of maybe-yes-maybe-no. 'Riggs, if I had to put money on it.'

Echo threw back her head and laughed. 'You've got to be kidding!' she whooped. 'Haven't you heard? You of all people?' She leaned forward and put her cheek against the columnist's face. It was the side away from Judy and she couldn't see or hear what was going on, but she was sure Echo wasn't telling him what a war hero Dalton was.

What in God's name is that woman up to? Judy asked herself, puzzled and worried. Within three minutes she had trashed three of Judy's closest friends. She looked around for George. By now another two hundred guests must have arrived. The party was about to 'crest', as she had heard caterers say. She squinted into the dense crowd and spotted Ian Vreen, Lady Maubry's companion.

Maybe Ian would know why this woman was spreading such venom. If George wouldn't tell her what all the threats and bad mouthing were about, hopefully Ian would.

Thursday, June 8, 1989 — 7:30 P.M.
Echo Bourne's Townhouse
P Street, Georgetown

Buck Sumner parked his car around the corner on Thirtieth Street and walked the half block back to Echo's darkened townhouse. Only the gaslights on either side of the front door illuminated his task as he let himself in with his own key. Why not? He owned the house, he thought bitterly.

He had phoned Echo that afternoon to give her one last chance to be straight with him. But she had lied.

Buck had been grooming Deirdre for weeks, ever since they had met at a reception at the Corcoran Gallery. He noticed her right away — a beautiful girl with an exquisite face and skin the color of polished mahogany. The daughter of a recalled Ghanaian diplomat, she could outthink any operative he had ever had. Perhaps, someday, she would turn on him, too. In the meantime she had been most useful, keeping him apprised of Echo's plans to set up the Saudi ambassador as she had done with so many others.

Coming for tea, indeed! he thought angrily as he

quietly closed the front door and reached for the low table lamp in the hall.

Buck looked about the tasteful living room that reflected Echo's preferences and his money. The most recent assignment he had given her — to help him in backgrounding Riggs, Ives, and Kirkland for the President — had turned into a disaster. Instead of searching for negative information, she had created it. The power had gone to her head, and now she faced a possible prison sentence for fraud, conspiracy, attempted blackmail, and he didn't know what else. She had been viciously angry and frantic when she had told him what Eliot Ives had done. It sounded all of his internal alarms.

Buck took one last look around the room before heading up to the second floor. Well, he vowed, whatever her plan was, she wasn't taking him down with her.

He had to hand it to her in one area, though. She certainly got things done. In one short week she had gotten his daughter to hire a transvestite who was clearly one of her operatives. She had set up her best friend with a phony tape that would blackmail the national security advisor and she was about to squeeze his wife Caroline over her extramarital affair. Echo could force George Lowry out of the US Senate and extort, for all he knew, millions of dollars from an Arab. This was all in the space of a week. Heaven only knew what activities she had been up to on her own before that.

What in God's name had he created?

Buck stepped directly to the desk in the small back office. He smiled as he pulled open the top drawer. Dear Echo. So confident that as a self-styled 'master spy' she had no need to hide anything in her own home, she had left her key ring lying in the drawer in plain sight.

On the third try he found the key that fit the walk-in closet in the hall. As he stood in the door of the open closet examining its contents he began to realize the enormity of her power. Shelf after shelf of tapes showing God knows what obscenities stood in mute testimony to her greed for power.

From his attaché case he retrieved a small high-density magnet. He held it to the front label of each video cassette and slowly moved down the row, chuckling at the titles on the tapes and noticing their dates. Deirdre had told him she was taping, but he had no idea it had been going on for so long.

Within minutes he had erased hour upon hour and several years of Echo's blackmailing sex tapes. When he reached the last one on the shelf he stopped. The date on the label, June 8, 1989, was written in her distinctive hand. The title was Outrageous Fortune.

He walked to the VCR at the foot of her king-sized bed and pushed it into place. He poured himself a drink from the bar by the fireplace and flipped the switch. He fast-forwarded through Deirdre and Ony working over the delighted Arab.

392

When Buck reached the last few minutes where he knew Echo would appear, he switched on to slow motion. He sipped his scotch and wiped his lips with the edge of her lace coverlet.

Naked, in a slow languid walk, Echo approached the bed. The ambassador was fully erect, his head propped on a half-dozen pillows. She beckoned to him to turn so his head was at the foot of the bed. When he was lying flat, she knelt beside him and straddled his head so that she was facing the camera. Slowly, slowly she began to move her body against his face.

So that's what she likes now. He felt himself go hard.

He watched for a few more minutes as Echo's beautiful and now contorted face writhed in passion.

He could stand it no longer. He quickly rewound the tape and removed it from the machine. This one, he smiled to himself, I'll keep. He placed it in his pocket.

Next Buck proceeded to Echo's small office in the rear of the second floor. When he had difficulty picking the locks on the fireproof filing cabinets he wondered if he'd lost his touch after all these years. Soon, however, he had opened all the file cabinets. He began going through the drawers, finding neatly typed and indexed transcripts of conversations, memos of meetings, calendars, and date books showing where various well-known people had been and with whom.

There was no way to know what was important

and what was not, so drawer by drawer he began carrying the contents into the bathroom down the hall. He put the plug in the drain and began filling the tub with the documents and water. When the drawers were empty and the tub filled he returned with his attaché case and took out a bottle of printer's dye. He poured it into the tub, stirring the black water with the handle of Echo's back scrubber. He knew these were all photocopies, except for one drawer he had not put in the tub. No one would ever be able to read these copies. The originals he carried to the fireplace.

Thursday, June 8, 1989 – 7:30 P.M.
Winterberry Farm

Dalton Riggs was seated next to Eliot Ives in the President's helicopter on the trip down to Winterberry.

'I hope Lady Maubry won't be offended.' Eliot had to speak loudly over the sound of the rotor blades, despite all the padding and comfort of the cabin. 'She didn't invite me to this do. My wife will have a fit when she finds out I'm here.'

Dalton laughed. 'No hostess is ever offended by anyone who steps off the President's chopper, Eliot. Don't worry about it. The President was pleased with the news you had on George Lowry's vote, and Lady Maubry will be delighted to see you.'

Eliot nodded. 'You're right, I'm sure. I'm just sorry Sinclare had a family emergency and had to leave the *Sequoia* before I got there. This trip would blow anyone's mind.'

Dalton couldn't have agreed more. Traveling in Marine One was always a heady experience, and he was delighted when the President spontaneously included Eliot as he left the party on the *Sequoia*. The craft seemed to be equipped with aeronautical instruments and gear not even invented yet. One's every wish was instantly satisfied by two marine stewards who moved silently from one plush seat to the next offering cocktails, snacks, and coveted Marine One matches bearing the presidential seal.

Dalton squinted down at the hundreds of people on Winterberry's terrace, hoping he could make out Caroline. He looked for the pinkish-red suit she had been wearing at the club, and one that nearly matched her hair. How beautiful she had looked when he met her at the club. And how guilty he felt for having troubled her with the damn tape business.

It was amazing how little she had changed over the years. Dalton smiled, remembering the night at Constance Maubry's when he looked across the dinner table at the beautiful young Johnson staffer spouting off about the Constitution in a thick Southern accent. He was thunderstruck but couldn't show it. He had been so afraid he would frighten her away. The difference in their ages, his marriage terminal but not yet dead. He remembered worrying that she would think he was some randy old army officer looking for a fling.

And when she did agree to a date he felt he had captured some rare animal, a unicorn perhaps, who without delicate handling and exquisite care would flee into the forest, leaving him alone with his secret knowledge that she had once existed.

But she didn't fly away. She fell in love with him. Then one night he took her back to her tiny apartment in Georgetown and she kissed him — over and over and over again.

'Caroline,' he whispered to the window, 'I wish I could find the words.' Dalton was not a verbal man, embarrassed and awkward around any kind of sentimentality. He supposed he was no different than most men of his generation and background. As a child of the Depression and the military there had been little reason to learn the vocabulary of romance.

He had hoped his actions would speak for him. He felt he was a good provider, a good father and husband. Yet always there was that yearning to explain to Caroline how much she had meant to him, how much he credited her with his success in life. The expensive piece of jewelry on some special occasion hardly seemed to express how he loved and needed her. She had given him their cherished Polly, and their beautiful, hassle-free home, an oasis of peace that gave him the strength he needed. She had been completely supportive of his decision to leave the military and follow Don Kane's political star. It had been risky, and he never kidded himself about the fact that it was her inheritance that made it possible.

Dalton sensed Caroline's increased drinking was more than her problem. His life was at its root and he blamed himself. The last year could not have been pleasant for her. His traveling, the long campaign, and now his preoccupation with the White House staff position. It couldn't have been much fun for her to be alone so much, he thought, with Polly gone as well. Since the first of the year she had gotten noticeably worse. She had gone far beyond social drinking, always asking if he would like one first, then drinking two to his one. She also took too many damn Valium and Seconals. Perhaps she should get a job. She was one hell of a manager the way she ran the house and entertained. That nice young Jan Kirkland was over at the Protocol office now. Perhaps there was something Caroline would like to do. He made a mental note to check it out.

Marine One began its vertical descent. The commotion it aroused among the party guests was amusing to watch. People seemed to appear from everywhere, out from under the trees and streaming out of the mansion itself. Dalton could see the Secret Service advance detail moving into position. The escort chopper that always accompanied the President when he traveled had just parked near the edge of the large flagstone terrace upon which stood hundreds of people with upturned, awed faces.

Once again Dalton scanned the crowd for a

glimpse of Caroline. Surely she would have made it down by now. He hoped nothing had delayed her on the road.

He wanted her to see him arrive with the President and talk to her as soon as he could. At the moment Dalton felt as though he were at the center of the universe. The only thing that mattered more than where he was, was sharing that place with the woman he loved as much as life itself.

'General Riggs?' the marine steward said over the noise of the landing. 'You'll be disembarking with the President. Senator Ives, will you escort the First Lady?'

Eliot, who had been deep in thought as he looked out the window, suddenly smiled. 'With pleasure!' he said, releasing his seat belt and quickly, confidently arising.

With the arrival of the President and five hundred and ninety-six invited guests, the tall iron gates of Winterberry Farm had been closed. Two Virginia state troopers with automatic weapons slung over their shoulders stood to one side. The tall young state trooper whom Sinclare thought looked like Don Johnson walked toward the driver's side of her bright red little car. She could see he noticed that her vanity plates read IVES 1.

As he bent down toward the open window, Sinclare put both hands on the steering wheel and pushed her upper arms against the side of her breasts. Her cleavage deepened another two inches. She didn't want any problems, she had too much on her mind.

'Hi, there,' she said in a little-girl voice.

'May I see your invitation, ma'am?' he said pleasantly.

'I'm Mrs Eliot Ives.' She lowered her eyes and smiled provocatively.

'Yes, ma'am. I'm Officer Neely. There's very tight security here tonight. We have orders to ask for everyone's invitation.'

'I believe special arrangements have been made for my arrival.'

'Are you meeting someone?' He lifted a clipboard and folded back the top sheet.

Sinclare could see a few of the names on the sheet. It read like page after page of *Who's Who in Government* and the *Washington Green Book,* the social register of Washington. She'd had a violent argument with Eliot when they dropped his name. Members of Congress and the administration were automatically included, and usually not removed when they left office if they remained in Washington – unless the bitches who compiled the book could find an excuse to drop you.

She thought she was the reason they had dropped Eliot, and it had hurt.

The trooper continued to study the list. 'I don't see your name on the list.'

Sinclare straightened her shoulders and ran her fingers through her hair. 'I'm sure there's been a mistake. If you'll call the house and ask for Lady

Maubry's confidential secretary, Ian Vreen, I'm sure he'll clear this up.'

'This list was prepared by Mr Vreen, ma'am.'

'Will you please, dammit, do as I asked.'

Sinclare and the officer locked eyes for a long moment.

'I'll see if I can reach him. The party's been going on for over an hour. I might not be able to locate him.'

'Well try,' she said, drawing her lips into a thin angry line. She couldn't believe it was happening again. If they didn't get her in at once she'd find some back way and sneak in. One way or the other, she was going to get to Echo – and soon.

The state trooper returned with a smile on his face. 'Mrs Ives, you can go in. Mr Vreen will meet you at the main house.'

As the gates swung open she shot up the long driveway toward the mansion, only to be halted by a large bus unloading thirty or so tuxedoed men carrying black musical instrument cases.

She waited, tapping her long nails on the steering wheel and thinking about how she was going to handle Echo. In any confrontation Sinclare let instinct be her guide. As she fumed behind the wheel she knew that the very sight of Echo would provide her with what she could or would say to her to stop her from her destructive plan.

A Secret Service agent approached her side of the car. 'Sorry for the hold, Mrs Ives,' he said, holding a small earpiece to his ear with one hand and pointing with the other. 'We've located a

400

parking spot for you just to the left there.' He walked alongside the car as she inched ahead into the spot and gave an appreciative glance as her short skirt slipped up near her bikini panties when she slid out of the little Ferrari, exposing her long legs.

As she got out of the car she saw Ian almost running down the long walkway covered by a beautiful canopy filled with thousands of lights. He was breathless by the time he reached her.

'Oh, Sin, such madness! Come walk with me. I'll take you down to the guest house.'

'Guest house?' she responded angrily. 'What am I, some after-dinner act that has to wait my turn?'

'No, no, no,' he said quickly. 'Look, I've got to go back up. The President's arrived. We're short three dozen lobsters, the wine I brought down is off. Well, one case. We've got waiters rooting around in Connie's cellar for something for the head table . . . I can't tell you.'

'But why me in the guest house?' she asked, trying to keep abreast of him as he scurried along a flagstone path.

'It's Echo, darling. She's going berserk. I don't know whether it's drink or craziness. You're her friend. You've got to get her calmed down.'

'Ian, what's she *doing,* for heaven's sake? Ian, slow down! I'm ruining my shoes.'

'She's going all around the party saying terrible things about everyone. I mean *terrible* things! Constance is hysterical she'll say something to the President. She's that crazed.'

They had reached the end of the walk. Ian opened the door of a house built of the same stone as the main house but a tenth the size. As she stepped into it she saw she could fit several of her Watergate apartments into it.

'In here,' he said, leading her through to a beautiful room. The walls were paneled in a dark burnished wood. Double bay windows faced out onto an English garden and every table held a ceramic pot of hydrangeas. 'Sit. Wait. I'll bring her down,' Ian said and disappeared back out the door.

Caroline had taken her seat early. Her table had a perfect view of the makeshift landing pad for the President's helicopter. She couldn't wait to see Dalton step out of Marine One with the President.

Most of the guests were still filing into the dinner tent looking for their tables. Some had already started to dance to Lester Lanin's bouncing society beat. Caroline noticed that Constance had put her and Dalton at her table, Senator Dole to Caroline's right and Henry Kissinger to her left. Elizabeth Taylor would sit with the presidential party at the very next table.

Lost in the delight of her surroundings Caroline suddenly became aware that someone was gently touching her shoulder. Startled, she turned to see a good-looking young man with sandy hair and wonderfully even teeth smiling at her. He was wearing an earpiece. 'Hello,' she said brightly, raising her voice above the music.

'Good evening, Mrs Riggs, I'm Bob Kadanoff. I believe Polly has mentioned me.'

'Oh, Bob!' she said. 'Mentioned you? My goodness. Oh my.' She started to laugh nervously. 'Oh, I'm so delighted .. please. Please sit down for a minute.'

'I really can't, Mrs Riggs. I'm on duty.'

'Well, aren't you sweet to drop by.'

'Mrs Riggs,' he said urgently, his smile disappearing.

She looked over his shoulder to see excited guests pressing forward to get a better view of the presidential party disembarking from Marine One and making their way toward the tent up the far lawn. 'Do you have to go? The President's coming now.'

'Not for a minute.' He reached into his inside jacket pocket and took out a small manila envelope. He handed it to her without a word.

'What's this?' she asked, puzzled. She lifted the flap and peered inside. For an instant she didn't recognize the bracelet. Fearfully, she looked up at Bob.

He cleared his throat and looked at her with clear, calm blue eyes. 'Please, I don't mean to frighten you. There's nothing to be concerned about. This will be returned to Jan Kirkland tomorrow. No one will ever know you were given this by the Secret Service when it's owner failed to claim it. No one. I know Polly spoke to you and I feel the same way she does. It never happened. You understand what I'm saying.'

Tears began to fill Caroline's eyes.

'Please don't, Mrs Riggs . . . It's just that I want you to know you have been completely protected. Put your mind at ease.'

Caroline stood in order to speak as quietly as possible. 'Bob, why are you doing this for me? I know it could cost you your job.'

He smiled another dazzling smile. 'I love your daughter, Mrs Riggs. And besides, you are going to be our child's grandmother. That counts for a lot.'

'I see,' she said, placing the bracelet back in the envelope and handing it to him.

'Would you like me to walk you through security so you can meet your husband? It will get you around the crowd.'

'Yes,' she said, 'I'd like that very, very much.' She took his arm and felt the taut muscles under the fabric of his jacket.

Well, good for you, Polly, she thought, as he cleared a way through the crowd. Good for my girl for loving a man like this.

Grandmother was a word that would have frozen her blood only days earlier. Now it sounded like the best thing in the world a woman could ever be.

Sinclare paced the solarium of the guest house. She *supposed* they called it a solarium — it had a high domed ceiling of etched glass, all swirls and curlicues, and colored bits that made a border all the way around the top of the huge room. It was

404

bigger than their entire apartment at the Watergate and positively crammed with overstuffed couches and chairs covered in flowered chintz. She could have stood straight up in the fireplace, and in an alcove of the main room was an enormous brass bird cage with tiny 'somethings' with wings flapping around.

Sinclare shuddered. She hadn't been able to bear the sight of birds ever since she trapped one between the outer shell and insulation of Ruby's trailer. She also hated being trapped in the guest house.

Damn Ian. He said he would be right back.

She wandered out into the backyard, if one could call it that. There was a small terrace and a pool full of lily pads. That meant frogs and those dreadful bugs with the long shiny tails. Ugh! She shuddered again and hugged herself. The thin cocktail dress she had worn to the yacht party did little to ward off the sudden chill.

Sinclare wondered why people wanted to live in the country with all the creepy, crawling things and the undependable air. In the city there weren't any bugs. You could control your environment with air-conditioning.

The only signs of life were the waiters scurrying back and forth inside a cook tent set up between the guest house and the mansion. She could hear their voices as she stood beside the pool: they spoke in a polyglot of languages trying to communicate with each other. Then she heard two familiar voices at the front door of the cottage.

'Right this way, darling,' Ian said. 'You can rest in here.'

Sinclare turned to see Echo half stumble into the room. Her pillbox hat practically covered one eye. *Was she drunk or had she taken some goofy pills?*

'Hi,' Sinclare said. It was all she could muster. She was cold and she was scared.

'Well, if it isn't my very own stool pigeon,' Echo said, lurching toward the chintz-covered couch and flopping into it. 'What the hell are you doing out here? I didn't think they invited lowlife to parties like this.' She took off her hat and threw it on the coffee table. 'Ian, get me a drink.'

'There's a bar in the hall,' he said hurriedly. 'I'll leave you ladies now.' He winked at Sinclare and fled.

Coward, she thought, leaving me alone.

Sinclare walked around to the front of the couch to face Echo.

'What's going on, Echo? Ian says you're wrecking the President's party.'

'He's just pissed because I called your husband a gangster in front of Henry Kissinger,' Echo said proudly.

'You what!! My husband isn't even here!'

'He sure the hell is. He walked off the President's fat-assed helicopter like someone elected him God. I gave him a piece of my mind and I'm going to give you one, too. You and your husband set me up, Sinclare,' she started to shout. 'Turned me in to the goddamn feds.' She rose unsteadily and

406

moved around the room picking up objects to examine and putting them down.

'Echo, I don't know what you're talking about.'

'Like hell you don't.'

'Well, I don't, Echo, and you don't have to believe me.'

'Why should I? You're nothing but a trailer park tramp. Always have been and always will be.' She dropped a crystal paperweight and picked up her hat. 'I'm getting out of here. The smell is getting to me.' She slammed through the screen door of the cottage yelling 'Where's the goddamn booze around here anyway?'

Sinclare stood in the middle of the room. Whatever Echo was trying to tell her had been completely obliterated after Echo called her a trailer park tramp. Sinclare could feel a bitter taste in her mouth and her hands shook with anger.

She caught up with Echo at the side of the pool just behind the tent where the cooks were busy at work. The smell of cooking food filled the air. Less than six feet away a chef's assistant was adjusting the flame under a row of gigantic chafing dishes.

'Echo, please wait. I want to say something,' Sinclare pleaded. 'I've always been your friend . . . I came all the way down here to talk to you, to try and understand . . .'

Echo turned and looked at Sinclare in a cold fury. 'The only thing I want to hear from you and your husband is that someone has put the fix in with the US attorney. I'm supposed to report

Monday morning to answer questions about that damn tape.'

Sinclare looked at the ground. 'Well, I'm sorry about all that.'

'Oh, give me a break, Sinclare. You knew that tape was fake, and you were ready to use it. You should be coming with me Monday morning and you know it. But what gets me is that you stood right there while your husband set me up on the phone.'

'You are out of your mind,' Sinclare said slowly, trying to control her rage. 'I didn't set you up, but if Eliot did then hooray for him. He's done the country a service. I hope you're good and scared because that's what you've been doing to a whole lot of innocent people.'

'Innocent,' Echo snorted. 'Some innocents.'

'They were until you got hold of them, myself included. You use people Echo and . . .' She couldn't go on. Her eyes were welling with tears. The emotions of one of the hardest days of her life were taking their toll.

Echo looked at her with an indifferent stare, her pale face lit by the eerie blue flames from the row of chafing dishes. She reached in her bag for a cigarette and lit it with a small gold and diamond lighter. She took a long drag and exhaled into the night air. She turned to Sinclare, who was standing dejectedly, slightly trembling. Sinclare could feel herself crying but could hear no sound.

'Stupid,' Echo hissed, 'stupid little trailer park tramp. Too dumb to learn the lessons I spent years

trying to teach you and now you've fucked everything up.' Echo spat at Sinclare's feet.

She spat at me! Sinclare had only seen someone
do that in some awful movie. She couldn't believe
it! Sinclare felt such a rush of fury that she felt sick
to her stomach. Her eyes seemed to cloud over as
if she were swimming underwater and her head
spun.

Without realizing it her arm shot up like a tennis
player ready for a forehand. With an open palm
she swung with a strength she never knew she
possessed. She didn't make contact, but in ducking
her blow Echo lurched backward on her high, thin
heels. She stumbled for a few feet and as she fell,
frantically trying to remain upright, knocked over
one of the flaming chafing-dish stands.

Sinclare stood transfixed as she watched a sheet
of blue flame pour across the tabletop as if in slow
motion. As she started to move toward Echo she
heard voices screaming, 'Get back! Get back!'

The puddle of flame hit the edge of a pile of
plastic sheeting at the edge of the table. Instantly
the horizontal flame became vertical as it exploded
skyward, igniting the side of the cook tent.

Someone pushed her from behind. Sinclare
heard words being shouted, but they seemed to be
in three different languages.

She backed up a few paces and then ran as she
had never run before. She was aware of people
behind her, noise, commotion, falling stacks of
dishes and flames. She only paused as she reached
a slight rise on the lawn. Behind her the blue-white

flames were devouring the side of the cook tent. Thick, putrid-smelling smoke began to fill the sweet night air.

'Echo,' she sobbed. The sound of her voice was only a hoarse whisper. She saw waiters running with huge cylinders in their hands. They reached the ring of fire that was now engulfing the side of the tent and began to back away from the heat. 'Echo,' she cried again. 'Oh God, I didn't mean it . . .'

Caroline had never been so happy. Connie's party was more a magical stage play than a social gathering, with the music, the beautiful setting, the Japanese lanterns swaying in a gentle night wind. The moment Caroline joined Dalton and the President's party the terrible problems of the week seemed to lift and float away over the rolling lawns of Winterberry.

Dalton had never looked more handsome, so at peace with himself. Earlier she had looked up at him as he moved from one guest to the other, smiling and acknowledging the wonderful things said to them both.

Now, seated in the huge white tent Connie had installed for the party, Caroline felt as though she was in some dreamlike fantasyland. Everything was white – the watered silk drops on the tables, the candles and flowers, even the dance floor was laminated white canvas over board. White swags of eyelet gathered at intervals and caught with enormous nosegays of baby's breath and peonies followed the scalloped edges of the tent. Each nosegay was tied with huge velvet bows, the long streamers falling ten feet to the ground.

Connie, in a white-and-silver-striped floor-length gown and swaying ropes of pearls, moved from table to table making sure everyone was taken care of. She never looked more beautiful.

The Riggs's table was next to the President's. As a waiter in a short white jacket and white pants leaned over to pour champagne, Caroline again placed her hand over her glass. There was no way she was going to ruin this evening.

The band struck up 'Isn't It Romantic?' Dalton pushed back his chair and offered her his hand. 'My darling, shall we?' he asked with a broad smile. Wordlessly, her heart too full to do more than nod, she stood and melted into his arms as he swirled her out on to the dance floor. As she glanced around she noticed they were the only couple on the floor. Slowly, couple by couple, the other guests rose from their tables.

She put her cheek against his. Her lips were against his ear. 'Oh, Dalton, I'm so — '

She didn't finish her sentence. The sound seemed to shake the universe. Reflexively they took two more steps and stopped. The band also stopped and an eerie silence suspended them in time.

The second sound was less sharp but equally terrifying, like nothing she had ever heard. Through the opening at the side of the tent she saw the escort helicopter lurch to one side on its temporary pad.

Suddenly, everyone screamed at once.

Caroline was wrenched out of Dalton's arms as people shoved by them. Dalton held her as tightly as he could, but he was swept away in the force of bodies pushing, falling about.

Her heel caught on the trailing cloth of an overturned table and she fell to the hard floor. She managed to crawl under a table. There was blood on her arms and clothes. She heard shouting as the Secret Service attempted to control the crowd. Someone had taken the band microphone and was shouting to people: 'Be calm! Do not panic. Please don't run!' She heard the band start up again feebly, a horn here, a violin there, as though half the members were gone.

Caroline could hear men shouting to get the President out.

Glasses and china started to fall around her as tables were pushed over. She struggled free of the tablecloth, terrified that someone would push the table over on her. A familiar form raced by her. 'Ian!' she screamed. He turned and started back toward her, pulling her to her feet. 'My God, what's happening!' Then she noticed the open gash on her knee.

'The cook tent is on fire! The gas tanks are exploding!' he said, his eyes wild. 'It's too close. We've got to get out before this tent goes up! Come on! Michael! Steve! Bruce!' he screamed, waving frantically at the waiters by the side of the tent. 'Get those garbage bags and fill them. The pool! Use the pool!' The four white-coated men

412

raced for a line of trash cans beside the tent and sprinted for the pool.

'I've got to help them. Caroline, you get out of here!'

Ian dropped her arm and bolted toward the waiters. 'Run! Now!' he ordered.

She took two steps before her knees buckled. The last thing she remembered was the color of the night sky — a sickening fiery red.

Mark Kirkland had noticed the light from the fire the moment he heard the first explosion. For a moment he thought Connie had pulled out all the stops and was mounting a fireworks show. Glancing toward the main house, he could see the mansion dimly lit by more small lights strung through a vine-covered trellis. Then he heard the crackle of flames. Windborne sparks from the fire in the tent jumped to the wooden trellis. Suddenly a whoosh of flame engulfed the thick vines then ran up and over the double door.

The men at the table jumped to their feet. A woman at the next table screamed, 'Fire!' Mark was vaguely aware of Dalton and Caroline Riggs rushing from the dance floor.

Mark sprang into action. 'I've got to find Jan!' he shouted to no one in particular. Then he was running toward the house. The sweet country air was now filled with ash and fear. Mark sped across the lawn and stumbled up the low steps leading to the terrace. Halfway across he saw Jan emerging from the mansion.

She was unaware that the outside of the door was ringed in flames. Just as he spotted her the fire-weakened trellis pitched forward.

'Jan! Look out!' he screamed above the chaos all around him.

Too late. The burning trellis crashed to the ground, flames and sparks shooting skyward, and Jan disappeared.

As the trellis began to fall it caught on the heavy extension cord that wove through it to light the lanterns. Now the wire lay snapping and throwing sparks across his path. He heard Jan scream his name as she disappeared under a pile of burning leaves and wood.

'Don't move!' a voice bellowed behind him. 'That wire is live! I'll get her! Stay back!'

Ian Vreen, his eyes wild, his face covered with soot, charged past the flaming heap.

'Vreen, for God's sake, man!' Mark watched in panic and disbelief as Ian kicked the snapping wire aside and pulled the flaming trellis off Jan with his bare hands.

The two men carried her limp body across the terrace and gently put her on the ground at the edge of the pool. Mark fell to his knees beside her and pulled her to his chest. She was out cold. He looked down to see a widening bloodstain on her skirt.

'Darling, darling,' he whispered. He looked up at Ian, his eyes pleading. 'Ian, get a doctor! Hurry!'

Ian raced back to the dinner tent. It seemed safe from the flames at the moment. He leapt to the makeshift bandstand and grabbed the microphone. 'We need a doctor!' he screamed. 'Please! Someone is badly injured!' Two men huddled at the back of the tent hurriedly approached the bandstand. 'Over there, by the house!' he pointed. The two men took off running in Jan's direction.

At the edge of the pool waiters were filling garbage buckets as fast as they could and passing them to a line of men and women in torn evening clothes that snaked across the lawn leading to the burning shed. In the distance Mark could hear sirens. He glanced toward the front of the house and could see a red light flashing in the darkness. The first fire engine had arrived.

The fire had reached the small shed near the greenhouse.

Ian looked around for Constance. Suddenly he realized his hands were completely numb. He had no memory of how they got that way. Without warning his knees went limp. He felt himself falling as though in slow motion. Helicopters whirled, the fire engines roared, he could hear shouts and screams but for the first time in his life he felt no anxiety or fear. On a night unlike any other he'd been put to the test. He could have been a shameless coward, but he'd done everything conceivable to save his friends. In the split second before he blacked out he heard his beloved Connie's voice. She was telling the band to keep on playing.

As Sinclare turned back to look at the growing flames that were consuming the cook tent she felt

415

confusion, then panic. Echo was still in there — probably out cold. Should she go back? Could she? She looked at the flames again. They were even higher now. There was nothing she could do. She turned and continued to run, faster, faster away from it all.

She was almost at the escort helicopter, which represented safety to her. Her lungs felt as if they were going to burst; her stockinged feet were torn and bruised. She reached the side of the helicopter and leaned against it, sinking into the soft grass. She was still gasping for breath when the butane tanks in the cook tent exploded.

Instinctively, she ducked down and lay face-down in the wet grass. She lay absolutely still, except for her legs, which jerked uncontrollably. Then she heard the President's helicopter revving its engines.

She turned her head and looked at the sky. A moment before it had been pitch black, now it glowed with an eerie, sparkling light.

Firelight, she thought. The place is on fire. She buried her head deeper into the grass at the sound of Marine One's powerful engine. It roared over her, shaking the ground where she lay.

'Help me,' she started to sob. Then she heard Eliot's strong voice calling for her.

'Sinclare . . . Sinclare, where are you?'

'Eliot, I'm here!' she shouted.

She felt his arms around her, lifting and holding her. 'Baby, baby . . .,' he said softly. 'Ian told me you were here. Thank God I found you. Thank God you're alive. I love you so.' He said it over and over again as she rested her head on his shoulder. She couldn't hear it enough.

Friday Morning

Friday, June 9, 1989 – 10:00 A.M.
The White House Press Room

The press room was filled to capacity. The lights were on and the cameras were rolling when Deputy Press Secretary Hildy Bornstein walked to the podium. The press corps became unusually silent. Big stories were expected to come out of the White House today, and no one wanted to miss a word.

'There will be no briefing this morning,' the deputy press secretary stated. Her opening remark was followed by a mild collective booing from the reporters. But the White House made the rules. Besides, everyone knew there would be time later for probing and follow-up.

Deputy Bornstein continued. 'I have a statement to read, and there will be two handouts this morning.' She put on her bright red half-glasses and began to read.

'The President and the First Lady wish to express their deepest sympathy to the families and friends of those who lost their lives in the tragic explosion and fire at Winterberry Farm. Those who lost their lives are the following:

'Miss Echo Bourne, a longtime public relations consultant here in Washington.

'Mr Edward Kauster, a chef for Foxcroft Foods, Leesburg, Virginia.

'Mr Alan DeSanta, a chef's assistant, Foxcroft Foods, Arlington, Virginia.

'Six other employees of Foxcroft Foods were injured. The President spoke this morning with each of the injured and their families. The doctors at Leesburg Hospital report that all are doing well, and President and Mrs Kane wish them a speedy recovery.

'The President spoke last night and again this morning with Deputy Chief of Protocol Mrs Janet Kirkland. Her injuries, while painful, are relatively minor, and she expects to be back on duty early next week. At her insistence, her husband, Press Secretary Mark Kirkland, will accompany the President on his mission to Moscow as planned.'

The press corps began applauding, whistling, and hooting. It was their way of saying that they were happy to hear that Jan was all right and that Mark was being a 'good soldier'.

After the assembled reporters quietened down Ms Bornstein continued. 'The President has sent personal notes of appreciation and commendation to the Virginia state troopers, and the Secret Service officers, for their bravery and heroism last night, and for preventing a tragic accident from claiming more lives. Of special note was the act of courage that saved the life of Mrs Caroline Riggs, wife of General Dalton Riggs, by Secret Service Agent Robert Kadanoff – '

'Hey, Hildy, I want to know if – '

'Sit down, Sam. I said no questions, and that includes you.' After the irrepressible ABC correspondent sat down, Bornstein continued. 'The President will be departing for Moscow in approximately fifteen minutes at ten-thirty eastern daylight time. The Vice President is in his office and will be holding a special news conference for release later tonight. The Vice President's news conference is scheduled for one P.M., with an embargo until three-thirty this afternoon. The news conference will focus on the cabinet nominations that I will announce shortly.'

This meant that all reporters would have an equal chance to file their stories if any major news came out of the news conference. A murmur went through the group.

'The first handout is the President's schedule for the next ten days. The pool reporters traveling with the President will be briefed on Marine One at noon eastern time by Mark Kirkland. The second handout, which as you can see has just arrived and will be passed out in a minute, speaks for itself. And, as I said, you can address your questions to the Vice President this afternoon.'

Knowing that the camera would want something more than a piece of paper, Bornstein gave them what they needed.

'The President has announced the following appointments: Senator George Lowry's name will be sent to the Senate on Monday for confirmation as attorney general. Also on Monday, General Dalton Riggs's nomination will be submitted to the Senate for the post of secretary of state. The attorney general will be named for the opening on the Supreme Court, and the secretary of state has informed the President he wishes to return to private life.'

A good press secretary always lets an announcement build, and Bornstein was a good deputy. 'Effective at noon today, former Senator Eliot Ives will become White House chief of staff.'

Suddenly, the press room erupted, as reporters clamored to get to the telephones or in front of their camera for stand-up comments, or to get copies of the releases being handed out.

Epilogue

New Year's Day, 1990
Washington, DC

The snow that began at midnight continued to fall. By noon on New Year's day, the nation's capital was covered and silent.

For those who had attended the *Madame President* ball the night before, the weather was a perfect excuse to stay home and recover by a cozy fire. The spectacular party was held in the recently renovated and refurbished Shoreham Hotel's main ballroom. The hostess of the ball was Deena Simon, who had invited several hundred of her friends to join her in celebrating the two-million-dollar sale of her first novel, *Madame President*, to a major New York publisher, as well as to a network for a soon-to-be major television movie. The gaiety of the evening did little to assuage the nervous whispers about just whom Deena would skewer in what was rumored to be the hottest novel about Washington in decades.

What amazed the several hundred guests was that Deena paid for the party herself. She looked marvelous. Two months at the Golden Door had shed enough pounds to reveal a startlingly good figure that need no longer be hidden under the

427

caftans and voluminous shifts she had once affected.

Jan and Mark Kirkland were unable to attend. Jan, who had completely recovered after the loss of her baby shortly after her accident at the Winterberry fire, was spending the Christmas holidays at the Swiss clinic where her mother had been a longtime patient.

The fire at Winterberry was still fresh in the minds of many of Deena's guests. Many there had witnessed it as it destroyed a caterer's tent, potting shed, and the guest house. Jan would have been hurt much more seriously had it not been for the bravery of Constance Maubry's companion, Ian Vreen.

Jan and Mark, the ambassador-designate to the United Nations, would be making their home in the Waldorf Towers upon their return to the States.

Jan phoned her Aunt Constance to wish her a Happy New Year and was amused to hear that one of the guests at Deena's ball had been Prince Seanoona. At the ball, the prince had introduced his constant companion, a rather extraordinarily tall, big-boned woman who mentioned in an oddly deep voice that she was an actress-singer-model. Once Jan stopped laughing, she told Constance her role as their matchmaker.

Jan also telephoned her father, who was living in the Bahamas. He had moved to Nassau's Lyford Cay after he married his long-time secretary, Belle. They had purchased a large home on the oceanside of Edgewater Drive, Lyford Cay's most exclusive street.

Ian Vreen, his hands nearly healed after months of skin grafts, was able to hold the *Washington Post* as he read the account of the ball in the New Year's Day edition. He had not attended, choosing to spend a quiet New Year's Eve minding Liza and Libby. The adorable pups had been so traumatized by the fire that they now required a nighttime baby-sitter.

Secretary of State Dalton Riggs and his wife Caroline were back in town after her successful stay at the Betty Ford Clinic. They were accompanied by Constance Maubry, whose necklace was the hit of the ball.

In the aftermath of the Winterberry fire, an excavation crew had unearthed a dried underground river and a treasure trove of priceless jewelry. Constance recognized it immediately and had had her jeweler clean and reset some of the more dazzling pieces for her niece Jan. She saved an emerald and diamond choker for herself. It went nicely with her emerald taffeta ball gown.

The Riggs were accompanied as well by their daughter and son-in-law, Polly and Robert Kadanoff, proud new parents. Their twins, Caroline and Bradford, had been born just two months earlier.

The Kadanoffs had been married a week after the Winterberry fire at Constance Maubry's Georgetown mansion. The two dozen Secret Service agents who attended made the President's presence secure.

Attorney General George Lowry was still thinking about Deena's ball as he turned on the Rose Bowl game on New Year's Day. It was the first time he had seen Sinclare since the fire. She looked radiant in a short red chiffon strapless dress and tiny velvet hearts glued to the walking cast on her left leg. She said the cast didn't bother her a bit and proved it by asking him to dance.

Eliot's move to the White House and the death of Echo Bourne had left Sinclare with time on her hands. The first week in January she would announce the establishment of her own public relations business. She would be careful to take clients who would not compromise Eliot's position. It seemed the perfect job for her. As she whispered to George as they moved around the floor, 'I'm told I'm very, very good with people.'

George smiled and pulled her closer. He knew how far she had come.

Washington is a city of dreams, great and small.